THE
AMBER
CROWN

JACEY BEDFORD

DAW BOOKS, INC.
DONALD A. WOLLHEIM, FOUNDER
1745 Broadway, New York, NY 10019
ELIZABETH R. WOLLHEIM
SHEILA E. GILBERT
PUBLISHERS
www.dawbooks.com

First Printing, January 2022
1 2 3 4 5 6 7 8 9

DAW TRADEMARK REGISTERED
U.S. PAT. AND TM. OFF. AND FOREIGN COUNTRIES
—MARCA REGISTRADA
HECHO EN U.S.A.

PRINTED IN THE U.S.A.

The Amber Crown

CHAPTER ONE
Valdas

THE DIDELIS BELL tolled the death knell of a king. It sounded from high on the Gura and echoed across the famed white city. Valdas Zalecki felt the sound in his skull. Its meaning clutched at his guts. He leaped to his feet, heart racing, dumping the whore on his knee onto the stone floor along with a flagon of the Winged Hussar's best Rhenish. Once on his feet he swayed and flattened his large, square hands on the wet wooden tabletop, trying to sober up between one breath and the next, and failing miserably.

He curled up his nose at the splashes of good wine down the front of his gathered pantalones. It looked as though he'd pissed himself.

"Valdas? Lover? What's the ma—" Aniela's voice at his feet drew his attention. She wiped a drip of Rhenish from the side of her face, licked her fingers, and froze, hand to mouth. "The bell . . ."

He reached down, pulled her upright, and dusted her skirts down.

"Grrnch." His wine-fat tongue would hardly obey him. He forced it to form words. "Get back . . . palace."

"Not in that condition."

"Oh, sweet Christ! Coffee." Valdas's voice slurred. "An' a bucket o' water."

He eyed the other customers: artisans, merchants' clerks, young bucks, and city rakes, plus a few tarts touting for business. A ripple of speculation led to a general exodus in search of news, shoving and jostling. They had no interest in Valdas, which was just as well. Out of uniform he was merely another big lug pissing away his wages with the best of them.

Aniela was well paid for her discretion.

The bell continued its funereal tolling.

"Come with me. Now!" Aniela grabbed Valdas's hand and pulled him across the room.

Numb, he followed her, scuffing up the sand on the floor as if his feet belonged to someone else. She dragged him through the narrow doorway under the stairs that led to her own room, the one where she didn't entertain customers, and yanked on his arm to remind him to duck beneath the low lintel.

"Sit down." She pushed him toward a chair and lit the stub of a candle from the embers in the small fireplace. He tried to focus on the battered fiddle hanging from a peg on the wall. *Concentrate on one thing at a time.* He swallowed hard and took a deep breath. His mind spun. *The king is dead. King is dead. King is dead.* He knew the words, felt their rhythm in his chest, but they didn't make sense.

"Sit," Aniela said again.

He let his knees buckle, and felt the chair catch him by the buttocks. The sinking feeling in his gut didn't let up.

"I've got to go." He grasped the chair arms and tried to lever himself out of it.

"Not in that state." Aniela pushed him down.

"My responsibility . . . The king's person . . . My men . . ." He put both hands to his face to scrub away the whirling sensation behind his eyes.

"Sober up first, lover. You don't make good decisions when you're drunk."

"Guhhh."

"See what I mean? Wait here."

What decision was there to make? He had a duty, even if it killed him. Valdas had always done his duty.

Aniela slipped out of the door, her sudden departure disquieting.

Valdas needed to move, but the alcohol inside him still struggled for mastery over his knees. One night off! One gods-poxed night, in—how many months? He fought down a wave of resentment.

Why tonight?

How had the king died? That was the big question. All may not be lost. Konstantyn himself had pardoned the High Guard when his own father had broken his neck falling from a horse while out hunting. Maybe Konstantyn had had an accident, or died of an apoplexy, or choked on a fish bone.

He didn't want to wish an ignominious death on such a good king—maybe even a great king—but if Konstantyn had been assassinated, heads would roll. His men would die, and he'd die with them.

A wave of melancholy swept over him. It almost seemed fair. A brilliant career so hard won and so easy lost.

The king is dead. Long live the king!

The thought tasted as sour as old Rhenish. The next King of Zavonia to wear the Amber Crown would be Konstantyn's fussy, middle-aged cousin Gerhard, a dithering ninny; a smoky lamp-glass to Konstantyn's shining light.

Konstantyn was a soldier, a scholar, a man of ideas, a man of the people.

Was. Had been.

Could the Didelis Bell be wrong?

No, the bell had never lied in two hundred years.

Gerhard on the throne would be worse than if Konstantyn had given his new queen a child and left a baby to rule.

Oh, if only . . .

Chancellor Skorny, a political survivor if ever there was one, could have held the regency for Kristina and a child. Wishful thinking. Valdas spared a little leftover pity—the scrap that he wasn't reserving for himself—for the young queen, wedded and bedded only last wintertide and secluded in the Queen's Court ever since, a leaf blown by the wind of politics.

The wind of politics was howling up Valdas's backside right now.

The door opened, pushed by Aniela's round arse. He focused on it. It was a spectacular arse. He loved women's arses, and their breasts; their hair, their hands, their slippered feet, the way they walked, the way they laughed, and even the way they talked. Some men liked their women silent and biddable. Valdas liked them to show a spark of something between their ears as well as the delights of what was between their legs.

Aniela checked over her shoulder and slid backward into the room carrying two glasses of pungent black coffee on a little tray.

She deposited a coffee on the small table by his elbow and poured a thimbleful of something clear into it. "Drink."

"What's that?"

"From the dame in Rivergate Yard. It's supposed to be magic, but I suspect it's just herbs. We keep some behind the bar for emergencies."

"You know I don't believe in all that old rubbish."

"Magic? Me neither, but I believe in herbs. Drink up."

He grasped the glass and gulped it down, shuddering at the bitterness. He could have sworn it was hot, but it felt like icy meltwater on his tongue. His fingers and toes began to tingle, but that was probably just his imagination playing tricks.

"Whatever it is, I feel better."

He tried to stand up, but Aniela pushed him down. "Give it time to work."

"What's the word on the street?"

"Poison! They say the king was poisoned."

"What?"

But she didn't need to say it twice.

Valdas dreaded poison. There were too many types of poison and too many ways to deliver it, even with the cook tasting each dish set before the king.

Valdas swallowed the rising lump in his throat. He had a duty, even if that meant dying, but he might be able to plead for his men—at least for the ones who hadn't been on duty. It was barely a shred of hope, but he clung to it.

"I have to get to the palace," he said.

"And then what?"

"Do my duty to my king—do one thing right, at least. Three days. They have to give me three days—until the funeral—to find the assassin."

She hesitated. "They're saying you are the assassin."

"Wha . . . ?"

"There's a hue and cry out for you."

"That's gods-poxed stupid. How could—"

"Only saying what's on the streets."

Valdas felt a snake roiling in his guts. His ballocks tried to climb up into his shivering belly. "I've got to go. My honor—"

"Honor be damned. They'll upend you and saw you in half on the gibbet. Where will your honor be then?"

He groaned. "I have to prove I didn't do it and find out who did."

"Will they give you the chance?"

He shrugged. "Probably . . . Possibly . . ."

Valdas pulled a gold ring from his finger, the wide band inset with three rubies, a gift from Konstantyn. "Take this. There's no point in letting . . . You deserve it. I know it's business between us, but you never make me feel that I'm paying by the hour."

Aniela stared at the ring but didn't reach out for it.

"Go on, take it." Valdas jerked his hand in her direction. Aniela was warmth and light. Where he was going was only darkness and death. He wanted her to take the ring. In years to come she might be the only one who remembered his name. They said a person didn't truly die until there was no one left to remember. Who would remember Valdas? Certainly not his family.

"Please, Aniela. I want you to have it."

She hesitated. He reached out and took her hand, sliding the ring on to her middle finger, which he guessed would be the best fit. He wrapped both hands around hers. "There. That's not so bad, is it?"

"Ah, Valdas." She swiped her free hand across her wet cheeks. "You know you've always been my favorite, don't you?"

"You say that to everyone, Aniela, but you say it very prettily."

Bugger the coffee. He felt his prick begin to stir at the sight of her low-cut gown. Two dusky half-moons peeked over the neckline. All he could think about was burying his face in her breasts and forgetting reality for a moment. Please let all this be a bad, alcohol-fueled dream. He knew it wasn't the time for sex, but the wine still had him by the throat.

Besides, it might be the last time.

"Aniela, come give me what I've paid for. Your potion worked. My ballocks are bursting. I can't walk through the streets with a broomstick poking through my pantalones." He sat back and sighed, his prick now fully at attention. "You said the potion was magic."

"I'm surprised you can get it up with all that Rhenish inside you." Aniela knelt before him and pulled the drawstring of his pantalones undone.

"I've never been let down by my prick yet. He knows his duty. Gahhh!" The latter sound was all he could manage as Aniela, all business, grasped him in firm hands, bent her head and began to work him with mouth and tongue until he shuddered. It was over in less than a minute and she spat into a kerchief as she raised her head.

"Better?"

"It'll do." He huffed out a shuddering breath. "Not what I'd planned for tonight."

"Another time, lover."

"I hope so. By any god you care to name, I surely hope so." His head was almost clear. "Give me that other coffee, darling girl."

Aniela patted his flaccid prick and tied his drawstring. Sighing, she rose to her feet and handed him the second coffee. It tasted vile, but either the magic or the coffee was doing the trick. He grimaced and swallowed it all down.

"Thank you—I think."

"Sober now?" she asked.

"Closer. Much closer."

"Good." She pressed her lips into a tight line and hugged her arms around herself.

"And I do appreciate your skill. You can do me one favor . . ."

"What, again?" She began to lift the hem of her full skirt.

"No, not that. Not now. Walk with me up to the Gura. I don't want to be taken in the street and marched back like a criminal. I'd rather deliver myself than have the High Guard come and find me. They're less likely to stop a couple out for a stroll."

"You're a noble soul, Valdas. I'd be halfway to the coast on a fast horse by now."

For the briefest moment he considered it, saw what might come next—a change of name, a sword for hire, moving on and on again until he reached somewhere he might not be recognized, maybe even where he didn't speak the language. Far from his men, his brothers in arms. Gah, no.

His duty lay here, grim though it might be.

He'd faced death in action many times before being promoted to the palace, but the thought of being tied upside down by his ankles to a stout wooden frame while the executioner placed a ripsaw between his legs to cleave him in two, live and screaming, turned his bowels to acid. It was a rare punishment, reserved for traitors and king-killers.

"What are you thinking, lover?"

"How much I hate carpentry!"

"Oh, for God's sake, run. I can't bear to think—"

He hugged her to him. "Sweet Aniela, let's go now, while I still have the courage for it. I didn't kill the king. Surely the truth's still good currency in Zavonia. If I return of my own accord it's a damn good point in my favor."

It wouldn't make any difference to his ultimate fate, but it might make a difference to the manner of his death, and to the fate of his men.

Perkunas, god of warriors, please let it be quick and dignified, not upside down on a frame with my ballocks under a saw blade.

CHAPTER TWO

Mirza

MIRZA HAD ALMOST ceased to notice the smell of sickness in the wagon, but Tsura wrinkled her nose as she poked her head through the opening in the canvas and pointedly looked at the heap of bedclothes beneath which Luludja eked out her final hours. Tsura's look said it all: *Isn't it over yet?*

Mirza shrugged slightly and gave an almost imperceptible shake of her head that said: *It will be over when it's over.*

The old woman had always been a vital presence among the Bakaishans, but now she was barely more than a heap of clothes, wispy white hair, and a ragged cough.

The illness had crept on slowly, but it was reaching the end. Mirza heard Lu'dja's breath bubbling in her lungs. The old woman was drowning in her own phlegm.

Tsura turned down her mouth and retreated.

The jolting of the wagon ceased.

Mirza heard Tsura mumbling to Koko while she unharnessed him. Her voice retreated as she led him away to tether him on the best roadside grazing she could find. The nightly routine of making camp went on around the wagon. Horses first, as always, then tents, cook fires, and finally the smell of food.

Mirza's mouth flooded in anticipation as the aroma of frying chicken tickled her tastebuds. Tsura had taken a fat hen in a snare yesterday. If it strayed from a farm, well, that was no one's fault but the farmer's for not looking after his stock. A fox could easily have taken that chicken, so if they stole from anyone, it was from the fox.

"Do you want a morsel of chicken, mistress?" she asked Lu'dja.

"Are you trying to kill me, girl?" The voice from the bed cracked.

"A drink then? Water?"

"Beer."

Mirza uncorked a flagon and poured a small amount of beer into a cup, then eased Lu'dja up against her pillow and held the cup for her.

Lu'dja took a sip, then turned her head sideways so the liquid trickled onto the blanket. "Pah. It's horse piss."

Mirza let her lie back. "Something to eat, then? Broth if not chicken."

"It all tastes of ash." The old woman's petulant voice trailed away. Mirza thought she'd fallen asleep, but then the bedclothes stirred. "I want to die under the stars." She clutched Mirza's sleeve and coughed. "I always thought I'd live to see us in a new home, but . . ." She gave the slightest shake of her head and sighed. "It's time."

Mirza pressed her lips together and nodded. She disentangled her arm from Lu'dja's grasp and leaned out of the wagon, looking to where Tsura was cooking over an open fire.

"Go find Stasha, Lu'dja says it's time."

Tsura abandoned the chicken and ran across the camp, skirts flying, ankles flashing, to find Stasha Hetman. Mirza heard Stasha call for Boldo, and Boldo calling for two of his younger cousins. The *shulam*'s request, possibly her last request, must be granted.

Mirza watched and sniffed the air. There was the tang of a storm, but it wouldn't break until morning. The clouds hung low overhead, hastening dusk. Springtime in Zavonia could be a mean season. This year it clawed its way reluctantly out from under the late winter snows. The ground would be damp and cold, not at all suitable for an invalid.

Stasha obviously had the same thought. Mirza saw him direct the men to cut a pallet of saplings and weave them roughly together before covering the whole thing with furs, including his own wolfskin, his pride and joy. Nothing was too good for the old shulam. After she'd gone, she would watch them from the other side. If they had not paid proper respect she might . . .

What might she do?

Mirza didn't know what Stasha's worst fears were, but Lu'dja had played on them. She'd been the band's shulam, their witch and healer, for all of Stasha's life, and though he was the band's hetman, he never dared go against the old lady's advice.

If only they'd known.

Mirza pressed her lips together. She'd been apprenticed to the shulam for six years. Lu'dja had seemed pleased with her progress at first. There had been no enmity. And then had come the long night, in the dark of midwinter, when Mirza had crossed over to that place which Lu'dja had never been able to find.

The realm of the dead.

Mirza wasn't sure what angered Lu'dja most, the fact that she'd crossed over, or the fact that she'd returned. There had been times when Lu'dja would have killed her with a green-eyed look if she could.

Lu'dja's own trances had always been feigned, her pronouncements entirely of her own making. She was a good actress. Her pronouncements were wise. No one had ever guessed. Even Mirza hadn't guessed until she'd experienced the spirit world herself and seen how different it was from everything Lu'dja had said. Without Lu'dja as a guide, she'd had to make her own way, but she'd make sure when it was Tsura's turn that she'd give the girl all the help she could.

If she hadn't been a true shulam, Lu'dja had been no fraud when it came to the healing arts, however, so Mirza had clenched her jaw and set herself to learn all she could, knowing that she would one day succeed her mistress as shulam of the Bakaishans. And, unlike Lu'dja, she would truly be both witch and healer.

It looked as if that day had come.

She wasn't sorry to see the old woman go, though she'd tended Lu'dja assiduously, keeping her clean and as free from pain as she could.

Lu'dja wheezed as Stasha and Boldo carried her out of the wagon and laid her on the fur-covered pallet. Mirza followed. Tsura ran forward to place a blanket over the shivering form, and then retreated to Mirza's side and reached for her hand.

Stasha knelt. "Is there anything else we can bring you?"

Lu'dja spoke to him in a low tone for a few minutes, then waved him away.

Mirza stepped back, too, but Lu'dja motioned her forward and down. "Closer," she said. "Come closer."

Mirza pulled up her skirts so as not to get them wet. She knelt, feeling mud squelch up with the weight of her knees in the wayside grass.

Lu'dja's voice rasped in her throat. "You think you're going to be able to take my place, don't you? That's all you've ever wanted, isn't it? Aye, well, you're a passable healer, and you've got . . . the other thing, but . . ." She coughed and Mirza wiped spittle flecked with blood from her chin with a clean rag. "But they'll never respect you." She grasped Mirza's forearm, her hand claw-like. "I told him . . ." Her gaze flicked toward Stasha, now casting long shadows in their direction as the central fire flamed up. "I told him you could have healed me, but you let me die."

Mirza rocked back on her heels. "But that's not true."

"Isn't it?"

"You know it isn't."

"When . . ." Another cough. "When I'm gone, if you tell them I faked a connection to the spirit world, they'll never believe you, not now. Not when they suspect you of getting rid of me for your own advancement."

Mirza wanted to protest again, but there wasn't much point. "Tsura knows I didn't," she whispered. But Mirza knew Stasha would never heed the younger apprentice. If Mirza had wanted to hasten Lu'dja's end, there were ways . . .

Lu'dja's breath rattled in her throat. Mirza hoped when it was her own time to go that she didn't choke on the phlegm in her own lungs. If she'd had a shred of pity for the old woman she would have squeezed her nose and clamped her hand over her mouth to hasten her end, but the only pity she had at the moment was for herself, so she knelt until her knees stiffened in the spring mud, listening. She thought every breath would be the old woman's last, but Lu'dja fought hard, keeping body and soul together breath by painful breath.

A last wet wheeze bubbled out.

And that was it.

Mirza glowered at Lu'dja's corpse and suppressed a laugh, which had little to do with mirth and more to do with relief that it was over.

She fancied the old woman looked smug.

As well she might.

Would Stasha and the rest of the Bakaishans truly believe that Mirza had killed her own mentor?

They had good reason, she supposed.

◆———◆

The Bakaishans didn't waste time. A band such as theirs, displaced from their own country and barely tolerated in this one, learned to bury the dead quickly and move on.

Mirza stood to one side while Stasha, Boldo, Himali, and Jeppa lowered the linen-wrapped body into the grave, dug as deep as they could between the trees where it was unlikely to be disturbed. Stasha lowered a rock the size of his head in a linen cradle to rest on Lu'dja's breast. She would not rise again.

"Ai-yai-yai." Nadia shook her head, the tiny gold charms around her headscarf tinkling gently. It should have been Mirza's place to mourn, but Nadia was the undisputed senior woman, and as such she stood in for Luludja's spirit, to make sure the Bakaishans displayed the proper respect for the dead, both at the graveside and, later, at the funeral feast.

Stasha fixed his gaze on the grave, but Boldo turned and glared at Mirza with ice in his eyes.

You killed her, his eyes said.

I did not, her own eyes replied.

Did it wound all the more because it was Boldo? He was the big brother she'd never had. She'd idolized him when they were growing up. He'd never seemed to mind the dark wine stain that disfigured the side of her face. The other men turned their eyes away, half in disgust, half in fear, for it was well known that a mark such as hers made her the very definition of a natural-born witch.

"Ai-yai-yai." Nadia's ululation caught Boldo's attention and Mirza saw the frown and slight shake of the head as he turned his focus on Lu'dja.

Mirza stepped back until she was pressed against the slender trunk of a silver birch. She stood unmoving until the grave was filled and covered with grass sods as if it had never been.

Everyone trooped from the grave silently. No one looked at Mirza.

As they reached the wagons, Mirza heard the sound of hoofbeats pounding along the road. As one, the whole camp turned. Two riders came into view, mounts lathered with sweat, reins carving foam along the sides of their necks. The men wore the red uniform mente of Zavonian hussars, but instead of looking crisp and neat, they were dusty and almost as weary as their mounts.

Mirza shrank away involuntarily. Hussars were always bad news, usually trying to move them on or inquire about missing property, but these two looked more like messengers.

The riders pulled to a ragged halt, each horse standing, head down, blowing hard.

"How far to the next inn?" the first rider demanded.

Stasha Hetman stepped to the front and answered with a shrug of his shoulders. "Two, maybe three miles." He looked at their horses. "You'll never make it if you push your horses so hard."

"Messages to deliver. We'll get a change of mounts at the inn." The second rider was more forthcoming.

"Must be important," Stasha said.

"King Konstantyn is dead," the first rider said.

"Long live King Gerhardt," the second rider added.

They gathered up their reins and pushed their horses into a gallop.

The king is dead!

The news went round the camp whispered from one to the other. *Konstantyn is dead.* What was the new king going to be like?

Konstantyn, unlike almost every other monarch from here to Gallia, had not expelled the Landstriders, but had allowed them to travel through Zavonia, and work whenever anyone offered them employment.

"Pack the wagons," Stasha called. "We'll have Luludja's funeral feast later. Let's get on the road."

Boldo strode up to Mirza. "Two deaths in one day, and no funeral feast for Luludja. Are you cursed with ill luck?"

Mirza had to remember to close her mouth as she stared at him. "What? You think I killed the king?"

"I think nothing good happens when you're involved."

"Oh, right, I'm an omen of ill luck. I killed Lu'dja and somehow managed to kill the king as well. I must be a very talented shulam." She somehow managed to stop her chin from quivering and blinked away tears. It simply wasn't fair, but life never was.

"They'll come around," Tsura said after Boldo had stalked away.

Mirza shook her head. "They'd rather have you than me as their new shulam."

"I've only been apprenticed for three years. You've been learning for twice that. Besides, you can walk the spirit world. I can't."

"You might yet. I was older than you when I first crossed over. Besides, they never noticed that Lu'dja couldn't."

"Are you going to the funeral feast when we get to the next campground? Everyone will make their own special dish for it. I could bake us a sweetloaf."

"I'm not sure I'd be welcome."

"Then I shan't go either."

"I was going to scrub out the wagon. You might prefer the feast."

Tsura set her shoulders. "I'll help you."

Mirza felt a sudden hot rush of tears. She hugged the younger girl. "Thank you, Tsura-mi. You don't know how much that means."

They moved the wagons ten miles along the road that day, and took refuge in a wooded clearing. As evening shadows lengthened, the Bakaishans came together to hold the delayed funeral feast for Lu'dja.

Instead of attending, the two young women hauled the wagon's canvas from its frame and turned everything out onto the ground:

bed, bedding, two chests of clothing, cooking pots, and all the para-
phernalia of everyday life. They burned the blankets that Lu'dja had
died in, for they were now unlucky.

"What shall we do with these?" Tsura threw open the lid of the
larger chest to reveal Lu'dja's clothes. She held up a dress, a bright
thing that rippled with jewel-like colors. "I've never seen this before."
She let it crumple to the ground. "Or this." She held up a baby's robe.
"Lu'dja never had children, did she?"

"A girl."

Mirza turned at the sound of a voice. Nadia had approached quietly
while they were occupied with Lu'dja's things.

"That's the dress she was married in." Nadia stepped forward and
squatted beside the jewel dress. "I was a tiny thing, but I remember
how glorious she looked on that day. She wasn't a young bride, she was
a woman in her prime, beautiful and confident, and her new husband,
Mihai, was dark and dashing and oh, so handsome that even my
grandmother sighed over him."

"She never said she'd been married," Mirza said.

"It was a long time ago and lasted only a short time. Mihai always
loved to wander. He was accused of stealing a horse as he passed
through some poxy village near the Ruthenian border. They hanged
him for it. In her grief, Lu'dja delivered the child she was carrying too
early. The little mite never breathed."

"What a sad tale," Tsura said. "I wish I'd known."

"Why? If she didn't tell you herself, there was no need for you to
know."

"What should we do with her things?" Mirza asked.

"I'll take them," Nadia said. "The cloth is good. It can be reused for
someone else. There will be more than one wedding after the next
gathering, and a few birthings after that."

"But—" Tsura began to protest.

"Don't worry. You'll not lack for anything." She turned to Mirza.
"Stasha and Boldo have discussed it. They will make you our new
shulam and give you whatever you ask for. Are you up to the task?"

Mirza straightened. "You know I am, but do they? They seem to
have some strange ideas." It was a mark of their feelings that they sent
Nadia to tell her. It should have been Stasha asking her to take Lu'dja's
place.

"They really don't have a choice," Nadia said.

"That's what worries me."

CHAPTER THREE
Valdas

VALDAS THREW HIS voluminous woolen *delja* around himself and Aniela, letting the pleated sleeves dangle behind. It was more for privacy than warmth in the summer night. He squeezed Aniela's hand as they stepped out into the street. He staggered slightly on the uneven cobbles, forcing himself to place one foot carefully in front of the other lest he turn an ankle. Maybe he wasn't as sober as he thought.

The Low Town, with its twisting ways and steeply gabled houses, nestled at the foot of the looming Gura, the home of the Amber Kings since Nikolaus, second son of Casimir IV of Kassubia, snatched the title of Duke of Zavonia and cleaved the Commonwealth in two, making himself king in the process.

They said the Gura had been created by magic many centuries ago. If so it must have been a marvelous working. There was a painting in the long gallery by Albrecht Dürer of the Gura being raised by five robed magicians, but it was only a hundred and fifty years old, so Dürer knew no more than anyone else. It was a fantasy of how it might have been. Valdas was prepared to believe that magic had once been a force in the world, but it couldn't exist in this modern age. No one knew the truth of it. Whether the Gura had been created by magic or by nature, the defensive qualities of the huge inclined plug of rock were not lost on Nikolaus, as they had not been lost on the generations of dukes before him. Atop the Gura sat the Citadel, a fortress that encompassed within its impenetrable curtain-wall a crumbling medieval keep, the barracks and stables, administrative offices, and a modern Italianate palace, Konstantyn's pride and joy.

This was where justice lived . . . had lived. Konstantyn had been a monarch determined to bring light to Zavonia's dark past. No one would easily forget three hundred years of oppression, starting with the Teutonic Knights and ending with the Church, but Konstantyn's reign had ushered in a period of stability. Could Gerhard hold the borders? Would he be an enlightened monarch? Valdas imagined the Zavonia he loved turning to dust and slipping through his fingers.

Damn.

The wedge-shaped Gura jutted out into the bend of the Biela River. From there it sloped so that the three-hundred-foot cliff above the river became a manageable hill on the city side, accessed by the Serpentinas, a switchback cobbled road, lit from dusk to dawn by burning braziers. The town homes of the nobility and the self-made rich lined the lower two thirds, tall and elegant at the front with stepped gables, yet squat at the rear where they were cut into the hillside.

Valdas had once harbored dreams of a modest house on the Serpentinas, with an agreeable wife (he had no one in particular in mind) and a brood of plump, biddable children, all funded by his fat pension. It would have been a fine achievement for the younger son of a minor house left to make his own way in the world . . . until tonight.

The city, itself walled, squatted on the south bank of the Biela. It teemed with men, women and children of every hue, from every walk of life, aristos, artisans, merchants, guildsmen, apprentices, laborers and beggars. Konstantyn had declared that all men should be able to follow their own religion without persecution, so while he followed the Church of Rome, in his city Christians, Jews, Muslims, and even a few Protestants rubbed along together without trouble. Thirty thousand souls jostled together in narrow streets and winding alleyways. Tall dwellings crowded shoulder to shoulder in the streets around the market. Tucked in behind them were stable yards, warehouses, and all manner of artisan workshops. In the main streets, traders set up booths crammed wherever they would fit, to take advantage of the crowds. They sold hot drinks and foods of all description, from traditional stuffed dumplings and pastries with lingonberry jam, to spicy delicacies from far-off Hindia. Street-hawkers shouted their wares— broadsheets, or tin cups, or lucky charms guaranteed to ward off the evil eye. A riot of colors, scents, and languages assaulted the eyes and ears and nose. The smell of money and shit, mingled side by side, fed by the trade from the fat, lazy Biela River.

Tonight people of all ages, all stations, all colors, thronged the streets. *Can it be true? Have you heard? What do you know?* Their words buzzed in Valdas's ears. The light from their lanterns rainbowed against his tear-wet lashes. He rubbed the heel of his hand across his eyes and cleared his throat gruffly before applying himself to looking unremarkable despite his height.

Valdas and Aniela left the busy streets behind and climbed the Serpentinas, cobbles still slick from the early evening rain. Though the road zigzagged to lessen the gradient for horses and carriages, a series of steeply stepped *crookways* cut directly upward between the high walls of the elegant townhouses. Maintained haphazardly, the brazier light at their entrances didn't penetrate the gloom, which made them almost impossible to traverse at night without a lantern. Valdas turned into the first crookway. His feet found the steps and he slid his fist along a smoothness in the wall, the tell-tale where many a hand had rubbed before, traveling blind, step after worn step. At the top he shrank into the shadows, protecting Aniela from view, while six riders clattered past, their horses' iron-shod hooves striking sparks. Once the road was clear, Valdas and Aniela crossed the Serpentinas and entered another crookway, this one smelling of piss. Valdas's leg muscles burned from the climb, and by the third crookway he could hear Aniela's breath coming in short gasps.

"Nearly there," he said when they were something less than halfway up. "Give me your hand."

They waited for a troop of foot-soldiers to pass before crossing the Serpentinas again. Another crookway swallowed them whole. He towed Ani up the last flight, panting with effort himself. The top crookway spat them out barely thirty feet below the main barbican set in the curtain wall that surrounded the Citadel. A crowd had gathered, anonymous, expectant.

"Wait a minute, lover." Aniela bent and put her hands on her knees to get her breath and he had a magnificent view of her breasts as a page with a blazing torch made way for a wealthy dowager to pass. Valdas leaned in, brushed Aniela's shoulder lightly with his fingers, and smiled. She was worth every bit as much as the aristocrats he bowed to on a daily basis.

At length she stood, puffed out her cheeks, and exhaled loudly. "All right. I needed to get my breath back. Do we go in there?" She pointed after the dowager to the long tunnel of the barbican, designed as a killing ground for unwanted visitors. "Only I've never gone in through the front before." She pointed to the carved inscription above the first portcullis. "What does that mean?"

Si Deus nobiscum quis contra nos.

"It's Latin. If God is with us, who is against us?" Valdas didn't need to read it in the flickering light from torches set in the sconces to know what it said. Who indeed? "We'll go round to the Cliff Gate. They've doubled the guard here . . . and, Aniela, love. You can't come in with me." He felt her fingers tighten in his and squeezed her hand. "But I'm grateful for your company this far."

"You don't want me to testify that you were with me all evening?"

"You'd do that for me?" He squeezed her to him and kissed the top of her head. "Bless you, but you might be implicated. Your coney's far too pretty to be sawn in half, my sweet. Best stay out of it."

Valdas led her past the main gate, around the ramparts, and along the very edge of the Gura to the last entrance, situated where the curtain wall met the cliff and squeezed the narrow footpath to nothing. Aniela pressed against him, shaking, until he changed sides and walked between her and the precipice.

Tomas should still be on duty. Tomas Gaida had been one of his trusted lieutenants in the High Guard until an accident in the training ring had honorably discharged him into the regular service on light duties while his knee healed.

Valdas recognized Tomas's outline with relief, but the watch had been doubled here as well, and he didn't know the guards under Tomas's command. He kept his face turned away.

"Can you attract his attention?" he whispered.

"Watch me."

He didn't hear what Aniela said to Tomas as she sashayed up to the gate, hips swinging, but she persuaded the young officer to follow her to where Valdas waited in the shadows, wrapped in the folds of the hooded delja.

"Tomas!"

"Captain Zalecki, sir. What . . . ? I've never . . . I didn't . . ."

Even in the flickering light from the torch set into the wall sconce, the young soldier's eyes were dark-circled in a face three shades paler than usual. Something was very wrong. Something besides the assassination of his king. It took a lot to rattle Tomas.

"Stop gibbering, man." Valdas spoke gently.

Tomas drew a deep breath. "Sir, yes, sir!"

"I have to get inside quietly."

"Begging your pardon. I'm ordered not to allow anyone to pass, especially you, sir. They think you're still inside somewhere."

"And you didn't tell them that I'd passed through this very gate earlier in the evening."

"They didn't ask about earlier." His voice cracked with emotion.

"If Henryk . . . Commander Zehrin . . . didn't see fit to tell them where you were, it wasn't my business."

Valdas nodded. "Good man. What happened? How did the king die? Was it really poison?"

"So they say." Tomas's face twisted. "I don't know what's going on. Someone had a plan, but it's not for me to say who. There's only me and you left, sir." He blurted it out and then clamped his mouth shut as if to stifle a sob.

"I'm going to hand myself over to Henryk—"

"It's too late. That's what I mean. Henryk's dead. They're all dead."

Valdas felt the strength drain out of him. "All of them poisoned?"

"No, sir. It would have been better if they had been. First thing Lord Ger—King Gerhard did. And not just because of the tradition." Tomas almost choked on his words.

"By tradition they should have been given time . . ." Tomas's hands balled into fists. "Collusion, he said. Reasonable suspicion, he said. Conspiracy, he said. Goddamned warrants were signed by Zygmund Kazimir." Tomas screwed up his face. "They allowed no appeal. None. They tied nooses round their necks and threw them off the curtain wall one after the other. You'll—oh, God in his heaven—you'll see them when the sun rises."

It was as if Valdas's being lost focus. His High Guard already dead? They would have followed him to Hell and back if he'd asked them to. His friends, his responsibility.

Now it was his turn to follow them.

What reason did he have to live? What right did he have to live? He clamped his teeth together and forced himself to count to three very slowly. The world around him steadied to a deadly calm.

Tomas's face was pale in the lamp light, a mask of pain. He and Henryk had been more than friends, in the way some men were, and now he wouldn't even be able to grieve openly. Valdas reached out and squeezed the lad's shoulder in mute sympathy.

"Anyone else?" He had a network of watchers throughout the castle, throughout the city, men and women who reported to him and were well paid for it. Most were known only to him, but Henryk had known some of his contacts. Had they put Henryk to the question before they hanged him? He hoped they hadn't had time, for Henryk's own sake as much as for the informants.

"No one else that I heard of, sir."

Valdas released a breath he'd barely noticed he was holding. "I didn't kill the king."

"Of course not, but with respect, you're not going in there to try and prove that. No swiving way . . . sir."

Aniela tugged at his sleeve. "Valdas. Let's go."

Tomas's upright posture slipped for a moment. "Henryk didn't let on. None of your men let on. Don't you think they were giving you a chance? I know it's not in you to run, Captain, but you can't do anyone any good if you go in there, not King Konstantyn, not yourself."

What good could he do if he stayed out here, honor-broke? Cast adrift from his position and resources, he was a useless lump of muscle and bone.

Tomas's voice hardened. "Whoever killed the king, it's obvious who's really behind it. Gerhard has proclaimed himself king, and Kazimir is chancellor already. Quick work, don't you think?"

"Already?" Valdas's brain slipped into gear and he nodded. "Quick work, indeed."

What had he been thinking? His king was dead. His men were dead and the little runt Gerhard had snatched up the Amber Crown before it was cold from Konstantyn's head. Was it a carefully worked-out plan, or merely opportunism?

Formless rage began to churn in Valdas's gut. He took three more deep breaths and pushed it down.

"What about Chancellor Skorny?" Valdas's voice shook. He swallowed to steady it. Gods, he regretted the Rhenish.

"I don't know."

Skorny was not in the palace. He'd left for his country home three weeks ago. Of course, the old man might already be dead. If this assassination was Gerhard's doing, he might have sent someone after Skorny, too.

Valdas straightened. An idea began to crystallize. A convenient idea to save his neck, right enough, but . . . it was his duty to avenge King Konstantyn and deliver justice for his men . . . and, by God, he would! The need burned in his chest.

"I will go, but right here and now, among us three, I swear that on whatever honor I have left, I will return and King Konstantyn's killer will pay. And by all that's holy, the men of the High Guard will have a stone on Soldiers' Fields to mark their loyalty to the crown."

He saw the look in their eyes. Had he been that intense? Yes, he probably had, and he'd meant every word. He didn't know how and he didn't know when, but he would return.

CHAPTER FOUR

Lind

HE'D NEVER KILLED a king before.

Lind clenched and unclenched his fists. The shaking had almost stopped. He didn't get the shakes while he was working, but once the job was over, reaction set in. He stared out at the rooftops from the small dormer window. If he let his eyes defocus, all he saw was a mathematical puzzle of shapes, gradients, and angles. He blinked to refocus. Beyond the rooftops the tilted slab of the Gura rose impossibly high. It had been the devil's own work to infiltrate the Citadel, but it was done now, so all he had left to do was get out of the city in one piece.

He'd made sure he was back here long before the Didelis Bell tolled, but he'd come via two other inns where he'd taken rooms and stashed certain items. In the first he'd washed off the stink of fish, shaved his dyed brown curls down to stubble that was his own fair color, and changed into fresh clothes. He'd shed the short tunic and workaday leggings in favor of an unremarkable drab green zupan, buttoned down the front and coming to just below his knees where his trousers were tucked into his boot tops. He'd burned the hair clippings and the fishmonger garb in the little bedroom fireplace, though the worn leather shoes had taken the best part of an hour to crumble to ash. He resented the time, but he daren't leave anything behind that they could use to track him. Even the best magicians couldn't track from ashes.

The nape of his neck prickled whenever he thought about magic.

In the second inn he'd washed again, never sure whether the stink of fish still followed him around or whether, after all this time, it had lodged in his nostrils permanently. Then he'd shaved his beard and mustache and exchanged the green zupan for a rich blue one, like those worn by the Zavonian nobility, largely of Kassubian descent. This one had braid frogging. The long sleeves ended in dog-ears that turned up to show the red silk lining. He matched the color of the lining with a long red sash tied around his waist with the ends hanging almost to hem level. It was an outfit he could wear a sword with, which he did. Having his own side-sword sheathed at his hip always comforted him. He placed concealed knives in his sleeves and his boots. You could never have too many knives. Once again he burned the discarded zupan rather than leave it behind.

The day being mild, his delja had been surplus to requirements, and besides it was bulky enough that if he had to fight for his life it would get in the way, so he'd folded it lengthways, tucked the bulky sleeves inside, and carried it over his arm. He'd always preferred a straightforward cloak, but a Zavonian gentleman wore a delja, and being dressed as a gentleman meant that he avoided the kind of questions the watch directed at the lower classes. He'd even had to take note of fashions to make sure he didn't stand out. This year the bravos wore their deljas with their arms through the open eye of the armholes with the cumbersome sleeves dangling backward from the shoulder; last year it had been de rigueur to wear the garment like a coat.

He'd left the second inn, striding confidently through the market, toward the quarter of town where whorehouses and taverns stood gable to gable. Trader Maksimilian's whorehouse had been his refuge in Biela Miasto twice before. Maksimilian didn't seem to mind Lind as long as he paid his rent.

Lind had considered trying to get out of the city before the news of the king's death broke, but the first thing that would happen would be troops out on the road asking questions. Better to let the fuss die down. He'd climbed to his attic refuge, wondering how long he would have to stay before it was safe to leave.

The last smear of daylight had departed the western sky when the Didelis Bell had begun to toll. He'd blown out his cheeks and whistled. Thank Christ it was over. If the poisoned fish hadn't found its mark he'd have had to think of another way to do the job, and infiltrating a second time would be damn nigh impossible.

Relief was short-lived, however, even more so than usual. Killing a king was the pinnacle of his career . . . So what now?

◆————◆

This attic room wasn't good for Lind's nerves. He had too much time to question whether he'd done something stupid. At first, killing a king had been a challenge. It wasn't, after all, his king. Lind had been born across the Narrow Sea in Sverija, where Karl Gustav ruled. He felt a slight twinge that his work had widowed Karl Gustav's youngest sister, only recently married to the Zavonian king.

But why should he worry? What had any royal ever done for him?

He shrugged and drew his chair up to the window to catch the light on the pages of his newspaper, the *Mercury*, borrowed from Trader Maksimilian. This edition was already three days old, still praising King Konstantyn on the twentieth anniversary of his coronation. Lind could imagine what the next edition would contain. This one contained nothing but the usual: European dynastic affairs, politics, and military campaigns. Not that he could read more than half of it. He could manage the Zavonian well enough, even though it wasn't his first language, but didn't have more than a smattering of Latin, and that was mostly bits of remembered church dogma. Why did they have to print so much of the damned paper in Latin?

The wind rattled the window catch and hurled a sudden squall of rain at the glass. A fine spray spurted round the ill-fitting frame and kissed his cheek. It reminded him of the feel of spray on his face at the falls in Tepet on the day he'd been offered the job.

The fine spray from the tumbling falls beneath his feet cools Lind's face. It beads on his eyelashes, conjuring jeweled rainbows which dance in the sun when he blinks. This is Lind's regular place of business, in the middle of the ancient bridge suspended over the gorge that divides the wooden Old Town of Tepet from the New Town with its limestone houses.

The man walks across from the New Town, alone as instructed. Close up, his eyes are curiously empty, the pupils large, as if he might have taken some calming drug, though surely any sane man would prefer to keep his wits sharp in the presence of a professional assassin on a narrow bridge above a waterfall. Neither old nor young, the man is dressed in dull colors. His zupan is closed and drawn in about his waist with a sash, but his delja is open and flaps in the wind, threatening to turn into a sail and carry him off the bridge into the gorge below. He's wearing it as a cloak, and the dangling sleeves are whipping about in the wind.

Lind half-smiled at the memory. One little jostle and the man could have met his end in the falls below. Lind amused himself by working out how he could have done it so that anyone observing was none the wiser. The answer to: *Did he fall or was he pushed?* would almost certainly have been: *He fell.*

The man had been a puzzle. He'd spoken with the slightly clipped tones of the Zavonian nobility, but he didn't quite have the imperiousness. Maybe he was one of those used to serving them.

Lind is curious. He's used to seeing emotion in those who offer him money to kill: sometimes agitation, naked anger, or self-righteousness, occasionally greed, and frequently fear, but this man displays only a curious detachment that makes Lind's hackles rise.

Lind turns and rests his hands on the rail. The lip of the falls is barely twenty feet below. He can see straight down to the stone-speckled riverbed. The water looks deceptively calm as it races toward the broken edge of rock and the sudden hundred-foot drop. However close Tepet's old city and the new crowd in on the rocky walls of the gorge, nothing can touch the crystal cold majesty of the torrent of water plunging over such a cliff edge.

The man joins him, elbow to elbow. The roar of the falls gives them privacy. The man holds out a purse between them.

Lind should have walked away right then. That he didn't was as much due to curiosity as to the obvious weight of the purse. He'd always made it a rule to avoid killing people important enough to bring down heavy retaliation. He was happy with a greedy merchant or two, or a corrupt councilor, or a man unfaithful in love, or the head of a family who was drinking and gambling away his children's inheritance. Once he'd even killed a bishop. He'd done that one for free when the parents of a young monk who had committed suicide had come to him with a story.

The weight of this purse alone should have filled him with alarm.

"Who sent you here?" Lind reaches out and brushes the purse with one fingertip. He's never been offered so much gold for one kill before.

"I cannot say." The man leans over to look at the drop. Lind waits for a reaction, but the man's face remains impassive.

"You don't look like a man with a hundred gold schillings to spend," Lind says.

"I . . ." The man clears his throat and wipes the sheen of water from his forehead, or maybe it's nervous sweat. *"I'm offering money. What more do you want?"*

"I want to know who I'm killing for."

"My master is paying you handsomely for your lack of knowledge."
He traces the lines of a symbol on the damp balustrade.

Lind's skin crawls. He's never had much to do with magic, but he recognizes the shiver of it. He quells the urge to turn and run for the nearest church where such devilry is outlawed.

The man reaches under the folds of his delja. Lind stiffens, his own hand close to the stiletto concealed in his sleeve. But instead of a weapon, the man pulls out another pouch, equal to the first. Lind stares. It's a fortune. He could retire.

Presuming he survives this kill.

"Double it." He swallows convulsively, wondering if he's being terminally stupid. It's not just the money, but anyone paying this much is going to give him a challenge he has never faced before, and maybe— just maybe—the challenge is as enticing as the gold.

The man drops the second bag into Lind's hand. It lands with a comforting crunch. "A sign of good faith."

"That would be your master's good faith, I take it?"

The man inclines his head. "Two bags now; two when the job's done."

Lind picks up the second bag, tests the weight, and nods.

CHAPTER FIVE
Valdas

WRAPPED IN THE anonymity of the woolen delja, Valdas and Aniela made their way down the crookways, feeling for each step with cautious feet.

His head was spinning.

King Konstantyn.

Henryk.

His men.

He began to recite their names under his breath.

"Henryk Zehrin, Lukas Grinius, Bartek Andrulis, Darius Kairys, Hector Bakaitis, Raulo Budrys, Feliks Kleiza, Iwan Matonis, Valter Mekas, Matis Liepa, Kajus Janutis, Eberhard Brunner, Vadim and Filip Rimkus, true brothers, Sandor Nowak, Fabius Adomatis, Tavas Varnas and Tavas Kleizer, Leonas Smetona, Jerzy Polonsky, Petras Mazur, Waldemar Konopka. Konstantyn, second of his name. King of Zavonia."

When he got to the end he began again.

And again.

Aniela tugged him toward the Low Town and the Winged Hussar, but that would be the first likely place they would look for him. He mustn't get caught now. He felt as if he had hot stones burning in his gut. He'd made a vow to bring Konstantyn's killer to justice and prove his men innocent. He stood tall and threw his shoulders back. After that, if execution was his lot, he'd submit with dignity.

And what if the perpetrator was the new king, as Tomas suspected?

That was the big question.

It seemed more than likely, but he simply couldn't imagine Gerhard ever having the ballocks to do that. Yes, he'd inherited the crown, but to Valdas's knowledge he'd never shown an interest in governance. He lived well and comfortably, so why would he want the work that came with the Amber Crown? Make no mistake, being king was hard work and a heavy responsibility . . . and that simply wasn't Gerhard's style. He preferred to mince around with his little lap dogs, follow the latest fashion—though never lead it—attend balls, dinners, and recitals, and be seen in the company of all the most prominent courtiers.

Valdas thought about all those courtiers. There wasn't one who would be better off with Gerhard as king. Though Konstantyn had kept his barons sweet, he'd never heaped favors on one over the others. Konstantyn's most trusted advisers were the ones who held responsibility—Chancellor Skorny, rock steady, but not a day on the low side of sixty, and General Klimt, who oversaw the disposition of the standing army, both the infantry and the husaria. He'd risen as high as a commoner could rise. Konstantyn's demise might see his years of service cast aside. Neither Skorny nor Klimt was guilty of Konstantyn's murder.

He turned Aniela down a side street. "To the docks," he said. "I'll find a boat going downriver."

Biela Miasto's walls surrounded three sides of the city with the river forming the fourth defense. Even so, there was a smaller wall separating the riverside from the Low Town. The Rivergate was usually open and unmanned in peacetime, but by the movement of guards through the city, they were strengthening troops at all the exit points.

Valdas pulled Aniela close and they slipped through the gate, arm in arm, while a young officer was barking instructions to a couple of soldiers to set up a barrier.

"I know someone," Aniela said. "Used to work for her at the Lobster Pot when I first came to the city. She got lucky, married the owner and inherited the tavern not two years later. She has a couple of riverboats, too. She runs a clean house and has contacts."

Madame Podory, modestly dressed in a high-necked linen letnik that hid her figure completely, greeted Aniela warmly with a kiss on each cheek. After pleasantries had been exchanged, she took a single candle and drew them out of the main room of the inn into a little cubby furnished with nothing but a bed big enough for two and a single chair. There she got down to business, naming a price for passage on one of her riverboats that made Valdas glad he'd brought a fat purse with him tonight.

She frowned when she heard who Valdas was, but the sight of his silver tolars put a smile on her face. They settled on six for passage safely beyond the city walls, but no further.

"She sails at dawn." Madame Podory placed the candle on the mantel shelf. "I don't want you hanging around the docks until then, so stay here. I'll throw in the room at no extra cost. I'm sure Aniela can keep you entertained."

The door closed behind her. Valdas dropped his delja onto the chair. His hand shook as he unbuckled his belt and scabbards. The alcohol was still in his system, dammit, fogging his brain, making him acutely aware that he was not at his best. He let Aniela take over, surrendering to her hands, quick and light and not at all sensual, as she stripped him naked and rolled him into the bed. She undressed quickly and simply stretched out beside him, her body warm against his, head pillowed on his shoulder and her hand unmoving against his chest.

The stubble on his chin caught in the tangle of her hair as he dropped a gentle kiss onto the top of her head.

"Sleep, Valdas," she said.

The sweet note of her cheap perfume tickled Valdas's nose. He stroked the silk of Aniela's shoulder, letting the sensation in his fingertips lull the whirligig of his thoughts and the churning mess in his gut. Images of Konstantyn, the man and the monarch, chased themselves around his head. They widened out to Konstantyn's plans for Zavonia. He was truly a modern king, instituting a charter that gave the common people rights: right to own land, however small the plot; right to a fair trial; right to marry without permission of their local lord; right to trade across borders without taxation. The people had prospered. Yet Konstantyn had not been a weak king. He'd retaken the disputed land of the Tevecor Reaches from the Ruthenian Tsar, and had protected his borders by marrying his sister to the tsar-in-waiting.

Valdas's thoughts were all too much. He'd never be able to sleep.

But he did.

He awoke in the middle of the night and found Aniela had lit a new candle from the stub of the old one. She lay on her side, watching him, not quite touching, though he could feel the warmth radiating from her.

"What's wrong?" he asked, listening for sounds from beyond the room. "Is someone here?"

She shook her head. "Where will you go?"

"Chancellor Skorny's estate—to see if the old man lives. If he doesn't, then to Konstantyn's sister Zofia in Bieloria. I hear she holds

Bieloria for the tsar while he holds Ruthenia. There has never been much love between tsar and tsarina, but she's a strong woman. Maybe I can return with Tsarina Zofia's strength behind me. Gerhard will pay. I know the Gura, I can take it with fifty men. There's God-pox-all I can do alone—not right now, anyway."

"You think you can make a difference." It wasn't a question.

"I have to try."

"Of course you do."

She put out one hand, not quite touching his face, then thought better of it and rolled onto her back, her figure making interesting shapes beneath the covers. She stared up at the ceiling.

"You don't think I can," he said.

She was silent for the count of ten heartbeats, then she took a deep breath and sighed it out. She raised herself up on one elbow to look into his eyes. "I think if anyone can, it's you, Valdas Zalecki. You'll find a way."

"I'm just a glorified guard—"

"Hush." She put her fingers to his lips. "You're more than that, Valdas. You never said, but I listened to what you didn't say. You protected the king, not just with your body, but with your brain, your network of informants—"

"Much good they did me . . . or the king."

"You said yourself that poison is the most difficult to guard against."

He didn't reply, lost in thought. How could it have happened? What could he have done to prevent it?

"Do you feel guilty?" she asked.

"Hell, yes."

"You've committed no sin, Valdas."

"Except, maybe, a sin of omission."

"Stop examining what you can't change. Think on what you can do. Make it right for King Konstantyn."

"For the man and the monarch, I will. And for my men, too."

Her mouth twitched into a half smile and she flopped down onto her back.

Her faith was humbling. In truth he was more than a little lost, but Aniela believed in him. Right now that was all that mattered.

If he'd had to choose someone to spend his last night with, Aniela would be the one. The thought surprised him even as he acknowledged it. He might never see her again. His eyes felt unaccountably prickly and damp. He ran his free hand beneath the blankets, over her generous breasts and down her little round belly, as if he were a blind man memorizing her shape by touch alone. "My lovely girl, I shall miss you."

"I'll miss you, too, lover. Good customers are hard to find . . . especially ones who want to snore all night."

"I've finished snoring. Time to earn that ring you're wearing."

"Oh, I forgot. Here." She started to pull it off.

"It was a gift."

"When you thought you were . . ." She swallowed hard. "You know . . ."

He nodded. "Keep it safe for me until I come back."

"It's worth a fortune, Valdas. You might need it."

"I can't sell it before I leave the city, and I'd never get full value for it in the country. Besides, it means something to me, and I hope that it means something to you, too."

"Men don't often give rings to women in my profession. Not that kind of ring. It's nice. Nice to imagine . . . Nice to have it for a while." She held up her left hand and waggled her fingers in the candle light, letting the reflection play along the rubies. "I'm not keeping it forever. It's still yours when you want it." She curled her fingers around it. "I'm just keeping it safe for you."

"Thank you."

He leaned over and kissed her on the cheek, then licked his lips. Salt. "Have you been crying?"

She gave a little hiccough, turned and buried her head in his shoulder. "Oh, Valdas . . . What do you expect? I'm not made of stone. How long have we been doing this?"

He tangled his fingers in her hair and lifted her head gently. Even in the flickering candlelight her eyes were rimmed with pink.

"Two years? Three?"

She smacked the palm of her hand on his naked chest. "You can be an oaf when you want to be, Valdas Zalecki. Try six."

"Six? Really? And you still a slip of a girl."

Her mouth began to twitch up at the corners.

"That's better," he said. "Now, send me on my way properly."

She pushed the covers away, kissed his mouth and his chest, awakening a growing heat. He guided her head downward, already throbbing with anticipation. He liked women—no—he loved women, young or old, fat or thin. Good, healthy sex with a warm willing woman always made his world come round right, and Ani was the epitome of warm and willing. He took care to give as well as take.

"Come on, big boy, get it up for Aniela."

Was there ever a time Valdas Zalecki had not risen to the occasion? He felt Aniela's tongue teasing a line from his belly button downward. His skin was on fire—all the heat and none of the pain. And . . .

"Yes, there. Ahhh . . . Lovely girl . . ."

He wasn't going to pop in less than a minute this time. He let her go on for just long enough, then gently pulled her face up level with his, his hands cradling her ears and his thumbs stroking her cheeks. Then he rolled her over onto her back, bent his head to nuzzle her nipples, and reached for her sweet spot with his fingers. He heard her gasp and felt shudders run through her body.

"You don't have to fake it for me, lovely girl. I know it takes a lot in your line of work."

She didn't answer for a few moments. When she did her voice trembled. "You're an ass, Valdas." She kissed him full on the mouth and whispered in his ear. "No sheath. I don't do that for anyone else, you know. And don't worry. I'm clean."

"Me, too." Ani wouldn't usually fuck without a sheath; pox being a bigger killer of whores than drunks. "What about, you know, babies?"

"It's the wrong time of the month. Don't worry, I won't make a father of you."

He didn't need a second invitation.

He felt the blood throbbing through his tackle, coursing through his chest and singing in his ears, or was that Ani's soft moans as she rose to meet him? Her warm, tight wetness sent shivery messages to his spine and hips to thrust and thrust again, deep and deeper still. He took his weight on his hands so he didn't crush the life out of her, but she had a lithe strength of her own. She hooked her legs up and still managed to rake the cheeks of his arse with her fingernails, rising and falling with his rhythm until a star burst in his belly and he spasmed inside her, then flopped, completely spent, between her legs, breathing hard.

She reached for him, grasping him around the ears, and kissed the top of his head before wriggling into a more comfortable position.

He was on the point of dozing, Ani curled in his embrace, his nose in her hair, his lips against the fine curve of her shoulder, when all hell broke loose. Three great thumps on the front door and a harsh voice yelling for admittance had Valdas shooting out of bed, reaching for his pantalones and his boots.

CHAPTER SIX
Mirza

A RIDER FROM the Uzgorzi people had arrived earlier in the day when the sun was high in the sky. What appeared to be chance meetings never were. Mirza had seen Stasha send out a rider the previous morning.

The Uzgorzi was another one of the nomadic bands that had fled the wide steppes, driven out by a decade of drought and the threat of the hordes sweeping from further east. The Uzgorzi and the Bakaishans had traveled together for a while, but soon learned that it was better to split into smaller groups so as not to seem threatening.

Whenever two bands came together it was an excuse for a feast, and an opportunity for the young folk to meet. Landstriders didn't mix with the local population, so the grandmothers of all the clans made it their business to promote healthy intermarriage.

Though there were no professional matchmakers here like there were at Djanganai, the grandmothers still brought together sons and daughters of good families, not too closely related, so that the bands would prosper. Healthy children made a band rich in ways that could not be counted in coins.

Mirza's hand drifted down to her belly. She might as well be barren for all the good her womb did. She hadn't found a man, but that didn't mean she didn't want children. What a scandal that would be, if she had children without a husband. Only widows could raise children alone, and there were always men, older bachelors or widowers, who would offer for a comely widow who had already proved fertile. Besides, children were raised by the whole band.

She shook her head to dismiss the thought of children. There would be other business now that she'd taken her place as shulam.

The last time they'd met the Uzgorzi, Lu'dja had still been well and Mirza and Tsura had attended a conclave with Sallia, the Uzgorzi shulam, and her apprentices, Esmaralda and Dina. The two shulams swapped information and traded herbs and recipes while the apprentices stared at each other in silence, wondering which of them had seniority, but not liking to ask.

Now it seemed as though it would be Mirza's turn to meet with Sallia as an equal. Was she ready for this? She didn't immediately seek Sallia out as the Uzgorzi made camp. There would be time enough tomorrow. Tonight there would be dancing.

Mirza sat on a thick rug and watched men and boys feeding logs into the central campfire in readiness for the evening to come. Stasha and Boldo directed some of the younger Landstriders in the task while managing to do very little work themselves. Young men from the Uzgorzi joined the Bakaishans with enthusiasm.

This gathering was informal, unlike the great meet at Djanganai each autumn, but the customs still had to be observed: food cooked together and shared; the young folk allowed a little more leeway for courting, as long as they remained chaste; the musicians from both bands playing together, and the dancing around the fire after dark.

❦

The flickering flames illuminated the side of Mirza's old wagon, fire and shadow twisting in and out to the music of the violins, jangling tsymbaly, and a pair of small drums struck with wooden beaters.

Mirza tapped her foot to the rhythm. She loved the sound of the violin, particularly when Sandor played it. He'd been the Bakaishans' primas for as long as Mirza could remember and now he established his dominance among the assembled musicians from the Uzgorzi, playing with virtuosity and passion, leading the others from lilting melodies to the high trills and harmonics that mimicked birdsong.

Sandor's son underpinned the melody with a three-stringed kontra, bowing three-note chords with the instrument against his chest rather than under the chin. Most musicians played violin or kontra, but the two Uzgorzi musicians played tsymbalys. The players of both bands had converged, to prepare for the dances to come, sparking off each other with lively tunes, thrilling runs along the fingerboard, or dramatic leaps.

One man, gnarled and toothless, played tsymbaly from a seated position, a faraway expression on his wrinkled face. The other tsymbaly player, strong-featured with a ready smile, strode among the crowd like a minor god, his instrument suspended on a strap around his neck with one edge anchored against his waist, the delicate hammers flying in his hands as he struck a tune from the strings, sometimes with more enthusiasm than accuracy, but always with flair.

Mirza's gaze was drawn to him, as were the eyes of every other female who had a pulse, but when he grinned in her direction, she looked away, hot and flustered.

Even though the dances had not yet begun, Florica stood close to the fire, swaying and twisting her hips so that her skirts swirled this way and that and the charms stitched onto her headdress jangled merrily and glinted in the firelight. She never missed an opportunity to show off her pretty ankles and her lithe grace. Sometimes she would even flick her skirts aside to show a scandalous glimpse of her calves. Oh, she tried to make it look accidental, but the women knew even if the men did not. Mirza smiled, as if Florica were a child with much to learn about the world, then pressed her lips together. Florica was her own age, vital and young, but since Lu'dja's death, Mirza had carried the weight of knowledge and responsibility.

Aiee! She was becoming old before her time.

Yet if she acted her true age, she'd never get any respect from the band. It was hard enough as it was, earning respect from people who had seen her struggling with her apprenticeship, clashing with her mistress. If only they knew why.

She sighed.

They wouldn't believe her if she told them, and she'd never be able to prove it.

"You should dance with the maidens." Tsura came to stand between her and the fire, casting Mirza's disfigured face into darkness. "It's your right."

"Right." Mirza waved her open fingers toward the witchmark that had separated her from the rest of the band's children ever since she could remember. It was her face that had caused Luludja to buy her from the family who had taken her in after her parents died, first as a servant and then as an apprentice.

Long gone to dust, her mother sat in a corner of her memory, more a feeling than an image. First her baby brother, then her parents and her sister got sick. Mirza remembered her mother begging other families to take Mirza, and finally one of them did. She never saw her parents or siblings again.

"Are you listening to me?" Tsura's exasperated voice broke into her thoughts.

"Sorry. What?"

"Ha! I thought not!" Tsura tapped her foot on the dusty ground. "I'm paying you a compliment and you don't even listen."

"You're my apprentice now." Mirza raised one eyebrow, teasing. "It's for you to listen to me."

"It's only a short while since we were both her apprentices." Tsura made the sign to ward off ill luck from speaking of the recently departed.

"I am the eldest by three years."

"You're changing the subject. I said you should dance because when the mood takes you, your dancing is every bit as good as Florica's."

"Ah, but she has the face for it. Unless I'm very much mistaken she'll find herself a husband before this meet is over. The young men have been falling over themselves to carry water from the stream, or fetch kindling from the forest."

"She's not interested in the young men."

Tsura's statement caused Mirza to look up.

"What do you know that I don't?"

"Since Stasha's wife died . . ."

"You think she's setting her sights on him?"

"Why not? As the wife of the hetman, she could lord it over the rest of us, even Nadia."

"Nadia would never allow that. She's the head woman, and no one is going to forget that in a hurry."

Tsura shrugged. "I'm only telling you what I gleaned. You should still dance."

"And then what, Stasha would offer for me?" She scowled. "I don't think so. No man here will offer for me. They are too afraid of what I might do to their manhood."

"He might." Tsura jerked her head toward the tsymbaly player. "He keeps looking over here and smiling."

"He's probably short-sighted. He smiles at everyone. Besides, I think it's you he's looking at."

"I'm too young to dance with the maidens yet."

"He doesn't know that. Definitely short-sighted."

Tsura shrugged. "Next year it will be my turn, but this year we should find you a husband. Stasha will know what a true gem he's lost only when you marry into another family and he has to find a new shulam for the band."

Mirza choked off a derisory snort. "As if that's likely to happen."

The music died away and the musicians leaned in toward each other as if deciding what to play next. Then the drumbeat counted them in. They struck up a chord, the sweetness of the violins offsetting the cheerful jangle of the tsymbalys.

Florica was first into the dance, as usual, leaping, swaying, and twirling to impress. Her eyes locked on Stasha. Even in the spins she kept her face toward his as much as she could.

"You're right, Tsura-mi. How did I miss that?" Mirza said.

"She's healthy and you're much more preoccupied with the sick."

"And so should you be."

"Yes, mistress." Tsura chuckled and sank down beside Mirza.

Mirza didn't dance, and neither did Tsura. Together they presented a united front.

<hr/>

"You do not dance, pretty lady, though I play good, huh?"

The voice, close by, startled her. The good-looking tsymbaly player, now divested of his instrument, hunkered down on his heels by her side. His words were accented, his dialect obviously Uzgorzi, but his meaning was clear. "If you are betrothed, I am too late. My heart will forever wither in my breast."

She didn't turn to look at him. While she kept staring toward the fire, the great purple birthmark was in shadow. Once she turned and he saw it, the flirtation would end. He would find an excuse and take his leave, or maybe just yelp and run away. Either way, he'd be paying court to one of the other girls within moments, trying to forget the splash of color and the roughly textured skin on Mirza's face.

For now, however, she enjoyed the novelty.

"You probably say that to all the girls."

"Not all of them."

"Only some? I'm glad you don't lie."

"Oh, I lie all the time, pretty lady, only not that way." He gestured with both hands, indicating lying horizontal.

"You are bold. Do you have a name?"

"Nicu Bihari, but my friends call me Mori."

"They call you Horse?"

"I am too modest to say why."

"Maybe it's for your ability to eat hay, or your strength when pulling a heavy wagon out of the mire."

A frown flashed across his face and then he laughed. "Or maybe it's because I'm hung like one."

"See, you are not too modest after all to boast of your giant kok to a woman you have only just met."

"A woman who does not blush at the word."

"I am a shulam. I do not fear to talk about a man's body, or about his soul. A boil is a boil whether it's on a man's neck or his arse."

He laughed again, a hearty, open sound. "I like you. You show no fear. We should make babies. They would be very brave and they would be able to talk down the moon."

"Why do I think you are not proposing marriage?"

"Alas, pretty lady, if you are the shulam of the Bakaishans I fear you are betrothed already and bound for another band. Why else would Stasha Hetman be making an offer for Esmaralda, who has only recently stepped out from behind her apprenticeship as a shulam in her own right?"

"Stasha is what?" Mirza heard her own voice rise to a screech. Nicu rocked on his heels as she whipped her head around. She didn't know whether it was her voice or the first sight of her wine-dark witchmark that startled him into a flinch, but right now she didn't care. "You're sure?"

"The grandmothers all whisper it."

Her throat burned. "Well, they can just stop whispering it. I'm not going anywhere."

She stood in one fluid movement. "Thank you, Nicu. I release you from your offer of babymaking. I would not wish your stallion kok to wither on my behalf. Take up your tsymbaly and find a pretty lady who is not so afflicted." She touched her face. "It's time I had words with Stasha Hetman."

Her boiling temper gave her courage. She marched across the camp, cleaving through waiting dancers like a wolf through a flock of sheep. The fire leaped higher as she passed, tongues of flame flickering toward her in sympathy.

"Out of my way!" This to Boldo, who positioned himself in front of the place where Stasha, Hetman of the Bakaishans, sat cross-legged facing a pretty young woman. A grandmother sat between them, holding Stasha's hand in one of hers and Esmaralda's in the other. She had not yet brought them together.

"Stop that right now!" Mirza snapped. "Whatever he has promised you, know that I am the shulam of the Bakaishans and I do not relinquish my place to you or any who would usurp it."

"Is this true?" the grandmother asked, dropping both her charges' hands.

Stasha raised both shoulders in a deep shrug and opened both hands, palms up, fingers splayed. "It is true that Mirza was the eldest apprentice of our much-loved Luludja when the dear lady went to paradise. What else could we do but accept her as our shulam, even though—"

"Even though what?" Mirza's shoulders stiffened. "When have I ever let you down? I served my time as Lu'dja's apprentice, and would have been released a year before she passed, but she was too mean to acknowledge me."

"Mean? Luludja was never mean, neither was she mean-spirited in her dealings with this world or the world above."

"Gah!" Mirza stamped her foot. "She never dealt with the spirit world. For forty years she faked it. Your father knew and let it pass, and so did you."

Stasha leaped to his feet. By now, everyone was standing, even Esmaralda and the grandmother, who had their heads close together, whispering.

"That's a lie. You can't say that," Stasha said.

"It's not a lie and I just did." Mirza stuck her chin out and folded her arms across her chest to hide the fact that her fists were clenched. "She faked it, and when she found out that I could do what she couldn't, she held me back, squashed me down at every opportunity, belittled me in front of the band. You thought I was struggling to learn, but I was struggling because I learned too well. Lu'dja was a healer, a good healer, but she was never a witch."

Stasha opened his mouth to deny it again. "But—"

"She tells the truth." Tsura pushed her way through the substantial crowd that had gathered, three deep. Her voice shook, but she had a determined look on her face. "Lu'dja couldn't bear to know that Mirza had found her way to the spirit world unaided. Every day she feared that Mirza would show her up as a fake, either deliberately or accidentally."

"She told me—" Stasha said.

"That it was the other way around," Mirza finished for him.

"How can I . . . ? How do I know what you tell me is true?" Stasha's sun-browned face had taken on a grayish cast in the firelight.

"Unless you can walk the spirit world, you'll have to take my word for it."

"No, he doesn't!" Esmaralda stepped forward. "I know a way it can be proven. My power against yours on the spirit plane, and if you lose, you stand aside and give me your place, your wagon, and your apprentice."

So Esmaralda was going to fight for it. Mirza couldn't give in or she'd be finished. She turned to the young woman, noting her perfect skin. No witchmark, unless it was hidden beneath her colorful dress. "You want my place so badly that you would risk—what? If you lose, what do I gain?"

"You keep your place. Isn't that what you want?"

"Mirza is right." The grandmother spoke. "If you want her wagon, you should wager yours."

"Fine. Right." Esmaralda spat upon the ground. "If you win you get my wagon. It's much better than yours. You're not going to win, anyway."

"We'll see about that." Mirza stared into Esmaralda's eyes. Who would blink first?

"You, boy, bring salt." The grandmother stepped between them and broke the staring match. "And you, girl, ask Jofranka to come and judge a contest."

"What's going to happen?" Stasha touched the grandmother's arm, received a sharp stare, and stepped one pace backward.

"A contest. See what you've started. They are both going to journey to the land of the dead. Maybe only one will return."

"A duel to the death? I didn't ask them to do that."

"Tell yourself that when one of them lies beneath the dirt."

Mirza felt her breath catch in her throat. To the death? The wagon was irrelevant. Tsura. What about Tsura?

She felt the girl tug at her sleeve and dipped her head to catch a whisper. "Don't worry. If you die I will kill her for you."

"If I die, you look after yourself."

The crowd stirred and parted. A wizened woman even older than the grandmother shuffled through, leaning heavily on a blackthorn stick as if her body pained her.

"Who calls Jofranka from her comfortable seat by the fire?"

The grandmother stepped forward. "I called you, mother of grand-mothers, to oversee a match of power between two foolish children."

"Ha, foolish indeed. What do they fight over?"

"Over who is to be the shulam of the Bakaishans. One has the posi-tion, but only claimed it recently. The other desires it, but the one will not step aside for the other."

"Hmm. Someone fetch me a seat." A young man stepped forward

with a box upon which he placed a cushion and Jofranka sat, leaning on her stick, both hands clasped together over its bulbous end. "Salt. Who's bringing salt?"

The boy who'd been sent for it proffered a wooden box.

"Well, what are you waiting for, boy? Make the circle. Mind there are no breaks in it. Give us plenty of room." She looked up at Mirza and Esmaralda. "Sit, both of you. Clasp hands. Wait for my word."

CHAPTER SEVEN
Valdas

THREE MORE THUMPS on the front door sent Valdas panicking for his shirt. A house-to-house search? Already? Or had someone seen them heading for the river?

"What is it? God in heaven!" Aniela rolled to her feet. "Valdas get out, quick!" She dropped her letnik over her head and let its folds cover her naked body, then stomped into her shoes, getting in Valdas's way as he fumbled for his tunic.

"Move, woman!" He pushed her onto the bed and grabbed his sword belt, looping it over his shoulder.

Above his head he could hear the sound of footsteps coming down the main stair as Madame Podory loudly cursed anyone who disturbed her sleep. Valdas turned to Aniela and kissed the top of her head.

"Sorry, lovely girl, I didn't mean to be rough. Look after yourself."

He wrenched open the door and turned toward the back of the inn, but Aniela grabbed his arm.

They came face-to-face with Madame Podory at the foot of the stairs, carrying a flickering lantern. "They're searching house to house. They don't know you're here yet. Get out quick. Hide on the riverboat until she sails." Madame motioned to the cellar door with a quick jab of her finger.

"Won't they search the boats?"

"Mine sails under a Sverijan flag. They wouldn't dare. They'll have a hard time getting past Captain Groeneveld. Don't get caught."

More thumps echoed on the door.

"Go! Sweet Jesus! If they catch you here we'll all swing."

Aniela tugged on his sleeve. "Quick, down the cellar."

He hesitated.

"Don't forget I used to work here." She yanked open a narrow trap door beneath the stairs. "There's an old smuggler's door through to next door's cellar and from there a barrel door opens into their yard."

She ran down stone steps into the gloom.

Thunk! In the hallway above their heads, Madame Podory drew one heavy bolt.

"Three bolts." Aniela beckoned. "She'll give us as much time as she can."

Valdas stepped cautiously down, feeling his way in the darkness.

"This way, lover."

Fists pounded on the door again, with an instruction to hurry up and open in the name of King Gerhard.

"Wait your hurry!" Madame Podory yelled through the door. "Even for the king I can move no faster. These bolts are stiff."

Valdas blinked and found his eyes adjusting to the gloom. He followed Aniela into the dank darkness, feeling his way between barrels and wooden crates and sliding his feet along the slick stone floor so he didn't trip.

"This way."

He heard the light click of a latch. She creaked open a door and shoved him through it.

"There you go, lover."

"Aniela, I . . ."

Thunk! The second bolt on the door upstairs gave way.

"No time. Come back and say it. Go now. Go and be a hero for King Konstantyn and your men. God speed you."

"I'll see you again. I don't know when, but I will."

Swiftly she pushed a bundle into his hands and closed the door. He heard the sound of crates being dragged in front of it and then her feet running up the steps.

Thunk! The third bolt.

The darkness was absolute until his eyes adjusted and he picked out a lighter patch of gray, the opening where barrels were rolled into the building down wooden planks.

He felt his way tentatively, finding a narrow space with stars twinkling above. At first he couldn't get purchase on the crumbling brickwork, but then he found the iron rungs of a ladder set into the wall of the pit. Cautiously he climbed, checking the deep shadows in the yard as he emerged.

He could hear feet in the alleyway behind the inn and a booming,

militaristic voice directing the search. He leaped and scrambled for
the high perimeter wall, got purchase on the ancient ivy crawling up
the crumbling brickwork, and hoisted himself to the top. He edged
himself into the shadow of the house wall, shrinking into the vegetation, sitting with legs stretched in front of him, hooked over at the
ankles, muscles aching from trying to stay balanced.

Soldiers crashed about in the yard, the top of their heads barely a
couple of handspans below his arse. He froze, trying to become another shadow in the night, trying to think himself into the leafy ivy. *Don't
look up! Please don't look up.* He thought his prayer to Perkunas,
venerating the old god of soldiers in his desperation, but not daring to
even mouth the words. The slightest movement or sound of breathing
would draw attention. He mustn't fart now. He hadn't wanted to until
he thought about it. Damn.

A spider half the size of his fist spun down from the ivy above his
head, brushed his nose, and landed on his mustache. He tried not to
breathe as it crawled beneath his nostrils, over his chin, and down his
neck. He began to itch all over. The miscreant was somewhere on or
in his shirt. If he ever got out of here he'd whack the bastard into the
middle of next week. Ugh! Now he had phantom spiders crawling over
every part of him. He pressed his lips together and tried not to twitch.

There were only two soldiers here, but he heard two more in the
yard next door. His fingers ached to draw his sabre. He could probably
take these two if he had to, but not without drawing suspicion onto
Madame Podory and Aniela, and not without alerting the others. He
relaxed his hand. Fighting his way out of here would be his last
resort.

Don't look up!

It was a standard search pattern. Groups of four soldiers with lanterns worked their way down the alleyway. It was likely there were
hundreds of teams abroad in the city, disturbing beggars at their rest.

Don't look up!

"What's that?" One of the searchers stopped his fellows and Valdas
heard the sound of steel being drawn.

"Didn't hear nothing," a second voice said.

"Yeah, over there."

Valdas pretended to be an ivy leaf, but his sword hand twitched in
anticipation. He had the moves worked out. Take the one with the
lantern first.

A loud feline yowl and a clatter sliced the night. One of the men
yelped as a dark shape leaped between them and up and over the wall

opposite Valdas. Another man laughed and they turned away to bumble their way into the next yard, and the next, and the next.

Valdas waited until the search moved past the end of the alley and then jumped stiffly down, patting his shirt for signs of the spider, but it seemed to have fled.

The cloth Aniela had bundled into his hands was a canvas pack containing a well-worn delja of some rough weave, less fine than his own. He drew it on over the bulge of his sword belt and slipped into the alley, turning away from the search and hunching himself over, shambling like a beggar in case someone saw him. It seemed an age before he reached the corner, but as soon as he was out of the direct line of sight he began to run from shadow to shadow and didn't stop until he reached the harbor.

He found the ship as the first glimmer of dawn cast rosy fingers above the Gura. The captain waved him aboard and pointed down into the hold. Valdas paused at the top of the gangplank and turned. He didn't want to look, but he had to.

Hanged men swung gently in the morning breeze, dangling from the curtain wall of the citadel, their red uniform mentes looking almost jolly from this distance. Toy soldiers in some particularly gruesome game. He supposed they were nothing more than toys to Gerhard. To Valdas they had been brothers. He couldn't identify them individually at this distance, but he knew who they were. He gave a salute, and as the captain ushered him belowdecks to hide, he whispered a litany of all their names. "Henryk Zehrin, Lukas Grinius, Bartek Andrulis, Darius Kairys . . ."

He swiped the heel of his hand across his eyes. *You shall have justice, my friends, my brothers in arms, my king. Justice.*

His heart hammered inside his ribcage. Konstantyn. His High Guard. Did they blame him as he blamed himself? Somewhere at the back of his mind, the door behind which the accusing voices screamed began to tremble. Valdas mentally barred it with a stout plank. One day he'd have to open that door—if he lived long enough.

CHAPTER EIGHT

Lind

LIND THOUGHT HE might solve the problem of what to do next by going quietly crazy.

Three days, and no prospect, yet, of it being safe to leave. They'd put extra guards along the wall-walks and arrayed three or four heads on pikes by each gate as a warning—the failed High Guard. The heads had looked surprised at first, but the crows quickly dealt with that. They couldn't look at all without eyes.

Lind was very, very good at what he did. He'd played the long game with the High Guard and the castle cooks, and had finally beaten them all.

The High Guard had merely been hanged, but the king's cook had met a much more grisly fate. Now, that had been interesting. Lind had never seen execution by sawing before, though he'd heard it was once commonplace in Zavonia. Now it seemed that they reserved it for people who killed kings—even unwittingly. He'd hidden himself on the edge of the crowd. Professional interest, he told himself. Would he have gone to see a public hanging? Probably not.

He'd heard about sawing, of course. It was true what they said: it really did leave the victim conscious and screaming for so much longer. It must be because hanging him by the ankles prevented the blood from draining out of his head. They'd split the naked cook from crotch to waist with a two-handed ripsaw, spilling guts and their contents before they'd hit a spurting blood vessel. His screams had finally faded as he'd bled out. A small mercy, too little and too late.

Interesting, but . . . Lind wrinkled his nose at the memory. He avoided the mess of blood, guts, and shit whenever possible. He preferred a quick, clean kill: a garrote or a stiletto to the heart. Sawing was a cruel death, and he didn't think of himself as cruel.

He thought of Tourmine, his first-ever kill. That had been personal. He'd not planned it beforehand, but had seized the opportunity when it had presented itself. Pity he'd had to make that one quick, though. Sawing would have been a good death for Tourmine. He squashed the memory. *Tourmine is dead. Tourmine is dead,* he told himself over and over again, his lips moving silently to the mantra.

Forget Tourmine. Think of the present, not the past. If he didn't want to end up dead himself, sawn in half from his ballocks to his brain, he needed to think.

The job at hand was escape. Escape from a city alive with squads looking for a High Guard captain and the man who'd supplied him with the poison. They'd have guessed it was the fish, of course. That was the only dish specially ordered for the king's pleasure. The fish-monger would probably have been made to watch the cook's execution, and by now he'd be in the dungeons answering pertinent and painful questions about his delivery man. Perhaps he'd already be watching his guts being drawn out through a neat slit in his belly. A good questioner could keep a man alive for days, even with a belly wound. The fishmonger voluntarily offering everything he knew would not stop them from torturing him to see if he was holding some-thing back. That was an advantage to Lind. First the man would give them the accurate information—as much as he knew, which was all Lind's fabrication anyway—and then under torture he'd invent whatever he thought they wanted to hear. That would cloud the issue beautifully. Lind appreciated the symmetry of letting the enemy's enthusiasm for information help him escape.

He was almost sorry for the fishmonger, even though the man was a skinflint who would cut a sprat in half rather than give good measure to a poor widow. Still, that was hardly a crime. At least he didn't prey on his apprentices. That was something Lind took very seriously.

He'd deliberately left fake belongings in a chest under his narrow bunk in the tiny storeroom behind the shop, hoping to lay several false trails. It was the curious detritus of an invented character: a small coin from Kassubia, a much-worn and crumpled letter written in a scribe's hand from an imaginary uncle in Posenja informing him his imaginary father had died. A silk shirt of Gallian design, too expensive for a fishmonger's man, and a note in Captain Valdas Zalecki's hand saying: "Tonight. Postern gate. I'll be waiting." A man should be careful about sending notes to lovers that could be stolen and misinterpreted.

Lind still worried about the threat of magic. His neck prickled if he let himself contemplate the possible consequences. He had never actually met anyone who could perform magic, but Tourmine had been highly superstitious and it had rubbed off on the rest of the household. Ewa had believed in magic. She'd told him how to protect himself from magicians. If only she'd been able to tell him how to protect himself from Tourmine as well.

Lind didn't want to believe in anything Tourmine had believed in. It was one of the reasons he never went to church. How could Tourmine have gone to confession and still done such things to the boys in his care? *Bless me, Father, for I have sinned. I have buggered three apprentices this week. Say three Hail Marys, my son, and drop an extra silver tolar in the poor box on your way out.* No, church was not for him. If Lind was going to keep any kind of faith in the Almighty, he would do it in his own way, privately.

And if he was going to believe in magic it would be because of Ewa, and not because of Tourmine. Lind had remembered Ewa's methods for outwitting magicians.

If his employer had magic, he could scry for Lind's whereabouts. With that in mind, Lind had never given his real name or, to his knowledge, left any possessions around that he'd handled with bare skin. He hoped that was protection enough.

He decided to stop fretting about something he couldn't control. He'd take himself downstairs. The girls always knew the latest news and town gossip.

The whorehouse's spacious kitchen was safer territory than the front parlor. Even during the day the parlor stank of expectation, desperation, and cheap wine. It became doubly unbearable when the doors opened in the evening and the customers poured through with coins in their hands and their brains in their pantalones.

Debauchery might govern the front of the house, but Klara ruled in the kitchen, and if debauchery came anywhere near it had better take off its hat, wipe its feet, and not spit on the floor. If it hadn't been for the dress, or undress, of the two girls chopping turnip at the scrubbed table, it might have been the kitchen of any busy household, with one corner of the room allocated to the ovens and an open fire belching woodsmoke up the chimney.

The whores themselves didn't worry him. Of all the beings in all the world they definitely didn't want sex with him unless he paid them, and he wasn't going to do that. They left him alone, thank God. Klara was the only one he had to worry about. Motherly, she tended to try to touch him when he least expected it. A floury hand on his hand, a pat on the arm. Touching, for God's sake! If only she knew how close she'd come to being filleted on the spot. It wasn't as if he even knew the woman beyond a couple of casual stays here in the past.

His usual cat-quiet approach didn't draw any attention. He stood in the doorway and watched for a few seconds, checking exits, assessing threats as he always did. Klara leaned over the wooden block in the far corner, wielding a cleaver and hacking into a lump of pale pink pork. Ruta, one of the older whores, maybe fortyish, chopped onions at one end of the table. She might be any respectable dame save that she showed an inappropriate amount of breast for the middle of the day. The two girls, whose names he didn't know, sat in their shifts, faces, one pink one brown, creased with laughter over some shared joke. It was a picture of lewd domesticity.

"Ludwik!" Klara greeted him with a smile that went all the way to her eyes, but, chopping hunks of meat and transferring them to a large iron pot, she did not cross the kitchen to *touch* him. "You want a griddle cake?"

He shook his head and stayed as far away from her as possible. "No, thank you, mistress. What's the news? Have they caught the assassin yet?"

"Not that anyone's heard." Ruta hooked a stray strand of hair behind her ear. She let her fingers trail down her breasts into the low neck of her loose letnik. The tease was a reflexive gesture. When he didn't react she simply picked up another onion, skinned it, and sliced it into the pot.

A heavy fist on the front door, two knocks, a pause, then two more, had one of the girls in the front parlor rush to lift the bar. Lind didn't realize his own hand had gone to his knife hilt until he saw Klara regarding him with narrowed eyes.

"It's Maksimilian," she said.

Lind unclenched his fist and forced it down by his side, hearing the door open. Two voices spoke urgently. One he recognized as Trader Maksimilian, the owner of this fine establishment and purveyor of smuggled luxuries to the nobility. The other voice was female and cultured by her accent. He didn't catch all of the words, but *"house-to-house search"* was enough for him. He needed to get out of the city now.

Something about the way the words were spoken gave Lind the idea that a house-to-house search was not something Trader Maksimilian wanted either. He was pretty sure that Maksimilian was more than a mere entrepreneur. Definitely a foreigner, though with a perfect command of Zavonian and only the barest hint of an accent. He guessed the man was an information gatherer in the employ of one of the countries on Zavonia's borders, though he was not sure which. Ruthenia, Bieloria, Kassubia, Posenja, or maybe even Danija, which had laid claim to the island of Bretlina, effectively blockading the Gulf of Riyja. And then there was Sverija. Her empire had spread right round the Narrow Sea, and only the recent royal marriage protected Zavonia from being next on the list for annexation. Sverija would be his best guess. Karl Gustav was a wily ruler, and greedy for more territory. He'd bet that Sverija had information gatherers in every major city throughout Zavonia, Bieloria, Ruthenia, and Kassubia.

He felt no affinity for the land of his birth, but as soon as he thought of Sverija, the memory of his mother's reindeer stew, served with tart lingonberries, came unbidden into his mind. How long since he'd thought about that? He didn't have many memories from before he'd been apprenticed to Tourmine, but that was one of the best.

"He's brought her here!" Ruta hissed.

"Oh my!" Klara dropped knife and meat and reached for a cloth to wipe her hands. With an uneasy glance at Lind, she bustled past him, causing him to step away quickly into the other half of the kitchen for fear of being touched again. With her standing squarely in the doorway, obscuring his view, Lind didn't get a good look at the person who was led to Maksimilian's private parlor. He heard a woman say, "He'll drive the country to ruin," and then the door snicked closed.

Klara turned round and stepped aside. "Why not rest in your room for a while, Ludwik? I'll send someone up with your supper." He knew the difference between a command and a request, but trapped in his room was the last place he wanted to be.

"My thanks, mistress, but I shall be leaving the city directly." He was going to have to risk the checkpoints on the gates.

"Finished that business that's been keeping you in your room for three days, have you?" she said sweetly.

"Maybe I have." He stared at her steadily, but she still blocked his view.

Behind her, Trader Maksimilian came out of his parlor, pulling the door firmly closed behind him. "Klara, Mistress Roza will take a cup of watered wine, and if you have some of your griddle cakes ready—"

"Ludwik says he's leaving the city directly." Klara addressed Maksimilian over her shoulder and inclined her head toward Lind.

"Indeed. Well, that could be very convenient. Out of my way, Klara, girl." He slapped her on the bottom and moved her to one side, looking completely out of place in the kitchen, still dressed in his delja and with a soft woolen *kolpek* on his head. "Friend Balinski, I might have a paying proposition for you."

CHAPTER NINE
Mirza

WITH THE SALT encircling Jofranka, Esmaralda, and herself, Mirza clasped hands with her opponent. She'd soon wipe that smirk from the girl's face. She turned her own head slightly to make sure that the girl got a good look at her witchmark.

Jofranka cleared her throat to get their attention. "I will wait for you on the spirit plane. I will see who arrives first and who dares to go farthest. If at any time you feel as if you are in mortal danger, unclasp your hands. The first to let go of the other's hands will be deemed the loser. Do not leave the salt circle without my permission. It is all that protects you from demons while you are voyaging above. I would prefer not to have to bury either of you by the roadside in the morning, but what will be, will be."

And that was it.

The old lady sank immediately into a trance that showed her skill and experience in traveling the otherworld. The speed of her going took Mirza by surprise. Through finger contact with Esmaralda, she felt the other girl start on her own journey and realized she would have to scramble to catch up. No, not scramble, that would never get her to where she needed to be. She took a deep breath to settle her nerves and reached out for that place where Lu'dja had never been while she lived, the place of the dead.

Mirza didn't remember the moment of transition, but all of a sudden she was walking through mist. It was different every time she traveled here. Sometimes the differences were subtle, sometimes they were massive, unlike anything she'd ever experienced before.

A rough hillside rose before her, a steep inclined plane that seemed to go up and up. Something had worn a track ahead of her zigzagging to left and right to make the journey less steep. A tiny figure was on the switchback, plodding upward, head bent. Was it Esmaralda? If so, she was a long way in front of Mirza. Surely she hadn't had that much of a head start.

Mirza ignored the path and climbed directly up, using her hands where necessary to grab at grass or clumps of rock to pull herself upward.

Gasping for breath, she paused and glanced back. Behind her was only mist. She couldn't even see the base of the hill, and ahead she couldn't see the top. The path had vanished as soon as she'd stepped off it. Where was Esmaralda? Where was Jofranka? Had she come to the right place? Had she taken the right path?

No matter, she'd set her course and she couldn't turn back now. She began to climb.

The next time she stopped for breath, the mist behind her was much closer, obscuring the way she'd come, but the mist ahead seemed less dense. It swirled and for a brief moment she thought she could see the summit. What lay beyond? Was there a beyond?

Head down, and breath rasping in her throat, Mirza climbed.

Ahead of her in the mist a figure moved. Esmaralda? Jofranka? It didn't look like either of them. A ghostly figure dressed in swirling colors stood facing away from Mirza. Lu'dja in her wedding attire.

The figure stopped and turned.

"So, old woman, you finally found the spirit world, but you had to be dead to do it."

Lu'dja said nothing, merely turned back to the hill and continued climbing.

This was stupid. Lu'dja was dead. She was alive. They shouldn't be traveling the same path. Where did it lead? Did Mirza really want the position of shulam that much that she was willing to die in the attempt to retain it? Stasha didn't value her. Boldo didn't value her. Only Tsura would miss her if she didn't return.

The mist cleared. Instead of the hill, she was in an encampment, one she recognized, the place where Lu'dja had died. The figure turned.

Mirza was aware that every moment she delayed, Esmaralda was gaining distance. She should turn and run past Lu'dja, but it seemed impolite.

Then Lu'dja laughed and vanished along with the encampment and Mirza was left on her own in the land of the dead. Lu'dja had returned to the mist she had come from, delaying her just enough for her to lose the contest.

❖———❖

Mirza climbed. Was it her imagination, or was the slope getting easier? Perhaps she was coming to the top at last, but the mist was more dense than ever.

It billowed, revealing a precipice.

One more step and she'd be over the edge. She gasped and flung herself back, landing hard on her arse and sending a searing pain through her left wrist as she put out a hand to break her fall.

Stupid, stupid, stupid. That was the way to break bones.

She rolled to her knees and using her right hand levered herself upright, cradling her left against her body. She felt light-headed and her knees trembled. Had she broken something? Wrists were complicated.

If she broke a wrist on the spirit plane would her real body have the same hurt? She hoped not.

She heard a voice chanting, accompanied by the sound of rushing water, far below.

The voice trailed off into a sob, but Mirza had heard enough to follow the sound. Esmaralda stood on the edge of the precipice.

She'd won the race. Where was Jofranka to announce the result?

"Is this the boundary?" Esmaralda asked. "If we go over the edge do we die?"

"I don't know," Mirza said. "I didn't see this the last time I came here. It's never the same twice."

"What did the old crone say? She said she would watch to see who arrived first and who ventured farthest."

"It seems to me that we've both stopped together."

"I haven't stopped yet." Esmaralda placed one foot behind and rocked back on it as if to spring forward.

"Wait! Do you want my place so badly that you are willing to go down there to get it? To cross the boundary is death. You'll never be able to leave this place."

"I'm strong enough to cross over and come back. Are you too frightened to even try? I'll never be shulam of the Uzgorzi. Our mistress is young and trained three apprentices, of which I am the third. My only chance is to find a place in another band. Why not yours?"

"Because it's mine."

"Not for much longer."

Esmaralda sprang forward into the mist.

"That was unwise." Jofranka stood an arm's length behind Mirza. "Are you ready to return?"

"We can't just leave her!"

Mirza dropped to her knees and peeped over the precipice, supported on her good right hand. The mist swirled again and she saw Esmaralda, still falling.

"Esmaralda! You win. Come back. Come back!" She swayed and dropped her forehead to the floor. "Please come back," she whispered to the cliff edge.

"Enough." Jofranka put a firm hand on Mirza's shoulder.

Suddenly she was back in her own body, her hands suspended in midair because Esmaralda had loosed her grip and slumped sideways, still within the circle of salt.

"Esmaralda!"

Mirza scrambled to Esmaralda's side and knelt. "Oww!" Her left hand wouldn't support her. It seemed that a bone broken in the spirit world was broken in the real world, too.

Esmaralda lay as if dead, her eyes open and unblinking, breath so shallow it was barely there.

"What's wrong with her?" she asked Jofranka.

"She's still falling."

"What will happen when she hits the bottom?"

Jofranka pointed to Mirza's wrist, injured in the spirit world, but also broken in this.

"She'll die?"

"She was dead the minute she stepped off the cliff."

"Can't she come back?"

"She could, if she had the strength that you have."

"Could I bring her back?"

"You could bring yourself back. Whether you have the strength for two, I do not know."

"I have to try."

"She wanted to take your place, make you an outcast."

"It doesn't matter."

Jofranka nodded. "Then go."

Mirza sat cross-legged by Esmaralda's side and took the young woman's left hand in her undamaged right, then closed her eyes and was instantly in the spirit world, this time at the top of the hill facing the abyss. The mist swirled and there, still falling, was Esmaralda. With her damaged left hand clamped against her chest, Mirza didn't hesitate. She jumped, feeling her stomach rise up to choke her. She'd thought it would feel like flying, but it didn't, it felt like falling. She knew she must not hit the bottom or there would be no return.

"Esmaralda!" The figure below her was getting bigger and bigger. "Take my hand."

At their relative speeds, Mirza might overtake Esmaralda in the blink of an eye. She concentrated on slowing down, on catching the air and riding it. The sound of rushing water from below was louder now. A great river, perhaps. It would be no softer landing place than the ground, not at this height and speed.

"Esmaralda, take my hand." She was almost close enough to touch her now, but the water below sounded much closer. The mist swirled and revealed a massive waterfall directly underneath, plunging hundreds of feet to a churning mass of white.

"Now! Take it. Last chance!" She held out her right hand and felt Esmaralda catch it with her left.

For an awful few seconds their descent continued unchecked, but Mirza concentrated on pulling out of her dive. She strained her head back and arched her body to follow in a great swooping arc until they were traveling upward. Now she was flying, except Esmaralda's weight dragged against her.

She looked up, fixed her gaze on the cliff edge, and pulled with all her might. Inch by inch, foot by foot, yard by yard, they rose. She didn't have a hand to grab on to safety, so she had to rise and rise until they were above the cliff.

"Let go, now," she said. "Drop to the ground."

"No, I'll fall again. Don't let me go. Don't let me go."

"You won't fall. Let go." She tried to shake Esmaralda off, but the girl's grip was iron, pulling them both toward the edge again.

Mirza angled her body toward safety and dropped with Esmaralda. They both crashed to the cliff top. Without her good hand, Mirza's broken wrist took the full brunt of their fall, and she screamed in pain, rolling away now that Esmaralda had let go.

She ran through her stock of curse words in her mind, but dared not utter them in this place. Counting to ten, and then onward to twenty, she held her broken wrist close to her chest. Her legs wobbled when she stood up.

"Come on." She grasped Esmaralda's hand and set off running down the hill until she realized that her legs were still and that the cold ground was beneath her backside and Esmaralda's hand was squeezing hers.

"Your judgment, good mother Jofranka," Stasha Hetman asked.

"Esmaralda arrived first and went farthest," Jofranka said.

Mirza's stomach lurched.

"Then it's Esmaralda who wins," Stasha said.

"I didn't say that. Esmaralda was rash and would have lost herself in the land of the dead if Mirza had not brought her home. Your shulam remains your shulam. You don't deserve her."

Mirza wanted to laugh with relief, but felt only tears coming to her call. She needed to get away before she broke down. With her left hand clutched against her chest, she stood shakily, bowed to Jofranka, and stepped across the ring of salt, to where Tsura waited.

"Are you all right?" Tsura whispered.

"Broken wrist. Take me to the wagon before I pass out."

Tsura slipped an arm through her right and together they walked through the camp until they gained the privacy of the wagon. Mirza sank onto the bed, tears streaming down her face, relinquishing her broken bone to Tsura's care.

Two days later, when Mirza had slept and slept, and her wrist, splinted and bandaged, was not aching quite so fiercely, she sat outside to listen to the tsymbaly players practicing for the evening's dancing.

"Look who's coming," Tsura said as Esmaralda marched across the compound and bowed her head as a sign of respect.

"I've come to pay my debt," she said.

"What debt?" Mirza said.

"We agreed that if I won I would take your place, your wagon, and your apprentice."

Tsura spat on the ground, but Esmaralda pretended not to notice.

"If you won," Esmaralda continued, "I would give you my wagon. It's a good one. I've removed my things and cleaned it. The one you call Boldo is bringing it for you."

Mirza contemplated turning it down, but was under no illusion that if Esmaralda had won the match, she would have stuck to the letter of their agreement and Mirza would now be homeless and outcast.

"Where will you live?"

"I have a place with my cousin's family. I know what you did for me. I need to say thank you, so I give you my horse as well. He's strong and willing and will serve you well."

With that she turned and walked away, head held high.

"Did she actually say thank you?" Tsura asked.

"I think that's as close as she could manage."

CHAPTER TEN

Valdas

A FAST HORSE to the coast, Aniela had said, but it hadn't quite
turned out that way. The riverboat captain had put Valdas ashore
at the first opportunity. He'd been walking for two days, and a hussar
on foot was an affront to God! Now he crouched in a ditch, heart
pounding, stagnant water up to his belly, while a line of horsemen
trotted past, two by two, heading away from the city. Without raising
his head, he estimated it was a full company, which was way too many
troops to be out scouring the countryside for one man. That was the
third today. King Gerhard might want him, but not that badly.

What was the new king up to?

Something moved in the water next to him and Valdas shot out of
the ditch onto the roughly paved road, feeling a cooling breeze bite
through wet clothes. His wet pantalones slapped around his legs as he
moved. Luckily his delja was rolled tight in his pack, which he'd managed to keep out of the water. That would provide a warm layer when
night came on, but for now he had to let his clothes dry on him as he
walked. He daren't take off his battered boots to empty them of water
in case he couldn't get them back on to his poor blistered feet again.
The rain had finally stopped, but not before it had soaked him through
to the skin even before he'd had to jump in the ditch. His soggy clothes
chafed in awkward places, and he shivered in the pale afternoon sun.
Summer it might be, but it rarely got *that* hot in Zavonia.

Chancellor Skorny, or probably plain Lord Skorny by now if he still
lived, had a country home on the outskirts of Fisk on the south bank
of the Biela River toward Riyja. It would have been a long day's ride
on a fit horse, but his gray, Zuma, was lost to him now. He patted his

pouch. He had enough for his immediate needs, but not enough to buy a horse.

Late in the afternoon, passing through an area thick with trees, he rounded a corner to find a loose horse grazing by the roadside, saddle askew and reins dangling. It was a sturdy beast, a mare, short-legged and round-bellied, with a common head, the sort of horse a farmer might ride, or put to a plow. His first thought was to thank Perkunas for providing him with transport, but then he felt guilty. Someone was in trouble, maybe injured. It looked as though the rider had taken a fall.

The mare flicked her ears toward him as Valdas approached, but continued snatching at grass. She made no attempt to skitter away when he spoke gently and reached for her reins. Once Valdas had the horse in hand, he undid the girth and settled the saddle, noting that she had the trick of taking a big breath to blow herself up as he was tightening the girth again. No doubt the saddle had slipped for entirely this reason, so he reasoned the accident might not have happened too far from her rider's home. He waited until she relaxed, then took the girth up another couple of notches, and patted her neck when she swung her head around and gave him a baleful stare. He checked her legs for damage, noting that one shoe was badly worn, but it didn't look as though she was lame because of it.

"Now, lady, where did you come from?" Any fallen rider would likely be the direction he was headed in. "Well, then," he told the mare amiably. "It looks as if we can help each other out."

He mounted, and turned the mare's head to the road. She was a sluggish ride, a plodder. It was strange to think that anyone could fall off her. It was like riding an overstuffed chair. The road wound between trees, but he'd only rounded the next bend before he spotted a mound by the roadside, a corpulent man, half hidden by a drab earth-colored cloak. As he approached, the man groaned and began to roll over.

Valdas jumped down from the mare and looped her reins over his arm. "Are you all right?"

The man groaned and Valdas leaned closer. "Let me help you." He reached down, but the man made no effort to help himself. "Can you get up?" Valdas knelt to see if the man had any serious injuries, but suddenly found himself on his back with the man kneeling over him, grinning.

As the man swung a solid blackthorn stick toward his head, Valdas rolled and came into a crouch. A second man rushed from the trees brandishing a pistol.

Valdas took it all in quickly. He'd been stupid not to see it for the trap that it was. Blackthorn man was short but stocky. Pistol man was thin-faced, with a ragged beard. The pistol wasn't primed, but it was still an effective weapon, even used as a club. He came up between the two men, trying to judge which was the more immediate threat. The mare threw up her head and skittered sideways, causing Blackthorn to turn his head slightly in her direction. It was a slim distraction, but it was enough. Valdas caught the end of the stick, wrenched the man off balance, and threw him at Pistol. That gave him a breathing space to draw steel. Sabre in his right hand, he parried the blackthorn stick as it crashed toward him and grabbed for it with his left as it came to the end of its arc.

The man was too quick and pulled the stick away, skinning Valdas's knuckles and drawing a curse.

Pistol waved his weapon ineffectively until he decided that threatening to shoot wasn't going to work, so he flipped it over and held it by the barrel. Valdas dodged sideways so the blow meant for his head caught his shoulder, sending numbing ripples down his left arm. He cursed again.

The thud of hooves and the jingle of bridles wormed their way into Valdas's consciousness. "Hussars!" he said.

Pistol broke off his attack and leaped for the mare.

Blackthorn must have realized his partner was running off without him. He tried to make a grab for the reins as Pistol clapped his heels to the mare's side. She leaped forward. Valdas grabbed Blackthorn's arm, swung him around, and downed him with a fist-and-sabre-guard punch to the jaw. Blackthorn dropped like a felled oak.

The sound of hoofbeats was closer now. Valdas sheathed his sabre. He dragged Blackthorn into the underbrush by the roadside and pinched the man's nose and mouth closed so he couldn't make a sound. He didn't mind if he killed the bastard. Robbing innocent travelers was a foul way to make a living. The world would be better off without him. One less bandit on the road would be a good thing for Zavonia.

A troop of hussars rattled past. It might have been the same troop he'd hidden from before, on their way back from wherever they'd been. Valdas crouched lower into the bushes and tried to blend in. The troop never broke stride. They were past and away before he felt Blackthorn stir. He lifted his hand and Blackthorn dragged in a tortured breath.

"Don't hurt me," Blackthorn said.

"What were you going to do to me?"

"Just take yer money and run."

"Didn't seem so." He picked up the blackthorn stick. "In fact, it looked to me as if you'd be happy to see me dead on the off-chance I was carrying a silver tolar or two. I take exception to that."

"But—"

"I don't care if you've got a wife and twelve children to feed plus your dear old mother. If you ever see me again, take a wide berth. Next time I'll spit you like a chicken." He didn't waste his breath on idle threats. He brought up the blackthorn stick and gave the man a sharp rap on the temple, felling him for the second time in quick succession. The man would have to take his chances.

Valdas set a brisk pace down the road, wishing he'd ended up with the horse for his trouble. Never mind, it was probably stolen anyway.

He left the trees behind and the land became marshy. The road had been built up, but to either side suspicious patches of bright green showed where the dangerously swampy ground offered to suck down the unwary. You could lose a horse in some of those bogs. There were plenty of tales of travelers disappearing along this road. Of course, the local banditry could account for some of them.

He should get off the main road, but the road was the only safe route. He'd have to trust to his sharp ears to warn him of danger. Hopefully the hussars wouldn't be back again.

Valdas jogged for a while to warm up, keeping the sun in his eyes. The jog turned into a walk, and the walk to a limping trudge, mile after mile. With each weary step the names of the fallen set up a somber rhythm in his head: *Henryk Zehrin, Lukas Grinius, Bartek Andrulis, Darius Kairys . . . Konstantyn, second of his name. King of Zavonia.*

He wanted justice for all of them.

Potholes, full to the brim with last night's rain, mirrored a heavy sky. The wool of his damp pantalones stank like a wet sheep from sleeping in the open, and the sticky clay on his boots weighed his feet down. His legs ached and his toes hurt. Who'd have thought that a bit of walking would bother a veteran of so many campaigns? He must be getting soft. He made a mental note that the High Guard needed more route-march training and then cursed himself for forgetting for an instant.

They were dead. Henryk, Lukas, Bartek, Darius . . . All dead.

It had been many years since Valdas had been on his own. He'd been serving in Konstantyn's hussars since soon after his sixteenth birthday. The army was the home of many a younger son with no inheritance. He was lucky to get a purse to equip himself for the husaria, and not sorry to leave behind an older brother, already wed and producing heirs, and a surly grandfather, bitter from his losses and turned too harsh to bear.

He'd found a better family among brother hussars. At sixteen he hadn't finished growing. By the time he'd reached his full potential, he'd grown to be, if not a giant, imposing in his height. It had singled him out and he'd found himself picked for contests of arms, winning them, rising through the ranks despite not having funds to buy a commission, being good at his job, the hero of Tevshenna, no less, and because he had brains as well as brawn, finally being recruited for Konstantyn's High Guard, and within a couple of years, their captain.

His life had changed. It had been more than a job. Konstantyn inspired loyalty. He had been a friend, often stopping to talk in passing, or sometimes inviting him into the library to share a bottle in the long hours of the night. Valdas had failed a man—a good man—as well as a monarch. He allowed anger to fill the empty place that Konstantyn had left. Anger drove him on, despite the blisters on his feet.

He mouthed the litany of the names of his men again and again. *I will bring you justice, my brothers.*

Toward the afternoon the cloud cover began to break apart. The sun came and went, came and went, until the clouds finally dissipated, but too late to save the reputation of this miserable day. As if to apologize for earlier behavior, the sunset blazed yellow and red, blinding him as he trudged. By the time it became barely a rosy streak on the western horizon he was exhausted. It was obvious he wasn't going to find any kind of shelter for the night, but Skorny's estate wasn't far now. He decided to push on.

Valdas topped the last rise as dusk descended to night, and saw Lord Skorny's estate spread before him, a fortified manor house built of red brick with a high perimeter wall that was worryingly unattended, its main gate open. He wondered if this was where the hussars had come. Had Skorny been with them when they returned to Biela Miasto?

The whole place should have been full of light, but it was strangely subdued.

Inside the outer wall was an inner wall, this time secured, all its gates firmly closed.

A little see-through hatch on the gate slid open as he neared.

He guessed that after days of living rough, a heavy beard shadow beneath his finely cultivated hussar-mustache, he probably would not be recognized. He might look too rough to gain admittance at all.

"I have a message for Lord Skorny," he called out, and raised his hands to show good intent.

"He can't see anyone." The voice at the other side of the gate was neither young nor old, neither peasant nor lord. "He's sick."

Sick? Valdas's guts churned. Had someone tried to poison Skorny as well? Had the hussars injured him?

"It's an important message, from Biela Miasto."

"Unless you've brought a message from God, be on your way. We've had enough messages from Biela Miasto for one day."

"Lord Skorny will want to hear this one."

"Pass it through the hatch."

"It's not a written message."

"Well, tell me, then."

"I was instructed to give it to no one except Lord Skorny."

"Who shall I say?"

Valdas didn't want to give his name. "Tell Lord Skorny the message comes from the loyal Zavonian who was in the room during the trade talks with Posenja."

The hatch closed and he was left standing there.

His blisters hurt more from standing than from walking. His calves and his thighs cramped. His back ached. He wanted to lie down where he was and rest. It seemed like he was waiting half the night, but it must have been less than a quarter hour when the bolts on the inside of the gate slid back. He blinked at the lantern held up to his face.

"I know you," a female voice said.

He narrowed his eyes to see the face behind the lantern.

"Yes, you do, Lady Danute."

"Tell me why I should take you to my father. Are you here to finish the job you started in Biela Miasto?"

"Whatever you have heard, Lady, I am not guilty of that great crime."

"So my father believes. Come, this way."

CHAPTER ELEVEN
Lind

BACK UP IN his room, Lind packed his bag. He'd left it here when he'd first come to the city and rented the room. It contained everything he needed for changing his appearance from fishmonger's delivery man to yeoman-farmer, plus some of the tools of his trade. He'd leave the city tomorrow at noon when the streets were busy. He'd entered the city gates a bachelor, but he'd leave as a farmer and family man, having agreed to take Roza Kushnir, one of Trader Maksimilian's girls, out of the city to her parents' farm to have her baby. Except he wasn't sure she was one of Maksimilian's girls, or a farmer's daughter, not with that little flurry in the kitchen. He wondered what was special about her that Maksimilian was getting her out of the city. Maybe the brat was Maksimilian's, and Maksimilian's wife didn't know. At first he'd taken Klara to be married to Maksimilian, but she had a husband and family close by. Maksimilian's wife was never seen in the whorehouse and apparently lived at one of his more legitimate businesses, a carter's yard.

Footsteps on the stairs brought Lind to his feet before the knock on the door. He crossed the room quietly and listened. Though he could have sworn he heard two pairs of feet out there, now he heard only the creak from one person standing on old boards.

"Who is it?"

"Roza Kushnir."

He turned the key in the lock and stepped away from the door, taking care not to silhouette himself against the light from the window.

She came in with a cloth-covered tray in her hands, her neckline not as low as Ruta's, but her bodice unlaced provocatively and her bright copper hair falling about her shoulders.

"I brought you some f . . ." Her voice faltered and died when she saw he had his hand on the hilt of his knife.

He saw where she was looking, kicked the door shut with his foot, and shrugged.

"Food. Nice. Thank you."

"I thought you might want to—you know—get to know me before we travel together."

"Get to know you . . ."

"You know . . . on the house."

She was a pretty little thing, even thick around the waist, but very young. She was no whore, despite trying to play the part for his benefit. He knew whores, knew the look behind their eyes. She puzzled him, but he couldn't quite work out why. Anyway, she stirred nothing in him. He sighed. He hadn't expected her to.

She took a deep breath and stepped closer to him. She was shaking. Had his knife unnerved her that much? He backed away, feeling slightly nauseous.

"Get out."

"What?"

"Out!"

She took one look at his face, put the tray on the bed, and almost ran, her gait made slightly ungainly by her belly. She yanked open the door and he heard her running down the landing. Damn, someone else *was* out there. In three strides he crossed the room and looked out. Nothing. But his ears were sharp. There were two sets of feet retreating to the floor below, and he heard a man's muffled question and the girl's breathless voice.

"You're right, he likes boys. I'll be sa . . ."

He ducked inside, picked up the tray carefully, and straightened everything on it. Blood pounded in his ears. *He likes boys. He. Likes. Boys!*

A band round his temples squeezed. Lind hurled the tray at the door, smashing pots to smithereens and splashing their contents down the unvarnished pine.

I do not like boys.

I do not like boys.

Please, God, let me not like boys.

<hr />

The following day Roza was already sitting, tight-lipped, on the front seat of Maksimilian's little wagon as Lind descended into the yard at noon. Her bags, two of them, both bigger than he'd expected, were installed in the wagon next to a pile of empty sacks smelling of turnips. Next to it was a sack of grain for the horse should fodder prove scarce on the journey.

"Mistress." He inclined his head politely as if he'd never met her before and she nodded back.

He threw his leather bag next to hers, his threadbare delja on top of it, and tucked the little cloth bag of hair dye and face plumpers in a corner under the sacking. With a polite nod he climbed up beside her. He was pleased to see that she was plainly dressed in demure layers, covered to the throat and wrists in a long, shapeless *szuba*, buttoned neatly up the front, and an embroidered cap over a linen *rantuch* which hid all of her very distinctive copper-colored hair. Altogether it was very proper, if a little too good for a farmer's wife. Definitely not a whore. He'd carefully chosen his own clothes to be nondescript, brown trousers and soft green linen zupan, tied around with a dark green sash. The zupan was unfashionably knee-length and thus marked him as one of the lower classes.

Trader Maksimilian, black-bearded, broad-girthed, and dressed neck to boot-tops in a highly embroidered but rumpled zupan that looked like he'd slept in it, hovered, a little too anxious, dark circles beneath his eyes and worry creases between his brows. The brat must be his.

"All right?" Maksimilian asked Lind, but his eyes flicked toward the girl.

"Fine," Lind said.

He pulled on a soft kolpek to cover the crown of his newly cropped head and took the horse's reins. Out of his eye corner he saw the girl nod mutely at the trader and some understanding passed between them.

"Look after my girl," Maksimilian said.

"Your money in my purse is as good as a contract."

"I know it."

Lind clicked at the horse, flicked the reins across its ample rump, and the beast plodded obligingly out of the yard and into the busy city street.

He could feel the girl stiff and silent next to him. He didn't know whether she was mad at him, scared of him, or both, but if they got questioned at the gate he needed her to play the part of his wife. Better make his peace with her. Politeness went a long way. It was one of his weapons that people responded to.

"I'm sorry."

"What?"

"Yesterday."

She didn't say anything and he felt the need to explain—but what explanation could he possibly give that would make it any better? The horse clopped on, and though the street was noisy, an awkward silence stretched out between them.

"Let's be clear. I'm not interested." Lind's knuckles stood out white as his fists bunched round the reins.

"I . . . er . . ." She half turned to him, confusion and embarrassment written all over her face. "If it makes any difference, I withdraw my offer." She looked modestly down at her fingers.

"Good. We understand each other." He wasn't sure they did, but that would have to do for now.

The horse plodded on a little further before she said, "So, we're supposed to be man and wife."

"That's what Maksimilian suggested. It works for me. But . . . don't touch me. I don't wish to be touched. Understand?"

"Yes."

Who was she? He guessed she was from a moneyed family, and she was nervous as hell, though whether it was of him or of getting caught he didn't know. He stole a sideways glance. Many a proud woman had been brought down by events—even noblewomen. Someone had paid handsomely to get her out of the city quietly. He had twenty silver tolars weighing heavily in his purse.

"There's a man," she said. "He's got some influence with the city guard. I don't want to be recognized."

"Keep your eyes down low. Don't look anyone in the face. And unless you can lose that fancy accent, let me do the talking."

She gave him a tight little nod. "I can talk this way."

"Passable if you don't say too much. Make your voice a bit flatter . . . heavier." He patted his chest. "Talk from here."

"All right." Her voice coarsened noticeably. "I've seen players." She licked her lips. "I can do this."

"I hope you can."

She nodded. "Roza Balinski." She tried the name for size. "I don't suppose I could borrow that name for a while?"

"Help yourself." The name wasn't his anyway.

Lind put together the lie they could both share. The trick was including enough detail without letting it get too complicated. "This is the story. We have a farm by Koplarr, a tenant holding of thirty-five acres, and we've been visiting your sister."

"My sister. What's her name?"

"I don't know, what name do you want?"

"Elzbieta."

"Elzbieta it is. Keep it simple. Follow my lead and don't talk unless you get asked something directly."

"All right . . . Ludwik."

He didn't trust that she'd got the gumption to lie well, but unless they aroused suspicion, she probably wouldn't have to say anything at all. He was conscious of his knives, sword and flintlock wrapped in his bag and only a plain knife strapped at his side and a stiletto hidden in his boot. He couldn't justify carrying a sword or flintlock if he was supposed to be a farmer.

They approached the city gate. Traffic, already crawling, shuffled to a standstill. Word filtered down from the line ahead that the guards were checking everyone who tried to leave the city, asking their business. That wasn't surprising. It wasn't every day that someone killed a king.

The guard on the gate gave the old woman in front a hard time, and Lind saw her reach into her purse and give him a coin. So that was their game—a little unofficial gate fee. He fingered his outer pocket, where he'd got ten coppers and even a silver tolar ready for bribes, and moved his horse and wagon forward into the line.

He heard Roza gasp beside him and she hastily linked her arm in his and turned her face into his shoulder.

Lind jerked away from her. "I said no touching."

"He knows me," she muttered. "From Trader Maksimilian's, I mean."

Unlikely. Lind thought quickly. This girl had never been a whore, no matter what the pretense.

"All right, stick to your story, but say it as if I made you say it."

"What?"

"Improvise. I hope you really are good at play-acting. And if you're going to leave them there, keep those hands *still*."

They had no more time for conversation. "Name and business." The guard was a burly, broad-shouldered cavalry sergeant with a military mustache and a scar on his chin. He was out of place on this kind of duty.

"Ludwik Balinski. Farmer from Koplarr. Been visiting my wife's sister."

"You picked a bad time to come visiting."

"I know. We been here about nine days. Never thought to see no royal funeral, nor no sawing a man in half. I got summat to tell when I get home." Lind coarsened his voice and dropped into the country way of speaking, a little slow and not very grammatical.

"What's your missis got to say for hersel . . ." The guard frowned. "Do I know you?"

Roza lifted her face up from Lind's shoulder. "We been to see my sister, Elzbieta."

"I'm sure I've seen you somewhere before."

"I said we been visiting my sister."

"That's lies. I know y . . ." He made as if to call his officer, when Lind turned to Roza and slapped her across the face. She squealed, bumped down on the seat, and put her hand up to her reddening cheek. The action drew the guard's attention to them rather than his duty.

"What's that for?" she asked.

"Is there any single man in this town who hasn't seen you in that damned whorehouse?" Lind yelled. "Has this one taken a poke? For pity's sake, Roza, I should ha' left you to rot in there. If it wasn't for the baby I would've."

She paused, almost for too long, and for a moment Lind feared she was going to dry up on him, but she compressed her mouth into a disapproving line and glared.

"There's men there, real men, that treat me better than you do."

Good, she was playing along with it.

"I gave you a good home, clothes for your back, shoes for your feet and food for your belly and you repay me by running away with a tinker man and ending up in a whorehouse. My wife! In a whorehouse."

He turned to the guard. "Did you know you was paying to sleep with someone's legitimate wife?"

"I never . . . Honest I . . . That's not where . . ."

"Wife? You didn't want a wife!" She raised her voice. "You wanted a dairymaid, cook, and housekeeper, and it was cheaper to marry one rather than pay one. I worked myself sick and got no thanks for my trouble." She got to her feet, balanced precariously between the seat and the brace-board of the wagon, her belly sticking out like she was more than six months gone. They'd begun to draw curious glances from the crowd and she responded to an audience.

"You couldn't even satisfy me in bed. How many times did you manage it? Once? Twice? Feliks Borski was ten times the man you'll ever be. Imagine how surprised I was when I found I was carrying your child. That's why he left me, you know. And where was I to go?"

Lind calculated that was enough. He responded with quiet dignity. "I know where you went. Sit down, Roza. We're going home." He turned to the guard. "Have you got anything to say about that?"

The man shook his head and stepped back. "Pass through."

They drove through without looking back.

"Well played," Lind said quietly. "And we didn't even have to pay the bribe. Now, please, I'd appreciate it if you would take your hand off my leg."

She giggled almost hysterically and withdrew to her own side of the bench seat.

"Sometimes the best way not to be seen is to be seen all too clearly as something you're not."

He didn't know whether she was talking about herself or him.

CHAPTER TWELVE
Valdas

VALDAS FOLLOWED LADY Danute's swaying hips, her swishing skirts, and the blessed brightness of her lantern across the courtyard draped in shadows. Rather than use the main entrance, she led him to a side door in a circular brick tower at one corner of the main building, and up a spiral stair, entering a darkened chamber by a narrow door. Her lantern threw the shapes of chairs and a small table into relief on the walls. The fireplace was dark, save for a dying red glow. Lady Danute, Chancellor Skorny's oldest daughter, unmarried despite reaching her middle years, and quite as formidable as her father, threaded her way through the room to a door at the far end, which stood open a crack, revealing the soft flickering glow of candles.

"You may go." Lady Danute nodded to a servant on watch by the door.

The woman nodded and left the same way Valdas and Danute had entered.

Chancellor Skorny lay abed, eyes closed. Valdas's heart thumped. "What's wrong with him?"

"Hush." Lady Danute pushed the door closed. "It's him, Father," she said.

Skorny opened one eye, looked at Valdas, then opened the other and sat up, going from corpse-like to animate in an instant.

"Captain Zalecki, good to see you." The old man swung his legs out of bed and stood up, pulling his bed gown down to cover his skinny calves. He slipped into a robe that his daughter held for him. "You look as though the road has not treated you kindly."

"My lord, if you're ill . . ."

Skorny's laugh turned into a wheeze. "A political illness, my boy. It seemed appropriate when the hussars arrived to escort me to Biela Miasto. Only my daughter knows. I don't wish to appear to be a threat to our new ruler. It seems he treats threats seriously." His eyes clouded over. "I heard what happened to the High Guard, and to the cook. I'm sorry."

"They hanged the cook as well?"

"Nothing so kind. Executed in the town square. Sawing."

"Sweet Lord have mercy." Not a religious man and as likely to call on Perkunas, the old god of thunder, as the church's One God, Valdas was moved to cross himself. At least his men had been spared that end.

"Amen to that, Captain Zalecki. A fate you would doubtless wish to avoid."

"I swear to you I did not kill the king."

"Of course you didn't. I'm a good judge of men, captain. Your loyalty to King Konstantyn is in no doubt. He spoke very highly of you."

"I have to deliver justice. My last duty on his behalf. I will find the murderer and make him pay. Gerhard—"

Skorny cut him off with a wave of his hand and gave him a measured look.

"Who killed him is not the question. I think you might find some nameless assassin to blame for the actual deed. Who had him killed is the real question. You think it's Gerhard, but what if it isn't? Gerhard is the obvious culprit. He has the Amber Crown, but I never saw anything in him to hint that he might want it, let alone take such drastic action to get it. If you had asked me a se'nnight ago I would have sworn that Gerhard had no ambitions toward the crown. He's ill suited to its weight."

"It's true I wouldn't have thought Gerhard an ambitious man either, but whether he killed the king, had him killed, or not, he summarily judged and put the High Guard to death within the hour. He was ready to fill the void Konstantyn left—him and his gods-poxed secretary Kazimir, now his chancellor. It was as if he was ready for it."

"An obvious choice, I agree."

Valdas chewed his bottom lip. "I know the Gura. Give me fifty good men and I can take it from the inside and get to Gerhard before anyone can mobilize the army."

"And then what? Put Gerhard on trial? Kill him? Who takes the throne then? Gerhard is a weak king, but having no king at all leaves Zavonia open to incursions from any or all of our neighbors."

"Aren't they just as likely to take advantage of Gerhard? I'm sorry for being so blunt, my lord, but Gerhard is . . ."

"I know, I know." Skorny held up both hands. "Gerhard may surprise us, but I honestly doubt it. He's more likely to leave all the decisions to his chancellor, and I know very little about the capabilities of Zygmund Kazimir." He screwed up his eyes and massaged his forehead with the fingertips of his right hand, then huffed out a long breath and inhaled steadily.

"Kazimir is a blowhard," Valdas said. "He's a nobody, unproven except when it comes to toadying up to Gerhard."

"Think, Valdas. Set aside your suspicions of Gerhard for the moment. Who else would want King Konstantyn dead?" Skorny began to count on his fingers. "Sverija is not at the top of my list. With the new marriage alliance it would seem to me that Karl Gustav's best interests lay with Konstantyn and Kristina, and their future offspring. He would not have wanted Konstantyn dead and his sister widowed."

Valdas scrubbed at his face and took a deep breath. "Agreed, though now Kristina has been relegated to dowager, Karl Gustav might think again. Sverija is a power to be reckoned with, and has ambitions to gobble up weak neighbors. He might take advantage of a new weak monarch."

Skorny nodded. "I concur. We can't rule out the possibility that Karl Gustav might move against us in the future, but I don't think he's to blame for this."

Valdas felt warmed when Skorny said "us." Skorny hadn't discounted him, not yet. He felt hope begin to stir.

The old man frowned and seemed to be looking deep inside himself. He counted off on his fingers. "Similarly, I think we can rule out Ruthenia."

"Why?" Valdas asked.

"I don't trust Tsar Ivan, but Tsarina Zofia would never have her own brother assassinated."

"You know her better than I do, my lord, but she is the mother of future tsars, and it must irk her that on her marriage, she and any future offspring were written out of the Zavonian succession."

"Even so, I truly don't believe her capable of fratricide. I knew Zofia from her childhood and can't believe that she would ever turn her hand toward her own brother. She never had much love for Gerhard, however, so I can see that she wouldn't stand in the tsar's way if he joined the vultures circling above the Gura."

"It would take a war for Ruthenia to annex Zavonia," Valdas said.

Skorny pressed his lips together and drew a long, slow breath. "The tsar may be a despot, but he's astute. I'm not sure he'd be prepared to wage a full-scale war, but I do think he might try to take the Tevecor Reaches while Zavonia is in disarray." He frowned. "It's also well known that Ruthenia wants a route to the Narrow Sea through our southern lands."

Valdas nodded. "I don't know Zofia well. She was in Ruthenia before I came to the Gura, but I understand she was unhappy to be married to the tsar-in-waiting, and blamed her brother for that."

"So she did." Skorny smiled at the memory. "She railed at Konstantyn like a fishwife, but she'd grown up knowing she was a pawn in the marriage game. Eventually she accepted it with good grace. Of all the eligible royalty at that time, Ivan was the least worst option."

"Which leaves Kassubia as the most likely," Valdas said. "If we're not counting Gerhard."

Skorny nodded. "It's true, Jonas Vaza of Kassubia has the motive." He shrugged. "All the kings of Kassubia have had the motive ever since Zavonia split the Commonwealth in two, but none has acted on it before. Besides, there's a blood relationship between King Jonas and Konstantyn."

"Distant," Valdas said.

Skorny nodded. "As you say. And when has blood mattered more than territory?"

"So, Kassubia, then?" Valdas grimaced. "If it's not Gerhard."

"One or the other."

"But how to tell which? I still say I can take the Gura, wring the truth out of Gerhard."

"You might make it in, but you'd never make it out alive. I still have people on the Gura whom I can rely on for information. Let's be subtle about this."

Subtle was the last thing Valdas wanted. His blood raged for action.

"Sit, Captain Zalecki. Valdas. Calm yourself and think."

Valdas dropped into an upholstered chair by the bedside and nodded. "I have a man inside the court of Kassubia, but he reports to me in code, by carrier bird, sent directly to the Gura. I have no way of contacting him now, unless I can get inside the Kassubian court myself and . . . well . . . look at me. I wouldn't get a job in the stables."

"I can do something about your looks, captain, but I no longer have the standing that would give you an introduction." He cleared his throat. "But Tsarina Zofia can. If she wants her brother's murderer, she might be willing to assist you. Ride to Bieloria and beg her to include you in her next delegation to Kassubia. You could be inside the Kassubian court in less than eight weeks."

"And if we're wrong, and she or the tsar is behind Konstantyn's death?"

"Then she'll have your head on a pike, my boy, and that will be an end to it, but at least we'll know if you don't come back. Are you willing to risk that?"

Valdas released a sharp crack of pent-up laughter. "To find my king's murderer I would risk Hell itself."

Skorny smiled a melancholy smile. "Ah, Valdas, wouldn't you rather find somewhere less dangerous to spend the rest of your life?"

"I have no skill for living a quiet life." He shook his head. "My king needs me. My men, my brothers in arms, deserve justice. I'll take my chances with the Tsarina Zofia in Bieloria. I made a vow to avenge my king and my men on the shreds of my honor."

Skorny clapped a bony hand on Valdas's shoulder. "You're a good man, Captain Zalecki. Go to Zofia with my blessing. Take your rest here for the night, and in the morning my daughter will give you horses, a purse, and suitable clothes. I can't give you fifty men to throw themselves against the might of the Gura, so let me do what I can. And remember, once you get to Bieloria, tell the tsarina that when you saw me last I was sick unto death."

"I will, my lord."

⊷———⊶

Fully rested after a night in Skorny's tower, Valdas was grateful for a tub of hot water and a razor the following morning, plus a breakfast of hot rolls, salt pork, herrings, and coffee with honey-drizzled sweet cakes. His filthy clothes had been removed by a servant in the early hours of the morning and replaced with a set of clothes fine enough to earn him respect on the road, but not too fine that he would be a target for brigands.

Valdas had always prided himself on being able to wake in an instant at the slightest sound, so he was somewhat perturbed that he'd not woken at the servant's entry, but he'd obviously not been robbed or murdered in his bed. He must have really needed that sleep.

He dressed in a fine shirt and slim-fitting trousers instead of wide-legged pantalones, pulling on new knitted socks and his old boots, now dry, over tender blisters. Skorny had provided a dark green zupan which buttoned down the front. It fitted him well enough that it might have been made for him, except that it was a little short, barely covering his boot tops rather than coming down to mid-calf, but the back was split for riding. There was a broad sash of a lighter green and, rather than a delja, a more practical hooded cloak in a serviceable brown. He rolled the cloak into a bundle and checked out the zupan in the looking glass. A hussar out of uniform stared back at him. It was the mustache, of course, a tell-tale if ever there was one. He reached for the razor once again. Having a naked top lip would seem strange.

He'd barely finished scraping the last few whiskers from his face when Lady Danute was announced by a servant.

Valdas gave a proper bow, but she waved him upright with one hand.

"My father says you're going to Bieloria."

"Yes."

"You're mad."

"How so, lady?"

"It's barely a plan at all, going to Bieloria and hoping to be sent to Kassubia by Tsarina Zofia's good grace. I'm older than you are. I was a girl at court with Zofia before she wed Ivan of Ruthenia. Headstrong, she was, and angry with her brother by the time he'd traded her into a political marriage that she didn't want."

"By all accounts she's prospered. She has beloved children and holds Bieloria for the tsar, but for all practical purposes she's ruling it in her own name. Perhaps she's forgiven Konstantyn."

"But if the tsarina is in Bieloria while the tsar is in Ruthenia, it's surely not a sign of a happy and loving partnership?"

Valdas shrugged. "Be that as it may, I have no better way of finding answers. My face is too well known for me to skulk about the Gura in disguise trying to overhear dark secrets. Your father has informants who might be better at that."

She sighed. "Maybe, but even if your plan succeeds, it could take months just to get to the court in Kassubia, and in the meantime Gerhard becomes accustomed to the feel of polishing the throne with his royal behind. And what happens to the country?"

"I shall have to play a long game, Lady Danute. I will avenge my king and get justice for my men, or die trying."

"I hope the dead have plenty of patience."

With no more dire warnings, Lady Danute led Valdas down to the stables where two horses were waiting for him. *No, not two; one and a half.* He revised his opinion. One, a red bay with a fine head and intelligent eyes was as decent-looking a mount as he might find any-where, but surely the second horse was a joke. A raw-boned, dull brown beast with a common head stood hipshot, over-long ears laid back, looking disgruntled with life. Next to the red bay, the contrast was startling. Well, beggars couldn't afford to be choosy. As long as the animal was sound, that would do. With two mounts he could make better time to Bieloria.

"My father has given you the best horse in his stable," Lady Danute said.

And the worst one, too, Valdas thought, *to make up for it.*

"There's food in the pack and here, a purse."

She held out a pouch heavy with coins, silver tolars by their feel. It seemed rude to look inside.

"Thank you. My sincere thanks to your father." He was aware that two grooms were working nearby. "And my best wishes for his return to good health."

He mounted the red bay, took the brown's lead-rein, and they clat-tered out of the yard on the road to Bieloria, the brown dragging heavily.

CHAPTER THIRTEEN
Lind

MILITARY TRAFFIC HAD been moving along the road since dawn. Lind was nervous—more than nervous if he was honest with himself. As each column rode past, Roza had shrunk against him. *More touching, though this time not her damned hands,* until eventually he'd sent her to lie down in the wagon, thus divesting himself of part of his disguise, but also ridding himself of her feverish energy.

What was she scared of? She wasn't who she seemed to be. She wasn't even Maksimilian's personal problem, he was sure of that now.

God's ballocks! That was all he needed!

It would be all too ironic if he got caught up in a hunt for her. He should dump her and move on, but he'd taken Maksimilian's money and that was his bond. The only business rule he lived by. That, and *"Don't get caught."* Besides, even if he'd wanted to, dumping her wasn't as easy as it might be. He ran through alternatives, from throwing her into a ditch with her head smashed in, to leaving her at a wayside inn. All of them ended up with the military on his tail. He'd always been supremely successful at his job because of the preparation. Yes, he was good at the kill, but he was even better at the infiltration and the exit. In and out of the pond without leaving a ripple on the surface. Dumping the girl, dead or alive, was a ripple he couldn't afford right now. Trader Maksimilian had a lot of contacts and would surely investigate if she went missing. It wouldn't take too much intelligence to ask why someone would need to slide out of the city in disguise barely a few days after the king's assassination.

Besides, she was pregnant.

It was his only taboo. He'd taken contracts on women, but he'd never knowingly killed a pregnant one. Not after what happened to Ewa. Tourmine had taken any contract that came his way without conscience. *Tourmine's face. "Two deaths for one cut. A bonus!"* The man had called himself a professional assassin, but in reality he'd been a swordsmith with a deadly sideline and a penchant for pretty boys.

Roza moaned. Lind twisted round. She was asleep, half resting on the sack of grain, one hand under her head, the other protectively across the bulge of her belly, obvious even under the layers. Her hat had fallen off, leaving the rantuch covering her hair.

She muttered something in her sleep that sounded like: *coming down now.*

"Are you?" He answered to see if she would absorb him into her dream and respond, but she lapsed into silence, so he turned back to the road.

He stopped by a ford to let the horse rest for its nooning. He unhitched it, slipped out its bit, and let it graze by the roadside.

"I fell asleep." Roza sat up in the wagon, her eyes bleary.

"You did." He looked up from searching through the bag of provisions stashed beneath the seat.

"Growing a baby is tiring work."

He shrugged. Truth to tell her belly both frightened and awed him a little. He had a thought that brought beads of perspiration unbidden to his hairline and upper lip. "When is it . . . ?" He nodded toward her stomach.

"Months yet. Another three."

"Oh!" *Thank providence for that!*

She came to the edge of the wagon and stood there as if she expected him to lift her down. Definitely high-born. *Damn!* He ignored her and she unbolted the backboard, sat awkwardly, and wriggled over the lip.

"Not much on manners, are you?" she asked.

He shrugged. "Figured you weren't used to being treated like a lady at Maksimilian's place."

It didn't get a rise out of her, so he concentrated on the food, finding black bread and hard cheese with apples and a separate pack of the ubiquitous journeycake. That stuff would keep for a year or more. "Want some bread and cheese?"

"In a minute." She trudged off over knee-high grass, skirting roadside nettles, and disappeared into a clump of bushes.

"Sorry," she said when she reappeared a few minutes later. "Not much room in here anymore. I'm afraid I have to . . . stop more often."

"Oh." What else could he say?

He handed her a piece of cheese and a roll. They chewed in silence, washing it down with water from the stream.

When he'd finished and hitched the horse, he fastened the tailgate, which she'd left hanging loose, and climbed onto the front board. She stood at the side and looked up at him until he gritted his teeth, reached down, and offered his hand to haul her aboard.

"Thank you," she said as she settled her skirts around herself.

Yes, definitely a highborn.

CHAPTER FOURTEEN
Valdas

STILL TOO CLOSE to Biela Miasto to risk staying in an inn where a stranger might be reported, Valdas chose to sleep beneath a hedge again, away from the road itself, but this time the rain had eased off, a gentle breeze had dried the ground, and he'd wrapped himself in the clean, dry cloak. Lady Danute's warnings chased themselves round his brain, but Lord Skorny did not have the same misgivings.

The grand old man of Zavonian politics was in his mind; maybe that's why he dreamed of his time as Captain of Konstantyn's High Guard.

The king and Chancellor Skorny are meeting with Lord Gerhard Zamoy after breakfast. Lord Gerhard is Konstantyn's cousin, his father's sister's only child, and fully fifteen years older than Konstantyn. He stands on his dignity as the king never does, as if he has something to prove. The meetings between Konstantyn and his heir can touch on many subjects, from the failing health of Gerhard's mother to delicate affairs of state. This is no assignment for one of the junior guards. Only Henryk or himself stands duty within that room. Valdas has learned a lot about politics while standing impassive behind Konstantyn's chair. When Skorny is invited, the meetings are often about foreign policy: trade agreements with Ruthenia, or how to counter the aggression of Sverija. A political marriage, Skorny suggested at the last meeting, and Konstantyn didn't immediately refuse, though his private grief over Queen Cecylia's suicide is still intense.

Valdas has seen the haunted look in Konstantyn's eyes when he glances at the garden below the colonnade. The fountain in the center is where they found Queen Cecylia's body shortly after her fourth stillbirth.

Today Valdas enters the small audience chamber before the king, quickly checking lines of sight and obscured corners. It's safe. The king follows and seats himself at the head of the table. Chancellor Skorny joins him without any fuss and the two exchange pleasantries.

Konstantyn looks up as a page enters and announces, "Lord Gerhard Zamoy and Zygmund Kazimir." Konstantyn includes Gerhard in these talks because Gerhard must learn how to be king in case he's called upon. What's the point of naming an heir if that heir is incapable of ruling?

Konstantyn mutters something under his breath to Skorny that is not very complimentary. Something about Gerhard not finding his arse with his hand without Kazimir giving him a map. The king spent some time in the hussars as a young prince and has retained a colorful vocabulary. The only reason Konstantyn tolerates Kazimir is that he's been loyal to Gerhard since long before there was any real prospect of Gerhard being named heir—before the death of Konstantyn's younger brother, and long before the late Queen Cecylia's four stillbirths.

Valdas dislikes Kazimir. The man presumes too much and takes on authority that's not his. It's pretty obvious that Konstantyn disapproves of him too.

The king keeps his face straight while he welcomes Gerhard cordially, and without looking at Kazimir says, "You may leave us."

Kazimir stiffens and looks pointedly at Valdas, then at Skorny, hesitating a moment too long, before glancing at Gerhard.

"Most noble uncle," Gerhard says. "Zygmund is my secretary."

"There are no secretaries required today."

Kazimir stands. He and Konstantyn are barely six feet apart and match each other for height and coloring almost exactly. Were it not for Kazimir's beak of a nose and his goatee beard, they might almost match in profile.

Valdas wonders whether the man might have taken insolence to new and dangerous levels. Konstantyn is not a wrathful monarch, but he is a monarch. Kazimir is not even a nobleman, though he plays the part. Valdas watches the silent interplay between the two men. Kazimir capitulates. He bows stiffly, turns on his heel, and strides out, thunder-faced. Konstantyn watches him leave, expression thoughtful. He nods to Valdas. "Captain Zalecki, please see that we are not disturbed until the noon bell."

⊷———⊷

Valdas woke from his dream, stomach grumbling, as a drip splashed into his eye. Gods-poxed weather. It was raining again. It probably hadn't been raining for long, because the accumulated droplets were only beginning to work their way down through the hawthorn he sheltered beneath. He took stock of his situation. He was lying on his side, head pillowed on his right arm, which had given him pins and needles in his hand. He was still mostly dry, but that wouldn't last long. He looked out from his prone position at the sleeting gray mist enveloping the grassy hollow. Oh, for coffee and fresh warm rolls. Breakfast would be dry rye bread and hard cheese. He closed his eyes against harsh reality and tried to sleep again.

His dream skipped along in time to the last full day before Konstantyn's murder.

⊷———⊷

Today the king leans on the parapet and gazes at Queen Cecylia's garden. His eyes do not look as haunted as they used to. Maybe the treaty bride from Sverija has eased his pain a little. She's a pretty thing, though barely half Konstantyn's age.

"It's a fine day, Valdas," the king says.

Valdas smiles. When the king calls him Valdas instead of Captain Zalecki, it makes him feel as though he is privileged to be more than a bodyguard. In private he feels as though he may be the king's friend, though he knows there is a world of difference between them. King Konstantyn has a way of inspiring more than loyalty, of making men feel as though they are still men, whether they are employed as the highest official or the lowliest servant. "Yes, sire."

"Many reasons for a man to feel privileged," Konstantyn says.

"Yes, sire." He doesn't think the king's good mood is to do with the fancy Amber Crown. He ponders on what it might be.

⊷———⊷

Valdas opened his eyes and instantly froze. A hoof as big as a soup plate occupied his vision. A brown velvety nose dropped down to the ground and yellow, flat teeth began to tear at the coarse grass inches from his face. All he could see was an ugly coffin-shaped head with ears that might have been borrowed from a donkey. Dammit, surely he'd tied the creature securely last night.

He glanced over. Yes, the red bay was exactly where he'd left him, but the brown was free.

"Damned Donkey." The horse seemed to have acquired a name.

The horse flicked one long ear at him and carried on grazing. Slowly Valdas rolled to his hands and feet. Donkey sidestepped nimbly until he was ten strides away. The horse seemed unconcerned. If it hadn't been for the twitch of his ears and the swish of his tail as Valdas stood slowly, he might have been deaf and blind. Trying not to spook the creature, Valdas reached into his pouch and broke off a corner of his breakfast bread.

"Nice horse. Good horse. Steady boy." He held out his hand with the offering of the bread. Donkey raised his head, stretched out his neck toward Valdas and, without moving a hoof, pointed its mouth at the treat.

"Good boy. Steady boy."

At full stretch the horse lipped the bread from his hand, but before Valdas could grasp his mane, the creature swung his haunches round dangerously close, trotted out of arm's reach, then turned to face him again. Damn.

He broke off another piece of bread. "Come on, fella. Breakfast."

Once again Donkey let him get close enough so that he could take the bread from his outstretched hand before retreating.

Valdas wiped rain from his eyes and broke off another piece of bread to try again. "Last time, Donkey, or I'll be eating grass for breakfast."

This time Valdas held the bread close to his body. As the horse stretched toward him, he noticed the small nick in his ear that proclaimed him to have been a hussar's horse. He'd been so disgusted with the brute that he hadn't really looked all that closely yesterday. As Donkey lipped his hand he rapped out, "Atten-shun!" The horse's coarse head came up, his ears swiveled forward, and for a moment he showed that he remembered his training. It was enough. Valdas stepped forward and grabbed a handful of mane. Knowing when he was beaten, Donkey relaxed once more into Valdas's ownership, and as a reward Valdas gave him another piece of bread.

He ran his hand down the horse's flank, then checked his legs. He'd taken no harm from running loose in the night. He decided to give the red bay a rest from carrying his weight. Today he'd ride the old plug.

He saddled up and put the light pack onto the bay, whom he'd unimaginatively started to think of as Red.

Donkey stood for him to mount, but as soon as he was in the saddle the horse began to trot purposefully. Valdas snatched Red's lead rein as they passed and managed to slow the jarring trot to a walk, but once he pointed Donkey's head to the road, Donkey broke into a high-stepping trot that required Valdas to post or grind his balls into the saddle with every step. He swore and settled into the rhythm of the stride.

"God pox you, Donkey. If I was ever worried about fathering a bastard child, I'll have no need after an hour or two of this."

With the rising sun in his face, Valdas trotted Donkey along the river road, Red jogging alongside. The rain had eased off once more and the late summer sun offered a small chance for man, beast, and road to dry off. He rested the horses and let them graze for a couple of hours at noon, then, throughout the afternoon, they jogged east along the riverbank, encountering nothing more dangerous than a couple of fishermen. As the afternoon drew on, Valdas saw a dust cloud in the distance that indicated a large party of riders, so he turned south to skirt Biela Miasto in a wide arc. No sense in taking risks.

CHAPTER FIFTEEN

Mirza

MIRZA LET BO, her piebald pony, amble along, head down behind the new wagon she shared with Tsura. It was so much smarter than her old one, and the stovepipe didn't leak smoke.

Since the duel, life had been a little easier. She didn't think she was any more popular, but the band—even Stasha and Boldo—gave her grudging respect, and no longer questioned her decisions. Boldo had even come to her with an inflamed cut, which she had cleaned and dressed with honey to take down the infection.

Her own wrist had now stopped aching, and she was regaining full strength and movement gradually.

Life was good.

A little plaited fringe of silks kept the stinging flies out of her pony's eyes, and Mirza thought she should wear one too. They were fierce today. She slapped at one that was intent on crawling across her sweat-dampened forehead, and another buzzed across the knuckles of her rein hand.

The pony's pace didn't falter as she dropped the reins on his neck, reached into the pocket of her riding skirt, and took out a little clay pot. Twisting off the wooden top, she scooped out a blob of pungent ointment and rubbed it into the exposed skin on her face, hands, and neck, taking care to thoroughly cover her witchmark. The ointment would protect her against the insects, but she never much cared for the smell. Heavy with herbs, it had made her eyes water at first. Fortunately the flies didn't care for it either. They went off to plague more appealing skin and left her and her pony alone for a while.

The brutal heat of the day choked her, but the weather would break soon and spectacularly. Weather sense was a part of Mirza's magic.

The scorched grass, hay-brown instead of summer green, would soon get the water it needed. The drought would give way to torrential rain probably followed by a few days of glorious late summer before the autumn frosts. They'd be almost to the border by then, always moving or being moved on, always looking for a place to settle.

She wondered whether she would have another death on her conscience by that time. A sick child was always a worry, but Mirza feared that Tamas would not survive the illness which had come upon him suddenly. The little lad's neck and shoulders had developed an unnatural stiffness. When she examined him she discovered a small puncture wound in his hand. It didn't look like much on the surface, but it was enough to let in bad humors. The disease was traveling through his body, and when it reached his lungs, Mirza knew that he would die.

Bo tossed his head and pricked his ears up as a shout passed from wagon to wagon. Mirza saw Stasha Hetman's family, actually three closely interrelated families in five wagons, begin to circle for the evening's camp, close to where a line of trees indicated a stream. Boldo's family followed suit, three smart wagons and her old one, loaned to a pair of newlyweds expecting their first child. They were followed by Himali's four and Jeppa's three.

Mirza traveled in her own family of one wagon, as Luludja had done before her. Her status, or lack of it, made her an outsider. She wasn't welcome at their fires or into their tents because she dealt with death. They conveniently put aside their fears, however, when they needed her healing skills. Only then did they remember she also dealt with life.

The band was on its way to the autumn horse fair, not only to trade horses, but to exchange news, and make marriage contracts. Young Landstrider women were prized for their virginity above all. As shulam, Mirza might be called upon to examine a prospective bride for purity. It was ironic that with her marked face, her reputation for shrewishness, and her history, Mirza couldn't give her own virginity away.

But what she had lost had been replaced by what she had gained. She was still trying to grow into the position of the Bakaishan shulam. Hiding her inner self behind a prickly exterior helped. She could ask for anything and it would be found for her, though she rarely did. Best not to push the goodwill of the band too far.

"Pull up by that tree," Mirza called across to Tsura in the driving seat of the wagon. A little shelter from the late afternoon sun would be welcome. Mirza slung her right leg over her pony's neck and slid to the ground. It wasn't far. Bo wasn't a big pony; he barely came up to Mirza's shoulder. "Size doesn't matter." She patted his neck.

"Is that Luka over there?" Tsura asked.

"You mean the boy whose ears turn pink every time you speak to him, and who can barely stammer out a sentence when you're nearby?"

"I hadn't noticed."

"Really? What? Blushing?" Mirza laughed. "I expect your parents have already received many offers of marriage for you."

"I won't cut my apprenticeship short, not for any man. My parents can't tell me what to do anymore."

"Good for you, but don't do anything out of misplaced loyalty to me. Do whatever you need to do to gain happiness."

Tsura grinned at her. "Don't worry. I will."

One of us has to be happy, Mirza thought.

⊰⊱

Mirza heard a noise outside her wagon in the middle of the night. Tamas had worsened. His father, Loiza, hammered on her door, but she hadn't really been asleep. She'd called in to see the boy after supper and seen the signs, so she'd been dozing, fully dressed, on the bed built across one end of the wagon.

"Wha . . . ?" Tsura sat up in her truckle bed on the floor, shuffling to one side as Mirza stepped past.

"It's Tamas. Where did you put the salt?"

"It's in the—uh, here." Tsura handed over a small bag of crushed salt, which had fallen down the side of her bed. "Do you want me to come?"

"No. There isn't room. Besides, we know what happens next."

Mirza clutched the salt, warm from where it had rested alongside Tsura's body, grabbed the bag she'd prepared earlier, and hurried to Loiza's tent, pitched a little to one side of Himali's *familia,* so Tamas's cries didn't wake everyone. It didn't matter. They were all awake. Himali himself was stirring the remains of the communal fire, and several shapes moved around the camp in the night. Loiza and Aishe's tragedy was shared by their extended family. No one expected the child to live.

Loiza had rushed ahead of her and held the tent flap open. Aishe held Tamas in her arms, rocking him as if he were a baby instead of a boy of eight summers. But all the rocking in the world could not quiet the boy's whimpers being forced from his body even as his breath shortened.

Mirza sat cross-legged next to mother and child. She took a piece of green ribbon from her pocket, tied three knots in it, and wound it around and between the fingers of her left hand, muttering to her ancestors to please help her now.

"Brave boy." She leaned forward. "Will you let me take him, Aishe?"

The glow from the campfire reflected upon the tent walls, illuminating the woman's tear-stained face. She shook her head.

"Ish, you must let the shulam help him, now." Loiza knelt by his wife.

Mirza remained silent. They might have held still for a minute or for an eternity, with nothing but the boy's whimpers between them. Eventually Aishe nodded and Loiza lifted the little boy, kissed his head, and placed him in Mirza's lap. Both parents rocked backward to give Mirza room to work, but neither took their eyes from their son.

Mirza handed her small bag to Loiza. "Light the candle, place it in the copper dish, and sprinkle on the herbs."

Mirza held the boy cradled in her left arm. When the scent of sweet herbs filled the tent, she reached for the salt with her right and sprinkled it round where she sat so that an unbroken line encircled them both.

"Whatever happens, do not break the salt circle. For the sake of your son's soul, hold steady."

Loiza nodded, and after a short hesitation Aishe did, too.

Mirza uttered a prayer to the spirits of Earth, Air, Fire, and Water, and finally to the god of all things. She began to tap a rhythm gently on the boy's chest.

The spirits were watching and they carried her over almost immediately. A small frail form, ghostly pale, followed her out of the mist and into a gentle golden light. There might have been rolling hills and trees and a silver river, but to Mirza's eyes it was indistinct. She suspected that if she ever saw it clearly, she'd never leave.

She took Tamas's hand. "Does it hurt now?"

He shook his head. "My neck doesn't hurt, and I can breathe."

"Yes. Your mama and poppa love you very much and they asked me to tell you that they will join you someday, but for now it's time to go to your grandmother."

"My grandmother is dead."

"Not in this world. Look, here she comes."

A shape detached itself from the mist and resolved itself into a dumpy elderly woman. All Mirza could really see of her was her smile. She put Tamas's hand into the hand of his grandmother, shivering as her flesh touched insubstantial spirit.

Tamas didn't even look back.

Mirza watched as the duo faded to mist, then turned and looked for the way home, following the light of the burning candle.

She gasped, breath returning to her body suddenly, as if without her spirit her body had forgotten to live.

"Ah!"

She opened her eyes. Tamas lay dead in her arms and both his parents clung to each other.

"Your son is with his grandmother. He says he loves you very much and will see you again someday."

"Aiyaiyai." Aishe began to wail. Loiza folded her into his arms, his own face wet with silent tears.

When Mirza had let their grief run for as long as they needed, she helped them lay out the body, sprinkle more herbs, and wind him in a sheet. Aishe gulped down a sob as they covered his face.

"Your other children?" Mirza asked.

Aishe shook her head, unable to speak.

"With Himali," Loiza said. "Like you told us. We've not allowed them anywhere near Tamas."

"Good. Don't let them back in here until you've burned the blankets and Tamas's clothes and toys."

Loiza bowed his head. "We won't."

"I am truly sorry for your loss, but Tamas is free of his pain now."

"We know." Aishe's voice shook. "Thank you."

As Mirza backed out of the tent she heard Loiza say, "She's not as bad as rumor has it."

CHAPTER SIXTEEN
Lind

HE WOULD HAVE slept in the open that night if he'd been alone, but mindful of Roza's condition, Lind stopped at a tavern and took a room, only one or it would have looked suspicious. She wouldn't leave her bags on the cart so he heaved them up the stairs, cursing women for not knowing how to pack lightly. He rescued his disguises and placed them in the bottom of his own bag before bringing it up.

"You take the bed." He wrapped himself in his delja and stretched out on the floor in front of the meager fire. He eyed a cockroach retreating into a shadow. "I'm not sure you have the best deal. At least the floor doesn't have bedbugs."

She gave him a look, threw back the covers, and examined the bed closely before climbing into it fully dressed. Yes, definitely a young woman used to finer beds than this place provided. He was only stuck with her for a few more days, until they reached the farmstead he'd contracted to deliver her to.

He heard her get up three times in the night to use the chamber pot, but he politely, or was that fearfully, kept his eyes closed. He must have fallen deeply asleep, but an early-morning commotion outside woke him in an instant. He knew the sound of many riders, and many riders sounded like a troop of hussars to him.

"God's ballocks!" Feeling slightly lightheaded, he crossed to the window in three strides and saw maybe twenty horsemen under the command of a young ensign. A sergeant snapped out orders while the ensign stood in the middle of the yard, every line of his body saying he was unsure of himself. His first command, Lind guessed. The sergeant spoke to him, putting one hand on his shoulder, and

Lind shuddered. The ensign nodded and strode purposefully toward the tavern door. A few seconds later Lind heard his sharp knock and then a louder one, followed by the landlord's voice.

"All right, I'm coming. Hold your horses . . ." Lind heard the door creak open, followed by a silence, probably a stunned one.

Something touched Lind's arm! His heart leaped into his throat and his hand started to go to his knife, but it was only Roza behind him, pressing close to see, warm against his back.

He held both hands up in front of his chest and breathed again.

"Don't ever creep up on me again if you want to stay alive!"

"I . . . I'm sorry . . . I . . ." Her voice trailed off as she stepped to the window and stepped away again very quickly. "What do they want?"

He looked at her. "What are you hiding? Who are you? You're not a whore, and you're not Trader Maksimilian's mistress."

She looked at him coldly. "That's my business, but I think I have no more need to be seen than you have." An edge in her voice told him despite her youth she was someone used to being obeyed. In a moment of clarity he understood that the mild-mannered woman-child that she'd been yesterday was also an act.

The silence hung between them, stretched out into forever. Neither gave way with an explanation. At length it was Lind who nodded sharply. "It seems we depend on each other for discretion."

She huffed out a short breath, nostrils flared. "So it's in our best interests not to attract any unwanted attention."

"Wait here." He slipped out of the door and assessed the long landing. In one direction the main stair, in the other a secondary stair down into the kitchen. There was a window on the half-landing and a ten-foot drop into the stable yard. Not too far for him, but Roza would certainly never make it. If he had to leave her behind, he daren't leave her in any fit condition to talk.

He balked at that. Surely he wasn't getting sentimental.

Sentiment doesn't enter into it.

He'd only kill Roza, or whatever her name was, if he had to, but not unless. He'd never killed for pleasure, except for Tourmine. That had been both a pleasure and a necessity. He brought up the memory of Tourmine lying in a pool of his own blood. His first kill. Unable to keep the thought out of his head, he stepped backward to the moment.

Tourmine, trousers at half-mast, buggering the new apprentice over the table in the workshop, so intent that for one vital moment he doesn't hear Lind, shaking hand reaching for new-made sword lying by the sharpening block. That instant of delicious decision. Contemplating shoving the blade right up the man's arse to his brain, but going for the safety cut instead. Swing hard from the shoulder, straight across the back of the bastard's thighs to the bone, leaving him hamstrung and helpless. Yelling to the crying boy to run and keep running. Slicing the blade across Tourmine's bare belly, watching his glistening guts exposed, smelling shit and knowing that even without another blow he's made his kill. Taking a final swipe, seeing Tourmine's prick fall away to the floor, strangely small for all the trouble it's caused. Hearing screams that are, finally, all Lind's own.

He slowed his breathing. Having butchered Tourmine yet again in his mind, he was conscious of an unpleasant tight feeling in his groin. It was still the only thing that stirred him to passion. He fought the feeling down and pulled himself back to the present.

At the top of the stairs, he stopped to listen. The ensign was negotiating breakfast of kasza, millet porridge, for his troop, with less authority than was usual in a hussar officer. He must still be wet behind the ears. He looked barely eighteen. Once his sergeant stomped in, broad-shouldered and towering over the landlord, the ensign got what he asked for, and the landlord set about waking the household.

Lind loitered, trying to catch snippets of conversation. He thought he heard *riding all night*, but the only thing that he was sure of was *red-haired woman*.

His heart began to race uncontrollably.

At least she'd had her hair covered when they arrived. That gave them a breathing space.

He slipped down the servants' stairs into the kitchen, where the pot-boy was stirring the big fire into life with an iron poker and feeding it dry wood for fast heat.

"Have you water heated?" Lind asked.

"Boiling it for the kasza for that lot out there." The pot-boy's mouth twisted downward and he sounded sullen.

Lind flipped a shiny copper penny to him. "They march in as if they own the place."

"Rutting hussars!"

"Won't hurt them to wait awhile longer."

"Let the Devil take 'em for all I care."

Lind flipped a second coin. "My wife's got a touch of the ague and fancies her feet in a mustard bath. You know how pregnant women get."

The pot-boy obviously didn't. Lind didn't give him the opportunity to question; he dipped hot water from the pot on the crane over the fire, half-filled a bucket, and looked around for another. The boy got the idea and filled a second bucket, and Lind took them upstairs.

"What . . . ?" Roza looked at the buckets.

"For a smart woman, you can be pretty stupid. I heard the ensign say something about red hair. You're walking about with a flag on top of your head, woman."

"I can't do much except keep it covered."

"Yes, you can."

He opened his bag and took out a closely woven cloth bag tucked inside a small copper bowl. With it was a pair of fine kid gloves, deep brown, but suspiciously darker on the fingers and palms than the backs of the hands. She opened the drawstring and looked inside.

"You carry henna with you?" She raised her eyebrows. "And you use kid gloves to keep the dye from your hands. I was once given a pair of these brought from Paris at great expense. Sir, you are a mystery. I'm not going to ask why you might wish to change your appearance in a hurry, or hide the fact from those around you. I'm grateful that you do."

"It's messy. You need to remove your garments, the outer ones at least. You don't want telltale splashes of dye on your dress."

She hesitated.

"We've already established that I have no interest in your body, but unless you can manage this alone, you're going to have to trust me."

She took a deep breath and unbuttoned her dark green szuba, under which she had a full woolen kaftan in brown. The collar was too high.

"Take it off."

Lind turned away from her, not sure if it helped. Out in the yard he could see the troopers had stripped saddles from their weary mounts and were sitting around the stable yard in small groups—all except for the sergeant and the ensign. Lind counted the number of horses and the number of riders to be sure. Yes, two fewer men than horses. The ensign and sergeant must be in the tavern, but as yet no one was actively searching the premises. It was barely past dawn; they still had an hour or two before their apparent sojourn in bed started to look strange. Maybe the troop would be gone by then, maybe not. He could hope.

Hope for the best, plan for the worst.

"Ready."

He turned around to find her standing in a silk chemise far too fine to have been made for anyone but a lady of some wealthy household.

He knew quality cloth when he saw it. She automatically crossed her hands over her full breasts.

"I told you, I'm not interested. Turn round, let me look at your hair."

She turned. Unpinned it rippled to below her hips, a mass of spun copper.

He ran his hand through it, judging the weight and volume. "I don't have enough to color all this. I'll have to cut it much shorter."

She drew breath as if to protest, but only said, "Do what you must."

He smoothed the hair down with his fingers to a long horsetail, folded it over to make a loop, took his knife and sawed through it, cutting it to less than half its length. She suffered his ministrations in silence. He dropped the strands into the embers of last night's fire, where they sizzled, curled, and finally flamed and shriveled, leaving a distinctive smell.

He mixed the crushed, dried henna leaves into a paste in the bowl with a splash or two of the warm water and looked at her hair. It spread down her back onto the white chemise. He couldn't avoid dye on that, and unless every trace was removed this was a futile exercise.

"I need some cloth, something I can burn afterward. I'm not so kind as to sacrifice my second-best shirt, and you seem to have an abundance of luggage. What have you got?"

He reached for the nearest bag and she almost yelped in her haste to distract him from it.

"Not that one. It's only baby things. Here, will this do?"

She rummaged in the second bag and brought out a linen night-gown, long sleeved and full skirted.

"Perfect."

He took his knife, sliced up the side seams, notched into it, and tore it along the warp so that he had four more or less equal pieces. The sleeves made two more irregular-shaped cloths.

"Drop your chemise at the back."

"What?"

"Loosen the drawstring and drop it at the back. Hold it at the front by all means, but get it out of my way before I strip it off you alto-gether. Modesty's gone far enough. There's more at stake here—for both of us, I think."

She did as he said, and he wrapped one piece of linen around her shoulders to keep the dye from her skin and pulled on the kid gloves— she was right—they'd cost him deep in the purse, but had already proved their worth. What price his life and freedom? Carefully he began to daub the henna mud onto her hair, rubbing it into every strand but taking care not to stain her face, ears, or neck, wiping it where he splashed accidentally.

"If you ever need a job you could hire out as a lady's maid," she said.

"You're obviously used to having one of your own."

That shut her up. When he'd used up every last bit, he wrapped her hair with linen, twisted it on top of her head, and tucked the cloth into itself.

"Keep still or that will fall off."

He watched the window while she continued to clutch the chemise to her breasts, standing far enough back not to be seen from the yard, should anyone look up.

"Thank you," she said.

"I'm doing it to save my skin, not yours."

"I mean thank you for not . . . for being . . ."

"Is it so hard to believe that I'm really not interested in your body? Are you so conceited that you think yourself irresistible?"

"I . . . don't know. I never . . . I mean . . ."

"I never took you for a whore. If you want to pass yourself off as one you're going to have to act a lot more forward, but that was a fine display you put on at the gate, I must say. I haven't figured you out yet."

"There's nothing to figure. A family quarrel."

"A family who can call on the King's Hussars!"

"My . . . uncle has influence."

"I'll bet he does. His baby, is it?"

Her eyes slid away from his and down to the dusty floorboards.

Well, he knew what it was to be prey.

As if she was reading his thoughts, she said, "You . . . you prefer men . . . boys?"

"No!"

"It's all right to say if you do. Where I come from women . . . often . . . spend time together."

"You don't look as though you've been spending time with women." He jerked his head toward her belly.

"We don't all have the luxury of following our inclination."

He grunted.

He let her make up her own mind about him. Any fiction would be better than the truth. He wasn't even sure what his inclination was. Best not to have one at all.

An hour later, with her hair dyed to a dark chestnut brown, she tied it up wet. Lind checked for dye marks on her fair skin, but she was clean. He left her dressing whilst he went down the kitchen stairs with the buckets, one thick with dye water, the other not quite so dark from the last few rinses. The pot-boy was ladling thick, creamy kasza into dishes while the landlord's wife carved slices from a side of fat bacon. They both looked up when he entered.

"She's feeling much better. My mother always recommended a mustard foot bath for what ails you," he said brightly.

The pot-boy made as if to stop what he was doing, but Lind shook his head. "I'll get rid of these. You look busy."

"Drain outside runs to the stream," the landlord's wife said without breaking her rhythm of sawing through the bacon.

"My thanks."

Out in the yard, twenty pairs of hussars' eyes stared at him as he walked out of the kitchen door.

"Good morning," he called. "Nice weather!"

"Only if you've been sleeping with a roof over your head and haven't been riding half the night." The hussar nearest to him cleared his throat and spat.

He kept walking. *Act normal.* He walked past the open drain right down to the stream, fast flowing, thank goodness. He tipped in the contents of the buckets and rinsed them out carefully, pleased to note that the wood was dark enough not to show the stain, at least when wet. He filled them both with clean water and carried them to the kitchen.

"My thanks for your buckets."

The landlady saw the clean water and her face softened into a smile. "I'm almost through feeding that rabble out there. Get you and your lady wife into the house-body and I'll bring you some breakfast."

He hesitated.

"I'll not take no for an answer."

"Thank you. We'll be down directly."

He couldn't ask if the ensign and sergeant were still in there, but he'd certainly not seen them in the yard.

Full of foreboding, he climbed the stairs. Roza was dressed.

"We are summoned to breakfast."

"We can't."

"I think we must."

"But the soldiers . . ."

"Are looking for a red-haired woman, not a couple."

She thought for a moment and unbuttoned the szuba from the hem to below her breasts and tied back the skirt with loops to reveal the kaftan beneath.

"Have you a spare sash, husband?" she asked.

"Only the one I have on."

She held out her hand. He removed his sash and she tied it round herself, under her breasts and above her bulging stomach. It made her look a lot more pregnant than she had looked yesterday.

"I've been hiding this for too long," she said.

Now it was his turn to puzzle.

"They're looking for a red-haired woman who isn't pregnant," she said.

Ah, that was it. She'd been hiding her pregnancy until she couldn't hide it any longer.

He nodded. "You're learning."

CHAPTER SEVENTEEN
Valdas

ALTERNATELY SWAPPING FROM Red to the appallingly mannered but seemingly tireless Donkey, Valdas made his way steadily toward Zavonia's eastern border, intending to join up with one of the trade caravans heading for Bieloria. The borderlands were teeming with brigands and there was safety in numbers. If he could hire on as a caravan guard he could save some of his tolars. Skorny's purse wasn't bottomless. He was cautious with his coin, however, keeping most of his reserves strapped around his middle underneath his clothes.

As the pale sun dropped down behind him, he spotted a village ahead, illuminated in the afterglow. It looked peaceful enough, so he risked the tavern, surprised to find it crowded. It seemed as though the whole village had gathered for a town meeting. In the aftermath, the locals were too busy grumbling about new taxes to take much notice of Valdas when he entered, but as he made his way through the crowd to the bar he noticed the noise in the room fell away.

"A room for the night, a stable for my horses, and a meal," he told the landlord.

Silence surrounded him now. Without turning his head, he checked for movement in his peripheral vision. None.

A low rumble of disapproval started somewhere to his right.

He turned, hand resting lightly on the hilt of his sabre. "Just passing through," he said. "Does anyone have a problem with that? If so, I'd be glad to solve it for them."

No one stepped forward or said anything.

"Good."

He turned to the bar, his back itching as if he had a target painted on it. "How much will that be?"

It took the landlord a moment to catch his breath. "Six coppers for the room, two for your horses' fodder, and thr . . . five for the meal." The landlord didn't quite meet his eyes. "New taxes, sorry."

"Fair enough."

Valdas put thirteen coppers on the bar and decided not to have more than one pot of home-brewed beer with his meal. He needed to conserve his money as much as possible. The new king was obviously not trying to make himself popular if his first decree had raised taxes. What was Gerhard up to?

Valdas watched from the doorway as the landlord's son, a stout young man, took Red and Donkey to the stable, narrowly avoiding the latter's sly nip toward his backside. Valdas was almost pleased to see that Donkey's disapproval wasn't only reserved for him. He'd go and check on the pair of them later.

Some of the crowd in the tavern left, others settled in for the evening. A few glances were cast in his direction, but no one seemed inclined to make trouble, though Valdas couldn't quite relax. He'd retire to his room long before the serious drinkers imbibed enough false courage to start anything.

The landlord hadn't asked him what he wanted to eat, so he settled at a table and resigned himself to whatever was on offer, probably borscht or something cabbage-related. When the meal came he was pleasantly surprised. Yes, there was cabbage soup, but it was flavored with ham, carrots, and onions and served with dark rye bread. A plate of surprisingly good cepelinai followed, the beef filling spiced with garlic to offset the blandness of the dumpling. It was served with boletus, the king of mushrooms, fried in butter with sour cream.

The landlord brought him a second pot of beer. Valdas looked at it and shook his head sadly. "I didn't order that."

"On the house. I feel bad about, you know, earlier. It's been a trying day for everyone."

"Taxes?"

The landlord nodded. "Penny on a cabbage. It doesn't seem much, but . . ." He shrugged. "These people don't have much to start with. Did you enjoy your meal?"

"I did." Valdas turned his spoon upside down to show his appreciation in the traditional manner.

"Good." The landlord sat down opposite and pushed the pot of beer toward Valdas. "There's no sleep on an empty stomach. My wife stirs the crockpot in her own manner. She is a good cook, yes?"

A female form appeared silhouetted in the kitchen doorway. Valdas's heart jumped. She was the same size as Aniela and for a moment there was a passing resemblance, but then she moved and the light fell upon her face. She was homely, even pretty, but she was not Aniela. He felt a sudden emptiness that he barely understood.

He smiled and nodded to the lady. "A very good cook. You are a lucky man to have such a talented wife."

The landlord smiled fondly. "And she's given me five strong sons, too."

"She is a paragon. When did you find out about the taxes?"

The landlord sighed. "The day after we heard about the king's death. This new king, Gerhard, must think we have bottomless pockets. He's the king. He's rich. What does he need our coppers for?"

Valdas avoided giving a lecture on the economy of Zavonia and the difference between the king's private fortune and the treasury that funded everything the local *sejims* didn't take care of, from the standing army to the maintenance of major roads.

"What, indeed, my friend," he said.

In the end he didn't begrudge his coppers for a fine meal and a clean bed.

He stuck a chair under the bedroom door handle, since there was no lock. No sense in being careless. That done, he settled into the somewhat lumpy mattress and drifted off to sleep with the usual litany in his head. *Henryk Zehrin, Lukas Grinius, Bartek Andrulis, Darius Kairys . . .*

And woke with the names still playing out in his mind: *Jerzy Polonsky, Petras Mazur, Waldemar Konopka. Konstantyn, second of his name. King of Zavonia.*

Despite all that, he awoke feeling more refreshed than he had since this whole nightmare began. Breakfast, another two coppers, was the inevitable bowl of kasza, but accompanied by a stack of pancakes with soft cheese and a slather of lingonberry preserve, all washed down with coffee. When he left, the landlord shoved a muslin-wrapped package into his hand.

"For the journey, my friend. Smoked blood sausage."

From the shape of the package, there was also bread in there, and an onion.

"Thank you." Unasked-for, he gave the landlord another two coppers. "For the taxes. I wish you well."

CHAPTER EIGHTEEN
Lind

R OZA PUT ON a good act at breakfast, behaving as though she hadn't a care in the world. Her confidence was her armor. Lind wondered whether she was as scared as he was. He'd certainly noticed her checking both soldiers from a distance, before stepping out into the tavern's tap room, so she had a certain amount of admirable caution. Good.

A fire already blazed up the chimney and the ensign and his sergeant both took full advantage of it, the ensign sitting a little way off while the sergeant roasted his buttocks, commanding the room from its focus. It was easy to tell who was in charge, despite their relative rank. Lind took an instant dislike to both of them, the sergeant for his bullying, oafish exterior, barely hidden beneath a veneer of civility, and the young officer for bending over for him without a whimper.

You're going to have to do something about him sooner or later, he thought, looking at the youngster. *Better to make it sooner and get it over with.*

The officer jumped up as they entered and offered a courteous greeting, introducing himself simply as Kaminski. The sergeant just eyed them up and stood his ground.

With Lind's sash under her breasts emphasizing the swell of her belly, Roza looked very pregnant. She'd twisted her brown hair into a simple knot, though even that had taken her three tries to get right, as if she was used to someone else pinning it up for her. He hoped anyone looking for a slim copper-haired woman would not look twice at Roza, and so it proved.

Fighting down his fears and playing the solicitous husband, he pulled a chair up in front of the fire for her, right by where the sergeant was standing.

"A share of your fire, sergeant, for my good wife." He glanced at Kaminski.

"Yes, sergeant, make room for the lady," Kaminski said.

Lind watched the subtle interplay between the two men, judging the child-soldier to be more conscientious in the carrying out of his duty, but the sergeant to be more dangerous. *In the event of a scrap, kill the sergeant first.*

"You're on the road early, Ensign Kaminski," Roza said.

Lind's belly knotted. *Don't talk too much, Roza, for pity's sake.*

"Indeed, ma'am."

"Might we hope you are on the trail of the devil who robbed us of good King Konstantyn?"

God's ballocks! Lind's bowels turned to ice water.

"I have good news on that account, ma'am. The assassin is identified and is even now being hunted down. The captain of the king's own High Guard, no less. Two of his accomplices, the cook and a spy masquerading as a fishmonger, have already been executed—by sawing. A further accomplice is thought to have fled to Posenja."

"That is excellent news." Lind felt a weight begin to lift.

"Ah." Roza barely managed a grunt. He turned to see that she looked quite pale.

"We are charged with a more grievous task." The young ensign's forehead knotted. "King Konstantyn's queen has disappeared and we are tasked with finding her. A young and beautiful woman, slight of build and with hair the color of copper."

If anything Roza paled even more.

All Lind's questions were answered at once. This was worse than he'd imagined. God's ballocks! He'd seriously thought about killing her! What a hue and cry that would have raised. He wondered if everyone else in the room could hear his heart trying to beat its way out of his ribcage.

He forced himself to sit very still and without looking at Roza said, "Queen Kristina? Do they think she's been abducted?"

"I am not privy to those details, sir."

The sergeant leaned forward. "Maybe she was the one paid the captain to do for the king? Maybe they were secret lovers."

The ensign's voice sharpened. "Keep that kind of talk under your hat, sergeant. The Amber Crown is not a source for gossip and speculation."

Lind resisted a sideways glance at Roza, who had gone very quiet, though her breathing seemed more rapid. Was she his employer? A young wife married against her will, taking matters into her own hands. Well, he could hardly blame her for that. It had certain parallels with his own life. Was Good King Konstantyn a monster when the bedroom door closed behind him? Was she merely trying to protect herself?

He shrugged away fanciful thoughts.

Don't get drawn in. She's too dangerous.

"I wish you well in your endeavors, sir," she said at last.

He was saved from further conversation by the pot-boy bringing in a board with freshly baked bread upon it and a hot ham. The boy smacked it down in the middle of the table, and wiped his hands on his tunic.

⬥———⬥

They were two miles down the road before Roza broke the silence. "Aren't you going to say anything?"

Lind scowled. "Like, 'I'm sorry for cutting off your hair, Your Majesty,' or 'Does Your Majesty wish me to arrange for a carriage and four at the next available opportunity?' Or how about I ask what's in that heavy bag that you don't want me to look in?"

"No! I mean . . ." She turned away from him and stared into the distance, at the low, rolling landscape of grassland broken by intensively cultivated patches around small farmsteads. When she turned back there were tear tracks down her cheeks.

"Don't start that. I don't have a heart you can melt with tears. You've done well up to now. Don't go snively on me."

"All right." She took a deep breath. "What do you want to know?"

"Did you?"

"Did I what?"

"Pay the assassin, or arrange to have him paid?"

"No!" She sounded horrified by the notion.

"So why run?"

She patted her belly. "This was . . . secret."

How could something so obvious be secret? He must have looked puzzled, because she untied the borrowed sash and let her dress fall loosely over her belly. In that outfit he could hardly tell she was pregnant unless she made a point of letting it become obvious.

"My ladies know, but they came with me from Sverija and are faithful. And Konstantyn knew, of course. It's hard to keep this kind of secret out of a marriage bed. I told him when he noticed . . . changes."

Ewa's breasts. That's what Lind had noticed first. Think of something else.

"Why the big secret?"

"Konstantyn's first wife, Cecylia, miscarried four times, despite being, or seeming to be, healthy. My family thought it strange—suspicious. When I married Konstantyn I made a promise to my mother that I would not give any ill-wisher the opportunity to do any babe of mine harm." She laughed, a brittle sound as near to a cry as Lind ever wanted to hear. "It turns out I should have tried to protect Konstantyn instead."

"A king is always a target. He should know how to protect himself from a professional assassin."

"And do you want to tell me how you know about professional assassins, Ludwik Balinski?"

He held his breath while seconds ticked past. It didn't seem to have come as a surprise to her. Had she simply guessed or did she know for sure? He wondered if he should kill her. The road was clear. He had a knife in his belt. One sure stroke and there would be blood pumping out over her breasts.

Two deaths for one cut. A bonus.

He breathed deep and made a final decision. "No, Your Majesty, I do not."

She shook her head. "What likelihood that you and I end up traveling together?"

"Not so strange. Trader Maksimilian has a certain reputation for discretion. There are few men would be so reliable in such adverse circumstances—for either of us."

She sat quiet for miles, then at length she said, "Tell me who employed you."

"I can't."

"Can't or won't?"

"Can't. I only saw a servant."

"And how much did they pay you?"

He looked at her, seeing for the first time a young widow, frightened for her life and for that of her child, but determined to take charge. If the new king was the man behind Konstantyn's death, as surely she must suspect, the very fact that she had an heir in her belly put both mother and babe in peril.

"In truth, not enough."

"And are you going to kill me?"

"No. I delivered what I was paid for. That's enough." If they'd known about her they would surely have included her death in the deal, but it wasn't up to him to exceed his orders. "Are you going to try and kill me, Majesty?"

"If I did, would I succeed?"

"No."

"That's what I thought." She put her hand on his wrist.

He froze.

"I'm sorry. No touching. I'll remember."

He nodded.

Roza or Kristina, or whatever he should call her now, didn't ask any more questions and left him alone with his thoughts for most of the morning. That was entirely good from one point of view and entirely bad from another. He tried not to think about Ewa, but it was difficult when she was still part of his nightmares.

She'd been a scullion in Tourmine's kitchen, the only girl in a household of men, and lower than a rat's belly in everyone's estimation but his. She might have been pretty if she'd ever been fed and washed properly. But pretty or not she'd taken pity on him when Tourmine had left him shamed and bleeding the first time. She'd been older than him, only by a year or two, but when he was eleven it had made her seem like the mother he could barely remember. By the time he was fourteen he needed to know if Tourmine had turned him into a molly or if he was growing to be a man. She'd proved it to him. Face to face.

It had been both not enough, and too much, and had led to tragedy.

He sheared away from the thought.

The rolling countryside slid past their wagon wheels, but Lind barely saw it. After fifteen years he was still taking Tourmine's punishment. Taking it, holding it, cherishing it. What was wrong with him? He needed to leave it behind once and for all. Maybe it started here.

Maybe helping Kristina would somehow balance what happened to Ewa.

CHAPTER NINETEEN
Valdas

AVOIDING MAJOR TOWNS meant that the journey to Dadziga took longer than it would have done on the main highway, but as he settled into the rhythm of his lone journey through the rolling hills, lakes, and forests of southern Zavonia, Valdas discovered it was the same story in every village. Increased taxes pushed the common folk into grumbling. Valdas was no expert on fiscal policy, but he knew a thing or two about people. A penny here and there might not be much to a king, but it was a burden on the common folk.

King Konstantyn had been careful not to tax the common people more than they could bear, though he'd taxed the nobles a greater share. Perhaps one of them . . . No, probably not. A king always demanded taxes; getting rid of one king and replacing him with another didn't guarantee lower taxes. If anything, quite the opposite. He wondered if Gerhard had increased taxes on the poor to reduce taxes on the nobles whose support he surely relied upon.

He wondered how the nobles had reacted. Were any of them suspicious, or did they all fear for their own necks, or more likely their ballocks, if they demanded Gerhard investigate Konstantyn's death more thoroughly? The High Guard dangling one by one from the Gura's curtain wall was enough to remind them that Gerhard considered the matter closed. It was likely that they were all playing politics right now. Maybe even some had feigned illness, like Skorny, and used it as an excuse to quit the capital until everything settled down. Maybe he could get some news in Dadziga.

In contrast to the country villages, Dadziga was bustling. The streets in the center were wide, new thoroughfares, rebuilt after a fire had destroyed a greater part of the city some thirty years ago. The old part of town, however, seemed to have no pattern to it. Streets twisted, crossed, and dead-ended for no apparent reason. The Leather Quarter gave way to the Mercanter Quarter, where trade warehouses lined Nowa Street.

He asked around in various taverns, and each time the answer led him to the Hindia Spice Company. Word on the street was that although the company didn't organize caravans of their own for the trek to Bieloria, they sent small quantities of expensive spices on a number of different caravans, and therefore had extensive knowledge of who was passing through and who was preparing to travel where.

He found the Hindia Spice Company on the ground floor of a warehouse shared by many merchants joined together under the banner of the League, a distant outpost of a once-powerful organization, now on the decline, but still influencing trade.

"What can I do for you?"

Surprisingly, the person in the office was a young, brown-skinned woman, self-assured enough to be in charge. If this was the Jadzia Lizovska he'd been told about, she wasn't what he'd expected. Valdas wondered how such an attractive young woman had come to be in such a position of responsibility. Maybe she had inherited the company from her father.

"I need to find a caravan going to Bieloria and I was told you could help me."

"You were?"

"By almost everyone I asked." He smiled. "The Hindia Spice Company seems to have quite a reputation for being up to date with information." He wished he'd known about her when he'd been intelligence-gathering for King Konstantyn. She would have been a useful, and pleasant, contact. "I'm told that nothing much happens along the trade route that you don't know about."

"I find out eventually, but caravans are slow. I hear a few rumors here and there."

"All I've heard on the road are mutterings about new taxes."

She sighed, her bosom rising and falling prettily beneath her lightweight summer letnik. "Here, too. The king thinks we're made of money. I can assure you that it's not the case."

"So why would he be raising taxes?"

"Maybe it's to start a war. The last caravan to come up from Luthlin reported Zavonian troops gathering on the border with Kassubia."

Valdas's first thought was that Gerhard had uncovered the assassin, but in his heart he knew Gerhard wouldn't go to war with Kassubia to avenge Konstantyn. A surge of anger almost overtook him. *What in seven hells is Gerhard up to?*

He pushed the anger down, but was perhaps still a little short with the girl when he said, "War doesn't make sense."

"War never makes sense to the common people, but kings fight among themselves just the same. We've had peace for a decade, but the Amber Crown still has blood on it."

"It does." *And not all from battlefields.*

"You look like a soldier."

"I was."

"And why would you be traveling to Bieloria?"

"To visit the sister of an old friend."

"Lucky girl." She smiled at him.

Valdas couldn't help but wonder if it was an invitation of sorts. "It's nothing like that. A duty visit."

"Well, walk with me. I have business with Lord Callender—an Angluman lately come to Dadziga with a caravan of pack mules bound for Bieloria. I need to arrange for him to carry a small consignment of spices for me. Maybe I can get him to take a passenger as well."

"I can work my way there. I'm told caravans need extra guards to pass safely through the borderlands."

"Are you good with that sabre?" She nodded to the blade that swung at his hip.

Was that a double meaning? He raised one eyebrow.

"As good as any." Whichever way she meant it, he answered truthfully.

"If I can get Lord Callender to take you on, you can keep a special eye on my spices. I haven't done business with this man before, so I'd be grateful if someone looked out for my interests. There would be a few tolars in it."

"I can do that."

Three days later Valdas gathered Donkey and Red from the livery stable, said good-bye to the lovely Jadzia, and joined Callender's caravan of fifty pack mules. It had been a pleasant and welcome interlude, but the journey promised to be tough. There were twenty teamsters and three guards—himself and two of Callender's foreigners. Their Zavonian was rudimentary and they jabbered in Anglu between themselves. Callender always addressed them in Anglu, so Valdas missed out on some of what passed between them. He spoke Sverijan a little, and Ruthenian passably well, but he had no Anglu at all.

He didn't like being ill-informed.

Callender was no lord, whatever he called himself. Valdas came from an ancient noble family, even though they'd fallen on hard times. He'd been around nobility for long enough to recognize it, and Callender, even accounting for his foreignness, didn't have the right demeanor. A lord said something and expected it to be done. Callender reinforced his instructions with blows and harsh words, even when the lack of obedience was entirely down to the incomprehensibility of his instructions. He didn't pick on Valdas, for they were much of a size and Valdas had eyeballed Callender and his men much as he had once eyeballed a sergeant-at-arms when as a young recruit he'd been picked on unjustly. The bullying had stopped then. He had not given it the opportunity to begin here, but some of the teamsters were not so lucky.

It was an unhappy outfit slogging through heathland, alternately stony and marshy, on a haphazardly maintained road. Valdas would have been ashamed to lead such a company. They were going into dangerous territory and half the men would be pleased to see Callender get a crossbow bolt in the neck.

Valdas kept to himself. He treated the men evenly and never lost his temper with anyone, though he'd been tempted to punch Rankin in the face a couple of times. Rankin was Callender's right-hand man and a cocksure bully. None of the teamsters liked him, though none stood against him for his petty acts of cruelty.

Valdas could have pulled this disparate bunch into a cohesive unit in just a couple of days, but any advice about morale would be lost on the Angluman. Valdas hated sloppy organization and poor attention to the needs of men under his command, but this really wasn't his business. It was hardly the hussars, and he was no longer in charge. Soon he'd be free of his responsibilities to Jadzia's spice consignment, which was only going as far as Kusko, while Valdas needed to travel on to Bieloria. Once past the border he'd make better time on his own.

It was late evening, two days shy of Kusko. Valdas looked up from the campfire to see Tommo, the youngest of the teamsters, hovering in the shadows. He was little more than a boy, but good with the mules and the horses. Even Donkey seemed to approve of him, and that said a lot. He'd taken too much time dressing a harness gall that one of the mules had developed and Rankin had deliberately upended Tommo's food bowl as a punishment and cuffed him away from the pot when he'd tried to refill it.

Valdas calmly got up from where he sat cross-legged on the ground, refilled his own bowl with the stringy meat and cabbage, and walked over to Tommo.

"Here, lad. Fill your belly."

Tommo grabbed the dish gratefully, but Rankin leaped to his feet from the other side of the fire.

"He sleep hungry. Be faster tomorrow."

Valdas got the gist of Rankin's poor Zavonian. He stepped between Rankin and Tommo and spoke slowly. "If he sleeps hungry tonight he'll be slower tomorrow. You can't march an army on empty bellies."

Rankin was broad, but Valdas had him for height by almost a handspan and he glared at Rankin without making a move for a weapon. It was enough. Rankin backed down.

Hobday, Callender's other Angluman, sniggered and Rankin wore a scowl fit to scare the devil. That wasn't well done. The snigger just added a layer of insult. Valdas would have to watch Rankin.

⬦⬦⬦

Trouble came the next day when they were far from the nearest village. Callender had ridden out early in the morning as if to scout ahead, but when he'd returned he'd said nothing to anyone except for a few words in Anglu to Rankin and Hobday.

When they stopped for their nooning, Tommo sidled up to Valdas and nudged his elbow.

"Psst! Valdas!" The lad twitched his head to draw Valdas away from the others. "Something's wrong," Tommo said.

"How do you mean?"

"I heard Callender talking to Rankin. He was telling them something he didn't want the rest of us to know."

"He always talks to them in Anglu."

"This time was different. He kept his voice low and kept glancing around to see if anyone was listening. I was crouched down dressing Mina's split hoof. He didn't see me."

"You don't speak Anglu."

"I know one word 'cos he's always yelling it: *getreddy*. He was telling them to prepare for something. I don't know what, but I don't like it. I've been with caravans all my life, but that Anglu bastard doesn't smell right. He's up to something. Be careful, Valdas. You've been good to me. Watch your back."

"Thanks, Tommo. You watch yours, too. If there's trouble, take my spare horse and run as fast and as far as you can."

By the middle of the afternoon, heavy clouds were rolling in, carrying a storm. The terrain, rough scrubland with low-growing vegetation, offered no shelter. Valdas's mind was temporarily on the rain he could see sweeping over the low hills. It had been a strange summer, weeks of drought followed by waves of rain and more rain.

The first arrows took him by surprise, not that he could have done anything about them. They'd ridden into a trap. At least twenty men exploded from the bushes, arrows nocked, and the first salvo brought down the lead teamster. It was then that Valdas saw Callender, Rankin, and Hobday riding off to the side together. They'd known this was coming. Were they in league with the bandits? Red screamed beneath him as he took an arrow in the shoulder and faltered. Another arrow took him in the windpipe. Valdas leaped sideways as the horse went down, spraying blood as a third arrow hit him in the ribs. Against arrows his sabre was useless. He ran to the mules, leaving Red thrashing on the ground bellowing as only a horse in pain can. Teamsters had let their charges go in order to save themselves. Chaos reigned.

The arrows stopped and the outlaws closed for the kill.

"Here, Valdas." Tommo shoved Donkey's rein into his left hand.

"I thought I told you to run."

"I'm taking Daisy. She's fast."

"Go!" He boosted the boy onto a rangy mule and slapped its rear, then turned and drew steel. The lead outlaws were almost on the caravan. He ran forward and engaged a beefy man with a sword in one hand and a long knife in the other. He parried sword with sabre and twisted to avoid the knife as it slashed toward his belly. He kicked out and heard the man's bone snap. He delivered a fatal slice to the man's neck and leaped over him to the next one.

He lost himself in the rhythm of thrust, slash, and parry, but he never saw the blow that laid him low, though he knew in that split second that he was done for. He heard a crunch inside his skull. Something behind him. His vision slipped sideways and he must have blacked out. Suddenly he was eating dirt and Callender's boots were striding past him toward the bandits. He blinked and tried to get up, and received a vicious kick to his kidneys.

"Stay down, bastard." It was Rankin's voice. Another kick took him in the ribs. Valdas saw the foot raised for another kick, but a sharp whinny rang out and Rankin staggered back. From low on the ground, Valdas realized that a plate-sized hoof had crumpled Rankin like a doll. Donkey whirled round and planted his front feet inches away from Valdas's head.

Valdas grabbed the horse round the foreleg and hauled himself to his knees. Donkey stood like a rock. Staggering to his feet, Valdas scrambled for Donkey's back, unsaddled, of course. The saddle had been on poor Red. Flopping forward onto the horse's neck, he clung to the scrubby mane. Donkey turned and bolted, almost unseating him leaping over an obstacle. The carcass of a mule flashed beneath him. Tommo, stuck with two arrows, sprawled across it.

He closed his eyes, blinded by blood and fogged with the blow to his head. It was all up to Donkey, now.

CHAPTER TWENTY
Mirza

A SHOUT UP ahead at the front of the band made Mirza's pony throw up his head. She gathered her reins and pushed him into an easy canter, past Boldo's *familia* to where a knot of men stood around something on the ground.

"Stasha, what is it?"

At the sound of Mirza's voice, the men stepped back, giving her the usual polite distance between them. Stasha stood upright over the body he'd been examining.

"A man. Dead, all but. His horse wouldn't let us near at first, but we've quieted the beast down."

"Let me see." She swung down from Bo and left him grazing while she knelt beside the man.

"It's already too late," Boldo said, looming over her.

"Someone fetch Rafal," Stasha said. "He knows about the Zavonians and how they should be buried. We don't want his spirit to haunt us."

A boy on the edge of the crowd turned as if to run, but Mirza flung her hand out. He stopped as if stung. "Not so hasty," she said. "No need to worry about the spirits of the dead yet. Do you think me such a poor shulam? He's hurt and dried out in the sun, but let's not send him over until it's his time."

They didn't meet her gaze, but the silence and a slight shuffling sound told her that she'd embarrassed them. Again. It didn't take much to wrongfoot their masculine pride. *Too bossy, Mirza. No wonder you can't get a man. No one would dare. It's not just the witchmark.* She sighed and gave her attention to the man. Beneath matted hair he had a fearsome head wound, but though he'd obviously bled freely, his skull was not depressed. If he didn't take a brain fever, he might live. She would have expected more blood on the ground if the injury had happened here. He'd either ridden this far and fallen senseless or been dumped and left to die.

She stood back, folded her arms, and tapped her foot on the ground. "Carry him to my wagon."

"He is a man," Stasha said.

"You are a man."

"I do not live in your wagon."

Mirza stared him down, her back stiff. "You think my virtue is in danger?"

That was a sour joke.

She clenched her jaw. "I appreciate your counsel, Stasha Hetman. I will call on you if the man looks dangerous."

Stasha nodded and motioned to Boldo to do as Mirza ordered.

Mirza stayed long enough to see that Boldo had set enough men on the task to ensure the man was carried safely and smoothly, then vaulted onto Bo and cantered back to prepare.

Tsura sat on the driving box with her feet planted against the brace-board of the wagon. "What news?"

"We have a sick man to care for," Mirza said.

"Who?"

"A Zavonian."

"A Zavonian? Here?"

"Don't worry, Tsura-mi. He's too sick to cause trouble. If he does, I give you permission to put another bruise on his head with the flat of your skillet."

Tsura looked at her round-eyed and then grinned. "I would do that for you."

"I really think you would, and I thank you for it, but I doubt the need. Brake the wagon and let the horse stand. Spread an old sheet across my bed. We need to scrape the filth from him before we can see what's wrong. You can light a fire and set water to boil. We'll not be traveling any further today."

Because she knew she could demand and it would be done for her, albeit reluctantly. She rarely asked. It was too easy to gain the habit of relying on others. This afternoon, however, was different. She called over Jeppa, from the neighboring familia, and asked him to send a youngster to see to her wagon horse and Bo. As the boy led them away, Boldo's party arrived with the man and she had them carry him up the narrow steps and lay him on her bed.

She bustled them out of the tiny space and stared down at the man. Water first. She sat next to him and dribbled a few drops of water into his mouth. He licked his cracked lips and swallowed reflexively. That was good—he was not so far gone. She did it again and again, wary that too much, too soon would be as dangerous as not enough if he couldn't keep it down.

Even though it was still daylight she clenched her fist, concentrated for a moment, and released a small witchlight, tossing it up to hover over the box-bed so that she wasn't working in her own shadow. She had Tsura come in and help her to strip off the man's dirt-encrusted garments. Tsura had long got over the giggly stage of learning to deal with men's parts, though she stared at the man and gave him a little prod with one finger. Even unconscious, his kok twitched.

"Tsura." One word was enough to bring her into line.

"It looks pale. Like a giant maggot."

Mirza sighed. "It's the same color as the rest of him, but cleaner and with no sunburn. And Zavonians don't circumcise their infant boys, though this one smells clean enough. Now if we can get past his impure parts and see to his wounds . . ."

"Of course, Mirza-mi. Only you said I had to ask if I didn't understand anything."

"You understand the way a man's body functions well enough. You're attracting those kind of glances from many a young man." She looked up. "Blushing?"

"No, I—"

The man groaned and she beckoned Tsura closer. "Am I a bad teacher, Tsura-mi?"

"Of course not."

"Am I too harsh with you?"

"Never."

"Good." She nodded once. "You are a good student. I don't know if I say that often enough. Now give me a hand."

Under the dirt Mirza could see a mass of bruises on the man's ribs, front and back, as if he'd been kicked. She ran her hand lightly over the area to see if bones were out of place. They weren't, but she found one crack, possibly two, on the right-hand side. She washed his body from face to feet, sending Tsura out twice for clean water. Even without the man being conscious, his body told her a lot.

He was a tall man, maybe in his middle thirties, give or take a year or two, well muscled, broad-shouldered, but lean-hipped, and, besides the recent bruising, he carried a number of old scars, mostly on his front, possibly sabre cuts, and one faded puncture wound on his thigh, maybe a scar from an arrow or a slim-bladed knife. Arrow, she guessed, already forming the opinion that he was a soldier who had fought in many battles. His top lip was slightly paler than the rest of his face. He'd had a mustache like the Zavonian hussars. That gave her a queasy feeling. Hussars were always on the side of the landowners. They'd fled from hussars before at swordpoint. It was no use appealing to the great lords of the area, they never offered justice for her kind.

She found herself resenting the fact that she'd chosen to take a hussar into her wagon and had to reprimand herself. She knew nothing about him, yet, except that he was a stranger in need of assistance, and she would not pass him by on the road.

Unconscious, the man was nothing but a dead weight, and it took both Mirza and Tsura to turn him face down. "Come on, General, over you go. Easy does it." She talked to him as though he could hear, speaking Zavonian, guessing it to be his tongue.

"Set his head sideways, Tsura-mi. We don't want him to suffocate, and besides, we need to clean up that wound. Examine it. Tell me what you see."

"He's been hit on the head."

"I didn't ask you to guess what had happened. I asked you to tell me what you see."

Tsura nodded and bent over the man. "He has a ragged triangular tear in his scalp behind his left ear. The wound is already scabbing over, so maybe it was done sometime yesterday or the day before."

"And how will you treat him? Do you wish to open the wound and clean it?"

Tsura shook her head and felt around the damage. "The skull beneath it is not misshapen. It has bled freely. Unless infection develops I would clean it as best I could and use tetri ointment to keep it sweet. I would be more worried about damage inside his head. The outside will take care of itself."

"Good girl." Mirza passed Tsura a pot of tetri. They could wash blood out of his hair properly later if he lived. She had no idea how long the man had been unconscious, but he'd probably had his wits knocked out of him by the blow. Sometimes a bad blow to the head caused a man's wits to leave him altogether.

She put her hand above the head wound and felt the wrongness of it roiling against her palm in cold waves. Closing her eyes and going inside herself, she called a gentle stream of healing magic, going past the outer wound and through bone to the delicate matter within, soothing, easing pressure, cooling inflammation. Tsura put one hand on her shoulder, reinforcing the power as she'd been taught.

"Good girl. That's enough for now." She patted Tsura's hand and stood up.

Together she and Tsura rolled the General over onto his back again. She turned his head so that he wasn't lying on the wound, then threw a light cotton sheet over his naked body.

"Tsura-mi, go and ask Nadia if you can take food at her fire tonight. Give her two scoops of rye flour and a pot of honey. You can stay and help her. I will not take a hot meal, but you can bring me griddle cakes."

Tsura nodded and started to leave, but Mirza called after her. "Arrange to sleep in Nadia's tent, too. I'll sleep on your bed so I can stay by the General in case he wakes in the night."

"I can sleep under our wagon. You might need me."

"Nadia has enough space."

Mirza turned to look at the stranger again. He hadn't moved. The longer a man's senses were away, the more likelihood of him being permanently damaged. She let the witchlight above him fade to darkness and closed her eyes to see if she had any kind of connection to his spirit.

She should try to reach him and bring his senses back. If he'd gone beyond the first gate, she would know that trying to hold spirit and body together was useless. If the spirit had gone it was a kindness to cut the body loose from life.

CHAPTER TWENTY-ONE
Lind

NOT WANTING TO risk a tavern again, Lind decided to spend the next two nights in the open, the queen in the wagon, himself under it. Thankfully the weather remained dry and the queen made no complaint.

The following morning she gave him the details of the farmstead where she was bound, a little way off the main road between Torek and Dadziga, close to the Biela River.

"Who lives there?" Lind asked.

"My father's agent," she said. "It's a place where we'll be safe." She patted her belly to show the "we" she spoke of was herself and the baby, not herself and Lind.

"Who else knows about it?"

"Only Maksimilian and Marilena, my . . . most trusted lady-in-waiting."

Lind grunted. "A handmaid and Maksimilian—that's two reasons for not going to your little hideaway."

"I trust them both with my life." Her voice took on a more imperious tone.

"You might," Lind frowned, "but I don't. That big bag of yours, is there anything in it that will convert into currency without arousing suspicion?"

"There's the gold plate that was part of my dowry."

"No wonder it's so heavy. I suppose it's got a very recognizable crest on it?"

She nodded.

"We'll have to see what we can do about that."

It was a plan of sorts.

The next village they passed through, Lind inquired for a forge and was pointed to a cluster of shacks some half a mile off. Good. It was as he'd hoped, the forge was situated away from the village so that stray sparks couldn't cause a fire.

The blacksmith, a squat young man with a scar above one eye, greeted them civilly enough, glancing at the feet of their horse.

"Your horse isn't in need of shoes."

"Indeed, not, but I'm in need of a forge and a few hours in which to use it." Lind glanced around. Yes, there was the sand he needed for casting and a mound under wet canvas that might well be clay. Good. "Are you a fisherman, friend? I noticed a likely looking lake where a man might pass a pleasant afternoon with rod and line."

"See here, mister. My forge is my livelihood. I can't afford for someone to play with my tools."

"Of course you can't. Would it help to know that I apprenticed to a master bladesmith? I was working the bellows in his forge by the time I was eleven years old, and I took up hammer and tongs as soon as I was strong enough to hold them."

"You can use the forge, but I stay here to watch over you, make sure you don't run off with my tools."

"I don't think so, friend. Here, take two silver tolars for the use of your forge, and two gold schillings for your discretion. I doubt you'll get a better offer."

The smith's eyes widened. He put his hand out and Lind dropped the tolars into it, followed by the gold schillings that were each worth half a year's wages. As soon as the smith's fingers curled around the coins, the deal was done. The smith stared at them as if hardly daring to believe his luck.

"Enjoy your fishing, friend," Kristina said to the blacksmith as he left the forge.

When the man was out of sight, Lind put all his old skills to good use. He fired up the forge, then uncovered the sand and the clay and mixed the two together with a little water to make it sticky and pliable. He packed the sticky mixture into a wooden frame and pressed the bottom of a thick glass bottle into it six times to make shallow disks. It didn't matter that the disks were not all exactly the same depth, all that mattered was that the gold was in smaller, anonymous lumps. He pressed his knuckle into the clay to make smaller, irregular holes that would make smaller nugget-sized lumps that would be easier to exchange.

He pumped the bellows to get the coals glowing. Then he broke the plate apart into chunks with heavy pincers, and melted it in a crucible.

Kristina watched him, fascinated as he turned recognizable items into plain gold, small enough to be exchanged one at a time without arousing too much suspicion.

As Lind repeated the process, Kristina got bored and went to draw water for their horse, then sat in the shade of a tree to shelter from the afternoon sun.

"Someone's coming." She alerted him to a figure walking up the track.

Damn. The blacksmith was back earlier than he'd thought.

"See if you can stall him," he snapped, checking the last castings to see if they could be removed from their molds safely. They could. He set about gathering the nuggets, still warm, and the disks, still hot, into the canvas bag that had held the plate.

Kristina was practically throwing herself under the blacksmith's feet to slow him down, and she might have succeeded, except the last disk, deeper than the rest, was still too hot to handle and Lind dropped it. The noise drew the blacksmith's attention.

Double damn!

The smith had seen the flash of gold.

Lind gave the man extra for silence without any explanation, and they drove away without looking back.

"He saw, didn't he?" Kristina asked.

"He did." Lind's answer was terse. He knew he needed to silence the man permanently. He drove far enough away from the forge to be out of sight. As the sun dipped toward the horizon, he left the queen in the wagon by the side of the road and ran through the trees.

The man was still in his forge, banking down the fire and putting away tools.

"Did you forget something?" the smith asked, and Lind walked casually up to the bellows.

"I think I left my kerchief here. My mother gave it to me, so I don't want to lose it. Maybe I dropped it under the workbench."

"Soon find it if you did."

The smith knelt to look under the bench. Lind stepped up behind him, and with the man's own hammer caved in his skull. He crumpled up like a raggedy doll cast aside by a careless child. Lind rearranged the body, making it look like an unfortunate fall resulting in bashing his head in on his own anvil. He wiped the blood and hairs from the hammer, then for good measure shoved it and the cloth he'd wiped it with into the still-glowing coals. Carefully he retrieved the silver to-lars and the gold schillings, leaving only a few coppers that would have been fair payment for shoeing a horse.

He turned and trotted to where he'd left the wagon.

"You killed him, didn't you?" Kristina said when he got back.

Lind said nothing as he drove down the road at a steady pace in the gathering dusk.

"Answer me!"

He turned to look her in the face. "Do you want your child to live?"

Her mouth straightened into a tight line. "Yes. I want my child to live and to inherit the Amber Crown, which is his, or hers, by right. I want my child to inherit a strong kingdom that's fair and just, so no more killing without my say-so. There's been too much already."

"When did you take charge?"

"The instant you knew who I was."

She sat there on the driving board of the wagon, dressed like a commoner and every inch a queen.

"Yes, Your Majesty."

"Do you doubt me?"

"No, Your Majesty. I wouldn't dare."

CHAPTER TWENTY-TWO

Mirza

MIRZA SAT BY the soldier-man, nibbling a griddle cake and waiting for the darkest hour of the night. She listened to the sounds of the camp unfolding around her: unharnessing, cooking, eating. Younger voices gradually subsided to be replaced by older ones. A fiddle began to wail a plaintive melody, at once sweet and sad, Pieta by the tone and style, playing the introduction to a set of sorrow songs. Someone sang. A faster melody followed, accompanied by clapping and shouts of appreciation. Probably Florica dancing, again.

Gradually the sounds died away and Mirza was left with the silence of the night and the breathing of the man. It was time.

She lit the stub of a precious beeswax candle from the rush light and set it in a small copper dish, then burned rosemary for protection and visions. She sprinkled salt all around the man and herself, enclosing the area within a circle.

She took her *dead man's string*, a worn piece of green ribbon about as long as her forearm, and tied it with three knots to call upon the spirits of her dead grandmother and aunt to protect her on her journey. *If you ever loved me, protect me now and guide my feet on the path to the first gate. Let me not stray so far that I cannot return home.*

She twisted the ribbon around her fingers and threaded it through itself so that only the slightest pressure from her thumb held it secure.

Sitting on the edge of the bed, she spat on her middle finger and drew the shape of her wine-dark witchmark on the man's cheek and down onto his neck, dragging it through beard stubble. There, that connected them. She took his left hand in her right, noticing the broad, strong fingers and the close-cut nails. There were old calluses on his sword hand. Yes, definitely a soldier.

She began to murmur to the spirits of the Sun, Moon, Sky, Earth, Wind, Fire, and Water, and to the one god who ruled them all, asking for aid. She could feel the higher spirits gathering and whispered a welcome in her own Bakaishan tongue to those she wished to encourage. Now she beat out a rhythm one-handed against her thigh, letting it pull her down into a trance.

Drawing a deep, calming breath, she reached out with her power to see if the General's spirit was close by. The beings in the spirit world didn't care whether you came or went. Occasionally they spoke— though only at their own whim unless you knew how to get their attention. If this soldier's senses were not yet wholly of the spirit world, if she could find him before he passed through the gate to the second level, she could lead him back. She closed her eyes and breathed deeply, walking in her thoughts through a gray void, a mist so thick that she felt the ground beneath her feet change from gritty salt-sand to vegetation before she saw it. She stepped out of the fog into sunlight. The grass, green and lush beneath her feet, had a luminous quality as if from the last rays of sun before a gathering storm, yet the sky, such as it was, was clear of all clouds. Clear and black and starless. Empty. And she was standing in sunlight.

She had never understood this place. Trying to dwell on its mysteries would only bring on madness. She needed to focus. Nearby she could sense something. She turned, but the harder she stared, the more elusive it was. The further you tried to look in the spirit world, the less you could see. Even though the light was clear, her vision was limited. So she had to keep walking and looking, using the link of hand and witchmark to seek him out.

Right in front of her, she saw her soldier sitting on a rock. He wore wide black trousers gathered into knee-high riding boots topped by a military-style *mente*, a bright red tunic of a similar style to the individually embroidered tunics many Landstriders wore, but with fancy gold frogging on the front such as she'd seen on high-ranking Zavonian officers. Maybe her soldier *was* a general!

Mirza felt a pang of disappointment. She hadn't wanted this man to be one of their persecutors, but it seemed that he was. Zavonians didn't understand Landstriders in general and Bakaishans in particular. Mostly they didn't even want to. They thought them lazy because they refused menial jobs and only ever worked as horse breakers and trainers. Didn't they realize what an indignity fruit picking or scything and mowing was? No, they probably didn't. And in their ignorance, the town sejims passed ordinances driving all Landstriders out into the marginal lands.

The man on the rock looked up and saw her, his gaze steady.

Have you come to lead me over? he asked inside her head.

No, I've come to take you back.

Wraiths roiled around them, insubstantial and mist-like.

Mirza stepped back, but they were behind her as well as in front. She touched her fingers to her lips, forehead and knuckles to her heart. *Grandmother, protect me now.* These wraiths were wrong, not merely spirit. Spirits of the dead were largely harmless, if frightening. No, these were spirits of the *unburied* dead, like in ghost stories. They were much more potent and powerful because their earthly bodies were not at rest.

What do you want? she asked, but they ignored her and clustered around her soldier, their uniforms the same as his. All soldiers.

Go with her, Valdas, one of them said.

It is not your time, said another.

"Henryk, Matis, am I dead too? I was too late to save you."

You couldn't have saved us, Valdas. You could only have died with us. Go back.

"Back?"

With the Bakaishan witch.

"Oh."

Valdas—that was obviously his name—seemed to see her for the first time.

The spirits' voices were indistinct, but separate. Mirza knew they were not one voice, though they all seemed to follow the same thought pattern as if they shared it. She took the opportunity they offered.

"Will you come with me?" Mirza asked Valdas.

"Why should I?"

"Because you are lost and I know the way home." She hoped that was true.

"I can't go home."

"So come with me to my home."

"Why should I? I should stay with my men."

"No, life is not yet finished with you. Your heaven will wait."

He seemed to think on that for a while, then shook his head. "I didn't protect them when I should have. Maybe my journey here is overdue."

I think not! A new shade appeared, solidifying from the feet upward, stronger than the wraith-soldiers, not an unburied spirit, but a spirit all the same, one properly laid to rest with all appropriate ceremony—except he was tied to the first level by something. Black boots peeked from beneath a traditional delja made of cloth so fine she'd never seen its like. It was fit for a . . .

Oh . . .

As the upper part of the shade appeared, the crown on his head became visible, a golden circlet, lined with sable and inset with amber. Valdas rose from his rock and fell—no, not fell, but flowed—to the floor, prostrating himself before the lordly form.

The shade's voice was soft but firm. Mirza wasn't even sure whether she heard with her ears or her head. *Valdas,* it said, *you have nothing to be ashamed of.*

"My king, I failed you. When the assassin came I was not there."

Ah, that was it—Mirza realized—a murdered spirit.

The shade, without breathing, managed a sigh.

Think not on past failure, but look to the future. Zavonia is in great danger. I have sown a seed. It must be allowed to flourish and grow. You have made me a vow upon your honor.

"Sire, what can I do? I am one man and dare not even show my face on the Gura. I swore to avenge you in the heat of my anger, but in truth I don't know where to start. Gerhard is . . ."

Poor deluded Gerhard. I had not planned . . .

The shade began to fade. *No! It's too soon.* It looked around as if speaking to another. He seemed to solidify a little.

Go to my sister, Valdas . . . She knows about Kristina.

The shade turned his attention to Mirza. *Landstrider!*

She bowed her head.

You have a part to play in all this. I refused to expel the Landstriders from Zavonia when you first came out of the east. I call on that debt.

"I'm but one person, Lord. Would you have me pay off the debt of all Landstriders?"

Yes.

"Why? Why me?"

Because you are here and there is no other. Because you have the skill and the power, though some of it is yet hidden. The duty is yours. Valdas will not remember when he wakes. It looked at her. *You will remember. You must go with him. Your skills will be needed. I charge you with this. A duty to the dead.*

Was that it? Mirza flushed with indignation. Did this shade think

itself as much a king in death as it had been in life? Did it not know
that Father Death was also called the Leveler? Did a dead king expect
her to leave her duties to the band and run away with a man? It was
not even *her* dead king! What about her people? Should she pack and
leave them without a shulam, because she had happened to be in
the wrong place at the wrong time? She had fought too hard to keep
her place.

The shade's eyes locked on to hers. Her protests evaporated. It was
a dead man's wish. Not doing her best to fulfill it was unthinkable.
The shade didn't know what this might cost her. And it wouldn't care
even if it did. Dead men were driven to pursue their own last earthly
desires. They forgot the concerns of the living.

"Sire!" As the shade dissolved, Valdas pushed himself up. "I am so
sorry," he called to empty air. He turned to Mirza. "Do you think he
heard me?"

"He knows. Come, let's return to the living."

"Wait. My men."

He turned to the soldier shades. "I will seek justice for you, for all
of you. You deserve better than . . ."

They began to fade.

Mirza held out her hand and he took it.

⊰⊱

Mirza returned to her own body with a hiss of breath. She sat perfectly upright, balanced by the part of herself she'd left as an anchor.
Nothing had changed—yet everything had.

She felt the soldier's rough hand in hers. She squeezed it.

"Valdas." The unburied dead had gifted her with his name, and a
dead king had burdened her with a task. She would deal with the
name now and think about the task later. "Valdas, can you hear me?"

He mumbled something indistinct.

She leaned over to touch his forehead, blessedly cool.

"Aniela?" he mumbled.

"No."

His eyelids flickered half-open and he made an effort to focus on
her, but his pupils were too wide. He raised his right hand to her face.
When his fingers touched her witchmark, she saw the look on his face.
Inwardly she sighed. That was ever the way with men. Too afraid of
the power in the mark. She took his hand firmly in hers and placed it
at rest. He needed to sleep now that she knew he was truly back in his
own body.

CHAPTER TWENTY-THREE
Lind

LIND EXCHANGED ONE small disk of gold in Torek. The elderly Jewish moneylender weighed it carefully and gave him full measure in coins less a five-percent commission—a very fair deal. He gave Queen Kristina a purse of schillings and tolars. He sold the wagon and horse, haggling for close to the market value so the new owner wouldn't remember a desperate man selling cheap, and bought two riding horses and a pack pony. Then he took the little queen to a whorehouse and in through the kitchen door.

"What is this place?"

"Like Maksimilian's—a whorehouse. Not the classiest, but far from the worst."

"I am not staying in a whorehouse."

"You stayed in Maksimilian's."

"That's different."

"How so?"

"I trusted him."

Lind didn't reply.

"Why does it always have to be whorehouses? Maksimilian I can understand. You can gather a lot of information when men are relaxed, perhaps a little drunk, thinking with their . . . you know. But why do you choose whorehouses?"

Because whores won't touch me unless I pay them for it. He wasn't going to say that out loud.

He lowered his voice. "You've got to be careful. Not every whorehouse is safe, but if you find the right one . . . Mostly look for ones run by women. You pay the same for a room with or without a girl in it and they're grateful for the break. No one notices whores. They're

invisible to polite society. You can hide among them without causing
a fuss. You'll be fine. No one will bother with a pregnant woman going
in and out of the back door. Obviously don't trust them with secrets.
Don't let them know how much gold you're carrying. If you need help
with . . ." He looked at her belly. "Help with anything . . . ask for the
madame."

Her eyes widened. "Are you leaving?"

"Only for a short while."

"Where are you going?"

"To check out your farm. Two days at most."

"You think it might not be safe?"

"I think your women will have been questioned."

"Marilena would never tell."

"I've seen hard men crack under certain kinds of treatment." He
didn't say that he'd been the one to administer it. "I don't think a
court lady would last two minutes with an experienced interrogator."

"You don't know Marilena."

"I do know torture."

"They wouldn't . . ."

He just looked at her, a sharp reminder that someone, possibly at
court, had had her husband killed.

She swallowed and said no more, but allowed him to lead her to a
small room on the third floor. "How do I know you'll come back?"

"You don't. I might have filled that bag with rocks and have your
gold in my saddle bags."

To her credit she didn't check.

"You haven't."

"How do you know?"

"I know."

"Fair enough."

◆——◆

Lind followed Kristina's directions. He spent one night sleeping uncomfortably under a hedge and arrived at the turnoff that she'd described to him early the following morning. *A farm by the river on a
bend by a clump of willow. By the gate is a lightning-struck oak. The
farmer's name is Benedykt and his wife is Elzbieta.*

He pulled up at the gate and looked around, trying to seem like a
casual traveler. The farmhouse looked neat enough, prosperous even:
a double-story brick building with red pantiles and steep gables. Three
dairy cows in the meadow crowded by the gate, one bellowing

pathetically, their udders distended. This farmer was late with his milking. Suspiciously late.

"Hey!" Lind turned his horse in through the gate and stopped in the yard but didn't dismount. He dropped his horse's reins and raised both hands in a gesture of *I mean no harm*.

A man came out of the house. He was dressed as a farmer, rough short tunic with rolled-up sleeves, but the boots protruding from his pantalones shone in military fashion, the soles too thin for regular farm boots. They were meant for riding, not for walking.

"May I buy bread and milk?" he asked. "It's a long way since the last tavern."

"We've none spare. Be on your way, stranger. Try the next farmstead." The man pointed.

Lind turned away, noticing the water in the trough was tainted with red.

He headed the wrong way down the road and only when he was well out of sight did he double back around the fields as fast as he could, arriving in Torek after dark. The whorehouse was busy, but he found Queen Kristina where he'd left her, fed, rested, and composed.

"Well?" she asked.

"Your farm's not safe, unless, that is, your farmer is in his thirties, wears hussar boots under his zupan, neglects his milk cows, and pollutes his water trough with blood."

"Damn!" She sat down on the edge of the bed. "They were waiting for me, you think?"

"I only saw one man, but it was too quiet. Yes, I'd say they were waiting for you."

"Maksimilian . . ."

"Possibly, but more likely your Lady Marilena."

"I told you, she wouldn't give me away."

"She might not have had any choice. I doubt she betrayed you willingly."

"If they tortured her . . ." The little queen paled. Her clenched fists and white knuckles betrayed her anger, but she didn't give way to an outburst. Lind admired that.

Eventually she took a deep breath. "What am I to do now?"

"I take it you'll be trying to go home to Sverija."

"It's a rough sea crossing, and with the animosity between Sverija and Kassubian shipping, not without its hazards. I'm not sure about trying until after the babe is born. Can I stay with you?"

"I'm a danger to you, for reasons that should be obvious. Certain people won't want to leave any loose ends. I plan to disappear."

"You can't leave me."

"I can, and you should be glad of it."

She took a deep breath. "I need to know what you know, about staying hidden, staying safe." She gave him a cool stare. "I need to know how to pick the right whorehouses."

He gave her as much information as he thought she could absorb, told her how to change her appearance, darken her hair even more, change the apparent shape of her face by wearing cotton plumpers in her cheeks or altering the way she wore her hair. He told her that if she wanted to sell gold for coin she should always find a reputable Jew and haggle, but not too hard. He told her where to buy secondhand clothes that were not flea-ridden, and how to walk as though she'd not been trained for the royal court. He warned her to coarsen her voice. "If you don't believe you're Queen Kristina, no one else will. If you put on airs and graces, people will notice."

She nodded. "I think I've got it now."

He certainly hoped so.

The following morning when he returned from the pastry shop, the room was empty and her bags were gone. She'd left him two gold disks and a handful of nuggets.

He didn't go after her.

CHAPTER TWENTY-FOUR
Mirza

THE MAN RECOVERED slowly. Sometimes he seemed sensible, sometimes not. The bruising and the cracked ribs pained him, but if he'd been going to cough blood he would have done so by now. For the first three days he answered to her calling him Valdas, drank what she dribbled into his mouth or held to his lips, and obligingly used the pisspot she brought him. His water was clear of blood despite one bruise dangerously close to his right kidney. His bodily hurts would heal, given time.

His mind, however, might not. Though she talked to him in Zavonian he didn't answer, so she thought he might be a foreigner. The fact that they had understood each other in the spirit world made no difference to the language he spoke. She tried the few phrases of useful Ruthenian that she knew and even one or two words in Sverijan, but it had no better effect and so she continued talking in Zavonian, trying to encourage him to answer.

On the fourth day he said "Thank you" in Zavonian, when she brought him the pisspot.

"Can you manage?" she asked.

He nodded and she left him alone with the pot, noting that he'd covered it when she went in to retrieve it. He was sitting on the edge of the bed, with the sheet across his lap, holding himself stiff as if each breath hurt. He looked up at her with tired but intelligent eyes.

"I apologize, mistress." He cleared his throat.

"For what?"

"Your trouble."

His eyes strayed to the covered pot. She shook her head and hid a smile at his obvious embarrassment by picking it up and handing it to Tsura outside.

"You would have rather we had left you to bake in the sun?"

"No . . . I . . ." He took a deep breath and winced. "Thank you."

"Can you stand?"

He stood up, clutching the sheet to him and wobbling slightly with the swaying of the wagon.

"We're moving."

She smiled. "That's what a wagon does."

"You are Landstriders." His eyes were guarded.

She waited for a curse-word or a slur. It didn't come.

"We are Bakaishans."

He nodded. "A blessing on your house. My thanks."

She nodded acknowledgment. He was polite, at least.

"Where to?" he asked.

"Northwest, to Fort Erta and into Bieloria for the autumn horse fair in Djanganai."

"It's autumn?"

"It will be by the time we get there."

"How long have I . . . ?"

"We found you four days ago."

"What's the date?"

The Zavonians were always counting: days; cattle; horses. "It's the middle of your eighth month."

He drew in his breath sharply and sat down again. "Already?"

"Are you in a hurry? Do you have somewhere to be?"

He pressed his lips together.

"You are a puzzle, Valdas, but I will solve you."

"How do you know my name?"

She smiled and thought of the wraiths. Was he ready for that information yet? "You managed to answer me when we first found you."

"Did I say anything else?"

"You asked if I was Aniela. Your wife?"

"Friend . . ."

"What were you doing alone out here?"

"I'm . . . not sure." He screwed up his eyes. "I was in Dadziga . . . looking to work my passage to Bieloria with a merchant pack-train. I remember doing the round of taverns. Somebody recommended a merchant . . ."

"Work your passage? As a mule driver?"

"Any way I could. I'd heard the trains hired guards."

She nodded. "It's a dangerous crossing. Some of the people who call the wild places home live by taking what belongs to others."

"So it seems. I didn't have much to steal except my sabre. I wish them well of my horse; it was a poor thing, ugly and stubborn like its master."

"If you mean Long Ears, you didn't lose him. We have him safe."

He almost seemed disappointed. "Watch him; he's a contrary beast. He can be quick tempered with anyone he doesn't know."

She laughed. "Tsura has tamed him with a share of her breakfast." She stepped aside to allow him to see out of the back door, held open with a cord.

Tsura, having dealt with the contents of the pisspot, was swinging herself up gracefully onto Long Ears's bare back. The creature stood kindly for her and plodded along, ears flopping sideways.

Valdas said something under his breath that could have been a curse-word, but it was too low for Mirza to catch. "He seems well suited here, mistress. Please keep him. I have nothing else with which to repay your kindness."

"Don't be so quick to give him away. He stood guard over your body and didn't give you up to us easily. He might have saved your life. Clever horses are worth more than all the pretty ones put together. Besides, I need no payment. I lack for nothing. The band takes care of me as I take care of them."

"You are their leader?"

She laughed, a mirthless sound. "No, Stasha is hetman. I am their healer, their witch, their shulam."

"Ah, I see."

The was a long pause. Maybe he was scared to check.

"Don't worry, you've still got them," she said.

"What?"

"Your stones."

He frowned and tilted his head to one side.

"I'm a shulam—and not always in their favor." She inclined her head toward the rest of the camp. "They think that lying with me will cause their kok to fall off and their stones to wither. It would be a brave man who spent the night under my roof."

"I have never believed in . . . witchcraft . . . or magic of any kind, for that matter. We are making so many advances in the sciences. The distance from the earth to the sun is imperceptible in comparison with the height of the firmament. Think of it. Could we but fly high enough we might meet God in his Heaven."

"Isn't that dangerous talk? Doesn't the Father on Earth burn people for less? Or are you a follower of the new religion?"

Valdas grinned. "I've never been one for the Church, but I do my duty and bend my knee where my king does. The Father on Earth can't burn all men of ideas! Besides, his palace is a long way away."

"You are an educated man."

"Alas, my tutor would not have agreed with you. I only came to see the value of education after most of it had passed me by, but latterly I worked for a very fine scholar. He gave me books to read, and sometimes in the depths of the night we would discuss—or he would talk and I would listen. He didn't believe in magic either. I'm sorry. I don't mean to offend."

She shrugged. "You don't offend. My power doesn't depend on your belief. In fact, it will be quite refreshing to have a man in my familia whose manhood is not threatened by me."

"In your familia?"

"While we travel, you must be in someone's familia. You are in my wagon, so you are, temporarily, in my familia. That doesn't mean you share my bed, but you are under my protection by our laws. You take my orders, and I am responsible for your good behavior. When you are well enough, you will sleep outside for the gnats to bite in the darkness."

"Of course. I understand. I am once more in your debt."

She pointed to a chest. "You'll find clothes in there. Yours were ruined, except for your boots. You can thank Stasha Hetman for the trousers and Rafal for his third-best shirt. It's not as fancy as your uniform, but it will keep you warm when the sun goes down. Nights can be cold at this time of year despite the heat of the day. Are you strong enough to dress yourself?"

"I'll manage."

She turned to leave.

"Wait . . . How did you know I used to wear a uniform?"

"I told you, I'm a shulam."

And with that she left him to dress.

⊷――⊶

The man seemed to occupy most of Mirza's time one way or another. She had a string of curious people turning up with slight ailments that had suddenly become urgent. If they were curious about the man, why didn't they simply admit it? On the day he decided to sit on the driving box of the wagon, a cadre of young men rode past so many times, Mirza thought they must simply be circling around.

Finally, late one night when Valdas had retired to her bed, she took Tsura by the wrist and led her down to the stream close by where they had camped. Donkey raised his ugly head and whickered at Tsura.

"I think you've made a friend," Mirza said, perching on a fallen tree trunk.

"He's asking for a treat." Tsura took a wizened apple from her pocket, bit into it, and gave the rest to the horse. "What do you want to talk to me about?"

"Can't we just sit in companionable silence?"

Tsura shook her head. "You've been fidgety since you led Valdas out of the spirit world."

"I know, I'm sorry. I'm going to have to go away."

"For how long?"

"I don't know. Maybe a few months. Maybe a year. Maybe forever."

"Why? How can you? I mean . . . You've only just established your-self. You fought Esmaralda for your place here."

"I did, but I have a debt to repay, on behalf of all Landstriders, to the crown of Zavonia. In return for us being allowed passage."

"That's a debt all the Landstriders owe. Why you?"

Mirza sighed. "Because I was in the right place at the right time."

"Or the wrong place at the wrong time."

"Ayeee! That too."

Mirza explained about meeting the assassinated Zavonian king in the spirit world and how Valdas was a bonehead and needed someone who knew magic.

"So, you see, I don't have much choice, and . . . I'm frightened. I'll never admit it to Valdas, of course." She wiped away a tear with one knuckle. "I'll miss you, my precious. More than I can say."

"I could come with you."

"No, you couldn't. You have to be shulam here in my place."

"But . . . I can't even spirit-walk."

"Lu'dja couldn't. But you will be able to, one day. That's why I've brought you away from the camp. Do you think that if I lead you over, you can follow? If we work at it while the man is recovering, I can teach you. There's time."

"You can teach me when you get back."

"What if I don't come back? Anything could happen. I have an awful foreboding that it might be a one-way journey."

"No! You mustn't say that. No matter how long it takes, you will come back. I say so. I will try to spirit-walk, but even if I'm shulam for twenty years I'll still give your place back to you when you return."

"Thank you."

"When will you go?"

"When Valdas is well enough to travel. A few days, maybe. A week. Two?"

"What will Stasha say?"

Mirza shrugged and waved her hand, fingers open. "I won't tell him until nearer the time. Don't let him bring another shulam into the band while I'm away. You'll manage very well."

"I'll protect your place—our place—like a mama wolf protects her cubs."

Mirza put her arm around the younger girl, her eyes suddenly overflowing.

CHAPTER TWENTY-FIVE
Valdas

THE LONG DAYS of traveling passed slowly while Valdas's hurts kept him confined to Mirza's wagon. He took each day as it came, fighting the headaches and nausea with sleep. When he was awake, he let life with the Bakaishans unfold around him without taking much of an interest. Whole days went by when the fog around his mind was so intense that he barely knew where he was. Yet there was one thought uppermost—his mission to seek King Konstantyn's murderer and avenge his men. It wouldn't let him rest.

Henryk Zehrin, Lukas Grinius, Bartek Andrulis, Darius Kairys, Hector Bakaitis, Raulo Budrys . . .

His body, normally quick to heal, took its own time to recover from the injuries. While his bones still ached and any movement resulted in a bout of dizziness severe enough to fell him, he couldn't leave the Bakaishans in order to ride ahead. Thank all providence they were heading in the right direction, toward the border.

When Mirza suggested he ride up front with her on the wagon, he didn't have the strength to argue, so he climbed up slowly, feeling his ribs protesting as he hauled on his arms to pull himself up to the driving board.

Watching the wagon ahead, and the round rump of Mirza's skewbald ambling along between the shafts, was almost hypnotic. He slapped a biting fly on the side of his neck and wondered if he should have slathered on some of the evil-smelling cream that Mirza had offered him.

After two days, Mirza put the reins into his hands and skipped down to ride her pony. Driving the wagon hardly stretched either his physical or his mental capacity. The horse would follow the wagon in front regardless of his presence.

He let his mind wander.

What had brought him here? Was he truly seeking revenge for Konstantyn, or merely trying to justify his continued existence? His honor had died with his men. Silently he spoke the litany of their names again.

Was he a coward? Was he running away from certain death, or toward something else, a justification for his life?

He'd never been alone before. He'd always been within a system, a hierarchy. When he'd first joined the hussars, he'd been a boy among men. Then he'd been promoted and become a man among boys, and finally a man among men. But he'd never been a man alone. In the Winged Hussars he'd taken orders from higher up. And as the Captain of Konstantyn's High Guard, he'd given orders to his men, but still taken orders directly from his king.

Now he had to think for himself.

There was no one to give him orders anymore. It was freedom of a kind, but a freedom he hadn't looked for. Could he simply forget who he had been and start a new life?

Even as he thought that, he knew he couldn't. He'd given himself a job to do. Maybe he did have some honor left after all.

"Wake up, Valdas, we're making camp!"

He was jerked out of his thoughts with a start.

Mirza rode alongside the wagon, swung one leg over the pony's head, and pulled herself up onto the driving board with practiced ease, keeping the pony's reins in her left hand.

"Swing round there." She pointed to a clump of saplings. "Yes, that's fine. There's grass for the horses and the stream isn't too far away."

"Stream?"

"Listen."

"Ah, yes." He heard a gentle burble of running water.

"Are all Zavonians as blind and deaf as you?"

He shook his head. "I was thinking."

She made a disparaging sound, and jumped down from the wagon as soon as Valdas drew the horse to a stop. She looped her pony's reins over one arm, unsaddled him, and rubbed his back where the saddle had sat. It reminded Valdas of one particular lover, an older, married lady, somewhat generously proportioned, who had always scrubbed at her sides and belly with pleasure after unlacing her corset. He supposed it must feel good after a long day. He smiled to himself. Maybe he shouldn't compare Beata to a stout pony of indeterminate breeding. She would take offense at that.

Mirza led her pony to the good grazing by the saplings and hobbled him for the night. He tore into the grass as if it was a feast, which Valdas supposed it was if you were a pony.

He climbed down from the wagon with much less agility than Mirza had shown. His ribs still pained him when he made sudden movements or laughed too much, or, god forbid, sneezed, but he could be useful if he moved carefully. The skewbald between the shafts had already lowered his head to graze. Valdas began to unhitch him from the wagon when he felt hot breath on the back of his neck. He stiffened and Donkey blew out a grassy, snotty breath.

Tsura giggled. "He says he misses you." Her Zavonian was accented, but she made herself understood.

"He can miss me for a bit longer. He seems to like you."

"He likes my breakfast."

"He's a military horse, or he was. He's used to a morning ration of oats and an occasional bran mash."

"You . . ." She searched for the word and tried another way when she couldn't find it. "You baby them."

"We look after them. They look after us."

"Makes plenty sense." She nodded. "You take Long Ears. I see to the wagon."

Donkey lipped his hair and then flattened his ears when Valdas turned to pat him.

"Oh, right, because you wouldn't want me to think you'd gone soft, would you?"

Donkey merely blew out another warm breath and followed Valdas to the grazing.

◦━━━━◦

Valdas awoke the next morning, stiff and cramped from sleeping under the wagon. The whisper of his litany of names faded as he opened his eyes.

Petras Mazur, Waldemar Konopka. Konstantyn, second of his name. King of Zavonia.

He crawled out and straightened slowly, supporting himself on the rim of the wagon's wheel like an old man. Tsura looked up from stirring the porridge pot over the fire and laughed at him. He tried a smile, but he feared it turned into more of a grimace. He could hardly blame her for her derision. Self-pity was not an attractive trait for a man. Self-pity and guilt. He still carried guilt for both the king and his men. Could he have changed things if he'd been there on that fateful night?

Enough dwelling on the past. Perhaps he'd spent too much time alone in his head. It was time to think of the future.

Mirza crossed to the fire, slopped some of the millet kasza into a wooden bowl, and handed it over. "Eat," she said. "You're thinking again."

He reached out and took the bowl automatically.

Mirza pushed a wooden spoon into his hand. "Eat."

He inclined his head in thanks to both Mirza and Tsura. No sense in being ill-mannered.

The kasza was tasteless but warm and filling. It would have been better with honey stirred into it, but that must be a luxury for these people. He would not ask for it. He ate the porridge and scraped the bowl, feeling guilty. An extra mouth to feed was no small thing when you had to carry all your supplies with you, never knowing where you could buy more because not all people, even those with grain to sell, would trade with the Landstriders.

Mirza looked at Valdas the way a farmer would look at a plow horse. "Arms up," she said.

He raised his arms as much as he could while still holding on to the porridge bowl. She poked him with a finger and he flinched.

"Stop it. You're favoring this side too much."

"Ribs," he said, as if it was an explanation. They bloody well hurt. He'd been lucky not to sustain any lung damage from the broken bones. Ah, dammit, he was feeling sorry for himself again. That had to end or it would become a habit he couldn't shake. Where was the hero of Tevshenna when he was needed? Where was the man who led the High Guard? He needed to move forward, but his head still ached and felt as if it was stuffed with wool.

"Start exercising gently," Mirza told him. "You've idled for long enough."

"I will." He meant it.

But he didn't have his sabre. Perhaps the Angluman, Callender, had taken it. He guessed that was who'd taken his money belt. Damn, but he'd been careless. He'd pieced together those last few moments before the blow that laid him low. He'd known trouble was coming, but he'd still been caught out, not by the attack, but by the blow from behind.

Right. Enough self-pity. It was time to do something positive.

He borrowed a knife and cut a stout blackthorn spur from a hedge. A stick was not a sword, but he wielded it with vigor, going through simple training figures until sweat dripped from his brow, his ribs ached, and his muscles cramped with unaccustomed use.

After the first time, he put his hand to his ribs, breathing heavily.

"I said gently!" Mirza called from the wagon's steps. "Don't undo my good work."

He grinned at her and she waved one hand dismissively.

He took to walking behind the wagon, building up from short walks, driving himself until he could walk half a day. Dammit, the women of the band often walked for a full day and then set up camp and cooked a full meal at the day's end. He should be able to do half that.

He found it a relief on the occasions when Mirza asked him to drive.

The motion of the rolling wheels beneath Valdas's backside and the rattle of the brace-board under his boot soles became comfortingly familiar. He was having fewer headaches and dizzy spells, and the pain in his ribs had subsided to a dull ache unless he did something stupid such as practicing his sword forms. He didn't know how long his ribs would take to heal completely, or how long it would be before he could swing a sabre with any accuracy or strength again. He frowned. If he had a sabre.

One day followed the last, settling into a pattern: walk for half a day, drive for the other half. His ribs began to hurt less. His muscles began to tighten.

Traveling with Mirza and the band brought a seductive kind of peace that he could learn to like. It surprised him. He'd never had much to do with the Landstriders. He's thought them all the same, but now he knew that they had their own identity. The Bakaishans were different from the Uzgorzi, and both were different again from the Kumpani. He felt shame. As a young ensign, he'd been part of a troop responsible for moving on several wagons—a familia, he now realized, related families all traveling together—from Zavonia across the Vironian border on suspicion of thievery, which, to be fair, was unproven one way or the other. King Konstantyn had always allowed small bands to pass through Zavonia, but the sejims, the local councils, were suspicious. The treatment the Landstriders received was often dependent on the pressure the townsfolk and villagers could bring to bear on any local landowner with troops at his disposal.

If Valdas had been asked then, he would have shared the same view of the Landstriders as most of the people he knew. Lazy at best; disrespectful, sly, untrustworthy, immoral; dangerous at worst. His own personal preference would have been to keep them moving, passing through with as little trouble as possible.

Now, living among them, he realized he'd been guilty of making false assumptions. This Landstrider band—Bakaishans—contained a huge variety of characters, some likable, some not. Some friendly and welcoming, others icily polite to his face, though probably not behind his back.

He saw no hard evidence of thievery, but as an outsider he'd hardly be privy to their secrets. He turned a blind eye each time a foraging expedition left the camp, often at dusk. He couldn't afford to be so discriminating, since he was living on their charity. He heard the word *crakev* several times, and though he spoke none of their language, it was a word he'd been taught when dealing with Landstrider bands in the north. It meant swindle, or more literally *switch in the bag*. He could hardly blame them for putting one over on the Zavonians, though.

The first time the band was moved on by a landowner, he'd been too weak and ill to do more than note raised voices and the juddering of his bed as they took to the road in a hurry. The second time he watched from the safety of the wagon as a small troop of local militia, dressed in somewhat work-worn versions of the splendid red mente he used to wear, laid down the law to Stasha Hetman. The ensign in charge was too big for his boots and might have been Valdas fifteen years ago. He felt ashamed. Now he saw it from the other side. Where were they supposed to go? How were they supposed to make an honest living? They were removed from their homeland, looking for a new place to settle. How would they ever find it?

The men worked with horses, being employed by any who could afford to pay—from wealthy farmers to impoverished lord holders—to break and train youngstock. Mirza explained that sometimes, if work was plentiful, they would stay in an area for a few weeks, but on this journey Valdas noticed they never stayed in one place for more than a few days, perhaps because they needed to be in Djanganai by autumn to sell their own horses at the fair.

He'd heard the band's women called sluts and whores, but nothing could be further from the truth as far as he could see. As in any close relationship, women were not always treated with great respect by their husbands or fathers, but much of the barracking was good natured, and a man who ill-treated his wife was censured by the hetman.

The level of politeness and formality between men of one family and women of another surprised him. The elderly of both genders were venerated for their wisdom and the matrons held their own against their—sometimes boisterous—menfolk with dignity. The maidens . . . ah, the maidens. The maidens were out of bounds, not only to him as a man, but to all men.

Valdas's sex life had always been feast and famine, but rarely had he been through so severe a famine with such a feast left untasted on the table. At night he ached with the lack.

But there were compensations. Being with Mirza and Tsura was like having family of his own. His father had died before Valdas's earliest memories. He remembered his grandfather's estate and a taciturn old man, broken by grief, but he had only a distant memory of a mother and sisters, overlaid by one of standing by a graveside with his older brother. In the year they became orphans, Zavonia had lost one in ten souls to plague.

While he'd been sick he'd relied on Mirza for everything. Now his strength was returning, remaining respectful and obedient wasn't always easy, but he knew instinctively that she'd react badly if he made any kind of sexual advance. She was a fine woman; small, but well-proportioned, and pretty in a dark, delicate, wild way. From one side her face was perfect, from the other, a blotchy mess, but in truth he mostly didn't even see the wine-stained witchmark anymore. Occasionally he found his eyes straying to the swing of her hips as she walked away from him, or the rise and fall of her breasts beneath her high-necked tunic as she laughed with Tsura.

She was tough, too, despite being small. She could handle a horse and run her wagon as well as any man, never asking for help. Being a Landstrider wasn't an easy life; he discovered that on the first night he slept under the wagon. The flies stung the tender skin around his eyes, making sleep difficult. Mirza took pity on him and gave him a pot of soothing ointment, which both eased the itchy swellings and kept away the tiny bugs. He used it despite the smell.

He looked forward to the rain Mirza said would come.

CHAPTER TWENTY-SIX
Lind

LIND BREATHED A sigh of relief as he rode into Tepet on Zavonia's far northern border and stabled the biddable gelding he'd acquired in Torek in the baker's yard, next to two sturdy dray horses. He had an arrangement with the baker, Pawel Dudek, a Kassubian whose cinnamon rolls were the best he'd ever tasted.

He entered the shop through the back door, nodded to Pawel's wife, and climbed the stairs to the family's rooms. The bedroom window overlooked the street and Lind's current place of business.

Was it safe to return or not?

He settled down in the small, cramped bedroom to watch the ebb and flow of Tepet's citizens.

Was it his imagination or was there a larger military presence in the town than there had been when he left? Tepet's military consisted largely of militia. Lind had always thought of them as hobby soldiers. Their ranks were drawn from local citizens who gave one day a week to train and patrol in their fancy uniforms. If it made their mundane lives a little more exciting, if it gave them a few extra tolars in their pockets, Lind didn't begrudge their activities, but he'd rarely seen so many patrols circulating around the town. Were they looking for something specific, or was it simply a show of force rolling its way through all Zavonia's towns?

Thank goodness they didn't seem to show any particular interest in his place of business.

Always cautious, Lind watched the tall, narrow building across the street. Its dull facade, oxblood plastered, was crammed in the middle of a row of nine tall, narrow-fronted houses. No two houses in the row were quite alike in shape or coloring. Some had stepped gables; others had dormers in the attics; several had upper balconies protected by iron railings of different designs and complexity. They offered a spectrum of smoky white through creams and yellows to dirty pink. They'd been built as elegant residences in better times, but now the upper floors were tenements and the ground floors were mostly businesses or taverns. Those who could afford it had moved across the river to Tepet's New Town while the Old Town gradually stagnated. The house he watched, however, was not split into tenements. It was run as a private club, essentially a gambling establishment and whorehouse, owned by Madame Dominique La Papillon. In reality that name was a front for a partnership of four women who'd bought the bricks and mortar with the proceeds of a life on their backs. Lind rented the attic room at the top of the house for a not ungenerous monthly sum.

He wondered whether Queen Kristina had found a safe place in an establishment such as this, or whether she'd risked the sea voyage to Sverija, to the safety her brother could offer. Did he have feelings? Regrets? Was he ready to admit that taking a commission to kill the King of Zavonia was a mistake? He thought of the money, a fortune even if the client never paid the second half. He could make good use of that, maybe even buy his way out of this lifestyle. He couldn't afford to become involved with the people he encountered on jobs—he might, after all, have to kill them. He cursed himself for his stupidity. He'd been more invested in Kristina's safety than he would easily admit. He hoped she'd found a safe place, but he might never know. He took a deep breath and decided he could live with that. The job was over. She'd been a complication he couldn't afford. He should put it behind him, forget about her and move on with his life.

He watched for hours while the Dudek family worked downstairs. Pawel, his wife, and eldest son and daughter baked bread and sold it on the premises. The younger children, too young for regular work yet, skulked in the street, the toddler kept in check by the six-year-old. The second son, Baz, a sly boy of twelve with a slight squint and bad teeth, delivered bread and ran errands, for a price.

This was as close as Lind came to home. He never slept in the same place for long, changing lodgings at random, but the attic room on the fifth floor of the pink whorehouse was what passed for Lind's office, though he hadn't been there in more than four months, not since he'd set off to deal with his recent business in Biela Miasto. He'd paid well for Madame La Papillon to keep the room secure for him and to take messages. He wasn't entirely sure it was safe anymore, but he was curious to know if his anonymous employers had tried to clean up after themselves by having him removed by a fellow professional. On a job of this importance, it was always a possibility.

If he was trying to kill the inmate of that garret, how would he do it? He ran several options in his mind, all of which he'd run before and prepared for. He even had a rope ladder in case anyone decided to burn the place down with him in it.

The whorehouse, known locally as Dominique's or the Butterfly, looked untouched. He needed to talk to Ludmila, the madame who called herself Lucille when she was working, but until he was sure no one was watching, he contented himself with the comforts of a small upright chair and the smell of baking bread drifting up from the brick oven in the yard.

He heard the stair creak, a light footstep, a child's. Even though he was almost sure it was Baz, Lind stood silently and moved three paces to take up position behind the door.

"Baz." A voice on the edge of breaking announced his identity.

"Come."

The skinny boy stepped into the room, his hands in plain sight as he'd been taught.

"What have you to report?"

"Nothing. An' I seen no one while you was away. As I said, it were all quiet. Only Madame's usual customers."

Lind tossed him a coin. Baz's eyes widened.

Lind nodded. "Don't tell your pa, and I won't."

The boy's fingers closed around it and he made a fist so tight it would take a crowbar to prize it open.

"Did you talk to Madame Lucille?"

"Yes. I said the words just as you said."

"What did she say?"

"It made no sense."

"I didn't say it would. What were her exact words?"

"She said, 'The sun sets at two,' but that's rubbish. Everyone knows the sun never sets at two, even in the middle of winter."

Those were the right words. He'd risk it.

He nodded to the baker and his wife as he exited into the yard. He made his way via an alley across the main thoroughfare, picking his way round piles of debris in the central gutter. Rather than entering Dominique's from the front, he strolled casually down a side street and slipped into an alley.

The back door creaked as he let himself in. Like Maksimilian's, but not as gracious, the kitchen was still the beating heart of this place, even though the money was in the bedrooms. An iron kettle dangled from a crane over the glowing heat of the fire, and by the steam issuing from its spout it was almost on the boil.

"I guessed you wouldn't be long once that bratlet came sniffing round."

Dressed in a wine-red satin off-the-shoulder robe, Ludmila Korolenko, also known as Madame Lucille, had an appalling French accent, but since few of her customers knew what a real French accent sounded like, she maintained an exotic image. She winked and grinned at him, showing teeth best kept behind a close-lipped smile. Crow's feet round her eyes gave away her age.

"Sit you down and take tea." She dropped the accent for pure home-grown Zavonian with a strong northern twang.

She took a key from the bunch at her waist and opened up a small, dark wood chest, scooped some dried leaves from it with a silver spoon into a small tin-plate pot, and poured boiling water in, setting it on an iron plate by the fire. Locking the box again, she set out two glasses and dripped honey into the bottom of them before grasping the hot teapot with a cloth and pouring dark brown liquid onto the honey and stirring it round.

Lind smiled to himself and accepted the tea without saying a word. Ludmila fancied herself a lady when she wasn't working, and had bought a delicate tea set to impress important customers.

"Business must be good." He held the tea glass up to the kitchen window and looked into the heart of the liquid. He didn't like to tell her he'd never acquired the taste.

"Booming, my boy. Booming."

"Have you had any unusual visitors?"

"There's been no one unusual inquiring for you, if that's what you mean."

She sipped her tea slowly and put her cup down again. "Though I have a few messages for you. One young man left a heavy purse."

"Did it come with sharp objects attached?"

She laughed. "I wondered why you'd been away for such a long time. I thought you'd angered some jealous husband or acquired a gaming debt."

He shook his head. "Had some business to take care of."

She held up both hands, palms out. "I don't want to know."

"That's good, because I'm not going to tell you."

He handed her the tea glass and, though barely touching his gloved fingers to hers, bowed low over her hand, making her giggle.

A man's voice from the direction for the front parlor called for Madame Lucille and she stood. "As I said, business is booming."

"Go earn enough to buy your tea-leaves, Madame. I shall be gone as soon as I've collected what's upstairs. Good health to you."

"And to you, Konrad Nizinski." She said it as if she knew it wasn't his real name.

He skirted around the rooms on the ground floor, where five men sat around a table, deeply involved in a card game. Gaming wasn't one of his vices. He walked lightly up the narrow stairs all the way up to the attic, taking care not to make any noise outside the doors he passed. One floor had had all its rooms converted into cubicles barely big enough for a pallet, several occupied even at this time of day. The two stories above had four luxurious boudoirs on each, all empty for now. Above that was Lind's own private room in the eaves, dearly bought for a space he hardly ever occupied.

On the table inside the only door was a bowl containing three envelopes and a leather purse. He glanced at the envelopes; more jobs for a good assassin. He sighed. People were always ready to seek a permanent solution to what they perceived to be problems. So be it. It was a strange way to make a living, but his unique upbringing had led to this. He picked up the purse. It was heavy and inside it a note nestled among the coins. He tipped out the contents in a flash of gold schillings. He hadn't thought to see the second half of his payment for dispatching Konstantyn. He counted it twice. Why send more than he was due? He opened the note and read: *We have more business. Unicorn Bridge. Usual signal. Three days. Noon.*

God's ballocks! He'd wanted to leave this job behind him, but it seemed it didn't want to let him go. He contemplated ignoring it, taking the money and moving to another city altogether. Maybe Tepet was getting too small. He'd drummed lessons into Roza, Queen Kristina, and now he should probably be taking his own advice. Maybe it was time for him to go to ground.

Although, with the money he had earned already, and the purse from another high-risk, high-pay job he could make enough to retire on. Yes, all right. He would put out the signal, two large stones and a small one on the front steps of the church of Saint Jozef in the New Town. Then in three days' time he would present himself at noon, on the Unicorn Bridge. He counted the ways such a meeting could go horribly wrong, but argued with himself that if they wanted him dead, they would not have paid the balance for killing the king. Even so, he would take precautions in case it was an appointment with death.

CHAPTER TWENTY-SEVEN
Valdas

WHEN THE RAIN came Valdas reveled in it, loving the feel of fresh water on his parched face. That lasted about half a day, but the rain never abated. After two days of water cascading out of the sky, every part of his anatomy was sodden and chafed. He was so wet that his clothes didn't dry out overnight even though he lay on a board to keep himself out of the mud. Wet clothing clung to the creases and folds of his skin. He longed for nothing more than a warm bath, a dry towel, fresh clothes, a roof over his head, and a blazing fire. Then he felt guilty. That was something the Bakaishans never had, yet he'd taken it for granted at the palace. He'd suffered hardships on campaigns, but he'd always known that there would be an end to it. Here with the Bakaishans, he knew that even if the rain stopped, there would always be another rainstorm and more mud.

Always mud.

The roads had been so parched that at first the rain had run off the surface, but now it was soaking in and the result was mud, heavy with clay. It clung to his boots, weighting every step. The wagons in front of them deepened the water-filled ruts in the road. Wagons bogged down. With increasing frequency the column ground to a halt. There would be a shout from up ahead. All the men would rush forward to put their shoulders to the back of some vehicle stuck in the mud.

The first time, he didn't follow what was happening. The second time, Valdas rushed with them. Stasha gave him a look that said, *You are not one of us,* but gave him room to grab onto a wheel spoke and haul as others pushed. The wagon came free of the mire with a sucking sound, and the men rushed to fill the worst of the boggy hole with roadside stones, cut branches, and whippy hazel saplings, so that the following wagons didn't bog down in the same place.

After the tenth such time, Stasha simply accepted his efforts.

When they pulled up for the night, there was still no respite from the wet. The ground was too muddy and the rain too persistent to light the campfires, so those without stoves in their wagons ate cold food, and the rest of them ate whatever they could cook on the tiny stoves, sheltering wherever they could. Valdas crouched in the doorway of Mirza's wagon, watching the copper kettle coming to the boil on the stove top. Their limited supply of dry wood and peat blocks, stored in a net beneath the wagon, would not last much longer, but whatever they had, they would share. The kettle began to boil, and Tsura wrapped her hand in a cloth and poured boiling water on herbs and dried whinberries in a chipped jug, allowed it to brew, and then poured the resulting tea into three cups. Valdas sniffed it and blew on the surface to cool it to a drinkable temperature. On the first sip it was sharp and astringent, but had a pleasant fruity aftertaste. As the warm liquid trickled down his throat and into his stomach, he smiled and sighed. Truly the small pleasures in life were the best. When you didn't have much, even the simple things could seem like great riches.

Mirza let him sleep in the doorway that night, jammed between Tsura's pallet and the stove, which still held some residual heat even though the fire had been allowed to die down. His body was too long for the space, but the discomfort was offset by the lack of mud. He fell asleep listening to rain drumming on the roof.

By the close of the third day, when the wagons had bogged down to their axles for what seemed like the hundredth time, Valdas never wanted to see rain again, but it kept coming. As the last in line, Mirza's wagon benefited from the semi-filled mud holes, but the skewbald was struggling against the fetlock-deep mud. Mirza rode her own pony and Valdas rode Donkey, still with no saddle, while Tsura, the lightest of the three of them, drove.

The wagon juddered as the front wheel ground against a submerged stone. The skewbald threw his weight into the harness collar and pulled, but he slipped in the glutinous mire and crashed down to his knees, floundering. Valdas jumped off Donkey and ran to the skewbald's head, placing both his big hands on either side of his cheeks to keep the animal from crashing over sideways in the shafts.

The beast's eyes were rolling in panic.

"Whoa, there, steady." He kept up a steady steam of nonsense talk in a low, gentle voice to settle him down.

Tsura leaped down from the wagon and she and Mirza unhitched the skewbald.

"Here, come and hold his head, and I'll do that," Valdas shouted, as Mirza and Tsura began to shove the wagon backward to allow the skewbald to get up.

Mirza didn't waste time arguing. She came and took the skewbald's head while Valdas leaned into the wagon, shoving as hard as he could, muscles straining, feet sliding in mud. Tsura, stronger than she looked, pushed on the other side, but the wagon barely moved, wheel firmly in the mud-filled rut.

Where was the rest of the band when they were needed?

The column was still moving forward, the front of it already hidden by sheeting rain.

Damn!

"Tsura, go and get help." Valdas jerked his head toward the retreating band.

She nodded once and ran to Mirza's pony, leaping onto his back and trotting off after the band.

With her efforts suddenly missing, the wagon settled into its muddy hole, and Mirza cried a warning as the skewbald began to panic. Help would come, but not quickly enough.

He put his shoulder to the wagon and began to push, thigh and shoulder muscles bunching, ribs in agony. Push. And push again. He felt the wagon rock as if coming free, so he redoubled his efforts. One more push might do it. He only had to move it far enough back to let the shafts clear the prone skewbald.

Yes!

The wagon wheel rocked over the offending stone and settled with a groan. Now the shafts were clear of the fallen horse. Valdas slithered and fell to one knee, but scrambled up and joined Mirza to coax the skewbald to his feet.

With Mirza on one side and Valdas on the other, they cajoled, pushed, and pulled. With a huge effort the skewbald staggered to his feet and stood, head down, blood dripping from a gash on one knee.

Valdas led the creature to the side of the road and Mirza ran to get a bag from the wagon. By the time Tsura returned with Boldo and three men, she was already dressing the wound.

"He can't go back in the shafts today," she said. "Maybe not tomorrow either."

"There's a campground up ahead," Boldo said. "I'll tell Stasha. Use your pony to get there and we'll find you another horse tomorrow."

Mirza nodded, preoccupied with the skewbald's knee.

"The wagon," Valdas said. "Before you go, it needs pushing forward over the pothole."

"Don't tell us what to do, man."

"He shouldn't need to tell you," Mirza called without looking up from the skewbald's knee.

The men muttered to each other, but Boldo jerked his head toward the wagon. With Boldo and Valdas lifting the shafts clear of the mud and hauling forward, and Tsura and three men pushing from the rear, the wagon rolled forward far enough to clear the worst of the rut.

"Are they always so unwilling to help?" Valdas narrowed his eyes and shoved his hair back, dripping even more water down his neck as he watched them returning to the band.

Mirza shrugged.

"How is the patient?" Valdas bent to look at the skewbald's wound.

"He'll be all right in a few days." She looked at the pony. "I'm not sure Bo is up to pulling the wagon in these conditions. Would Long Ears oblige?"

Valdas wasn't sure Donkey would settle between the shafts of a wagon, but under the circumstances it was the best course of action. They stripped the harness from the skewbald and with much adjusting of the leathers, transferred it to Donkey, who stood, ears back, head poking up unto the air, disapproval in every line of his face. When it came to placing the collar over his head and around his neck, he shook his head from side to side as if saying no.

"Come on, old boy, I'm sure this isn't your first time in harness," Valdas said.

Donkey flattened his ears and took a nip at Valdas's sleeve.

"I'll make it up to you, I promise."

"He doesn't believe you." Tsura stood a little way off, hands on hips. "Wait." She ran to the wagon and came out with a stale piece of bread in her hands. "He do for me, yes?"

Valdas stepped back.

"You hold this way." Tsura positioned the collar in Valdas's hands and stuck her arm through it with the bread held out.

Donkey moved in for the treat and Valdas slipped the collar over his head and settled it gently. He received a baleful glare from the horse for his trouble, but it appeared that somewhere in his past Donkey had been used for harness work. Once harnessed and coupled to the shafts, he threw himself into the collar and hauled the wagon through the mud with Valdas walking at his head the whole way, and Mirza leading the skewbald while Tsura rode Bo.

The other wagons were settled into the campground by the time they arrived, but Stasha sent the same three men to help them make camp and Nadia, the head woman, brought a pot of soup big enough for three.

CHAPTER TWENTY-EIGHT

Mirza

IT WASN'T SO much the fact that Valdas had joined the men in pushing wagons out of the mud, or even the fact that he'd made it plain to Stasha that the band should be doing more to help Mirza. It was the way he'd held the skewbald's head and, almost by sheer force of will, stopped the fallen horse from panicking. That's what finally got to her. Dammit, Mirza was beginning to like Valdas.

She'd cared for him at first because his life had been put into her hands, and healing him was her job, her vocation. He became a challenge and she liked a challenge. Then, when the worst was over and the long recovery began, he irritated her: his lack of knowledge of their ways, his automatic assumption that he knew best, even when he didn't, and the way he used the intimate form of their names as if he considered both Mirza and Tsura belonged to him.

And then the skewbald slipped in the mud and Valdas ran to prevent him from further harm, and Mirza saw the innate kindness in the man that even a life in Zavonia's husaria had not been able to train out of him.

She began to study him—watch him when she thought no one was looking. Valdas might not have noticed, but Tsura certainly had.

"You like him," she said, almost accusingly.

"I do not," Mirza said. "He's my patient. I need to keep an eye on him."

Tsura just gave her a funny, sideways look, and didn't bother to answer.

Mirza would have protested more, but she knew how that would look, so she tried to watch him less, and avoid watching too closely if Tsura was present.

In the end, the next thing that gave Mirza a further insight into Valdas's character was something the whole band saw.

CHAPTER TWENTY-NINE
Lind

THE UNICORN BRIDGE joined the Old Town and the New Town across the fast-flowing Brudny River. The bridge ran across the falls. From it, Lind could see upriver to the boulder-strewn rapids and downriver to the basin, the last safe harbor for shallow-keel boats. It was a long footbridge slung across the water, suspended as if by magic, and paved with wooden cobbles that looked set to crumble. Two people could pass, with extreme care, but it wasn't the sort of bridge you wanted to start any kind of argument on. High winds caused it to judder sickeningly, and were almost strong enough to pitch a man into the churning waters below.

It was a good place for an accident to happen.

Some people called it Suicide Bridge.

At noon on the appointed day, Lind stepped carefully out onto the bridge, a loaded and primed flintlock tucked into the strap round his thigh, one dagger up his left sleeve and one down each boot. He felt the first gust of wind tug at his shoulders and he braced himself for the blast as it swept down the river.

At the opposite end were two figures. That wasn't right. By common accord, meetings like this were one to one. Lind hesitated, but one of the men stepped forward on his own. His delja fluttered around him. The delja was a mistake. It might cover any number of weapons, but it would catch the wind. As if to agree with Lind's assessment, the heavy cloth billowed out and made the man stagger, causing him to grab the balustrade on the leeward side. Good. Even if he was armed, it would take him a vital split-second longer than Lind to reach his weapon. Lind kept his left hand on the balustrade. His right was held loosely at his side, within easy reach of either pistol or dagger.

The man drew closer and they met in the middle. This man was new, but like the other he had a slightly unfocused stare—his pupils wider than they should be on a day as bright as this.

Damn. Lind recognized the stink of magic.

The man half-bowed. "My master send his regards."

"And I thank your master for his prompt payment."

The man looked puzzled, briefly. Obviously this one wasn't aware of the previous transaction.

"Is that your master over there?" Lind nodded to the figure at the other side of the bridge.

"A messenger only." He moved his hands in a series of patterns and the messenger replied in the same fashion.

"He doesn't hear," the man said. "He talks with his fingers, but his memory is excellent, so he will take back exactly the message I give him and no more."

Lind wondered why the man couldn't carry his own message.

"You have a job for me?" Lind asked.

"Two. There's a soldier called Valdas Zalecki, sometime Captain of the King's High Guard, now doubtless fleeing for his life. That life must end."

"Valdas Zalecki. I know who this man is. I'll recognize him. But if he's fleeing for his life he won't be easy to find."

"My master said that you would know him, and also said he's paying you enough for the search to be part of the job."

Lind nodded. "When was the last time Valdas Zalecki was seen?" he asked.

"On the day of King Konstantyn's death."

"More than three months! The trail has surely gone cold by now. Your master asks the impossible."

"That's why he's asking you."

Lind grunted. "Your master has a lot of faith in me."

"You have a reputation among those who know about these things."

Hmm, Lind couldn't afford to become too well known. Retirement began to look even more appealing.

"And the other?" Lind asked.

Standing precariously, one hand still on the balustrade, the man handed over a cloth-wrapped miniature, bound with an anonymous seal. Lind risked letting go of his handhold and lifted his other hand away from his weapons to break the seal. It was a small likeness of Queen Kristina, painted by someone with a very good eye for detail. The gold and amber circlet on her head would have told Lind immediately who she was, even if he hadn't fled Biela Miasto with her. The bridge shuddered as a gust of wind hit it, and the man dropped to a crouch. Lind's guts did a somersault that was nothing to do with balance. He shoved the likeness into a pocket and took firm hold on the balustrade again.

"My master wants this lady alive—and her child—for their own safety."

Alive? Thank God in his heaven! Lind made a hurried calculation. Yes, even if she hadn't had Konstantyn's child by now, she certainly would have had by the time he located her. If she survived alone. If she survived the birth. If she hadn't already left the country and made her way to the safety of Sverija.

"What do you know of the lady?" Lind asked.

The man's eyes were drawn to the miniature as if he hadn't seen it unwrapped before. "I know nothing. Everything is in the package."

So the messenger knew as little as was necessary to deliver the message.

Lind contemplated not taking the job, but wondered whether he'd survive that decision. He already knew too much, but if he was bound by a new contract he remained useful to whoever was behind this. At least he could make the man and his master pay. And besides, if not Lind, then a man with the resources of the man's master would simply find someone else to do it.

"My fee will be two hundred gold schillings, in advance, for each person, whether or not I have any success."

The man nodded.

"And a further hundred for each job on completion."

"Agreed."

Damn, he should have asked for double.

The man shuffled his feet and braced against the wind before taking one hand off the balustrade again. He kept it where Lind could see it and pointed to a pocket for permission. Lind nodded and he fumbled inside, bringing out two weighty pouches. Lind transferred them to his own pockets and the man clutched the balustrade again, then leaned against it for stability while he sent his message to the man on the end of the bridge by a series of rapid hand signals. He received a simple affirmative signal in return.

"How should I contact you when this is done?" Lind asked. "Where shall I bring the lady?"

"Send word to the North Star Coffeehouse by the East Gate in Biela Miasto. Ask for Chazon and wait for a message."

Lind half-turned and paused. "Chazon is your master?"

"No."

"Who—"

The man's lips clamped together. He fished in his pocket and placed an additional bag of schillings on the balustrade. "You work too cheap, assassin. My master was prepared to pay more. You might as well have it. I will have no further use for money."

Before Lind could ask why not, the man lurched across the width of the bridge and tumbled heels over head into the falls. Lind made a grab for him as soon as he realized what was happening, but his fist closed on empty air. The man was gone, the roar of the falls covering any sound he might have made.

Lind was used to death, but the man's suicide shocked him to his core. This had more than a stink of magic about it. And what if someone should accuse him of murder? That would be a bad joke, to be arrested for a murder he didn't commit. He took a deep breath and walked calmly to his own side of the bridge, slipping into the midday pedestrians who had either not noticed or didn't want to notice a body plummeting into the foaming waters.

He would have to leave Tepet. It was no longer a safe place to do business. Damn it, he was ready to get out of this business altogether. He'd fallen into the trade by default, and he was good at it, but surely he could be good at something else. He simply had to discover what.

CHAPTER THIRTY
Valdas

AT ESTEDGE, CLOSE to the Tevecor Reaches, Stasha Hetman approached the lord holder, Antoni Kafel, about selling two horses. He didn't make a sale, but Kafel set the band on breaking some youngstock and so they decided to stay for three days, camping on the southern side of the ramshackle town, within sight of the lord holder's crumbling stone keep.

Valdas knew of Kafel, an elderly widower who never put in an appearance at court. It was unlikely that they'd ever come into contact with each other, so when Stasha Hetman invited him to watch them starting the three- and four-year-olds—he never called it breaking, for what use was a broken horse—Valdas climbed stiffly onto Mirza's pony and rode to the keep. Mirza leaped nimbly onto the skewbald, now recovered from his injury, took a leather satchel from Tsura's outstretched hand, and followed half a length behind.

Up close, the keep was in an even worse condition than it had appeared from a distance. Valdas worked out how close it was to the Ruthenian border. If he were King Gerhard, he'd invest a little in building up the area, maybe by giving Kafel a small force of infantry who could be put to good use rebuilding the keep's curtain wall, and also give Kafel's eldest son, Ulryk, a taste of commanding men who were more than a bunch of farmers with pitchforks.

Kafel himself came down to the yard, where six young, flighty horses, each one taller than the band's own smaller, more compact mounts, had been corralled.

"What do you think of my beauties?" Kafel asked. "Are they not fine?"

"Very fine, lord," Stasha said.

"Three silver tolars," Kafel said, "for three days of your time. You think you can break them in that time?"

Valdas saw Stasha's lips tighten at the word *break*.

"We can start them, lord, without breaking their spirit, but your own horsemaster must continue their training."

"I want the colt for my son. Take special care with him."

"Of course, lord, as you wish."

Valdas leaned with his forearms resting on the top rung of the stout wooden fence. Mirza stepped silently to his side.

"Does Stasha always act so subservient?" Valdas asked quietly.

"Is there any other way to act? If the Landstriders show pride, it's often knocked out of them. Or worse."

"It hardly seems fair."

"What's that got to do with anything?"

"Well, for one thing—"

She cut him off with a hiss and a wave of her hand. "Watch this."

Stasha and Boldo, with four of the younger men, slipped inside the pen that held the six horses.

"He'll go for the colt first," Mirza whispered.

The young horses, two mares, three geldings, and an uncut bay colt, raised their heads, most ready to flee, but the colt, head up, ears pricked, stood his ground.

"That one." Stasha pointed toward the colt. He walked steadily in the colt's general direction without making eye contact or looking as if he was interested. He got to within a couple of lengths and deliberately turned his back, feigning indifference. The colt stretched his nose toward Stasha, ears twitching warily, but didn't move.

"Stasha's got his attention," Mirza said softly.

Boldo and the men inserted themselves between the colt and the remaining five horses and smoothly drove them toward the far side of the paddock, where a second gate led into a smaller enclosure. Once alone with the colt, Stasha, patience itself, waited for curiosity to overcome wariness and for the colt to take his first step.

"How long will he stand there?" Valdas kept his voice low, not wanting to intrude upon the moment.

"As long as he has to," Mirza said. "Don't be too quick to count the minutes and hours. This can't be rushed. The colt must come to the man. They must form a bond of trust so the rest can follow."

Valdas didn't know how long it was before the colt finally made one step toward Stasha.

"One small step on a long journey," Mirza whispered.

It didn't take as long for the second step, and then a third.

Finally the colt was standing with his nose almost touching Stasha's shoulder. Slowly, so slowly, Stasha turned and put out a hand for the colt to sniff, then moved his other hand to touch the colt's neck. The colt stiffened and twitched, but did not shy away.

"There! It's done," Mirza said. "The rest will come with time and patience."

And so it did.

On the fourth day the band rolled north again, but they'd barely traveled half a day beyond the hold when the sound of hoofbeats on the road made Valdas pull the wagon's sturdy cob to a standstill and twist around to look behind. Ulryk Kafel thundered toward them at the head of a gang of maybe twenty liegemen-farmers mounted on sturdy native ponies. They quickly closed the gap, so the band pulled to a ragged halt. Stasha, Boldo, and several of the Bakaishans rode to meet the lordling. Valdas could hear raised voices and see gesturing. He waved Tsura close.

"Want to drive for a while, Tsura-mi?" he asked her.

She blushed and wagged her finger at him in the universal gesture of reproach, then she gabbled at him—words he couldn't understand. Apparently her Zavonian wasn't up to whatever she was trying to tell him, despite it being the language of trade common to all the northern kingdoms. As near as he could work out, the band spoke a guttural dialect of a language from the far eastern steppes, full of sharp sounds, which he couldn't begin to get his tongue around apart from a few very basic words.

Eventually she scowled, said something to the sky, and called Mirza.

"My young apprentice wishes me to inform you that you should not address her by the familiar, as you are neither her father, her brother, her cradle-friend, nor her lover."

"What?"

"You keep addressing her as Tsura-mi. That's only allowed by family or intimate friends."

"Oh." He thought how many times he'd copied what he'd heard and called Mirza *Mirza-mi* and felt his cheeks heat up. "I'm sorry. I didn't mean to give offense."

"I know."

"I've called you Mirza-mi in public."

"I know." She looked as though she found something amusing in that.

"Was that very rude of me?"

"Stasha wonders if you are my lover. He's wondering whether to call a meeting and have you judged and castrated for my shame, or to pity you for the damage I may have done to your kok. Forgive him if he tries to follow you and watch you take a piss. He wants to know if you can still point and aim or if you have to squat like a girl."

"You're laughing at me aren't you?"

"Only a little."

"Does it cause trouble for you?"

"No. Let them wonder." She waved Tsura alongside and spoke to her rapidly. "You want to ride Donkey."

"If Mistress Tsura doesn't mind." He was careful not to use *Tsura-mi* again.

"She doesn't."

"I'm curious as to what's happening up there." He gestured toward what was rapidly becoming a confrontation.

Mirza rolled her eyes. "Ulryk Kafel is looking for an excuse to reclaim his father's expenses by taking the coin that has been paid over for honest work. Maybe he's discovered something has gone missing. It's surprising how often that happens. Possibly something to the value of the purse his father has paid over."

"That's criminal!"

"Not when you are the law."

Valdas scowled, handed over the cob's reins to Tsura, and slid off the wagon into Donkey's saddle, an old one lent by Boldo's brother-in-law.

"If you're going to play the part of a good Landstrider, learn to look down and not up," Mirza said. "And bow when the little lord speaks. Don't get yourself—or us—into trouble!"

"Who says I'm going to play the part of a good Landstrider?"

Valdas rode to the rear of the wagons where Stasha, Boldo, and several heads of the various families that formed the band were nose to nose with Ulryk Kafel and his ragtag army, noticeably armed with cudgels, billhooks, and a couple of rusted sabres that had not seen military service since before King Aleksander's time. Valdas was conscious that his own sabre had been lost along with everything else but Donkey, and all that he had was a borrowed general-purpose knife tucked into his sash and a stout blackthorn stick. He was sure that he could do some damage with it if he had to, but it mustn't come to that.

"I have an indictment from the magistrate in the name of the Amber Crown." Kafel was waving a scroll as Valdas approached. "A fine of two tolars, and the return of the three tolars you were paid for your work, plus the stolen property."

"That's five silver tolars, and we were only paid three in exchange for three days of our skill, lord." Stasha's voice had become ingratiating, his pride swallowed in order to deal with a man who might literally have the power of life and death over the band. "And we stole nothing. Took nothing but water from your stream."

"Here's proof." Valdas found himself the unwilling focus of Kafel's attention. "That's a horse belonging to the King's Hussars."

Donkey tossed his head and pricked up his ears, something he did rarely. The clip mark was obvious even from a distance.

Stasha had two options now, neither good from Valdas's point of view. He could either give away Valdas's identity as a found man, in which case there might be a warrant out for him, or he could weasel his way by handing over Donkey and paying the extortionate fine. Valdas knew which he'd do in Stasha's position, so before Stasha could say anything he used his best parade-ground voice.

"Enough! Do you presume to accuse me of stealing my own horse?"

Stasha flashed him a brief look of panic. The hetman was obviously used to backing down in these sorts of situations rather than standing his ground. Was Valdas doing the band a disservice? Should he have let them handle it? Too late now.

Kafel's eyes narrowed as he looked at Valdas. What would he see? The military mustache had gone, though there might be a slightly paler mark where it had been. He was dressed completely in borrowed clothing except for his boots. *Ah, make sure he sees the boots.* Valdas didn't give him chance to draw breath. He quit his anonymous slouch, and sitting up in the saddle like a hussar, he rode forward until Donkey was almost nose to rump with Kafel's horse and snatched the paper out of Kafel's hand. Most Landstriders didn't read. Kafel would likely know that, so the paper could be anything, but wasn't likely to be real. He unrolled the document and scanned it quickly, confirming his suspicions.

"Lord Kafel, your scribe has sadly misled you." He dropped his voice so that Kafel would not be embarrassed in front of his men. An embarrassed man could get irrationally stupid to save face. "This isn't an indictment for the Bakaishans, but one for a petty thief, signed by a magistrate some months ago in the name of the late King Konstantyn. King Gerhard holds the Amber Crown in Biela Miasto now. I'm lately come from there on an errand that necessitates me traveling across the Ruthenian border incognito. If you have intentions to detain me here, you must explain your reasons to King Gerhard himself as to why I have not completed my mission."

"I . . . you're traveling with the Landstriders?" Kafel wrinkled his nose.

"For the Amber Crown I would travel with the Devil if I had to. Now, may we pass in peace?"

Kafel's face ran the gamut of emotions, starting with anger, but ending as thoughtful. At length he nodded and reined back a few paces.

Valdas breathed again.

"Lord Kafel . . ." One of the farmers carrying an old sabre obviously thought his lord's authority flouted.

Valdas stared him down and Kafel wheeled his horse. "A misunderstanding. Let them pass."

Stasha cast a glance at Valdas, and almost imperceptibly Valdas twitched his head in the direction of *away*. Without wasting time Stasha waved to the lead wagon, driven by Boldo's wife. It began to roll forward. The others followed.

Valdas sat with Kafel as the band departed. "Lord Kafel, I trust I can rely on your discretion in this matter."

"May I know your name, sir?"

Valdas shook his head. "It would be better for you if you did not. The king takes the security of his realm very seriously. The king—"

"The king may be assured of my best service at any time."

"Thank you." Valdas inclined his head. "You might wish to have a care when dealing with the Landstriders. It's not unknown for the king to send couriers with them."

It was the best he could do to assure that Ulryk Kafel and his father dealt fairly with the next Landstrider band that passed through, but he couldn't do much more. *Not criminal when you are the law,* Mirza had said. If Landstriders had to live with this kind of treatment all the time, no wonder they were clannish. If what they earned honestly could be stolen from them so easily, why not take recompense where they could?

That night he sat at the campfire with Mirza and Tsura, eating thick pancakes stuffed with small pieces of meat, feeling that he'd at last begun to sense what being Bakaishan really meant, though he couldn't begin to guess the long-term effect of being driven out of one place and met at the next with hostility. They could never answer their accusers or fight back except by stealth because there were few countries where they were welcome. They couldn't afford to be banished from one more. No wonder the band was wary of outsiders. He should thank them again for taking him in without awkward questions.

Ah, and here come the awkward questions now, he thought as Stasha and Boldo approached Mirza's fire. Mirza nodded as they asked for permission to approach and sit. She offered them tea and they sat politely while Tsura fetched extra porcelain cups and poured the brown liquid into them, using honey for sweetening.

Ah, they have honey after all.

Duty done, Tsura took her leave politely.

"I came to thank you, my friend," Stasha said. "Without your intervention, this afternoon might have gone badly for us."

"I'm glad I could help."

Boldo cleared his throat. "We heard what you said—about the king—and . . ."

"And you wondered whether I should have told you before." Valdas opened his hands, palms out. "It was nothing but a bluff, a crakev, and I feel that continuing our journey without undue delay might be a sensible precaution."

"You seemed to know so much about the king's business," Stasha said.

"Luckily Lord Kafel did not. I . . . worked for the old king, King Konstantyn. I was . . . I am . . . loyal to him—to his memory. If the new king finds me, my life would be forfeit. If you feel that puts the band in a difficult position I will leave at once." He shrugged. He'd told Mirza his whole story but didn't see any need to unburden himself on Stasha.

"Pah!" Stasha spat. "The king sits in his white tower many miles away wearing his Amber Crown. You are welcome to stay as long as you like. We will make you Bakaishan yet."

That was the biggest compliment a Landstrider might ever pay to an outsider. Valdas bowed his head in recognition of the honor. "Once we're over the border I must leave, but I thank you for your hospitality."

He heard Mirza clear her throat. "When Valdas leaves I must travel with him."

"What? It's true then." Stasha looked at Valdas and Mirza and his eyebrows met on the bridge of his nose.

Valdas put hand to heart. "I swear . . ."

Mirza waved one hand to silence him. "I have spirit-walked to the first gate, and there I was given a task by the shade of Valdas's dead king."

"What?" Valdas asked the question at more or less the same time as both Stasha and Boldo.

"I told you before, Valdas. Surely your wits were not that addled. When I say something I mean it."

Valdas wanted to say it was all hogwash. He couldn't believe he was sitting around a campfire with adults having this conversation as if it were real.

"Tell us." Stasha seemed to accept the spirit-walk nonsense without questioning it.

"I saw the *far country*. Valdas's spirit was searching for the first gate."

"I said he was dead, all but," Boldo said.

"The spirit of Valdas's king turned him back, saying he still had work to do. That he, King Konstantyn, had planted a seed and Valdas was to see that it grew fair."

"But what has this to do with you, Mirza?" Stasha asked.

"Valdas is a bonehead. Dead to spirit dreams, and so he doesn't believe them. The spirit king told me that I must go with him, that I would be needed. He called in the debt of the Landstriders for the freedom of traveling within Zavonia."

"Bakaishans don't serve the Amber Crown!" Boldo said.

Stasha shook his head slowly. "No, but a shulam must serve the spirit world." The two of them fell to arguing ethics.

Valdas listened, bemused.

Did they object to Mirza leaving as strongly as they should have? Valdas suppressed a little knot of anger rising on her behalf. Maybe Stasha and Boldo would be somewhat relieved to see the back of her, even though it would leave them with only Tsura to tend their ills. When they'd finished discussing between themselves, the matter appeared to be settled. Valdas would leave the band after they'd crossed into Bieloria at Fort Erta and Mirza would accompany him. Boldo would lend her a long-striding horse and Stasha would lend them ten silver tolars for the journey, which Valdas would repay twice over when he returned Mirza safely.

And if Mirza didn't return—well—possibly ten tolars and a long-striding horse might not be too much to pay.

CHAPTER THIRTY-ONE
Lind

EVEN IF LIND could find Kristina, he didn't want to deliver her into the hands of the man who'd had her husband killed and likely wanted to kill both her and her child. He ignored the fact that he'd been the actual instrument of Konstantyn's death, since he'd not been the instigator. At least the messenger had asked that he deliver the queen and her child alive, but how long would they stay that way?

He'd keep all his options open for now, though, and at least make a show of looking for her. The last thing he wanted was someone else on the job. He wondered whether he was the only searcher. Well, he couldn't do anything about any others.

What he could do was start with Zalecki.

Valdas Zalecki had been the worryingly efficient High Guard captain whom Lind had watched closely when looking for the right opportunity to poison Konstantyn. It had taken more time than he had anticipated because he'd waited until Zalecki was out of the castle before he'd poisoned the fish. Hence, Zalecki had escaped the grisly fate of his fellow High Guards. He didn't owe Zalecki anything. His life, or death, meant nothing, so he'd search for the man first.

Before Lind reached the edge of the Unicorn Bridge, he'd decided that Zalecki was as good as dead already.

As Lind let himself in through the back door of the Papillon, Ludmila Korolenko was waiting for him.

"I heard someone fell from Unicorn Bridge?"

"Really?"

"Konrad Nizinski, please do me the courtesy of not underestimating either my intelligence or my circle of contacts. A man of your description was seen leaving the bridge immediately afterward."

"Not my doing, madame, I assure you."

"That's what you said when you left me with a corpse on my hands after your last visit. I begin to think that despite the rent you pay, you are more trouble than you are worth. I hear the city watch are looking for someone to blame, and they have a good description."

He nodded. He'd have to make sure he didn't match that description. Being innocent of murder did not guarantee safety, any more than being guilty guaranteed arrest.

"Give me a quarter hour and I'll be on my way, madame. I thank you for your past hospitality and ask only that if the watch comes calling you say you don't know where I've gone." He handed her five gold schillings. "For the room rent, and your discretion."

He ran up to his room and changed into a tunic and wide pantalones, then hastily stuck a ginger false mustache to his top lip, and jammed a soft kolpek on top of his head to hide his hair. He had a better disguise in his rooms in the New Town, which Ludmila Korolenko knew nothing about. He grabbed the bag that held his weapons and his disguises, hair dye, face plumpers, and unguents to change the flesh tones of his face. He didn't want anyone to know that disguise was his stock in trade. He bundled two outfits into a bag, but the rest of the clothes weren't worth rescuing. There was nothing in the room that he needed to keep, nothing to identify him. Let Ludmila Korolenko sell it or burn it as she saw fit.

"Nizinski!" Madame shouted from the bottom of the stairs. "There are four watch soldiers two minutes away."

God's ballocks! That was quick.

He ran down the stairs.

"Oh!" Madame stared at him. "Quite the master of disguise, aren't you?"

"When I have to be."

"I won't ask how often that is."

"Don't and I won't have to lie to you. I'll go out of the back door."

"No, they have men at the end of the alley. The front door or nothing."

"But—"

"I'll see you safely away. At least no one will recognize you. Come here."

She tucked her hand into the crook of his arm and led him to the front door, opening it wide and pausing on the front steps. "Kiss me," she said softly, "as if we're old friends."

He drew in a sharp breath.

"What's the matter? Too good for an old hag like me?"

He swallowed hard. The touching was bad enough, but kissing? He shuddered.

"Well, Konrad Nizinski, do you want to be accused of murder?"

He swallowed hard and bent to kiss her.

"Not on the cheek, idiot, on the lips as if we'd just spent a passionate hour together."

He swallowed hard and kissed her full on the lips. She tasted of bad teeth and tea. He wanted to vomit.

"There, that wasn't so bad, was it?"

Yes it was. It was almost as bad as being hanged for killing a man who had, for whatever reason, committed suicide.

"Good-bye, my lover." She raised her voice so the watchmen couldn't fail to overhear. "See you next week."

"I look forward to it." He answered her at the same volume.

She sighed as he left. "I love a man who's easy to please," she said to the sergeant of the watch as he approached her door.

Lind didn't hear the rest of it. He walked away, not too fast, not too slow, and when he was far enough down the street that the watch had lost sight of him, even if they were looking, he slipped into a narrow alley that smelled of piss, and started to work his way back the way he had come.

CHAPTER THIRTY-TWO

Valdas

VALDAS'S APPREHENSION GREW as the Bakaishan band approached the border. It was as though he was on a cord that stretched tighter and tighter the further he traveled from Biela Miasto. Leaving Zavonia felt wrong, deep in his gut where reason gave way to feelings. His gut felt that he owed Konstantyn instant justice, but his brain told him not to be stupid. What could he do? Rush back to Biela Miasto and kill the new king?

Was he even sure Gerhard was guilty?

If not Gerhard, who? The country itself was as stable as it had been for many a year, so the likelihood of a homegrown political malcontent was distant. According to some of his critics, Konstantyn was too soft, but that trait tended not to breed rabid enemies from within.

Soft wasn't the word Valdas would have used. He'd captained a company in the King's Hussars in that white-knuckle time when the old Tsar of Ruthenia had annexed Bieloria. There was speculation that he might turn his attention to Zavonia next, but Konstantyn made a decisive and genius move. Instead of acting defensively, he had immediately attacked and retaken the disputed land of the Tevecor Reaches while Ruthenia was otherwise occupied, securing that tract of wild land, which had previously been too close to both the Ruthenian and Bielorian borders for comfort.

No, indeed, Konstantyn was not soft, but he wasn't cruel either. He had a keen sense of justice and a knack of knowing how far to go. He'd immediately appeased Ruthenia's aging tsar by marrying his sister Zofia to Ivan, the Petrov heir, with a dowry that almost paid for the land he'd taken. He'd won the loyalty of his new subjects in the region with lower taxation and had given them better roads, increased trade, two schools, and three small hospitals. He'd set up town councils, se-jims, taking a certain amount of power out of the hands of the fickle border barons and putting it into the hands of the people. This, of course, had made him a popular king—with everyone except the barons.

Valdas mentally added any number of Tevecor's disenfranchised minor barons to his suspects, but he didn't really believe any of them guilty. If it wasn't Gerhard, Kassubia was still top of the list.

If whoever it was had waited much longer before making his move, Konstantyn's new queen might have presented the country with an heir.

Oh, if only . . .

Valdas didn't know Queen Kristina well. After the wedding she'd retired to the Queen's Court, the palace within a palace, with her faithful retinue. Though there were two decades between the royal couple, it seemed to be as successful as any political marriage might hope to be. Valdas himself had stood guard outside their bedchamber on enough occasions to know that the couple did their duty, though he didn't know whether they found joy in each other. He hoped they did.

He sighed. If he eliminated Kassubia, it still came down to Gerhard wanting the Amber Crown for himself.

As the night closed in around them and everyone went to their beds, Valdas laid his blanket by the dying embers of the campfire. First he recited the litany of the names of the High Guard, and then he thought about what being Zavonian meant to him. He'd fought his way across a dozen battlefields for Konstantyn. Why did this battle feel so very different? Was he a coward now? It was as if the rock that had been sitting on his chest exploded into a thousand shards, each one cutting like glass, stripping away his outer layers and exposing a raw and bleeding inner. He let out a great shuddering sob, which he covered with the rough blanket, stuffing it into his mouth to stifle the sound.

He'd been brave once.

The Battle for Tevshenna had been his first as a captain in the Third Hussars. He'd thought himself invincible. The sight of winged hussars charging the enemy was enough to break an army. A hundred men on tall horses with great wings of metal and eagle feathers strapped to their backs to make them ten feet tall. They rode in loose formation on the approach, not close enough to make a solid target for the enemy musketeers. Their horses were eager to be off, but they reined them in, saved their strength until needed. As they got close enough to see the fear in their enemy's eyes and smell their sweat, they closed up, knee to knee. The trot became a canter, still controlled, until they let their mounts spring forward into a gallop, muscles pounding, pennants flying. And those wings on their backs sang in the wind of their charge—sang the enemy to damnation. That's when they knew why they went to the trouble of strapping them on. They were the Angels of Hell come to reap the souls of their enemy. The charge carried all before it into and through the enemy lines, breaking them like matchwood.

At Tevshenna, though, it had all begun to unravel. They were ordered into the field against Petrov's rabble. As it turned out, the intelligence was wrong. Petrov's army was not a rabble. Behind their musketeers they had field guns. Valdas had lost half his company to grapeshot as they closed.

He remembered the truth of his bravery then. He'd been terrified, but he'd squashed his fear, or maybe he'd used it. Nothing to do but go forward. Race into the enemy lines, get behind the dreaded guns.

Bravery wasn't being without fear, it was being shit-scared and doing what you had to do despite it.

They'd won the battle, but winning came with a price.

And now he faced an even bigger battle than Tevshenna. Bigger and so very different.

Three days later, at Fort Erta, Valdas packed what he could call his own into Donkey's saddlebags. As he was preparing to leave, Stasha Hetman approached him with a cloth-wrapped bundle, long and narrow.

"You will need this, if you are to take care of yourself and our shulam."

Valdas could tell what it was by the weight and the feel. Unwrapping it, he saw that he was right. It was a sword, longer than his cavalry sabre and showing signs of age. The blade cried out for a whetstone and the leather of the scabbard was beginning to peel where it had dried out. He knew better than to ask where it had come from.

"She intends to come with me. I've tried to change her mind, but she insists."

Stasha inclined his head.

"And you don't mind?"

"She is her own woman. I doubt anything I could say would change her mind. Even so . . ."

"You think she owes her allegiance to the band, not to some stranger."

"She owes her allegiance to the spirit world. I didn't see her worth at first, but she has proved herself."

"I thought you disliked her."

"I don't have to like her. She's our shulam."

"You have Tsura."

Stasha nodded. "But there will always be a place here for Mirza, even though she is not . . ." He pursed his lips. "She is not always a comfortable person."

Valdas twitched his lips down, but there was a smile in his eyes. "I agree with you there, but she's a good person."

Stasha grinned, a rare moment of mirth for him. He dipped his head once in acknowledgment and turned away, saying over his shoulder as he left, "Look after her, Valdas, or you will answer to me."

"What did you tell her?"

"I told her to look after you."

The band was heading to the fair at Djanganai. Valdas felt as though he was about to cut off a part of himself. The band had replaced his troop. He wasn't a man who liked to be alone, and Bieloria was a different country, even if, this close to the border, they probably spoke some Zavonian. The border had fluctuated several times over the last couple of centuries. The common folk probably didn't mind which ruler they bowed to as long as their farmlands were not ravaged by armies. Bielorian was similar to Ruthenian, so he could get by if he had to. Mirza probably spoke the language better than he did, though . . .

"You don't have to come," he said to Mirza. He didn't tell her what Stasha had said. She wasn't used to compliments and she'd think he was manipulating her if he told her that the band valued her and tried to use it as an inducement to get her to stay behind. Without being offensively rude, he'd not been able to tell her what a load of horseshit he thought the whole concept of spirit-walking was. "What's Zavonia to you?"

"Nothing, but I have a promise to keep."

"A promise?"

"A binding promise to the spirit of a dead man. I told you."

She always talked in riddles, as if she liked to confound him with her mysteries. He'd seen her attending to minor hurts as they traveled: a broken collarbone and a gashed leg, but he'd seen no indication of her witchery. It was all in the mind, he thought. The Bakaishans believed her to be a witch, and so in their eyes, and her own, she was.

In truth he wouldn't mind the company, but he might be riding into danger and he was reluctant to take her with him. Besides, a Land-strider traveling with him would slam some doors in his face. Doors he wanted to remain open. For an instant he was ashamed of Mirza, then he was deeply ashamed of being ashamed.

"You think I'll slow you down," Mirza said.

"That too."

"I'm Bakaishan, Valdas Zalecki. I can ride the wind. Boldo has lent me a horse, a long-striding, iron gray that will match your Donkey step for step. I'll wear pantalones. You won't even think of me as a woman."

He thought that most unlikely, but he knew when he was beaten.

CHAPTER THIRTY-THREE
Mirza

MIRZA WANTED TO slap Valdas. How could a man be so obstinate, so stupid? Give him a sword and he thought he was a god. She'd told him to take the right fork and he insisted it was the left.

"The farmer back there said to follow your nose!" He glared at her, slowing Donkey to a walk. "It's obviously the left fork."

"But he pointed to the right. Besides, I don't think he understood your Ruthenian. I knew what you were trying to say and even I didn't understand it all." She settled her own mount and fell in step beside him. "Have you ever traveled this road before?"

"No."

"Well then."

"That farmer needed a lesson in manners." Valdas scowled.

"They don't like Landstriders around here. If you're going to take issue with one man, you're going to have to knock some sense into all of them."

"Where do they like Landstriders?"

"I don't know."

"Didn't they expel the Landstriders from Bieloria fifteen years ago? Are you going to be safe there?"

"Fifteen years ago Bieloria belonged to Kassubia," she said. "Then it belonged to Bieloria, now all of Bieloria belongs to Ruthenia, or maybe it belongs to the tsarina. It's hard to tell."

"That's true. Ivan rules from Ruthenia and his tsarina holds Bieloria against Kassubia with a heavily fortified border."

"And the Landstriders are allowed to cross that border. Ha!" She slapped the pommel of her saddle and her horse's skin twitched on his withers. Patting him, she softened her voice. "Do you want me to wear a bag over my head?"

"Don't be silly. I'm not ashamed of you."

"No?"

"Of course not."

"But you are afraid of being treated like me."

"I . . . Not afraid, but it will make it more . . . difficult. And I'm worried for you."

She let out a groan, but really she wanted to scream. He didn't know how afraid she was, away from the protection of the Bakaishans. Landstriders rarely traveled alone unless they were *unclean*, outcast. She missed the band. Mostly she missed Tsura's solid friendship. She'd been worried for the girl, but a few days before they left, Tsura had found her way into, and out of, the spirit world alone. She still had a lot of learning to do, but she'd overcome the most difficult hurdle. Oh how Mirza wished she could be with her to guide her.

She scowled at Valdas.

"Your king gave me this task. I didn't seek it."

She hissed out a breath as Valdas briefly glanced up toward heaven. He might as well have told her that she was talking horseshit. He obviously didn't believe.

Mirza put her hand on his arm. "Your king had green eyes. Tell me how I could know that?"

"I must have mentioned it when I told you the whole sorry tale."

"No you didn't. Why would you? Think about it."

She gritted her teeth and rode forward, taking the right fork without looking back. A few minutes later she heard Donkey on the road behind her and smiled to herself.

They camped that night, and the night after, finding sheltered spots close to the road. Valdas spent the evening honing his new blade and, stripped down to the waist, going through the sword forms, right handed and left handed, until he learned its weight and length, and it became an extension of his own limbs. He was moving more easily now. Mirza assessed his fitness as she might a good horse, trying to remain detached.

During the day Valdas rode in front as if proving his manhood. Mirza didn't try to catch up or even keep up. She wasn't going to have a pissing contest with a pigheaded outsider. She'd give him this little quirk. If he was used to being up front, she could easily lead from the rear.

Stubborn he certainly was, but she'd observed good qualities in Valdas while she'd been nursing him. Afterward, too, he'd fitted into the life of the band as well as any man might. In time he might even be accepted as Bakaishan. She truly didn't think he was prejudiced against her kind, but once away from the band his Zavonian nature might reassert itself. He was caught between two worlds, not knowing how to reconcile them. He'd been a polite guest, kind to Tsura, and good with the horses. He'd even stumbled over a few phrases of their language, which, Rafal had informed her, was difficult to learn for all Zavonians because it was so different from their own tongue.

Valdas had also been respectful to her, always proper, though she knew he was a virile man. She slept a few feet away from him, separated by the wooden planking of the wagon. She could hear him at night, what he was doing for ease. He wasn't the sort of man she could ever spend her life with, but he was a man who didn't seem intimidated by her reputation, and that might be enough. Stasha more than half-believed that Valdas had stolen her virginity, and the fact that he hadn't cast her out had told her what she'd already known, that no one in the band was ever likely to offer her marriage. Did her witchmark make her so unattractive or was it her power they feared? Maybe it was neither. Maybe it was her tongue. They feared taking a wife who would turn into a scold. They also feared one who might kill them and make it look like a wasting disease. As if she could! As if she would!

She'd always thought she'd go to her bride-bed a maid, but at this rate there would be no bride-bed. She'd die a wrinkled old virgin, regretting missed opportunities, unless she decided to do something about it herself. Could she, should she take that ultimate step toward self-discovery? If she did, she would surely be wrenching the wheels from her wagon. No man would ever take her tarnished.

Was she ready to let go of her last hope?

She tossed and turned through the night, tumbling the choices over and over in her head. In the morning she was sluggish from lack of sleep. They hadn't traveled more than a few miles when Mirza saw a familiar sign.

"Here," she called out to Valdas, who was, as usual, riding on ahead and had missed the bunch of twigs tied around with red twine and hung in the branches of an oak by a farm gate. "The people here will deal with my kind."

They turned along the farm track. As the sign promised, the farmwife didn't mind selling to a Landstrider. Valdas's Ruthenian was court, but these farmers spoke a country dialect. Mirza, well-traveled as all Landstriders, spoke not only the language, but the dialect fluently. They bought fresh soft cheese and hard rye bread, some for now and some for later, and drank a cup of kvass each, the farmwife's own brew. When asked how far to Bieloria, all she could tell them was many days, but they were heading in the right direction.

Valdas seemed to be ashamed that he had to rely on the Bakai-shans' money, as though it was some great sin to have lost his own. He didn't even remember it being taken.

"Konstantyn's quest is more important than your pride," Mirza said.

"I had money, I'm sure."

"You still can't remember what happened, can you?"

He shook his head and ran his fingers behind his ear to the scar on his scalp. "Some. Not everything. Maybe that's for the best. Otherwise I'd be distracted by thoughts of trying to find my sabre. It was a beautiful weapon, perfectly balanced, a precision instrument made from folded steel by Starost the Elder." His eyes grew dreamy. She wondered if he looked at women that way.

They rode on in silence for a little longer, but he looked as though he had something on his mind. He seemed to be building up to something.

At length he said, "Witchcraft."

"What about it?"

"You're the band's witch."

She nodded. "Witch. Healer. Both. Shulam."

"What does that mean exactly?"

Now he asks! What did it mean? How to put it simply. How to say: *I balance the powers of dark and the powers of light*, or *I draw on the elemental powers of the land* or *I walk with spirits*. Would he believe that?

"Do you do spells, make potions? Make people do your bidding? Turn lead into gold?"

What did he think she was? "I do not! Ignoramus."

"I didn't mean to offend. I told you I've never believed. I only know what others think they believe—the men who skirt the edges of what the church allows and style themselves sorcerers."

"Oh, you should believe," she said. "Believe and be afraid. There are those who seek out old forbidden knowledge. Blood magic, body magic. It requires pain and sacrifice by the user as well as the victim. It's destructive. Unnatural." She shuddered.

Valdas gave her a puzzled stare. "But you use magic."

He barely believed in magic. How could he be expected to understand what she herself knew in her bones? How could she make him see?

"Not blood magic. I use natural magic. It's different. A shulam is both healer and witch. I spirit-walk."

"You mean you have herb lore and can draw an astrological chart?"

She drew a slow breath and sighed it out. This wasn't going to be easy. "It's true I can earn a few coppers mixing potions for the Zavonians, but that's not what magic is all about."

"You cheat them?"

"No. The herbs are good, the potions are true, though the best healing comes from within. If they believe in what they want to happen, they are more likely to make it happen for themselves."

"What about ghosts? You see ghosts."

"Yes."

"All the time?"

"Only when I look."

"Oh."

He lapsed into silence and their horses' four-time hoof beats, not quite synchronized with each other, sounded out a comfortable rhythm against the hard-baked road surface. One-two-three-four. One-two-three-four.

"And you saw my ghost before I was dead."

"I saw your spirit. You wore a red mente, a hussar's red mente, but with gold braid, here." She patted her chest. "There's a spirit plane where the dead and the living may sometimes meet. If you don't know how to walk it, you can easily lose your way. You had become lost."

"And then?"

"Without its spirit a body usually dies, though sometimes it lives on for months, or years, a shell empty of reason, unable to perform the simplest of tasks."

He shuddered. "I'd rather someone slit my throat than leave me like that."

"I'll remember that. I have a sharp knife."

She saw a smile light up his face when he finally realized she'd made a joke of sorts. Humor was the most difficult thing to translate into a language not your own.

As dusk fell, they found a deserted barn tucked away in a hollow behind a grove of trees. The central double doors were long gone, but the red pantiles had been repaired at one end at the expense of the other. It looked to have been used within the last year or two for storing hay. The dry remains, not too musty, offered a softer bed than the solid ground. They left their horses hobbled safely outside on what had once been a meadow and had a supper of the cheese and bread they'd bought earlier.

As the last of the light faded, Mirza put one hand on Valdas's arm. "You asked about my witchcraft. Watch." She curled her right fist loosely and concentrated on the warmth in the palm of her hand, letting it build. When she was confident it was strong enough, she turned her hand over, palm up, and opened her fingers. A pale glow, soft as moonlight on water, sat lightly against her flesh. She tossed it upward and it hovered in the rotten rafters above their heads, bathing the barn with silvery light.

"Oh." Valdas watched it, wide-eyed, but not terrified. He turned to her. "It's beautiful. Is it a trick? How do you do that? Glowworms?"

She hissed out a breath. "Watch." She pulled up her sleeve as far as the elbow and took his hand, rubbing his fingers across her palm. Then she wrapped his fingers around her wrist and began to create light again. This time, instead of folding her fingers over her palm, she kept them straight out. A tiny ball of light no bigger than a pearl began to glow in her palm. She concentrated hard and the glow grew.

Valdas drew a sharp breath.

"Now tell me it's a trick," she said. "Touch it."

"What?"

"The light. Put your finger in it and tell me if it's a glowworm."

"I . . ."

"Not afraid, are you?"

"N . . ."

"Then touch it. What are you waiting for?"

Slowly—very slowly—he raised his free hand and touched his pinky finger to the light, as if he'd decided that was the one he could most afford to lose. He touched it and jerked back, then looked at his finger and, seeing no damage, touched the light again.

"I can't feel it. I can only feel your hand."

"That's because it's—"

"Magic."

"Yes. Have I made a believer of you?"

"How . . ." He swallowed hard. "How do you do that?"

"You train for years." She smiled. "But you also need talent. Only a few can learn. And you never, ever, do it where the Zavonians can see. Not if you want to keep your skin whole."

"I'm a Zavonian."

"You're different. I trust you."

"Thank you." He said it very quietly.

As the witchlight faded, they snuggled into bedrolls, a safe distance from each other. Everything went quiet except for the creak of old timbers and the sigh of the wind in the yellowing autumn leaves outside.

Valdas broke the silence. "Which is strongest?"

"What?" Mirza was already drifting away in the darkness, more comfortable than she had been since leaving her wagon.

"Blood magic or natural magic. Which is strongest?"

"Oh, Valdas! That's just the sort of thing a soldier would ask." For a clever man he could be so dense. If he didn't understand, she couldn't begin to explain it. "It doesn't work like that. You can't duel with magic. You can't test a rapier against a sabre or a pistol ball against an arrow."

"So . . ."

Oh, for pity's sake . . . "Good night, Valdas. Sleep well."

CHAPTER THIRTY-FOUR
Lind

LIND CHANGED HIS disguise when he reached the room in the New Town where he'd been sleeping for the last few days. He needed to prepare another Lind to return to Biela Miasto. He'd already let his hair grow out again, and true to form, it was long enough to curl. He heaved a couple of buckets of water up the steps to his garret and dyed his hair a convincing red-brown, a startling contrast with his fair skin and gray-blue eyes, but it would do. He could touch up the roots as he needed to.

He changed his clothes, selecting a blue zupan and a darker blue delja in good-quality wool, seeking the outward appearance of a minor noble's son. He looked in his glass and the face that looked back at him was still too pretty, too young, with a too-sensuous mouth and too-firm chin. He scowled at his reflection. This would have to do. He could certainly pass for early twenties, fully fifteen or more years younger than his fishmonger guise.

He'd entered his room wearing tunic and pantalones, with his hair covered and a large mustache dominating his face; he came out a dark-haired young man, clean-shaven and bright-eyed. This time he'd be Lukasz Kowalik, a feckless younger son looking to take up a new career with the Winged Hussars. That would give him every excuse to hang around the taverns in Biela Miasto where the off-duty hussars and Palace Guard spent their free time.

Stopping downstairs only to leave two tolars for the rent on his room, even though he wouldn't be returning, and then calling in briefly to see Simeon, the young and very astute Jew who acted as his banker, no questions asked, Lind made his way to the river docks.

There were three sail-barges loading for the trip downriver. He eyed them all and chose the most workmanlike of the three, though it was not the fanciest by any means. It was a family-run vessel with husband, wife, and two sons. They asked him no questions and only spoke if they needed him to move or to come and eat. They chatted among themselves at mealtimes, topics that would only interest a bargee and his family such as the cost of docking fees and the warehouse fire that had put one of their best customers out of business.

At Sigrida he left the barge and paid a carrier for a place on a cart heading south. On reaching the Biela River, he paid handsomely for the captain of a clinker-built work boat to make room for him among the boxes that he was ferrying upriver from a square-rigged brig anchored in Riyja. Rowed by six men when they couldn't catch a breeze in their single gaff-rigged sail, they made steady time, anchoring up only between dusk and dawn and making every use of the tidal flow.

Lind asked around wherever they stopped, finding the right people to talk to and distributing coppers and tolars where necessary. If Queen Kristina had made her escape to Sverija on a ship sailing down the Biela River, neither the boatmen nor the sailors ashore from the oceangoing ships had noticed. Good. That was entirely as he expected and hoped. A woman and baby should attract little attention. She might be away by now if she'd borne her child safely.

He hoped so.

CHAPTER THIRTY-FIVE
Mirza

MIRZA LAY AWAKE listening to the rain during the night. Water fell from the sky, plinking into puddles, and battering the fragile tiles clinging to the barn's sagging roof trusses. It found its way in through cracks, dripping and pooling on the floor at the far end, but luckily not on their sleeping place.

In the morning she dug into their pack for breakfast. She had millet ready-pounded to make kasza, but that would mean lighting a fire in this tinder-dry barn, as it was too wet outside, and it would take too long to cook the grains to a proper porridge consistency. Instead she had some black bread, a little dry now, and some walnuts and dried mushrooms. It would have to do.

Valdas stripped down to his trousers to keep his clothes from getting soaked in the warm rain, and went out to get the horses, intending to let them dry off a little in the barn before saddling up. Mirza sat on her heels in the doorway and watched him. Even the worst of his bruises had faded to a sickly yellow discoloration.

She was still trying to make up her mind. Valdas wasn't Bakaishan, of course, but he was a good man, decent by all the standards of the Zavonians, and not unattractive. He hadn't tried to force himself on her or on any of the other women in the band; in fact, he'd been polite and respectful. She didn't know how the Zavonians viewed sex outside of the marriage bed. She knew they paid for it sometimes, and that well-brought-up young women were supposed to go to their marriage bed virgin, but what of that gray area between maidens and whores? Sometimes desperate women came to her as the band passed close by towns and villages, asking her to twine them from the bastard in their belly. To some she gave the bitter herb. Others needed more positive help. Some were too far along their course and she could offer them nothing except to hear their sad tales without judging. These were women afraid for their reputation, in some cases afraid for their lives. The infidelity of lovers who withdrew respect once they'd taken a woman's flower was manifest.

Would she lose Valdas's respect? She didn't want him to think that she gave herself lightly, but she also didn't want him to think that she was pledging herself to him. Valdas wasn't the sort of man she wanted for a husband, not if she wanted someone to grow old with. The number of scars on his body showed how often he'd cheated death. He would not always be so lucky.

Still thinking, she stood to let him lead the animals past her. Donkey flicked an ear in her direction, every line in his face saying that he hated being wet. Valdas pushed his own dripping hair off his face and blinked water out of his eyes. He grabbed handfuls of dusty hay and rubbed down both animals. Since time wasn't pressing, they could afford to wait until the horses' own body heat completed the job and the saddles could at least go on dry. Besides, no one liked riding through this kind of weather if they didn't have to, even Landstriders. By Mirza's reckoning the storm would blow over before noon.

As Valdas tossed away the last handful of hay he glanced at her, saw her watching, grinned and patted his well-muscled chest. "You like what you see? Heh?"

"I was thinking you're going soft." She tried not to smile at the lie.

She'd been thinking about the rain, wondering whether she could walk the spirit world and give it a nudge with her powers, but decided it wasn't worth the possible consequences of a flash flood somewhere else.

"What?" Valdas let the horses nuzzle for old hay on the barn floor. He looked a hand's width taller now he was standing upright. That was better. He'd been losing himself, but now he knew who he was again. The sword work was helping, but she mustn't let him grow complacent.

She chuckled. "You had more muscle when we found you, half-dead as you were. Call yourself a soldier?"

"I don't call myself a soldier. I am a soldier."

"You were."

"I am."

She inclined her head, glad to hear him sounding so positive.

"I'm as strong as an ox."

"A spit-roast one." She walked over to him, digging her fingers into his chest. "If you were a horse I'd say you'd been out to pasture for too long. Keep still." She ran her hand down his chest where the curly hairs gave way to smooth skin, moved behind him and felt his back from shoulder to waist, probing where the ribs had been cracked. He didn't flinch, though by the way he held himself it was still tender. She guessed he'd rather die than admit it.

She rubbed her hand round the back of his waist. He began to twitch away and then steadied. "Kidneys working properly?" she asked.

"Fine, thanks." His voice was tight.

She felt as though she had a lump of wax in her throat. If she didn't want to, she shouldn't do it. But if she didn't do it she might never know what it was like.

She moved close behind him and reached round the front. He smelled of warm man and faintly of horse and the dust of sleeping in a stable.

"No blood in your water?"

"None. Do we need to . . ."

She slipped her hand down the front of his trousers. "All other functions normal?"

He gasped. His spine stiffened against her breasts and his kok jumped under her hand.

"There's my answer," she said, and wrapped her fingers round it as it grew warm and hard. "That's splendid." It seemed as though she'd made up her mind. She took a steadying breath, encircled his waist, and with her left hand unfastened the drawstring. His trousers dropped and, caught in his boot tops, puddled around his feet. He laughed and sat on the blanket.

"Boots first, darling girl. It saves getting into a tangle."

When he looked up she was still standing in the same position, frozen by not knowing what came next. Her eyes were drawn to the planes of his chest. He was sitting on the blanket, knees drawn up, but apart, and between his legs that which she'd had nothing but a healer's interest in—until now.

It was awake.

He rose and stepped so close she could feel his hardness against her belly.

"Close your eyes, Valdas. You needn't look at my face."

"Why not?" He kissed the clear side of her face and the other, not seeming to mind which was which. With his right index finger he traced the wine stain down her face and to the neck of her undershirt. "How far does it go?"

She'd left her shirt open at the top. His hand quickly found a way in, stirring all kinds of *feathery* sensations that her own touch didn't. Her heartbeat pounded in her ears. *Stop thinking. Give yourself up to it. Trust him.* Eyes closed, she let him pull off her shirt. The cool air made her shiver and . . . Oh, her nipples . . .

He closed his hands round her ribcage and ran them upward.

She giggled, a nervous reaction.

His breath fluttered on the side of her neck as he put his lips to her throat. "Are you sure? Really sure?"

She held her breath and nodded, anything but sure. "What's the matter? Don't you want me?"

"Oh, yes." He breathed out the words. "I can hardly . . . but . . . I have no sheath and unless you do . . ."

"I looked after your body while you were out of it. I know you don't have the pox. You don't think I do, do you?"

"Of course not, but a sheath prevents more than the pox. I don't want to get a bastard on you."

"You won't. I'm a shulam. Trust me."

"Then let's join with goodwill and good grace."

He quickly unfastened her pantalones, and already bootless, she stepped out of them as they fell.

He stepped back. She felt him hesitate and her heart fluttered. Was she not good enough? He didn't seem to mind her face, and surely if he could stand her wine mark, he'd find nothing to complain about in her body; her breasts were firm and full and her belly and buttocks round and welcoming, not too bony.

"What's wrong?" Suddenly she was aware of the surroundings, the drafty barn, the pounding of the rain on the roof and the drips it made in the far corner.

"Nothing. Nothing at all. You are as lovely as a picture. I want to drink you in with my eyes."

Her hand went involuntarily to her face and he reached forward and pulled it away. "You have nothing to be ashamed of."

"The mark. It . . . frightens the men of the Bakaishans."

"They're fools." He smiled and pulled her down into the soft nest of his bedroll, stretching his warm body beside hers, causing all kinds of skin-on-skin sensations she hadn't expected. She felt the stiffness of his kok against her leg. Soon it would be inside her. She began to shake as Valdas folded her into his arms.

A soft whicker from above froze them both where they lay. She opened her eyes to see Donkey's coffin-shaped head filling almost her entire field of vision as he lipped Valdas's ear.

Valdas dropped the blanket over her as he got up, led Donkey across the barn floor to Mirza's incurious iron gray, and tied his sash around the horse's eyes. Donkey whickered.

"Serves you right, wretched beast. This is not for spectators."

He came back, lifted the blanket, and looked down at her. "Sorry about the interruption, my lovely girl." He slid beneath the blanket and held her once more, not rushing.

"Are you sure?" he asked.

"You've asked me that before."

She trusted that if she said no he'd let her go and nothing more would be said, but she'd gone too far to stop now. She felt one of his hands warm in the center of her back, steadying her while the other cupped her left breast.

"I'm sure."

His lips came down on hers almost before she'd finished speaking the word. For the longest time his mouth didn't stray lower than her throat, but even so he brought forth feelings in her belly that made her shiver despite the heat radiating from him.

"All right?"

She swallowed. "I want you to touch me."

"Where?"

"Everywhere."

"Let's start here."

His big warm hand started on her belly and moved upward, stroking, teasing.

"And if I kiss you here?" His voice had gone soft and breathy.

"Oh yes."

"And here?"

"Oh yes."

"And here?"

"Can you do tha—? Oh!"

He came up for air, grinning. "Oh, my lovely, you have so much to learn. There's no rush. We have all the time in the world."

He gently nudged his knee between her thighs. She opened for him, feeling more vulnerable than she ever had in her life before. Could he feel her shaking? Apparently he could. He stroked her flank as though she were a frightened filly. He kissed her wine mark, each breast, down to her belly button and her mound, his lips leaving little circles of heat and little ripples of . . . undoing. He came back to kiss her forehead and eyes, not rushing, and very gently, her lips again. She parted them and kissed him back, feeling his teeth on her lower lip and his tongue-tip against hers. His kisses became more passionate, deeper, and he swept her along with him on a rising tide of sensation. She pushed up to meet him. They rolled over together and his fingers rubbed her belly, kneading her flesh gently, slipping further and further down until they burrowed . . .

"Oh!"

"Oh!"

They said it together.

CHAPTER THIRTY-SIX
Valdas

IT TOOK ANOTHER three days to reach Bieloria. Three days and three nights.

Valdas was happy. Mirza could be a sharp-tongued harridan during the day, never letting up for a moment about his fitness, always finding fault with something; but at night she was a delight, snuggling up to him, at first trusting him to guide and to teach and then experimenting, testing the boundaries of what two bodies might do—whether they were fully dressed, out in the chill autumn night and working round layers of clothing, or—like tonight—fully naked in a clean bed in a warm room after a good tavern meal of hare, pot-roasted in beer. She was a fast learner, already a partner and a teacher rather than a student.

"Tell me about Tsarina Zofia." She snuggled into his side and traced the line of an old scar down his chest with one fingertip. "How well do you know her?"

Valdas was starting to drift off. Good food and good sex always meant good sleep. He lay on the bed, feeling boneless, the after-tingle from his gently wilting cock still warming him, and now Mirza was yammering in his ear wanting sensible answers.

"Aww, Mirza. Will tomorrow do?"

"Tomorrow we reach the city gates. I want to be prepared."

He sighed. "I don't know her well. She married before I came to Biela Miasto, but I was already Captain of the High Guard when she last came to visit. She might remember me, but if not, Konstantyn's name should get an audience." He briefly pondered whether it might get him sawn in half. He ignored the stab of fear and the ache in his ballocks at the thought and took a deep breath. He'd have to risk that.

"I believe she was fond of her brother, even though it's common gossip in the palace that when her marriage was arranged she ran off and had to be brought back."

Konstantyn had once said something about his sister's barbarian husband and had laughed as if it was a huge family joke, but Valdas hadn't been privy to it.

"She's got three boys. She brought them to visit her mother a few months before the old lady went to God. The oldest must be eight or nine years old by now. She seemed very . . . regal."

"I've heard tell," Mirza said, "that leaders quickly forget the people they leave behind."

"Royal eyesight, yes. They want people to forget how they were before they came into their power, so those people who remember find they are no longer in favor. That might have been especially true when she visited the place she'd grown up in."

"The tsar's father hated my people," Mirza said. "He tried to purge all the Landstrider bands from Ruthenia, but mostly only succeeded in casting them out of the big cities."

"I know and I'm sorry. The tsar's father had a reputation for being intolerant and warlike. Always pushing outward, taking more territory. That's why Konstantyn sought to wed Zofia to the young tsar-in-waiting, to keep his nose pointing east instead of west. Though from what I hear, Zofia has acquired a certain reputation for ruthlessness as well. You should let me see her alone."

"How do I know you'll come back for me?"

"Because I say I will, sweet Mirza." He kissed her forehead. "Trust me."

She was silent for a few heartbeats as if thinking. "A Landstrider begging an audience to see the tsarina is a risk, I admit, but you're Zavonian. You know how the court works. I'll stay in your shadow, quiet as a mouse. I would rather risk coming with you than hide in some anonymous tavern, not knowing what's happening until I see your ugly head on a pike."

"You could wear Zavonian dress. Your skin is no more brown than that farmwife who sold us cider."

She glared at him. "And if I'm caught I'll be hanged for trying to pass myself off as something I'm not."

"Fair point. Zofia is Konstantyn's sister, and he was the most enlightened monarch of his time, but even so, I'm sorry to say it's a risk. The whole damned enterprise is a risk. I'm the Captain of the High Guard who's been accused of her brother's murder." He shook his head. "Oh, yes, she's going to invite me in for tea and tidbits. Unfortunately I can't see any alternative."

—◆———◆—

Less than a day later Valdas and Mirza were sharing a damp cell deep under the tsarina's palace, a crumbling fortress built in the time of the Northern Crusades. Ruthenia had taken Bieloria from Kassubia and now the tsarina held it, but resources were poured into troops, not into architects and builders for royal comfort.

If the nobles were uncomfortable in their drafty chambers, then Valdas and Mirza were wretched in their cramped stone cell with dampness oozing from the walls and floor, and only the rats and each other for company. Though barely the end of summer, it felt cold enough to freeze the marrow in Valdas's bones. Anyone in here through the winter would surely die of it.

Valdas didn't want to hear Mirza's accusation, but he knew he'd handled it all wrong. He should have sent a note of explanation to the tsarina, not relied on some fool footman to repeat his words exactly. So far, Mirza had not cursed him for his stupidity, but she had every right to. The slimy stone of the cell floor was all they had for a bed. Mirza should use him for a mattress. After all, this had been his idea, even if she'd gone along with it. Perhaps she'd not believed that a Zavonian would get such poor treatment. Did she think it was reserved exclusively for Landstriders? Even with his cloak wrapped round him he was chilled through. She must be frozen because her cloak had been in her pack. He'd offered his, but she was sulking.

He opened his mouth to speak, but she put one hand out. "Don't say it. Just don't. All right?"

"I was only going to say that we'd both be warmer if you came and sat here by me. That corner's as cold as this, but I'm warmer than a wall and we can share whatever heat we have." He raised a corner of the cloak.

"I'm not sure I can move."

"Here."

He got to his feet, slow and stiff, and reached a hand down to her. How long had they been in here? It was difficult to judge when they couldn't see daylight and hadn't been fed. He was hungry, damned hungry.

Wisely, she hadn't attempted to make a light out of magic stuff. If, indeed, that's what she did to make light. He was still puzzled by the whole magic thing. He couldn't deny that she'd done magic, because he couldn't see how else she had made a cool light, but he was still puzzled by it. He'd always been so sure that any magic exhibited must be trickery, but Mirza couldn't have used trickery in that barn, a place neither of them had been before. Every time he thought about it, he had to question his long-held beliefs. And if he was going to question his beliefs, what did he think about her strange tales of the spirit world?

She took his hand and he pulled her to her feet, glad she couldn't see his expression in the darkness. He didn't want to change the way he treated her just because he now knew something about her that he hadn't known before. She was still Mirza, magic or not.

"Come on. Stay healthy." He turned her round and began to rub her shoulders and back, massaging down to her waist and buttocks, the shape of her body familiar to his hands. He rubbed her arms next and finally her fingers.

"Stretch, like this."

He shrugged off his cloak and did some simple stretches and movements from his army training, deceptively gentle moves to energize the muscles. He felt his own blood begin to flow again. It seemed to have pooled in his veins for a while.

"Better?"

She nodded.

"Konstantyn's sister doesn't seem to have taken after him, does she?" Valdas said.

"Obviously companying with a Bakaishan woman wasn't the right approach."

He refrained from saying he'd told her that.

"Or perhaps giving your real name and position didn't help."

Oh great, now Mirza was saying *I told you so*.

"What else could I have done? Added lying to my catalog of crimes?"

"I suppose not. Turn around."

She tugged his sleeve and he turned so that she could massage his neck and shoulders. It wasn't going to turn out as well as last time they'd stood like this. He didn't think she'd go for sex in a cell.

"Stop it," she said.

"What?"

"Thinking about sex."

"I wasn't."

"Of course not."

"I wasn't. I was thinking about . . . how to get out of here." He pulled the cloak around his shoulders again and she slipped inside it with him, tucking herself up under his arm for warmth like a mouse burrowing into its nest.

"Why are you here, Valdas?"

"You said—"

"I know why I'm here, but you . . . What made you start this quest in the first place?"

He thought about the night on the Gura, hearing from Tomas that all his men had been executed, supposedly complicit in *his* murder of Konstantyn. It was as if a hand gripped his heart and squeezed until it was a hot coal within his breast. Anger, sorrow, despair, but mostly anger swelled inside him.

"It's something I have to do. Konstantyn was assassinated and I vowed—"

"Yes, but why did you vow?"

"It's who I am. It's what I do." Valdas took a deep breath. "Konstantyn was my king—a good king. Intelligent, even handed, a wily politician when he needed to be, but always ruling for the benefit of his country and his people. He didn't hold the Amber Crown for the sake of his own power, he made life better for those in Zavonia. It's not always given to us to like the people who govern us. An apprentice may not like his master. A child may not like his parent. A captain may not like his general. But I admired the king, and liked him too. He made me feel as though I was his friend. Oh, I know on one level we could never be friends, but I felt as though he respected me for my skills. Skills that let me down, that let him down. It was my job to protect him and I failed. My life should have been forfeit and I failed even that."

"So your life should have been over. You should have accompanied your king into the lands beyond. Is that what you wanted? Is that what you still want?"

"I . . . I don't want to die." He lowered his voice to a whisper. "Does that make me a coward?"

"Sometimes it takes more courage to live, to do something with your life."

"I vowed to get justice for my men, and to avenge Konstantyn."

"I don't think he wants vengeance."

"But I want it."

"You are angry for yourself, for the disruption of the life you had, not for your king."

"No . . . Yes . . . Maybe. I think I'm angry for both of us. I'm angry for my men. I'm angry for Zavonia. I'm angry for the peasants who are having to pay taxes on cabbage! I'm angry for the little queen, widowed before she's had time to be a wife. I'm angry that the new king is not worthy to touch the hem of Konstantyn's robe."

"And you think it's your job to do something about it?"

"If I don't, who will?"

She sighed. "Did you come up with any bright ideas or are we going to stay in this dungeon until we rot?"

"If we had pen and paper I could write and explain things to Zofia."

Mirza's face told him what she thought of that idea, even in the semi-darkness. "I have a better way," she said. "A way she can't ignore. I'll spirit-walk in her dreams."

Oh yes, great idea. He thought it, but managed not to say it out loud. Yes, he'd seen her make light without fire, and granted, she did seem to know things that she couldn't possibly have found out any other way, unless, of course, he had rambled and talked in his sleep.

"Valdas!" Mirza's sharp voice brought him back to the present. "Sit here and let me lean into you."

Doubt squatted like a toad in his chest, but he did as she directed, sitting on the cold stone floor of their ten-foot-square cell. He leaned against the wall in the blind spot from the small grille in the stout oak door. Their only light, such as it was, came through that grille. It was surprising how little light you could get used to.

Mirza sat in the fork of his thighs, leaning against him. It was only when he wrapped himself round her that he remembered how tiny she was. She had such a commanding presence that sometimes she seemed eight feet tall, but she was a scrap of a thing who hardly came up to his chin.

"What do you want me to do?" he asked.

"Unless you have a bag of salt, nothing. Be my anchor."

"Do you mind telling me what you're doing?"

"I'm going to enter her dreams and see if I can show her the shade of Konstantyn and convince her that us being here is his idea."

"What if she's not asleep?"

"Why then, this experiment will be very short, one way or another."

"And what if she is asleep?"

"She'll either believe us or burn us."

Valdas didn't know whether to hope the spirit-walk was successful or not. He would have asked more questions, to prevent her from starting, but he felt her spine stiffen against his chest and realized that she was not *at home* anymore. He wrapped his cloak around both of them and began to count slowly and steadily, wishing she'd told him how long this would take.

He reached a hundred and nothing had happened. He could feel that she was breathing, but light shallow breaths, not ones that could sustain a body for long. At a thousand he wondered what would happen if he interrupted her. Would it be dangerous? Would he even be able to reach her through her trance? At two thousand he began to worry. Could she get lost up there, cut off from her own body, a living corpse? Should he try to rouse her?

He put a hand lightly on her shoulder. She was icy cold except for where their bodies touched. He wrapped his arms round her and tried to pour warmth in her direction, not that he had much warmth to start off with.

At three thousand he was chilled to the bone and seriously wondering whether he'd ever be warm again. Maybe—if Zofia decided to make good on his destiny to follow Konstantyn into death—he'd have the fires of hell to warm him in the afterlife.

At four thousand he decided enough was enough. He put both hands on Mirza's shoulders and shook her gently, speaking her name softly, and then louder into her ear.

Nothing.

He started again from one. At fifty-six she drew in a great shuddering breath and came into herself.

"Well?" he asked.

"She was asleep, but she's awake now."

Mirza started to shiver. He put his arms around her again, hugging her tight. The shivers almost became spasms before they died away again.

"Come on, get on your feet."

He pulled her upright and began the rubbing-down process once more, working her stiff muscles and massaging life into her arms and fingers. He was still working on her hands when the sound of footsteps echoed in the corridor outside, low voices followed by the key grating in the lock, and their door swung open. Though the jailer hovered in the background, instead of guards, a well-dressed man held a lantern.

"Captain Zalecki, I am Igor Karel. You will come with me. Not the Landstrider witch," he said, as Valdas took Mirza's hand.

"She's a healer."

Karel sniffed. "They're all as bad."

Briefly Valdas considered refusing to go unless Mirza came too, but she gave him a little push. "Don't forget where you left me."

He removed his cloak and draped it around her shoulders. "There, I have to come back, now."

She gave him a little smile of acknowledgment.

CHAPTER THIRTY-SEVEN

Lind

ARRIVING IN BIELA Miasto's bustling riverport, Lind paid off his boatmen and made his way, on foot, toward the market square in the Low City, feeling as though the ground was still rocking slightly beneath his feet. He'd never make a sailor; even the river upset his sense of balance. He needed to sleep in a bed that wasn't moving beneath him.

He'd spent a lot of time in the city in his fishmonger guise. He liked to think he had a feeling for the mood of the place, and today's mood wasn't good. It was as if everyone was angry or worried, or short of cash. The easiness had gone out of the street. It felt mean.

He began to make the rounds of the taverns, staying in each one long enough to observe the customers. This one was favored by market traders, that one by butchers fresh from the shambles. His fourth tavern, the Bell, yielded what he sought, a group of off-duty hussars. You could tell them a mile off by their boots and their bearing. They all walked as though they still had those damned eagle-feather wings strapped to their backs.

He called over the landlord and bought himself a room for the next two nights, choosing one of the ones with access from steps in the yard. Needing to sleep off his river journey, he flopped down on the bed, fully dressed, grateful that it seemed reasonably clean and the room had a fire in the hearth.

Four hours later, spruced up and fully rested, he made his way down the steps, shivering at the temperature drop, and pausing at the doorway to the tavern as the heat, smoke, and noise hit him in the face. By the looks of it the ale was flowing well. A fire blazed in the large inglenook hearth and several tables were occupied by off-duty military types. He circulated, bought a few flagons of beer, engaged a few of them in conversation, but learned nothing specific except that the ranks were uneasy about troop mobilization on the southern border and rumors of war.

The following night was more of the same.

It wasn't until the third night, having extended his stay, that he struck lucky. As he came down from his room into the bustle of the main bar, a group of seven hussars, two still in uniform, sat round a table. Most of the other tables were taken, giving him an excuse to pick up a three-legged stool and swagger toward them.

"Gentlemen, may I join you and offer my hospitality for another flagon?" He tossed two tolars on the table, which made a couple of them sit up and take notice, and a third began to laugh.

"Landlord!" the laughing one called out. "That will keep us drinking all night. Bring us your best."

"Who said he could buy his way in here? Jumped-up little prick." One of the uniformed men scowled into his drink.

"Forgive my friend Tomas, here. He's a little morose when in his cups," Smiler said, putting one hand on Lind's shoulder and gesturing theatrically with the other. "I'm Longin Klavons, and who might you be, my fine, rich fellow?"

Lind stiffened at the touch, but forced himself past the familiarity. "Lukasz Kowalik."

"Kowalik? That's a Kassubian name?"

"My grandfather was Kassubian. I'm in Biela Miasto to join the hussars." He inched his shoulder away and Longin's hand slipped off and did not return.

"Are you, by God? Well, you're drinking in the right place," Longin said.

The landlord brought a jug of beer and Longin poured for everyone, sloshing it onto the table as well as into the flagons. Across the table, Tomas took his, stared into it, stared at Lind, then raised it in a half-salute and downed it in one.

Longin poured him another. "So first of all, Lukasz, before you can call yourself our brother and gain your wings, we need to test your fitness. You need to be able to drink like a fish, fight like a demon, and rut like a boar. First things first. Drink up!"

Lind drank and Longin poured him another, and another. Damn, he should have had food before coming down here. He called for cold pork, cheese, and bread, enough for all, and chewed it down when it arrived in the hopes of preventing his head from swimming too early in the evening.

Piotr and Pawel, who it turned out were genuine brothers as well as military ones, dipped into the food. They seemed excited by the prospect of action and hoped their regiment was going to be called south. They began to regale him with stories of recent campaigns, how the hussars had carried the day against all odds, winning through against overwhelming numbers.

"It's the charge that carries it," Tomas said over the top of his flagon. He slammed the vessel down on the table, splashing its contents high. "You strap those wings on your back and it's as if you can fly."

"Are they difficult to manage if you're unhorsed?" Lind asked.

"Friend Lukasz, you're going to be a hussar," Pawel said. "If you're unhorsed, you'd better be dead."

They all laughed, even Tomas.

"The wings are worth the effort," Piotr said. "They scare the shit out of the enemy. Imagine a hundred winged horsemen riding down on you like devils. Aieee!"

"The wings didn't do us much good at Tevshenna," Tomas said quietly.

"I beg to differ." The other uniformed hussar previously introduced as Serafin spoke up for the first time. "I was on the wing with Kosiorek, but I saw Zalecki lead the charge straight into Petrov's guns. Chain shot. They used chain against men and horses! Half of them were blown to hell in the first salvo, but they kept on going. Zalecki was right out ahead. How he wasn't blasted in half, I'll never know. He jumped that big gray horse of his clean over the artillery line, sabre slashing, and his men followed him. Bravest thing I ever saw."

"You were on the wing, were you?" Tomas's mouth set into a hard line. "I followed Valdas Zalecki over that God-damned artillery line. Bravery? Pah! If I'd had time to shit in my britches I would have. There's a moment when you're too scared to go forward, but it's death to stop, and your horse is galloping, and the wind is screaming through your wings, and you're screaming as well, probably for your mother. That's the bravery of it." He blinked once, his eyes dark pools of memory. "Think on that, Lukasz Kowalik, before you get yourself a pretty horse and march up to the barracks gate to buy yourself a commission. With the wind blowing cold from the south, it's likely that you'll see action sooner rather than later."

"This Zalecki, he must be quite some man!" Lind said, jumping at the opportunity.

"He is," Tomas said, and then raised his flagon to his lips and drank deep.

"He was," Pawel said. "He could outfight a bear."

"And out-fuck a rabbit," his brother added. "They say he was hung like a horse."

"Not *was*," Tomas muttered under his breath. "Never say *was*."

His fellows ignored him.

"Gentlemen," Klavons said. "They call me Longin for a reason. I challenge any of you . . ." He stood and reached for his belt.

"Sit down and have another drink." Pawel pulled him down by the elbow. "Besides, I have it on good authority from Aniela Kolano . . ."

"Who?" Lind asked.

"Captain Zalecki's favorite whore. I have it on good authority that I beat you both by two inches, easy."

A guffaw of laughter went round the table. "Not by the size of your boots," Piotr said.

Lind reached for the jug, realized it was empty, and called for more. He left it another half hour or more before he stretched and said, "So what's next, the fighting like a demon or the rutting like a boar? I'm for the rutting, personally. Where do you gentlemen recommend?"

"There's Maksimilian's," Longin said, "or Madame Irenka."

"What about this famous Aniela whateverhernameis? If I'm going to measure up to the hero of Tevshenna, I should stand up and be counted." He gestured an enormous erection, bringing another peal of laughter.

"You'll find her at the Winged Hussar at the other end of town." Pawel waved an arm in the vague direction of outside.

"Right." Lind stood, knocked over the stool he'd been sitting on, wobbled, and fell into an undignified heap on the floor. It wasn't altogether feigned. He'd lost track of how many jugs had been passed around, but he was certainly not *that* drunk.

"Steady there." Someone from another table picked him up and set him upright. He shrugged off the strange hands and didn't even look round.

"Gentlemen." He leaned on the table and grinned foolishly at his new friends. "It seems I have exceeded my capacity for refreshment, and should I follow you all to the Winged Hussar, I should indeed be fucking like a bear—a hibernating one. Have a thrust of your sabres for me. I shall retire to my bed while I can still get there and take advantage of Mistress Ani-nelly's pleasures another day."

And with that he wove his unsteady way to the door, out into the yard, and up the steps to his room, shaking from the contact, but extremely satisfied with his evening's work. Aniela Kolano would be getting a visit from him tomorrow. She was as good a place to start as any. Someone had to know where Valdas Zalecki had gone to.

CHAPTER THIRTY-EIGHT
Valdas

VALDAS FOLLOWED KAREL along labyrinthine corridors and up a spiral stone stair, which he was positive was narrower than the stair they'd entered by, though at the time he'd been busy trying to keep a step ahead of the point of the guard's murderous halberd.

"Are we going to Tsarina Zofia?" Valdas asked.

"Speak not her name, peasant!" Karel huffed the words between gasps as the steps began to take their toll. He was older than he looked. "Bow when brought into her presence . . . and only answer what she asks. Do not . . . turn your back on her."

"I know how to behave, Igor Karel, don't worry."

Karel stopped, turned, and held up the lantern to look at Valdas's face, getting his breathing under control before saying, "She asked to see you in private. Rest assured the room is secure, and it will only take one word to see you dead at her feet."

"I mean the Tsarina no harm."

"So she seems to think."

Karel turned. They were now at the top of a long stone corridor, narrow, bare, and cold, probably a servants' access corridor. He stopped and tapped on a door. It opened a crack and after a whispered conversation with someone on the other side it swung open. A tall dark-skinned woman ushered Valdas through into a brightly lit antechamber, then left. The door clicked shut and he was alone.

He blinked. After the dim prison and the flickering lantern, the blaze of expensive candles glittering off crystal was almost painful. He screwed up his eyes as if he was in bright sunlight.

"They say I am the light of Ruthenia, but I fancy they're only looking at my surroundings. The tsar believes in keeping up appearances."

"Majesty." Valdas turned quickly and swept a low bow to the woman who had entered the room behind him. He'd had his back turned. That was one of Karel's rules broken. He stayed where he was, chin almost on his knees.

"Get up, man. I'll wager Igor has been trying to preserve my dignity again."

"Majesty."

He stood and looked at her properly for the first time. A shiver ran through him. Zofia was a female version of her brother. She had Konstantyn's slender nose, his green eyes and slightly pointed chin, but what had been strong features on Konstantyn were, if not beautiful, remarkably striking on Zofia. She wore no baubles or outward sign of her position, yet he would have known her for a queen in any crowd.

"I do remember you." She studied his face. "You were captain of my brother's High Guard the last time I visited my lady mother."

"Yes, Majesty."

"He had trust in you."

"Yes, Majesty."

"And now he's dead by your hand and you stand here before me." The tone of her voice made Valdas's blood run cold. "Tell me, Captain Zalecki, why I should not have you sawn in half and your head boiled and sent to your king."

"Majesty, truly, I did not kill your brother nor by any action did I cause him to be killed. I would be more than foolish to present myself here if I did. If you don't believe me, say the word and I will sharpen the saw myself. I'm here seeking justice."

"Justice, you say. For whom? Yourself?"

"Majesty, for my Lord King Konstantyn and for my men."

"They say your accomplices named you as the assassin. They were executed."

"Under torture any man may be made to confess to crucifying the Christ himself, Majesty. And now they are too dead to recant."

"You have doubts?" The flash in her eyes when she said that told him that if he did have doubts he'd better be able to justify them. He pushed down the lump in his throat that was rising to choke him.

"Doubts? I wouldn't presume, but I have questions, Majesty."

"Let's hear them, man!"

She spun round and sat in a velvet-upholstered chair. Valdas remained standing, unconsciously at parade-ground attention until given permission to relax. She gave him no such permission.

"On the night that King Konstantyn took his last breath, I was not in the Gura . . . though I can't think that was any more than chance. The king had chastised me for not taking time off, and I had gone down to the Low City. When I heard the Didelis Bell, I tried to return to my duty, only to find that within an hour of my king's death Lord Gerhard had declared himself for the Amber Crown. The High Guard, all except me, were dead by his order and I was already a hunted man."

She drew a sharp breath. "So quickly?"

"Yes, Majesty."

Valdas let the silence work for him. Her face was a mask, brows drawn together. She rubbed her lips with one finger.

"Majesty, may I speak?"

She inclined her head.

"Once I learned that, as well as my king, my men were also dead—twenty of them, Majesty, all good men and loyal to King Konstantyn with their last breath—it seemed to me that fleeing the city was the least of the crimes that had been committed that night. I entertained some foolish notion of living to bring the king's assassin—or better still the power behind him—to justice."

"You think it's Gerhard?"

"I don't know, Majesty. I would have sworn Gerhard had no such ambitions, but who knows what a man will do for the Amber Crown."

She waved one hand to tell him to continue.

"When my blood cooled I realized that one man, especially one whose face is known throughout the Gura, can do nothing alone. I went first to Chancellor Skorny's country estate only to find him sick and dying." If she didn't believe him, Zofia would kill him—slowly. "I could have fled to Kassubia or Sverija or even over the wide sea to the Anglu islands, but I swore an oath of loyalty to my king, and his killer is still free and unnamed."

"And so you have come to me."

He nodded, not sure how convincing he'd been so far. Time for all-or-nothing.

"I didn't know what to do. An assassin could have been employed by Kassubia, by Sverija, or . . ."

"Or even by the Ruthenian Tsar. You can say it. I would have thought the same, but I can assure you that we had no hand in my brother's murder."

Valdas felt one worry fade away. "Nor is it likely to be Sverija, so the finger points either at Kassubia or at someone inside the Gura itself."

"It's not Kassubia. I have an ambassador there, and the ambassador has a shadow man whose information he trusts."

Valdas dipped his head. "When first I set out to come here, I thought that I would ask you to send me to the court in Kassubia with one of your delegations so I might discover the truth for myself, but . . . things happened on the way." He shrugged. "Majesty, do you believe in dreams—that in dreams we might find that wisdom that escapes us in our waking hours?"

She sucked breath in through her teeth. "My belief is not for you to question."

"Of course not. I apologize. I don't believe in things which I cannot see." *Oh, go on, Valdas, dig yourself a deeper hole.* "Except for our Lord God in Heaven and the counter-world below, of course."

"Stop rambling, man, I'm not your confessor. You had a dream."

"I was injured on my journey; beaten, knocked senseless. The Bakaishans saved my life, nursed me back to health. Whilst I was recovering, it came to me that those forgotten dreams of the night should be remembered." He tried to minimize Mirza's involvement. "In the spirit world my Lord King Konstantyn said to me: *Zavonia is in great danger. I have sown a seed. My seed must be allowed to flourish and grow.*"

"You're sure?" Tsarina Zofia's voice took on a new quality, sharp and excited at the same time.

"Yes, Majesty. Sure of what was said, but less sure of its meaning. I think I should return to Zavonia, but Mirza said . . ."

"Mirza is your witch?"

"She's a healer. I don't entirely believe . . ."

"Does she spirit-walk?"

"I . . ."

"It's a simple question. Does she spirit-walk?"

He nodded. "She says so, Majesty."

God in Heaven, he hoped he hadn't signed Mirza's death warrant.

Zofia fell silent. She rubbed her lips again with the fingers of her right hand and stared at her knee as if looking for enlightenment, then she looked up. Valdas stood a little taller, a little straighter, a little more at attention.

"Oh, relax, soldier. At ease," she said.

He came to parade-ground rest again, feet slightly apart, hands clasped in front of him.

"The news from Zavonia is not good," she said. "My Uncle Gerhard has made some . . . odd decisions for a man newly thrust onto the throne." She frowned. "Did you know Queen Kristina has disappeared—and that she was with child?"

"What? No!" His demeanor slipped, but he hurriedly regained his position.

"It seems my brother did sow a seed. No one knew, apparently. Except maybe Konstantyn himself, and most probably Kristina's trusted court ladies. I had the news two days ago from one of my informants. It took a long time to reach me and I'm unsure as to the timing of this event."

"If Konstantyn has an heir . . ."

"Quite. Kristina's child, not Gerhard, is the rightful ruler. Yet Gerhard didn't declare himself regent, he declared himself king. We are invited to his coronation at the midwinter feast, three months hence."

"Majesty, has anyone had news of Queen Kristina since the king's death? Is she . . . well?"

"You have asked the very question I want an answer to. I have sent to King Karl Gustav to see if he has had word of Kristina, but even the fastest courier I have can't return from Sverija before the month is out, maybe even six weeks. In the meantime, my brother's seed may be in grave danger if it is all that stands between an ambitious man and the Amber Crown."

She tapped her lips with her index finger and gave him a piercing look. "You would recognize Kristina?"

"Yes, of course. Copper hair and a face you don't forget in a hurry."

"Then you shall return to Zavonia. I want my brother's child out of harm's way, and political channels are too slow. My informant tells me that a trader called Maksimilian may have more connections to the Sverijan Royal House than any Zavonian trader might safely boast of. That may be a good place to start."

"Maksimilian. I know him. He keeps a clean whoreho . . . tavern. Good God! A Sverijan spy in my city and I didn't know it."

"I charge you with this, Valdas. If you want to regain your good name, find Konstantyn's child. I want him—or her—here, safe under my roof, and Kristina too."

I bet you do, my Lady Tsarina. How would it be if you had the heir to Zavonia under your control?

Was this another attempt to steal Konstantyn's throne? Maybe. Oh, God in Heaven, if he brought her the heir, he would be delivering Zavonia into Ruthenia's hands.

He wanted to turn and bolt from the room. Instead he bowed.

"Majesty. I will find and protect the heir." *But not for you.* He didn't add that.

"The Landstrider witch."

"Mirza, Majesty."

"Take her with you and don't bring her back. If I find her in Bieloria again I'll have her burned at the stake. Do you understand me?"

"Yes, Majesty."

"You can requisition a purse and whatever you need for your journey from Igor Karel. A troop of cavalry will accompany you to the border, and I'll be sending someone into Zavonia with you. You will know them by my token." She held out a small gold disk, intricately engraved. "My insurance that you'll do as you say."

His heart sank.

"Thank you, Majesty." He bowed low, sensing the interview was at an end. By the time he stood up, she'd left, and he never spotted where her private door was.

◈━━◈

"We're meeting Zofia's agent? Who?" Mirza glared at Valdas as though it was his fault.

"I don't know." Valdas shrugged. "He'll be joining us at the border, I think."

"As long as it's not that Igor Karel," Mirza said as she stood shivering on the doorstep of the guard room. "He gives me the ants."

"The what?" Valdas put his arm out and pulled her under his cloak. She hadn't really warmed up yet from her stay in the cell, and her own cloak had disappeared from her pack when their horses and gear had been returned. Valdas wouldn't have allowed petty pilfering in the Gura.

"The feeling that ants are running all over my bare skin."

"Euww." Valdas pulled a face. "I don't think Karel could keep up with us. He doesn't look very fit. Though it would make him easier to lose."

"An extra fighter through the Tevecor Reaches could be useful," Mirza said. "I heard the jailers talking about trouble there recently."

Valdas dropped his voice even lower. "Zavonia is vulnerable. With the dowager queen and the rightful heir in the hands of Ruthenia, there would be war within months. Maybe we keep him with us through the Reaches, but we'll need to lose him before we find Kristina."

"But Zofia is from Zavonia—she's Konstantyn's sister—surely she won't want to destabilize . . ."

"Zofia is a Petrova now, mother to the heir of Ruthenia's throne. She probably wants to deliver Zavonia lock, stock, and barrel, to her son. She may even believe she has more right to it than Gerhard, and she probably has. If she'd still been at home and unwed, the crown would have been hers. It's only the fact that she renounced any claim by marrying into Ruthenia's royal house that gave Gerhard the throne in the first place."

"From what you've told me, if she'd still been at home, she'd be dead by now."

"Possibly."

They were interrupted by the guard captain and a small troop of ten leading twelve horses into the yard, ready to ride. Donkey was nowhere to be seen.

"Where's my horse?" Valdas asked.

"And mine," Mirza added.

The captain's eyebrows knitted together in a frown. "I was ordered to outfit you with two good horses, and these are two of the finest from the tsarina's stable."

"I don't doubt that they are fine, but I want my own . . . our own horses returned to us."

Igor Karel came out of a door opposite. "Is there a problem?"

"Our horses," Valdas said. "Mine's a dull-looking thing with long ears and Mirza's is an iron gray."

"It sounds as though there would be others better suited," Karel said.

Valdas ignored Karel and eyeballed the captain. His voice dropped to the kind of low whisper that carried to any errant recruit in the training yard. "Our own horses, Captain. Thank you."

The captain looked uncertain.

"We'll come with you and identify them."

Without being openly discourteous, the captain had run out of arguments. He indicated the way to the stables. Valdas and Mirza stalked past him.

The stable yard was in better condition than the palace. The building, four ranges around an open quadrangle, showed signs of recent repairs, and the quadrangle, paved with stone setts, had been swept clean of muck. Valdas drew breath. It smelled clean and well run. At least their horses would have been well taken care of.

A stableman came out at their approach, and dipped his head in deference to the captain.

"Two horses, belonging to these people. They would have been brought in yesterday."

"Morning," Mirza added. "An iron gray and a brown with long ears."

The stableman's mouth turned down and he rubbed the cheek of his arse.

"I see you know the one we mean," Valdas said. "Quick with his teeth."

"He is, indeed. Needs a good thrashing, that one."

"That's not for you to say or do," Valdas said. "I used to think the same, but he's proved his worth. Where is he?"

A loud braying whinny announced exactly where Donkey was. Valdas pushed past the stableman and stalked into the left-hand range of stalls. He blinked at the sudden gloom. The whinny came again, accompanied by a plate-sized hoof stomping on the cobbles. Valdas followed the commotion to where a stable boy hovered outside a stall with tall sides. Donkey's tail swished angrily and his hind feet stomped side to side, giving the lad no chance to slip into the stall with the bucket of feed.

The lad said something in a strong dialect that was close enough to Ruthenian for Valdas to recognize the word for devil.

"I suppose he is if you don't win his trust," Valdas said, taking the bucket from the lad. He reached out to put a hand on Donkey's rump.

"Nonono!" The stable boy put a warning hand on Valdas's arm.

"It's all right." Valdas shook off the boy's hand as Donkey's rump swung toward him. "Ha! Donkey, it's me." He slapped his hand down on donkey's hindquarters. "Move over and mind your manners."

Donkey's braying whinny turned into a loud whicker and he stilled.

"That's a good boy. Steady now." Valdas edged up past the horse's side to the front of the stall. Donkey was tied tight, too tight, with his nose up against the wall. Valdas kept his voice low as he unbuckled the head-collar rather than trying to pick at the knot in the rope, pulled tight by Donkey's antics. "There, boy, that's better, isn't it?"

Valdas lifted the bucket of feed. Donkey didn't wait for him to pour it into the manger; he stuck his nose in the bucket and began to munch. When the bucket was empty, Donkey tossed his head and rolled his eyes as if to say: *You left me!*

As Valdas placed the bucket in a corner, Donkey snaked his head around and his teeth snapped on empty air about a finger's width from Valdas's backside.

"I love you, too," Valdas said and called for the stable boy to bring Donkey's tack.

In the next stall, Mirza's iron gray was much better mannered, but he could hear her laughing and thought she was probably laughing at him.

At length, with both horses saddled, they emerged into the stable yard. The captain eyed up Donkey and shrugged, as if to say, *you prefer that to a mount from the tsarina's stable?*

Valdas simply smiled.

Igor Karel had followed them to the stable yard, trailing a page loaded with two packs and two bedrolls. Karel motioned for the page to hand them over, never looking Mirza in the face once. Ridiculous prejudice. Konstantyn would have been furious with his sister.

Valdas took Donkey's reins, and the big horse laid back his oversized ears and snaked his mouth toward Valdas's backside again, snapping yellow slab teeth in empty air.

"I missed you, too." Valdas slapped the side of the horse's neck affectionately.

He checked the packs, handed one to Mirza, and strapped his behind Donkey's saddle.

Turning to Karel he said, "My sword?"

Karel gave him a sour look and said something to one of the guards in rapid Ruthenian. The young man returned with the ungainly sword. Valdas strapped it on and loosened the blade in the scabbard to make sure it hadn't rusted solid. He felt on safer ground with Karel since the tsarina had given her orders.

"We'll need something warm for Mirza to wear. Her cloak is missing. It doesn't seem to have been returned." He reached out and brushed an imaginary speck of dust from Karel's fine fur-lined cloak. He wasn't too much taller than Mirza. The garment wouldn't bury her like his own would. *Come on, Karel. Get the idea!*

Karel shrugged the cloak off his shoulders and stood in the yard in his kaftan. Handing it over to Mirza, he still managed not to look her in the face.

"Thank you, Igor Karel." She settled the cloak on her shoulders, sighed and smiled. "Ready warmed. Very nice." She fastened it at the throat and swung into her saddle easily. "I will return it to you via one of my family one day."

He made a choking sound. "Please, consider it a gift."

"A gift given freely to a Bakaishan shulam. That earns you both a blessing and a fortune."

Because he kept his eyes fixed somewhere around her knee, Karel didn't see the sparkle in her eyes, or the corners of her mouth twitch as she leaned down from her saddle and touched his head as a priest might do. Valdas suppressed a smile and noticed the captain of the troop did the same.

Mirza was enjoying herself now. "May the light of the one god shine on you, Igor Karel, your wife, your strong sons and fecund daughters. I see an old age surrounded by many fat grandchildren."

"Err . . . Thank you. I think."

Valdas mounted Donkey and with a nod to the captain made ready to ride. He barely kept the laughter in check until they were out of the gate. "Fat grandchildren? Did you really see fat grandchildren?"

Mirza looked at him sideways and grinned. "The art of a good fortune teller is always working out what they want to hear. I happen to know that he's recently taken a bride twenty years his junior."

"How?"

"I *listen*."

CHAPTER THIRTY-NINE
Mirza

MIRZA WAS GLAD to be safely leaving Bieloria with Valdas at her side. Waiting alone in that dank cell had been fraught with imagined bad ends, from being left there to rot, to burning on a pyre. Bieloria didn't welcome her kind, and she was doubly damned: Landstrider and shulam!

It was a two-day ride to Fort Tevec at cavalry pace, and their escort, Captain Hirokov, not having had any instructions to the contrary, commandeered rooms and food for them as well as for himself and his men, first at a wayside tavern and then at a farmhouse. Mirza would not have consigned the owners of a farm to sleep in their own barn so that she could sleep in a bed, but it seemed to be normal practice for Hirokov and his men, so she said nothing.

Valdas muttered quietly when Hirokov wasn't listening. "It's not a good way to get support from the locals when you most need it. Konstantyn always insisted on paying for goods requisitioned whilst on campaign. You have to treat country people right if you want them at your back rather than circling around behind you with sharpened scythes."

"Your Konstantyn sounds like a wise commander."

"He was."

Still, the bed was comfortable. Mirza shuffled over to make room for Valdas, naked and already erect.

She threw one leg over him and sat upright.

"Oh, my lovely girl."

He ran his hands down her body, then held her hips and guided her into place.

"Ah!" She loved the feel of him inside her, solid and enthusiastic. It was the safest feeling in the world. It was the opposite of lonely. Was there a Zavonian word for that?

"Do all men make love every night?" she asked him as she flopped by his side afterward.

"It's not every night."

"It has been so far, at least since the first time."

"I was making up for the number of times I slept under your wagon alone."

"Alone except for your hand."

"Mistress Hand and her five lovely daughters have often kept me company." He chuckled. "We don't take the fairer sex on campaign, and I've never craved the company of men, even pretty ones."

They lay together, Mirza comfortably curled up in the crook of his arm, waiting for sleep to come.

"What's that you whisper every night? I know you're saying something, but I don't hear it properly. Are you praying?"

"No. Yes. Almost. It's the names of all my men who were executed by Konstantyn's successor. I've vowed to avenge them. I'm sorry, I didn't mean to disturb you."

"You didn't—disturb me, I mean. Say them out loud. I want to hear. I met them, don't forget, in the spirit world."

"All right. Henryk Zehrin. He was my second in command, a good man and a good commander. Then there's Lukas Grinius, Bartek Andrulis, Darius Kairys, Hector Bakaitis—he used to play practical jokes on the others and once caught me with a bucket of water balanced above a door. To be fair, it wasn't meant for me. I was in the wrong place at the wrong time and got a soaking for it. Then there was Raulo Budrys, Feliks Kleiza, Iwan Matonis, Valter Mekas, Matis Liepa, Kajus Janutis, Eberhard Brunner, Vadim and Filip Rimkus, birth brothers. Vadim was the oldest by just eleven months. Sandor Nowak, Fabius Adomatis, Tavas Varnas and Tavas Kleizer—we called them by their surnames, otherwise it got complicated. Leonas Smetona, Jerzy Polonsky, Petras Mazur, Waldemar Konopka. And then there's Konstantyn, second of his name. King of Zavonia. I owe them all. I hope they don't think I've forgotten them while we search for the queen."

"I'm sure they know you'd never do that."

At Fort Tevec, arriving late afternoon, they were given a rye-bread-and herring-heavy meal with the troopers, and for the night a spartan cubicle with two narrow cots, which were impossible to make love in without alerting every sleeping soldier in the other cubicles. Hirokov had delivered information about the Tevecor Reaches while they rode, so Valdas updated Mirza as they prepared to roll into their mean beds, too tired to do more than strip off their outer garments and footwear.

"Hirokov knows much more than I'm comfortable with." Valdas shook his head. "He's altogether too interested in the disputed lands, as if Ruthenia is planning to take them back. If they did, I'm sure the people would welcome them. Konstantyn poured his own money into the Tevecor Reaches to build roads. He even built schools and hospitals. He was determined that if Ruthenia ever tried to take the region its own people would not support the invaders. In just a few months Gerhard has reversed all that."

"It can't be that bad. Not so soon." Mirza sat on the edge of her bed and dragged off a boot.

"Here, let me." Valdas pulled off her other boot and rubbed her foot, working his thumbs gently but firmly round her arch and cupping her cold toes to warm them. "Hirokov says that the first thing King Gerhard did was withdraw the money for the hospitals, and Cardinal Pieritz recalled the ministering brothers to Biela Miasto. The hospitals were looted and stripped clean almost immediately. There were conflicting reports, according to Hirokov. Some say it was bandits calling themselves Cossacks, though they're not really; others say it was the locals, sharing out supplies before bandits could take them."

"The Tevecor Reaches have always been dangerous, haven't they?"

"It seems there are more bandits than ever scattered throughout the hills now and the border barons are taking no action. Secretly they'll be pleased if the country goes to hell and they can wrest power from the sejims. Swap." He let go of her foot and signaled for her to give him the other one, which she did.

"I thought we'd cleaned a lot of the bandits out, but when the living is marginal and it's already ingrained in the culture, there are always those who'll take the easy way. Gerhard is playing into their hands. He's placed a tax levy on the towns and villages and a one-in-ten manpower conscription to augment the infantry."

"The new king is planning a war."

"Defensive or offensive, though?"

"Does it matter?"

Valdas looked up from Mirza's delicate foot. "It matters. Something is very wrong."

Hirokov rose at dawn to see them on their way and walked through the walled town with them, their horses' hooves clopping on the cobbles of the main thoroughfare.

"I understood Tsarina Zofia was sending someone with us." Valdas looked around.

"I imagine whoever it is will meet you a little way down the road. Tsarina Zofia's agents are not from our ranks. She keeps their identity secret, even from us, though from time to time someone will ride across the border with a token that ensures our absolute cooperation."

"I know the token."

"Anyone carrying one of those from the tsarina may command any officer of any rank, maybe save for the general himself, and even then I'm not sure." He shrugged. "But what do I know of politics? I'm only a simple army captain."

Valdas gave him a sideways look and raised one eyebrow. "I used to think that, my friend, but the world changes."

"I wish you safe travels." Hirokov shook Valdas's hand and gave a half bow to Mirza and smiled. "Mistress Mirza, please don't wish fat grandchildren on me."

Mirza grinned. "I wouldn't dream of it. For you, Captain Hirokov, a natural death beneath the silken sheets of an expensive whore, many, many years hence."

"I'd take that one myself, Hirokov, if she has something similar in her store of fortunes." Valdas laughed.

"Don't ask me about yours, Valdas, not ever." Mirza shook her head. She saw the look on his face and quickly smiled once more at Hirokov.

"Come on." She urged her mount forward and into Zavonia.

CHAPTER FORTY

Valdas

THE TEVECOR REACHES had changed.

Valdas had been stationed here after Tevshenna. They'd been rebuilding, trying to heal the wounds left by two warring armies. By the time he'd been transferred to Biela Miasto, he'd been able to see some real improvements. Two years ago he'd returned with Konstantyn and had been happy with the changes made by ripping some of the power out of the hands of squabbling border barons and putting it into the hands of local sejims. His new roads and innovative ideas, schools for the sons of artisans and freemen-farmers, and church-run hospitals for the sick had been popular with the locals.

The people here were honest and hardworking—mostly—but for many years there had been a culture of small rebellions against the barons, with popular local heroes living as bandits, overturning the rule of law for a time, usually with country support, until they met their fate on the gallows or ran for safety. Konstantyn had known that it would be easy for the crown to become the new target for angry young men full of righteous indignation and hot blood, so he'd channeled their energy into fair employment.

That seemed to have been abandoned.

For the first half day after leaving Fort Tevec, their road ran broad and level, with stone-paved wagon tracks that kept it from degrading to mire and ruts. As the road began to wind up the side of a deep valley toward a high moorland plateau, they passed a small quarry that cut a bite some sixty feet wide and thirty feet deep out of the hillside with a stack of paving slabs made from the quarry's own stone leaning against each other in a neat block, ready for laying. Yet, within a mile, the paved wagon track ended. Earlier wheel ruts still showed in the summer-baked earth, though autumn and winter would soon re-map it into fresh channels. A little further along, a second quarry that had barely been broached told the story of work abandoned. Whatever stone had been cut had been removed, leaving a few broken flagstones in a jumbled mess.

"The local economy is already reabsorbing Konstantyn's goodwill." Valdas scowled. "When I think what so many gave to win this land, and the efforts Konstantyn put in to ensure that we keep it and the goodwill of its people . . ." He shook his head. "It's a terrible waste. What's King Gerhard thinking of? Does he want another border war? If he does, he's going about it the right way. Ivan Petrov will be across that border in an eyeblink if he thinks he can retake the Tevecor Reaches while Gerhard is napping."

He lapsed into silence, letting memories of Tevshenna and its aftermath chase themselves around his head. He remembered little of the battle itself except noise and stink, dust in his throat and grit in his eyes. Being celebrated as a hero afterward had always been an embarrassment, but eventually it was one of the things that had singled him out as being worthy to promote to Konstantyn's personal service. He'd promoted young Tomas Gaida shortly afterward, the only one of his men to survive Konstantyn's assassination—at least he hoped Tomas had had the good sense to get out of Biela Miasto. He might even be here in the Tevecor Reaches, though according to Hirokov the hussar units had been the first to be withdrawn after Konstantyn's death.

It was as if King Gerhard was inviting Ruthenia to attack. But why? It made no sense.

"Ahead."

Mirza's warning snapped him out of his recollections and he silently cursed his foolishness. This road was too dangerous for dreaming.

A lone mounted figure faced them some two hundred yards distant, sabre sheathed, but fully armed. Valdas's hand went to his own weapon, but he didn't draw it.

"Our watchdog, do you think?" he asked Mirza quietly.

"Could be."

"Keep a little behind me and stay clear of my sword arm."

"I won't argue with you."

"For once."

He nudged Donkey forward and Mirza dropped behind half a length. The rider didn't move. He gave no telltale glance to either side of the road to where others might be hidden and, indeed, he'd picked a section of road clear of cover for some distance.

Valdas reined in about two lengths in front of the rider and felt Mirza pull up behind him, still giving him room to maneuver if he needed it. *Good girl.* She might argue endlessly, but he was glad to see that when it counted she knew how to take orders, though she'd probably give him hell later for giving them so high-handedly.

The man was tall, with skin black as midnight, younger than Valdas expected, with a fine-boned and beardless face and short dark hair that curled tightly to his head. Three ridged scars ran parallel down each cheek from ear to chin. He wore a black, high-necked kontusz, tightly fitted to the waist and closed with six parallel sets of braid. Below the waist it was flared and split for riding, and beneath it peeped black trousers and boots.

"Well, not what I expected at all." Mirza spoke low under her breath.

Not what Valdas had been expecting either, but when the stranger held out a token he recognized it instantly.

"Valdas Zalecki at your service." Valdas inclined his head and half turned. "And this is Mirza of the Bakaishans."

"Dahnay of Ethiop, in the service of Her Majesty Tsarina Zofia Petrova of Ruthenia," the man said in a light tenor voice, his accent slightly clipped.

There didn't seem to be much to say after that. Dahnay turned his horse and rode in front while Valdas and Mirza rode together silently, about ten paces behind, not feeling at ease to talk about the one subject he wanted to discuss, as the subject himself was riding within earshot.

"It will be dark within the hour," Valdas eventually called out.

Dahnay nodded and pointed ahead. "A way-hut up ahead," he called back.

"He must have eagle eyes," Valdas said.

"Even an eagle can't see round corners," Mirza said. "My bet is on an earlier scouting trip, or more intimate knowledge of the country hereabouts."

Whichever theory was correct, Dahnay's way-hut materialized around the next bend. Built in the time-honored manner in which man had sheltered from the elements in years gone by, it was a circular hut of stones lime-mortared together into a single, windowless, beehive-shaped vault with a center hole for smoke to leech out, once the inside was so full that breathing was damn near impossible. It was

trenched into the ground about two feet deep with a low doorway that
Valdas practically had to bend double to get inside. He'd been in
worse accommodations. The floor of stamped earth held a flat hearth-
stone in the center. Around the inner circumference ran a foot-high
ledge that served as seating or beds. A couple of crumbled peat bricks
showed where the fire-fuel was normally stacked. It was customary for
travelers to use fuel and replenish it for the next traveler to follow, but
it was obvious that the system had been much abused of late.

"I didn't want a fire anyway." Mirza shrugged. "We have bread and
cold meat for tonight."

Dahnay paced around the hut, which didn't take long because it
was barely fifteen feet across on the inside.

"I'll take first watch," he said.

Valdas went outside to see to Donkey and to fetch what food they
needed for the evening meal. Mirza followed him out and saw to her
own horse, glancing first at Dahnay and then making wide-eyes as if
to say, *What do you make of him?*

Valdas shrugged. He didn't know the answer yet. The tsarina's
agent didn't look like a soldier, but he wasn't stupid enough to underestimate him. He wondered whether he'd get the opportunity to see
Dahnay in action, then grinned to himself. *Be careful what you wish
for, Valdas.*

Dahnay seemed pleasant enough. They shared supper and incon-
sequential small talk.

"You're a long way from home, Dahnay."

Dahnay nodded.

"How many languages do you speak?" Valdas asked.

"Including my own, six, though my Sverijan needs improvement
I'm told."

"You must travel a lot," Mirza said.

"For my tsarina." Dahnay inclined his head.

"Do you ever go back to your home? To Ethiop?"

Dahnay shook his head. "I have nothing there . . . except,
perhaps . . ." He looked up at the overcast gray sky. "I miss the sun."

Valdas nodded. "Home is never as you remember when you go
back. Take it from me." He'd been to visit his grandfather only once,
after Tevshenna. The surly old man he'd remembered had shrunk into
old age. His brother had married a buxom widow with three sons and
had another child on the way. The estate was prosperous, but unwel-
coming. His grandfather railed at him for leaving, was unimpressed
with his promotion. His new sister-in-law eyed him with suspicion lest

he want a share of the estate. The sons largely ignored him, taking their lead from their mother. His brother had studiously addressed his food and said little. Valdas had not even stayed the night.

Mirza's eyes teared up. Valdas put out a hand and touched her shoulder briefly. "Homesick?"

She sniffed. "It seems silly, doesn't it? I haven't lived in the same place for more than a few weeks since I was a child. Always moving on, or being moved. Always hoping to find a new homeland."

"Home is people, not places," Dahnay said, and stood to take first watch.

CHAPTER FORTY-ONE
Lind

LIND SLID INTO a seat by the window and stared round the almost empty room of the Winged Hussar. The walls were plain rough plaster, soot-marked from the cheap tallow candles in the wall sconces. A woman, probably one of the whores by her dress, scraped a passable tune out of a rough-hewn fiddle. Another whore sat as if listening, her skirts bunched up to show a great deal of calf and ankle. Above the fireplace was a badly executed painting of a hussar in full armor, wings strapped to his back, riding a flashy white steed rearing above the barrel of a cannon that was discharging shot while the gunners fled for their lives. Smoke swirled around horse and rider, making it seem as if they were flying out of Heaven like avenging angels. Tevshenna, Lind thought, the greatest battle fought by the winged hussars in the last fifty years and always the one they harked back to. Zalecki had been at Tevshenna, had led that mad charge into a line of artillery and somehow managed to beat the odds and rout the Ruthenians once and for all.

Not only Zalecki, of course, but Zalecki had been the hero of the day and it had earned him a place in the High Guard, the King's chosen men.

The door opened and three youngsters entered, young enough, or poor enough, to be still in tunics rather than in full-length zupans. They took a table by the fireplace and one smiled at the whore showing her legs, only to receive a dead-eye stare in return. It was early enough for the whores not to bother touting for business. They had a long night ahead of them.

A skinny boy brought Lind a jug of ale and a tankard and sloshed almost as much over the table as he managed to get in the pot. Lind tossed him a copper for the ale and a copper for himself.

"Aniela Kolano?" he asked.

The lad nodded toward the woman playing the fiddle. On his way back to the serving board, he gave a short sharp whistle and jerked his head toward Lind. The woman bent forward from the hips without missing a note and swayed in time to the tune.

A middle-aged man stomped in and let the door swing shut noisily behind him. He wore a fine zupan, buttoned up to the neck and tied with a crimson sash under an open woolen kontusz trimmed at the edges with fur. The pot-boy picked up the jug of sour ale again, but he waved him away and instead called the landlord for a pint of Rhenish and a plate of goulash.

Lind flipped a coin in the air and caught it again, then raised one eyebrow at the overblown whore still fiddling on the other side of the rapidly filling room. She was older than he expected, thirty-some at least, and her fair hair was more like straw than gold. Could this be Zalecki's favorite fuck? She must have a lot more going for her than was apparent on the surface. She left Lind unmoved. He hadn't expected anything else.

The tunic boys started stamping in time to the music and some of the newcomers clapped along, driving the rhythm until the whore finished with a flourish that left them applauding. She handed the fiddle to the other whore, who scraped a note or two and then began to sing a bawdy song, something about a bull, a billy-goat, and a fine mare.

Aniela Kolano cupped her breasts and pushed them up so her cleavage bulged over the neck of her letnik and waggled her shoulders at Lind. The pale flesh wobbled slightly. She inclined her head. The question was obvious. *You want some?*

He flipped the coin again and nodded. Four off-duty army types passed between them on their way to an empty table, but when they left a clear view the whore was gone.

He stood up to look for her and nearly jumped out of his skin when a voice close to his ear said, "For four coppers I suck you off, eight coppers for a fuck, and an extra two coppers for a sheath. I don't fuck without a sheath. House rules. A silver tolar gets you all night and as many fucks as you can get it up for. Sheaths included for free."

The hand that had been automatically reaching for his knife reached into his purse instead, and he pulled out a whole silver tolar.

"Come with me, lover. You'll not be disappointed."

"Oh, I'm sure I won't be."

She led him up a wooden stair to a corridor with four doors and pushed open the first one. There was a low bed covered in a relatively clean sheet, a chair and a chest with a bowl of water and a towel. Next to it was a pile of gut sheaths. He looked at them with distaste.

She saw where he was looking. "You got your own?"

He shook his head, feeling himself freeze under her expectations. Even knowing this was just a ruse to get her on her own, the very idea of sex weighed heavily on him.

"Come on then, lover, no need to be shy." She unbuttoned the let-nik and instead of layers of undergarments she was stark naked beneath it. She shrugged it off her shoulders, let it drop, and stepped away from its folds all soft curves and bobbing breasts. "You like what you see?"

He was going to lie and say yes, but his voice let him down and the word came out as a choked gurgle.

"Not shy, are you, lover? Only we can take it steady and get you in the mood." She stepped in close and cupped his ballocks.

He flinched and cracked her backhanded across the jaw, snapping her head back and knocking her flying onto the bed. He hadn't planned it this way, but his heart raced and he was committed. Before she'd had the opportunity to cry out, he was on her, straddling her naked body and stuffing a corner of the sheet into her mouth until she gagged. She beat at him with her fists but he caught them easily and held both her wrists in one hand and shoved them down hard onto her breasts. A thick gold band inset with three rubies drew his attention. It was too fine a thing for a cheap whore. Where did she get it? With his weight on her thighs and both hands pinned against her chest, he drew out his stiletto as she bucked against him.

"Keep still or I'll fuck you with this!"

Pink fury drained from her face to be replaced by pale fear. She stilled.

"Understand?"

She nodded.

He rested the point of the knife in her belly button, drawing a bead of bright blood, then leaned over it until it was wedged point down between his chest and her naked flesh.

"Move and this dagger's in your guts."

He took a length of silken cord that had been wrapped around and around his wrist and twisted it twice round her neck, and then tied her wrists to the front of her throat with a knot that tightened with every move she made. Wisely, she didn't move.

"All right. I'm going to take the sheet out of your mouth. One squeak and they won't recognize this room for blood and piss and shit. All yours."

She nodded again.

He shuffled sideways and stuck his knee between her legs, opening her up and sitting on one thigh with the length of his stiletto measured against the inside of her other one. He let the point draw blood up close to her cunt and grinned at her indrawn breath. He felt an unaccustomed tightness and his worm of a prick began to stiffen. It was nothing to do with sex and everything to do with power. For a moment he contemplated turning her over and fucking her up the arse like Tourmine used to do to him, but at the thought of Tourmine he wilted.

Business as usual. Better get on with it.

He reached up and pulled the gag out of her mouth. Her breath came in ragged gasps, but she didn't try to scream or call out.

"Good. We've reached an understanding."

"If I'd known you wanted it this rough I'd have charged you a gold schilling."

He slapped her across the cheek, hard, and then the other cheek back-handed.

"You don't get it, do you? I don't want your body, I just want information."

"What information could I possib . . ."

He cut off her words with another slap. "Valdas Zalecki," he growled in her face. "Where's Zalecki?"

"Valdas? How should I know?"

"Because on the night of the king's death he'd gone whoring in the town, and according to some very drunken hussars, that probably means he came to see you."

"Valdas didn't kill the king."

He almost laughed.

"But does he know who did?"

"How should I know?"

"Where is he?"

"I don't know."

"Oh, come on. From what I've heard, Zalecki can't keep it in his pantalones. You want me to believe he hasn't needed your services since the king died. Where is he?"

"I don't know."

"Are you prepared to die for him?" He pricked the inside of her thigh with the point of his stiletto, wondering if he might have to go all the way, but if he killed her he'd never get his answer. He needed something non-lethal but painful. Maybe he'd have to kill her later, or maybe not. He hadn't been paid to gut her and if he didn't need to, he wouldn't.

He straddled her hips again and reached up to her hands, crossed and tied in front of her throat. He touched her gold band. It wasn't on the correct finger to be a marriage band. He turned it idly around her finger, still thinking. Three inset rubies came into view. Curious. The ring took on a meaning of its own. Did she have the protection of some noble lord? Downstairs in the bar he could hear the music. As a rowdy song came to an end and applause and catcalls swelled, he turned his attention to her right hand, took firm hold, and twisted the little finger back. Back and back until it cracked. Her scream sounded loud in his ears but would have been drowned out in the bar. He clamped his hand over her mouth.

"I said no screaming."

She whimpered. Her eyes were wide above his clamped fingers.

"So where is Zalecki?" He moved his hand away.

"I don't know. Gone."

"Gone where?"

He reached for her left hand. "You play the fiddle so prettily. Maybe you can hold the bow with only three fingers on your right hand, but can you finger a tune without the pinky on your left?"

"No, please. Don't."

He pulled the finger back.

"Please . . ."

"Zalecki. Where?"

"Gone from the city. Away. Run away."

He'd been half prepared to believe her until she said that. Zalecki was not a man to simply run away.

"Is he looking for the assassin? Does he know who poisoned the king's fish?"

He pulled her finger back a little more and she gasped.

"I don't know."

He pulled again and she flinched, tightening the cord around her neck.

"What do you know?"

"Valdas didn't kill the king. Please, you've got to believe me."

"Oh, I do, but I still need to find him."

The music below swelled and the crowd gave a roar. He yanked and she screamed again, the little finger on her left hand now twisted to match the right.

He grasped the ring on the middle finger of her left hand. "Eight more to go."

"No, please . . . take the ring. Leave me alone."

"I'm not a thief." He transferred his grip to her third finger and began to twist.

She yelped. "Skorny." She gasped out the word. "He was going to find Chancellor Skorny."

"I heard the old man was dying, though he's taking his time about it."

He pulled her finger back even further. She closed her eyes, but tears leaked out anyway.

"And then . . . to Bieloria. To the tsarina. You'll never catch him there."

"Oh, I can catch him anywhere. Thank you, Aniela. You've been very enlightening."

He eased himself off her hips and retrieved his stiletto. With a couple of practiced moves he untied the knot at her wrists and unwound the cord from her pretty neck, then flipped her over, face down. He twisted the cord around her neck once more, then tightly round both thumbs behind her back, ignoring her bruised and swollen fingers. He crossed her ankles and bent up her legs at the knees, tying the silk around both ankles. If she arched her back and kept her head up she wouldn't choke, but if she moved or even shuffled, or, God forbid, managed to roll off the bed, she'd strangle herself. Just to be sure, he stuffed the corner of the sheet back into her mouth.

He'd paid for the whole night. If he could slip out of the back door unseen, it would be morning before they found her and he'd be long gone from Biela Miasto. He was sick of this place already.

CHAPTER FORTY-TWO

Valdas

VALDAS WOKE IN the dark to take over the watch from Dahnay. He estimated he'd slept for about four hours. His bones ached from the solid bench. On the opposite side of the hut, Mirza mumbled and stirred in her sleep as he quietly shook out the cloak that added an extra layer of warmth to his bedroll. He'd need that outside; the air was chill. Summers were short in the uplands of the Tevecor Reaches and autumn came early. He strapped on his sword and slung the cloak around his shoulders, but didn't fasten it.

His bladder twinged so, bending double under the low door, he stepped outside. Dahnay was nowhere to be seen, but the scrape of boot on dry earth and the splash of liquid told him that the man was about the same business. He undid the drawstring of his pants and pissed against the side of the hut, nodding to Dahnay as the man came round from behind the building. Valdas shook and fastened the drawstring. Settling his tunic and cloak, he looked around.

"Quiet out here," he said.

"I like it that way," Dahnay replied.

"Get some rest. I'm awake now."

Dahnay nodded and ducked into the hut.

Valdas started to turn and heard a hollow thunk. As he fell, he realized that the noise was the sound of something hard hitting the back of his skull as heard from the inside. The ground came up to meet him and he had an oh-no-not-again feeling.

He came to his senses lying on the floor, shivering, hands tied behind him, painfully aware that his cheek was on a sharp rock and his mouth tasted of blood.

He risked opening one eye. His cloak lay in a heap beside him. The sky had paled to mid blue. Christ on a pig, how long had he been out?

Mirza and Dahnay were sitting on the ground outside the stone hut about twelve feet apart. Two men stood over them, flintlocks drawn. Pistols were notoriously inaccurate at anything much more than ten to twenty feet, but close up they were a weapon you didn't argue with.

His heart began to pound. Two there, what about the rest of them?

Another two brought the traveling packs out of the hut. Rather than look through, they tipped the contents of each pack in turn onto the ground, prodding, poking, checking. Unless Dahnay was carrying a lot of coin, they'd be disappointed with their haul. Neither he nor Mirza had much worth stealing. Tsarina Zofia had been generous, but mostly with goods rather than coin. They had a small bag of silver tolars and five gold schillings, which were safely sewn in the seam of Valdas's trousers. He wriggled. No, he didn't think they'd been stripped off him and put on again. That didn't seem likely. If they'd found it, he'd have been lying bare-arsed on the ground. They seemed delighted about something and he realized they'd found the fresh food in the packs, bread, cold meat and hard cheese, some coarse sausage and a couple of onions and some apples. Bruised apples now, he guessed.

Ouch! He tried to move and pain shot through his head. He counted feet within his field of vision. Four of the bastards to deal with. Four against three. Not bad odds if Dahnay could fight. Perhaps he should cause some kind of distraction to take the attention of the men with pistols.

Someone behind him said something about taking turns. That made five. Someone else answered him. Six. Christ! At least six of them. The odds weren't so good now. He fought down fear and began to work calmly at his bonds, slow and steady. He hoped not too slow.

One of the men he'd not been able to see before stepped in front of him, a big bastard in country dress, short, ill-fitting drab green tunic and linen trousers tucked into half-boots. He held his hand out and one of the pair going through the packs handed him a lump of cheese. He pulled his knife from his belt and carved a sliver, tasting it cautiously and then chewing with obvious pleasure. It should be good, it was from Zofia's royal kitchen.

Others took food from Green Tunic. So he was their leader, by the looks of it. Valdas's heart sank. Not six but seven and none of them small except for one, a boy maybe thirteen or fourteen years old, as dark-skinned as Dahnay. Another man spoke. Eight, by God and Perkunas!

Valdas eased his position on the hard ground and drew attention. One of the pair who had been emptying their packs, a barrel-chested man, cursed, stood, and walked over to him, followed by a weasel-faced man. Valdas never saw it coming, but a sharp pain in his side introduced him to the man's boot. God's ballocks! That felt too familiar.

He breathed in, waiting for the stabbing pain, but found only a dull ache. Hopefully no new breaks in his ribs.

"Leave him alone!" Mirza yelled.

No, Mirza, please. Shut up. Don't draw their attention.

Barrel Chest crossed the space to Mirza in four strides and pulled her to her feet. "You're not in a position to be giving orders." He pushed his hand between her trousered thighs and cupped her.

Valdas felt his temper rise, pushing the fear away, but got a kick from the boy, this time in the muscular part of his arse, which wasn't so fragile. He yelped loudly even though on the scale of things the pain hardly registered, but it drew Barrel Chest's attention from Mirza. *Yes, that's right, you bastard, come over here and leave her alone.*

But Barrel Chest wasn't so easily diverted. "Check his bonds," he told the boy. "Make sure they're nice and tight." He turned to Mirza.

Valdas looked over to Dahnay. The man was sitting very still, trying not to draw attention, but a very slight movement in his shoulders showed that he was working on his bonds. Good. Maybe all Valdas could do was to distract these oafs from noticing. His own bonds had been pulled tight again, though he'd felt the boy's hands shaking as he tugged the knots and hoped they weren't as thoroughly tied as before.

Mirza took advantage of the distraction to bend herself almost double, taking her crotch out of Barrel Chest's reach, but the hut wall was behind her. She hit it backside first and catapulted herself at the man's chest, smashing into it as if it was a stone wall, winding herself more than Barrel Chest. Great God, but the man was built like a bear.

The man with the pistol thrust the muzzle right behind her ear and pulled the doghead back. Mirza froze. Valdas held his breath, but Barrel Chest pushed the flintlock muzzle upward to point harmlessly at the sky.

"Don't waste her, Vasily." He turned to Mirza. "It's a little early . . .

I was going to eat first, but if you insist, sweetheart. I like a spirited mare with a few bucks in her."

Valdas began to work on his bonds again. The boy who was supposed to be guarding him was wholly absorbed in the scene that was unfolding a few feet away.

"I'll have her next." The man with the pistol, Vasily, jerked it suggestively and Barrel Chest laughed. "I've seen you work a woman with that thing before, and you left nothing for anyone else. You'd better go last."

He undid his loose pantalones and walked out of them with hardly more than a shuffle. He didn't even need to touch his cock, it was engorged already.

"Who said you could go first?" Green Tunic looked up from the food and jumped to his feet.

"Aww, Martyn, you said you fancied trying the dark one. Come on, man, this thing is ready. I've got to stick it in before I burst." He jerked his hips in a thrusting motion and grasped his cock as if willing it not to shoot too soon.

Valdas's blood seemed to curdle in his veins. The implication wasn't lost on him. There were two others Martyn might try if his tastes ran to sodomy. Another man laughed and Valdas was aware that Dahnay was still sitting very stiff and very still, a pistol practically in his eye. How far had he got with his bonds? Valdas was still working on his own. The boy hadn't tied a very good knot and the rope was already loose.

"Please, Martyn." Barrel Chest almost whimpered.

Martyn's face creased into a grin. "Go on, then. I'll take the other, then little Yusuf here can have a thrust. About time he wet his tackle."

The boy behind Valdas whimpered quietly.

"You want me to hold her for you?" Vasily lowered the doghead on his pistol gently and tucked it into his sash and grabbed Mirza from behind, groping her breasts through her tunic. She struggled, but was held fast. He kicked her on the back of the knees and smacked her down onto the ground. Another man came to help and they took an arm each.

Valdas pulled at his ropes, using more brute force than finesse, his wrists slick with his own blood. They were looser now, but he was running out of time.

Barrel Chest bent over and pushed up Mirza's tunic, then yanked the draw-cord and pulled off her trousers. Her feet were already bare, she must have been sleeping when they came. Naked from the waist down, she looked so vulnerable, but she neither screamed nor begged. Her face had gone beyond terror and her eyes narrowed. She looked more angry than terrified.

"You don't want to do this," she spat at Barrel Chest. "You really don't want to do this."

"Oh, I really do." He took out his long-bladed knife. "Look at me, woman." He held the knife alongside his cock and made obscene thrusting gestures. "Which would you rather have stuck in you, me or sharp steel?" He grasped his cock, angry and straight, and bent to her.

She lashed out with both legs, catching him on the thigh. He roared wordlessly, rubbing where she'd already begun to raise a bruise, and waved the knife.

Martyn laughed. "Don't fillet her yet. You said yourself we shouldn't waste her. Jawel, Lew, a leg each for pity's sake before that proud cock wilts. You can have her next. I'll take the other."

Valdas started forward, hands still tied, but a yank on his bonds and a knife at his throat froze him instantly. He could only watch helpless and seething, impotent with rage and frustration. It took four of them to hold Mirza still and even then her body arched as Barrel Chest descended.

Descended and then recoiled.

Mirza shrieked a curse—primal, raw—words Valdas didn't understand, but every fiber of meat on his bones did. He felt his own cock turn icy cold and his balls pull upward as if they were trying to climb out of his scrotum and cower in his belly. The boy with the knife must have been affected in the same way. His hand wavered and it was all the opportunity Valdas needed. The ropes around his wrists were loose enough and slippery with his own blood. One almighty pull shook them off. He grabbed the boy's knife and twisted one arm behind his back until he felt the shoulder joint pop. The boy screamed in agony and he would have sliced the lad's throat right then and there, but a second high-pitched scream cut through. He turned, thinking at first it was Mirza.

Dahnay had taken advantage of the distraction, and the man who had been holding the pistol over him was now on the ground, motionless. Dahnay had the pistol in his hand but stood transfixed, eyes wide, staring at Mirza and her attackers.

Valdas followed his gaze.

Barrel Chest staggered back, screaming. He dropped his knife and clutched his wilting cock. Smoke rose from between his fingers. His hands began to singe. He let go of his cock. Burned sausage was all that came to Valdas's mind. The man's ballocks began to glow, then smoke. He flapped his charred hands ineffectively and screamed again, one long keening sound that seemed set to never end until he ran out of breath and collapsed to his knees, falling over to hug himself, his bare arse toward the rising sun. For a few seconds no one moved and no one spoke. More smoke, black and greasy, curled upward from between his legs. He stank of burned meat.

His screams turned to whimpers, but were drowned out by a roaring whoosh as his shirt caught fire. Barrel Chest's body was consumed by flames as quickly as if it had been oil-soaked kindling. His corpse—God, Valdas hoped the man was dead by now—flopped over sideways and folded in on itself, burning away to ash, bones and all, in less than a minute.

The four holding Mirza dropped her as if she was a hot coal—which indeed she might have been for all Valdas knew.

Oh, sweet Christ on a pig. What had she done? This was different again from the light she'd made, but Valdas knew instinctively that Mirza had done this with magic.

With magic!

His spine crawled.

"Anyone else?" Mirza's voice rang out shrill.

No one moved.

"Get out."

No one moved.

"Go!" she yelled.

They went, minus the two that Valdas and Dahnay had immobilized, leaving their booty scattered, scrambling for their horses. Three riderless mounts pulled at their tethers but were held fast.

Dahnay sprang to his feet and reached down to pull Mirza upright, seemingly unafraid of her despite what she'd just done. He held out her pantalones.

Drawing a deep breath, she pulled them on.

"Are you all right?" she asked Valdas and Dahnay.

"I should be asking you that." Valdas forced himself to step toward her but she retreated from his embrace, and he hesitated. Of course she wouldn't want that kind of contact, not right now. He should have known better.

"I was afraid they'd bust your ribs again and we'd be stuck here while they healed."

"My ribs were the last thing I was worried about. What did you do?"

"I don't know." She gave a slight shake of her head. "Something I should not have done. I'm going to suffer for it, but I'm not yet sure how."

She turned away from him and retched. He wanted to touch her, as much for his own comfort as hers, but he daren't. Was this why the men of her band were too afraid to bed her?

"What shall we do with these?" Dahnay asked.

The black boy, Yusuf, lay weeping on the floor where Valdas had left him, babbling in an unfamiliar language, one hand clasping the other arm. The man that Dahnay had tackled was dead, his neck broken quickly and efficiently.

"What's the boy saying?" Valdas asked.

"That he's scared and in pain and he's asking the witch-lady please not to kill him," Dahnay said.

"You speak his language?"

"No, but I know what I'd be saying in his position. Are you going to kill him?"

"No, but I'm going to hurt him." Valdas stood over the boy, took his injured arm in a firm grip, by the hand and above the elbow. He planted his boot in the boy's armpit, pulled, twisted, and shoved. The boy screamed again, but when Valdas stood up, the arm looked to be in a more natural position.

"Crude but effective." Mirza passed judgment on his technique. "Remind me never to have you manipulate a dislocated shoulder for me."

"Are you all right?" Valdas could see her cheeks were flushed and her eyes glittered feverishly.

"I think it's starting."

"What?"

"The reaction to . . . doing that." She indicated the pile of ash, already being disturbed by the breeze.

"Where's Dahnay?" He couldn't see the black man.

"She's probably gone to weep where we can't see her now it's all over. That was close. If they'd started with Dahnay I couldn't have done . . . what I did. It was only seeing that . . . thing coming toward me directly that brought out the . . . instinct and called up the power."

The world fell from under Valdas's feet and pitched him on his arse. "She?" He looked toward where Dahnay had disappeared down the path.

"She?" he said again.

"Oh, Valdas." Mirza touched his face. "For a smart man, you can be such an arse sometimes."

CHAPTER FORTY-THREE
Mirza

IT'S WRONG, she knows it's wrong, but she's trapped and helpless. A huge kok, ten feet long, is coming at her, engorged and purple, glistening at its tip. Bloated stones beneath it, pulsating, a pumping heartbeat. All she can see of the man looming above it is a hideous gap-toothed grin. Her legs are open wide, as wide as they can go, muscle and tendon stretched to tearing point. Between them, an aching void, fragile as a cobweb. The purple kok's color deepens to steel blue, sharpens until it becomes a huge knife with a manic face above it and shining stones of steel below. In seconds the tip will rip into her—split her wide open like a herring—spill out her guts, purple and glistening.

Steel.

Forged in fire.

Made and unmade.

She draws on the nature of steel, the heat of the forge, hot as the sun in the sky. Draws it into herself, hurls out raw power, sun power, light power, and unmakes the knife.

The gap-tooth grin twists into an open-mouthed scream and a man hovers before her, naked, arms and legs spread wide as if stretched on some invisible frame. His crotch is blackened meat with a smoke wisp rising, intensifying, darkening. A small flame flickers in the center—turns to a dense oily swirl. The flame grows and grows. The man becomes a flaming torch. The heat—unbearable heat—scorches her.

"Hot . . ." she heard a voice say.

Something told her it was her own, but it didn't sound like her. It sounded . . . dry. Cracked. Old. Exhausted.

"Mirza." Another voice. A man. A man with a burning kok and stones of steel. She began to gather power to herself.

No. Not the man with the burning kok, though she was pretty sure this man had a kok. Valdas!

She pushed the power away, but its heat was inside her. She needed to strike out to release it. She felt herself being raised by an arm round her shoulders, and ice-cold water, tasting of blood, jangled all her teeth, dribbled down her chin, splashed between her breasts.

Cool . . . A blessedly cool cloth to forehead and face.

She reached out. A hand grabbed hers.

"Mirza. I'm here. You're not alone. He's gone. You're safe. God's teeth, Dahnay, I don't know if she can hear me."

"I'll ride for more water." Another voice, tenor, clear. The black man who wasn't a man.

"For God's sake, hurry."

The voice receded . . .

It's wrong. She knows it's wrong but she's trapped and helpless and a huge purple kok, ten feet long, is coming at her again . . .

Mirza felt herself slipping into madness and could do nothing to prevent it.

The burning man begins to spin as if pinned through the exact middle, his hands and feet trail fire, spinning faster and faster until he becomes a wheel of fire, burning orange, then yellow, then white hot. He trails sparks as he spins away from her. She knows she should feel relief at his going, but above her, above the whole land, hangs a cloud. Definitely a cloud, not a pall of smoke from her burning man. A thunderhead cloud, channels energies vast and dangerous, preparing to vent its power to the ground. The cloud begins to spin, not like a funnel, but like a disk. It spins and shreds itself, fine tendrils fly out from the center, two, then four, then eight until it looks like some giant spider with a dense body and eight knotted legs.

A voice whispers on the storm wind. "I know what you did. You will do it for me."

"Never!" She screams at the wind, but her pathetic little voice blows away like an autumn leaf.

❦———❦

"Mirza?"

"Valdas?"

"Oh, thank God, I thought I'd lost you." His voice was wobbly, or else her ears were.

"Not going anywhere." Her teeth felt as though they belonged to someone else. She worked her tongue against the roof of her mouth, trying to draw enough saliva to swallow.

"Here."

That same strong arm around her shoulders. A cup to her lips.

She swallowed water a sip at a time, grateful for the feel of it trickling over her tongue, down her parched throat.

"How long?"

"Three days. You're in Zefalos. We carried you here. Five miles."

"He carried you," Dahnay said. Mirza hadn't realized there had been anyone else in the room. In fact, she hadn't even been aware of the room. She opened her eyes and saw Valdas's worried face. He looked as though he hadn't slept in a week.

She looked beyond him. The room about her was small with too many personal things in it to be a tavern room.

Dahnay unfolded herself from a stool by the door. Mirza hadn't noticed her on the first pass; she'd blended with the shadows. She was tall and angular for a woman, very flat-chested, no wonder Valdas had been deceived. He obviously hadn't noticed the lack of bobbing lump in her throat when she spoke or the rich, low female voice. All the signs were there if you knew where to look, but she made a passable man especially dressed in zupan and delja. The dark scarification lines on her cheeks, obviously a deliberate marking, almost made up for the lack of beard. In their own way they were, if not beautiful, striking.

Pity she needed to squat to pee. The outlaws had obviously been watching the camp. They'd not been taken in.

"Are you hungry?" Dahnay asked.

Mirza thought. She wasn't really, but she knew she should eat. "Something small, light. Broth, maybe."

"I will ask. I fear it might be borscht again. They seem to live on it. What wouldn't I give for pelmeni or pirozhki, or anything to get my teeth into. The people here are dirt poor and thus not very hospitable, but Valdas has impressed upon them the urgent need to assist travelers, or suffer the consequences." Dahnay left.

"This isn't a tavern." She looked around the room.

"Their village hetman's own house. He has found alternative accommodation for his family, temporarily."

"What happened to the boy?"

"Yusuf? He's here in the village. It turns out he's only twelve. He'd fallen in with the gang a few weeks ago and he was too terrified to run away. The villagers think more of him than they do of us. Dahnay seems to get on with them, too. I guess it's just Zavonians who aren't welcome here right now. This is exactly what I feared. The Tevecor Reaches will devolve to Ruthenia of its own accord unless King Gerhard does something about it soon."

She looked at Valdas. How their positions had reversed. "I need to piss," she said. She became aware of herself beneath the covers. "And I need a shirt or a chemise of some kind."

He squeezed her shoulder gently. "I'll get you one."

<hr />

"A magic presence in the sky? Mirza, are you sure? You were pretty far gone for a while."

Valdas was arguing with her again; she must be on the mend. What a bonehead he was. Mirza took a deep breath and tried again.

"Delirium can open a door into the spirit world, Valdas. It shows us tides within ourselves that flow in the dark." Mirza glanced across at the black woman sitting still as a statue in the corner of the bedroom. "Dahnay? What do your people believe?"

"My tsarina insists that I pray to her God and attend mass, but there are things which only the spirit-touched can see. The ancestors guide our footsteps in my childhood home."

"See?" Mirza turned to Valdas. The man was hidebound and narrow-minded. He was ready to believe that she could burn a man's stones off and fry him from the inside merely by looking at him, but not that she could sense something on the spirit plane.

She tried again, speaking slowly. "I felt a presence. It wasn't in the sky, not literally, it was on the spirit plane, dark and malevolent. Imagine a spider waiting at the edge of its web, always feeling with its feet for the vibrations that tell it when a fly is enmeshed. It . . . felt my vibrations, the echo of what I did in the spirit world. It knows. It's waiting. It's tasted me."

"Speaking of taste, have you finished pushing the remains of that soup around the bowl?"

"Mmm? Oh, yes, thank you."

Valdas stood and took it from her.

"I'm ready to get up now, please. Phew. I stink. I need to wash."

"I'll ask for water." Dahnay unfolded herself from her stool and slipped out of the room.

"However did you think she was a man?" Mirza asked.

Valdas shrugged. "I don't know. Seems obvious, now, that she's a woman. Good with a sabre, though. We've been training each morning. She's taught me more than I've taught her, I can tell you. What she lacks in weight she makes up for in hard muscle and suppleness. Her reach is almost as long as mine. God, she's tall."

Mirza smiled. "That's almost respect on your voice."

"Respect? She scares the shit out of me."

Dahnay returned with the good news that the household was heating water for the tub.

"A tub? No, I can't. I'll go to the stream."

"Nonsense," Valdas said. "A hot tub is the least they can do for you."

He didn't understand. The thought of sitting in her own filth made her feel sick. "It's not our custom."

"The Bakaishans take baths. I saw you."

"In the river, yes, where running water can take away the filth. A tub means sitting in your own dirt."

"Hmm . . ." His brows drew together. "I don't think you're strong enough to walk all the way to the stream and I certainly don't fancy carrying you. How about we compromise? Stand in the tub and when you're washed I'll pour a bucket of clean water over you. Will that work?"

It took such a short time to heat enough water that Mirza suspected buckets had been brought in from neighboring houses. Valdas led her into the cramped living room where a wooden tub, really a half-barrel, stood in front of the fire, water steaming. Dahnay had tactfully disappeared.

Mirza pulled off the borrowed chemise and without waiting to be invited, Valdas lifted her bodily and stood her in the tub. With a jug he poured the warm water over her head and shoulders. She sighed. It felt good. Better than she'd expected. Warmer than the stream would have been, too.

"Bend your head."

She did as he ordered and he soaped and rinsed her hair, tangling his blunt fingers in her curls until she yelled one time too many and slapped his hand away.

"I'll do it."

As good as his word, Valdas poured fresh water over to rinse her clean, lifted her out of the tub, stood her in front of the fire, and turned to get a sheet to dry her. She shook the water off her hands and wiped her face, then froze. Where her purple witchmark was, the skin felt different.

"What's this?" She prodded it with her fingertips. "It's changed."

"It's fine," Valdas said in that voice that said it wasn't fine at all.

"Show me."

"I said it's fine."

"There's a glass in my pack."

"Mirza . . ."

"Get me the glass, Valdas. Let me see for myself."

She read what she needed to know in his eyes as she took the tiny cracked glass from him and unwrapped it. She almost didn't need to see, but she looked anyway. Her witchmark, hitherto a wine stain on her skin, was puffy and swollen, like a fistful of blackberries had been squashed onto her face, dark purple and glistening.

She tried to breathe as if she really didn't mind the change, as if living with one mark was no different to living with another, but this made her wine stain beautiful. She'd always wanted to be normal. Now she wanted her dear, familiar wine stain back rather than this hideous, bulging, alien . . . thing which had attached itself to her.

"I . . . knew . . ." *Breathe, woman.* "I knew I'd have to pay a price for what I did, but . . ."

She felt the mark again, trying to let her shaking fingers get used to the new Mirza.

Valdas took hold of her hand and slowly and deliberately he kissed her cheek. How could he bear to let his lips touch . . . that?

"It's not so terrible," he said.

"You're a bad liar."

"And you're a lovely woman." He put his right arm around her back and drew her to him, cupping her right breast gently with his left hand, caressing her nipple until it awoke from its bathwater stupor.

She gasped and pushed him away. "I can't do this."

"Not yet. Give it time."

"Not ever. Not with you. Not with anyone. I'm too dangerous."

"I'm not afraid. This is me, Valdas. Balls of steel." He held her again, but this time only enfolding her in a hug.

Stones of steel, blade for a kok. The vision from her delirium washed over her.

"I'd kill you, Valdas." She rested her head against his shoulder. "I wouldn't mean to, but I'd kill you."

The rule of three. She was paying threefold for her transgression against nature. First the fever, then the witchmark, and now the loss of that very normal human comfort which she'd only just come to know.

Tears soaked into Valdas's shirt.

She let herself cry once to mark an end to self-pity. The darkness wasn't just coming, it was here already. That was why Konstantyn had told her to work with Valdas. It all became horribly clear. He'd said she had power. He'd known!

More than anything, right now, she wanted to be with the Bakai-shans, back in the days when all she'd had to worry about was a dark birthmark and being a virgin, but she'd foolishly spirit-walked into an obligation she couldn't refuse.

It didn't matter about her face.

It didn't matter about not being able to take comfort with a man.

What was coming was darker and more dangerous than she'd ever faced. Even if she managed to defeat it, she wouldn't survive. The world wouldn't have to look at her overripe blackberry face for much longer.

CHAPTER FORTY-FOUR

Lind

LIND RODE SOUTH from Biela Miasto through the fertile district known for its produce. Cabbages! Well, somebody had to eat them, but it wasn't going to be him. He'd had his fill of cabbage soup as a child.

He silently cursed Zalecki. He'd been hoping the man had gone to ground in the city, but he was pretty sure he'd got the right story out of the whore eventually. You couldn't use the same threats on whores that worked on other people. Hell, what they did every day was his worst nightmare and they didn't seem to mind it, or if they did they kept the fact well hidden.

In the end it had taken nothing but straightforward pain.

He hadn't enjoyed it.

It was safe to say she'd enjoyed it less.

But he had his answer. Zalecki had been heading for Chancellor Skorny's estate, but he'd have found no welcome there. The old boy was mortally sick. Lind suspected it was a political sickness, since it started on the day of the assassination and still had not carried him off. Zalecki's next destination was Bieloria, to Tsarina Zofia. It seemed likely Zalecki would have taken the shortest route to the border so as to minimize the possibility of running into patrols. If Lind had been trying to lie low and get out of Zavonia, he'd have gone via Dadziga, joined a merchant caravan, and crossed the border at Fort Erta.

He'd stared at a parchment map, looking at the latticework of roads, wondering whether to ride directly for Bieloria and start at Zalecki's possible finishing point, or follow his supposed trail. In the end the latter won. He'd cast around for a while, see if he could find any leads, carefully avoiding checkpoints on the road.

He found nothing. It was a cold trail, if, indeed, he'd actually passed through this area. No one remembered a single man on foot. They'd had other things to worry about after King Konstantyn died. That was when the new tax had been brought in . . . and since then they'd had to send produce to the troops manning the new checkpoint on the Tildich road . . . and who thought a checkpoint on the Tildich road was a good idea anyway, for heaven's sake? Did the new king think cabbages were a dangerous commodity?

He heard all those grumbles and more.

"A copper on the price of a cabbage," the landlord of the only tavern in Szichy said. "Good King Konstantyn, rest his soul, would have barely been cold in his tomb. The soldiers came and brought the notice and the whole village turned out to talk about it. Talk! It got a bit more heated than just talk, I can tell you."

He placed a dish of cabbage soup in front of Lind with a fat sausage, a loaf of dark rye bread, and a pot of butter.

Lind sniffed at the soup and sighed. Cabbage. You couldn't disguise it.

"Five coppers." The landlord held out his hand and Lind dropped the coins into it.

"Now come to think of it, a stranger came through here that day, a big man with two horses, one of 'em lop-eared and bad-tempered." He dropped onto the bench at the other side of the table and idly tore a strip of bread from the loaf Lind had just paid for.

"Help yourself."

The man didn't notice Lind's sarcasm, but drew his eyebrows together.

"Big, you say?" Lind prompted the man's memory.

"Tall, muscular. Not fat. Short hair, military type, but I remember thinking his top lip was pale, as if he'd shaved a mustache. I see a lot of people, you know. I can't remember all of them, but I put my prices up that day, too. He was the first to pay the new price and I felt . . . well . . . let's just say I remember."

Lind tore a hunk of bread off the loaf before the man could beat him to it, buttered it, and munched. It would be a cold day in hell before he'd eat cabbage.

"Which way was he heading?"

"He asked about the road to Dadziga."

Lind's guess had been right. He smiled around the sausage.

Lind couldn't wait to leave cabbage country behind. He headed straight to Dadziga where the caravans gathered for the trek to Ruthenia and Bieloria. He planned to hang about in the taverns frequented by merchants, and perhaps see if he could find which caravans had set out around the right time. The two-day journey stretched to three because he had to skirt two more checkpoints in the pissing rain. His horse threw a shoe in the mud and pulled up lame. He ended up making an expensive trade and acquired a rangy chestnut to replace the compact bay. He never got attached to his mounts. One was as good as another.

Dadziga must have been the last place God made, a trade crossroads where traffic came through from Kassubia and traveled north to intersect with the route from Biela Miasto to Bieloria. Rumor had it that you could buy anything here from a body-slave to Hindian opium or field artillery and ordinance to any one of fifty books on the church's *List of Proscribed Works*.

Cutting straight to the heart of the matter, Lind took a room at the Gatehouse Tavern on the corner of Nowa Street and West Gate. He saw that his horse was taken care of, checked that his room had adequate emergency egress, and returned to the bar, where he found a cozy corner by the fire and listened. He was an unobtrusive listener when he needed to be.

The following morning, having learned quite a bit about how the system operated, he asked the landlord where he might find the offices of the Hindia Spice Company. They traded small but important quantities of spice to Ruthenia and Bieloria, sent as add-on freight with almost every merchant caravan. If anyone had records of which caravans left, and when, it would be them.

He found the office on the ground floor of a warehouse building shared by several merchants. Surprisingly, it was occupied by a brown-skinned young woman in western fashions, a cream day-dress with large ruffled sleeves and a wide square-cut neck.

"May I speak with the man of business?" Lind asked.

"Yes." She sat behind a desk that was two sizes too big and tilted her delicate chin up at him.

He waited.

She waited.

Neither moved.

"Are you going to keep me sitting here all day?" she inquired.

"I asked . . ."

"To speak to my man of business. I know. I heard. I am my own man of business. Jadzia Lizovska." She held out her hand and he didn't know whether he should shake it or bow over it. He settled for the latter.

"Lind," he said, and then realized he'd given her his real name. How long since he'd done that?

"Just Lind?" she asked.

He shrugged. He'd had a first name once—when he'd been young and vulnerable.

"What can I do for you, Lind?"

He looked at the delicate creature, straight black hair framing her serious face, and estimated her to be in her mid-twenties at most. He tried to forget he was speaking to a young woman and explained the situation as he would to a man. She was obviously well versed in trade and the comings and goings of the various caravans.

He told her he was looking for an ex-military man and described him.

"Ah, and would this man have a name?" she asked.

"Zalecki."

"Ah, Zalecki. Valdas Zalecki." She knotted her brows.

Lind hesitated. "You know him?"

"He came here asking about caravans to Bieloria. I introduced him to the Angluman, Callender. The others have their regular men."

"And you've heard from him since?"

"Why should I? He was only a brief acquaintance. Besides, I might have seriously misjudged the man, though I think and hope not. You probably need to talk to Callender. In fact, I'd recommend it." She checked a paper of scribbled notes on her desk. "Callender, Lord Callender as he calls himself, though I doubt his credentials, is in town now, preparing another caravan."

It was obvious she didn't think much of Callender.

"What aren't you telling me?"

"Callender lost cargo. Mine was a small package, thank goodness, but a number of my colleagues were left out of pocket. I shall not use him again. He blames the loss on Zalecki, says he was in league with bandits."

"Surely not every cargo gets through unscathed."

She pressed her lips together. "That's why I send my spices in small quantities, split between many merchants. Most are honest. It's been many years since a merchant returned with all his goods missing and no scars to show for it."

"Callender?"

She nodded.

"You have suspicions?"

"Nothing I can prove."

Jadzia Lizovska's demeanor didn't alter by more than a fraction, but Lind knew that this young woman wasn't someone to cross. Callender had made a mistake. She was not only pretty and intelligent, but very determined and possibly quite ruthless. Women who didn't smell like victims were the only ones he found it comfortable to be around.

"How does . . ." He was going to say: *A woman like you.* He stopped himself. "It's unusual to find a business run by . . ." *God's ballocks, he was digging himself a hole.*

"How does a dusky maiden come to be running a business?" She laughed. "When you have nothing, the only way is up. What! Do you think I inherited it from a merchant father?"

He raised his hands, palms outward. That was precisely what he'd thought.

"Your life is your own," she said. "However others may treat you, what you do with it is up to you."

She gave him concise directions to where Callender's caravan was assembling. "One favor in return," she asked.

He nodded. "If I can."

"When you've spoken with Callender, if you discover anything of interest, please come and tell me. I have waited too long for a true accounting from Lord Callender and I'm thinking it's overdue." She half-smiled. "Maybe I can treat you to dinner tonight?"

Was she . . . ? No. Of course she wasn't. It was business. He understood business.

"Very well." He bowed, thanked her, and left.

Callender was easy to find but difficult to talk to because of his appalling accent. He spoke Zavonian badly and interspersed it with words in Anglu to fill gaps in his knowledge. Constant interruptions— men and horses coming and going in the yard and a large chest belonging to a middle-aged lady passenger—all took his attention away from Lind's questions about Valdas Zalecki.

Yes, probably, he didn't know; yes, he always took on at least two guards; yes, he'd had problems on his last trip.

He met Lind's eyes too readily. He was a good liar, but Lind smelled untruth.

"Lord Callender." Lind stood squarely between the man and one of his teamsters trying to ask him a question. "Jadzia Lizovska has already told me Zalecki hired on as a guard on your last trip. What happened?"

"James and John are over there. Been with me for years. The other fellow was a new man. Local, well, Zavonian anyway. Must have been in league with the bandits. All his fault that we lost everything. He ran off after a fight." His hand went unconsciously to the sabre at his hip, not an Anglu weapon, but a hussar's sabre. Callender wasn't Zavonian, so he probably didn't recognize it, but it carried not the royal crest but a silver feather from the wings of a winged hussar, the emblem of the house guard of Konstantyn.

"Ran off, you say?"

"Like a dog."

If Lind knew anything about Valdas Zalecki it was that he was as straight as a plank. Not the type to throw his lot in with thieves and bandits.

"Thank you. I shall trouble you no further."

He would, but he'd do it much later tonight when the man was alone.

In the meantime he would take the news to the Hindia Spice Company.

CHAPTER FORTY-FIVE

Valdas

VALDAS SAT ON a log outside the cottage, putting a fine edge on his sword with a whetstone. He wasn't really taking much notice of the job in hand, but the swish swish swish as he slid the stone down the length of the blade was comforting. He shoved all thoughts of magic and its consequences aside and lost himself in the repetitive action of whetstone upon steel. He'd think about magic later. Maybe his heart would get used to the idea and stop trying to pound its way out of his chest every time he pictured the brigand blazing to ash.

"Are you determined to wear away the steel to a sliver?"

Dahnay followed him out of the cottage and perched next to him on the log, not touching.

Now that he knew she was a woman, he wondered why he hadn't seen it before. He wanted to turn and study her face, her neck, her hands, for signs that he shouldn't have missed, but instead stared at the tip of his sword resting on bare earth.

"You saw what you expected to see." Dahnay answered his unspoken question.

"Huh?"

She repeated herself.

"How did you know what I was thinking? You're not magic as well, are you?"

"Sadly, no."

"Sadly?"

"Mirza's magic saved us all."

"I suppose it did." Damn, he'd been stupid. He hadn't considered the effect their narrow escape might have had on Dahnay.

"Has she done that before?" Dahnay asked.

He swallowed convulsively to clear the lump in his throat. "Not to my knowledge."

"How long have you and she been together?"

Together? Were they together? He supposed they might be, for some value of together.

"Her band took me in when I was injured. I've known her a couple of months. She's a healer, not . . ."

Not what?

Mirza, what are you? What have you become?

"Not a warrior?" Dahnay finished for him.

He shook his head. "She always said she was a shulam, that's a witch and a healer combined, but I've only ever seen her help people, never harm them."

"She helped us."

"So she did." He tapped the point of his sword on the ground and kept his eyes fixed on it. "Are you all right? I mean—"

"I am alive and uninjured. The rest will pass in time."

"You must have been scared."

"Were you?"

"No." He swallowed again. "Yes. Terrified. But I've been scared before. If you let it control you—"

"You're lost. I know."

He glanced sideways quickly and then back to the sword point. Was it worse for a woman to be held helpless? To be threatened with rape and murder?

"Don't ask," she said.

Blast it, was the woman a mind-reader, or was his face an open book?

He shook his head. He wouldn't ask.

CHAPTER FORTY-SIX
Mirza

THE FOLLOWING DAY Mirza pronounced herself ready to travel, and though she let Valdas saddle her horse, she wouldn't accept a slower pace. She noticed Dahnay glance in her direction a couple of times, but the tall black woman had already fallen into a pattern of saying little unless she was asked a direct question, and direct questions were hard to find.

So, Dahnay, how long have you been a secret agent for the Tsarina of Ruthenia? No, that didn't work at all.

So, Dahnay, how did they make those pretty scars on your face? Another bad question, though Mirza was curious. She'd heard about ritual scarring, made with a Y-shaped knife and rubbed with charcoal so the cuts healed into cicatrices. *And do you mind having them?*

Valdas was curious about Dahnay, too. Mirza had seen him looking sideways at the black warrior woman when he thought she wasn't looking. She was, of course. Dahnay missed very little. She was a watcher and a listener. She could freeze into a stillness so profound you almost forgot she was there. It was as if she divorced herself from the world around her. But of course she didn't. She remained perfectly connected at all times.

Perhaps Valdas would try to bed Dahnay now Mirza had rejected him. Mirza thought about it and decided she wouldn't mind. It wasn't as if she was in love with Valdas. She'd used him as much as he'd used her. No—*used* wasn't the word—*taken comfort in* was a better term, because they'd surely both enjoyed the experience and neither had asked for anything except warmth, pleasure, and intimate knowledge of each other. It had been lovely while it lasted, but she'd known all along it wasn't permanent. She'd never envisioned Valdas as the father of her children. He was, after all, a Zavonian, but he was still her friend.

She'd never envisioned Valdas as the father of anyone's children, though he was a generous soul and would have made a good dada. No, when she looked, Valdas's future was occluded. She sincerely hoped that it wasn't because he had no future.

Dahnay was easier. A warrior's death in the service of her tsarina. But whether that was next week, next year, or twenty years from now, she couldn't say. Dahnay would, no doubt, be satisfied with that. She seemed to take delight in her physical prowess. Even on the trail she exercised each morning, testing her sabre against Valdas's sword, and for a part of each day running alongside her horse, her hand on the stirrup.

On the third day their trail took them through a large village. They stopped and Valdas negotiated for bread, curd cheese, kefir, and permission to refill their water skins and water their horses at the well.

People stared.

Of course they stared, Mirza told herself. What else would they do? A big man on a donkey-eared horse, a Landstrider, and a tall black warrior traveling together was an unusual sight. They would be stared at in most villages. It didn't take the squashed raspberry mark on her face to make them instantly noticeable. No, of course not. She had a hard time not putting her hand up to cover the side of her face as they rode away from the well, but she clutched her reins and straightened her back.

It was when a guttersnipe picked up a stone and threw it that she discovered another price for what she'd done. The stone arced toward her and her temper blossomed hot and strong. Something inside her opened up. She held out her hand. The rock flared brightly for a second and disappeared. She snapped her head round to find the child who'd thrown it, but he was already running for his life. She pushed down an urge to make that run his last one.

"He's only a child." Dahnay inserted her horse between Mirza and the fleeing urchin. "Save your strength for what you say is coming."

She was right, of course.

But Mirza had been so close to letting go. She'd opened a door and hated what she'd found behind it.

"Are you all right?" Valdas put his hand on her arm.

She gave him a brief nod.

"Sure?"

She took a deep breath and huffed the air out of her lungs. "I'm sure." *At least for now!* But she didn't say the last bit out loud. She'd seen the look in their eyes. Even Valdas was scared of her. And with a good reason.

Mirza wrestled intermittently with sudden and unexpected desire to kill things that annoyed her.

"Can't you feel threatened by a nice fat woodpigeon?" Valdas asked the following night when they found no better shelter than a stand of trees and no better food than the two-day-old bread and cheese in their packs. "If you got annoyed enough, we could have it ready roasted."

She glared at him until he got the point that he was currently at the top of her roasting list. That shut him up!

Heavens above, what am I thinking? I'm threatening my friend!

She placed her hand above her heart and started to apologize, then stopped before she made it worse.

Dahnay picked up one of the rotten logs they'd gathered for the fire, and looked across the flames at Mirza. "Do your people have a way of controlling such magic?"

"I've never heard of any of my people having fire magic. Do you know of a way?"

"Perhaps." Dahnay dropped the log into the flames.

A fire salamander, patterned black and yellow, exploded from the flames. Valdas jumped back, startled. Dahnay just watched it scuttle away with a thoughtful look on her face.

"It is a sign," the black woman said. "What do you know of salamanders?"

"Fire lizards," Mirza said.

"There are many legends, going right back to ancient times. My tsarina has a library. I have read of these things. My people also have legends . . ."

"The little critters hide in rotten logs," Valdas said. "It's no wonder that they get thrown on the fire by accident sometimes. Hey, I'd jump out of the flames pretty quickly if someone threw my log on a fire."

"My people say they are fire elementals." Dahnay put her head on one side.

"As do mine," Mirza said. "But they also say that a salamander's cold can extinguish flames. Thank you, Dahnay. I have to think about this."

The solution came to Mirza when she was sleeping. She didn't recall a specific dream, but she woke with the knowledge of what she needed to do.

When she told him her idea as they rode along through rolling scrubland, Valdas refused outright to do what must be done.

"Dahnay, tell him," Mirza turned to the black woman.

"It's true that the salamander symbol will help." Dahnay nodded.

"It's not magic in itself," Mirza said. "It won't take away my fire magic, but it will act as a focus to help me control it."

"How?" Valdas asked.

"Because I believe it will."

"But to cut it into your skin . . ."

"I can't cut it myself. That's why I need you."

Valdas shuddered.

"I will do it, if you will permit me." Dahnay touched her own scars. "My people have a tradition and I am a fair hand with pen and ink."

"This isn't a pen and ink drawing." Valdas's voice rose. "You're talking about cutting a design with a knife."

Dahnay nodded. "And rubbing ash into the wound to leave a scar. It will hurt, Mirza."

"I know."

They camped early while there was still plenty of daylight. Valdas lit a fire and Dahnay sharpened a wickedly thin knife. Mirza tried not to think of what was to come. What if she burned Dahnay in her pain? She must not. She. Must. Not.

"You have to hold me, Valdas."

"I want nothing to do with this. It's foolishness. What if you take an infection?"

"I won't."

"How do you know?"

"Trust me. We're going to do this with or without you. With will make it so much easier."

"Ready," Dahnay said.

Mirza stripped off her embroidered blouse and wriggled out of the straps of her chemise, leaving herself naked from the waist up, then thought again and stripped off all her clothes.

"I don't want to get them soaked in blood," she said.

"You must hold her very still." Dahnay positioned Valdas on the floor and settled Mirza on her back between his legs. "And hold these out of the way." She indicated Mirza's breasts. "But don't stretch the skin. I'm going to be cutting between them. It's delicate. We don't want the salamander to have a kink in its tail."

Mirza settled back into Valdas's embrace, feeling his arms clamped around her and his big, warm hands flattening her breasts and holding them slightly apart.

"Are you sure this needs to be . . . here?" he asked.

"Over my heart," Mirza said.

"Are you sure you can do this?" he asked Dahnay over Mirza's head.

"I have prayed to my god for a steady hand."

"Please. Stop talking and get on with it." Mirza closed her eyes so she wouldn't see the knife coming toward her.

Dahnay placed a leather strap between her teeth. It tasted of horse sweat, but the taste was soon forgotten as the knife bit home, sweeping across her chest, down between her breasts.

She tried to scream, but chomped down hard on the leather to hold it in.

"Brave girl," Valdas muttered in her ear. "Not long now."

That was a lie. Dahnay had hardly begun.

Slice. Slice. Dab with a linen more used to other blood. Slice again. Dab. Dab.

The pain, intense at first, burned her chest until she got the sudden urge to laugh with the exquisite pleasure of it. Laugh or cry, she wasn't sure which to do. She did both.

She felt every move of the knife as Dahnay etched the head of the salamander above her breasts, its blunt nose just below the base of her throat. Its front feet trampled the cushions of her breasts and its lizard-like body fitted neatly in the valley between them. The hind feet gripped her ribcage and the tail hooked round beneath her left breast.

"I've finished the cutting," Dahnay said. "No, keep it in." She repositioned the leather strap between Mirza's teeth. "This next part will hurt."

And it did.

Dahnay rubbed sooty ash into the cuts to ensure that the wounds scarred visibly. By the time she finished, Mirza was drenched in sweat and shaking, but the bleeding had stopped.

"Does it look all right?" Mirza's voice shook.

"It will do. Allah guided my hand."

"It looks like raw meat." Valdas's voice choked off. "Can you sit up by yourself?"

"Yes."

He eased her upright and her chest stabbed. She gasped and her hands flew to the hurt. Dahnay smacked them away.

"Don't spoil my handiwork."

Mirza bent her head to look down, but all she could see was puffy and inflamed flesh around dark welts.

"Tomorrow. Sleep now," Dahnay said. "Take your own medicine and see how you feel in the morning." She handed Mirza a cup of one of her own brews.

Mirza drank it gratefully and slept naked from the waist up beneath two blankets and her cloak. She woke sometime in the night and cried out when the sharp stabbing pain from her dream turned out to be real, but Dahnay was there with more of the sleep-inducing tea and Valdas reached out for her hand.

CHAPTER FORTY-SEVEN
Lind

LIND HADN'T EXPECTED that Jadzia would serve him dinner at her own house, a tall, narrow townhouse, built of red brick and set third in a row of six on the edge of the market square. It was simply furnished, but not cheaply, he noticed. And it was in the respectable part of town, small though that was.

A servant girl opened the double doors for them and took Lind's delja. Jadzia led him straight through the narrow hallway to a square room, paneled with oak and warmed by a fire set in a blue and white tiled fireplace, in the Delft fashion. The light was beginning to fade outside, so she drew drapes across the small leaded panes of glass and the servant girl brought two lamps.

Why was he here? Lind didn't usually get involved with the locals unless he needed information. And he *never* told anyone his real name. If she knew too much he'd have to silence her. He imagined snapping her delicate neck and found he didn't like the idea much. He'd do it, though, if he had to.

Within what seemed a very short space of time the serving girl brought the meal to the table. Jadzia bade him sit at one side and seated herself opposite him, leaving the head of the table empty.

As was traditional, bread was placed on the table first.

Jadzia kept a fine table. Pork-stuffed dumplings, capons smothered in blackened mustard, spit-roasted and served with pot-simmered vegetables, and little pan-fried blynai, wafer-thin and with grated apple mixed into the batter. She poured beer from a jug, but aware of the business to come he drank sparingly. He noticed she did the same.

"My cook is the finest in all of Zavonia," Jadzia said over the capon.

"I wouldn't swap her, even though she does think she's my mother as well."

"Your real mother?"

She shrugged. "Long gone. A good Zavonian Lutheran girl cast out by her family when it became obvious that my father was from much warmer climes, and probably returned there before she even knew she was pregnant. She went whoring. Died of the pox eventually. I grew up on the street, in and out of the whorehouses and the gambling parlors. Does that shock you?"

"Should it?"

She looked at him levelly. "I didn't think it would. I learned a lot about economics and human nature in those places. I financed my first purchase of cardamom and ginger from the proceeds of selling my virginity a week before two different whorehouses had rich gentlemen lined up to take it. I thought the profit was better in my pocket, so I sold it for less, but kept all of it and immediately put it to use."

"Good for you. Did you get into trouble?"

"One of the whorehouse owners tried to take it out of my hide, but I went to ground."

She laughed and put one hand on his. He stiffened, but tried not to snatch it away. She moved it herself and made no more attempts to touch him.

"I regained my virginity the day my first caravan came home with a profit." She smiled. "I bought the whole damned whorehouse when I was nineteen—through a man of business, of course. They do come in useful sometimes. The girls run it themselves now and pay me rent on the property. My cook came from there. She's a much better cook than a whore."

"Your errand-girl too, I bet."

"Born there, the daughter of some mule-drivers from To-Kayat."

"You are a financial success-story, mistress."

"And if the first merchant I'd trusted with that tiny consignment of spices had cheated me, I'd have been on my back, probably poxed by now, or beaten to death. I hate cheats. It's the little people who lose out. I take it that you have something interesting to tell me about Lord Callender."

"The man lies. I'm going to have a private conversation with him later tonight. He doesn't know it yet, though."

Her eyes shone. "Tell me more."

"The man I'm looking for, Zalecki, is . . . well, let's just say I believe him to be an honorable man. Your Lord Callender tried to tell me he was in the pay of the bandits who attacked his train and that he ran off with them, yet at his hip Callender carries a sabre that almost certainly belonged to Zalecki. I don't think Zalecki would easily be parted from that sabre."

"Oh!" She drew her brows together and then her face opened up into a smile. "In that case, I may not have misjudged Zalecki, and that would make me feel so much better. Except, of course, if Callender has his sword, he may be dead." Her face clouded again. "May I come with you?"

"I don't think that would be . . ."

"It's important to me. I usually pride myself on being a good judge of character. When Callender came back with his story I was angry with myself that I was twice mistaken. I . . . liked Zalecki. I too thought him honorable."

Lind's backbone began to creep. He really didn't want to have to snap this pretty neck. It would be such a waste; she was so . . . alive.

"How much did Zalecki tell you?"

"About who he was or what he was running from?"

Lind started.

"Oh, relax," she said. "I didn't ask him. And I'm not going to ask you either. It was obvious he was running from, or to, something, but it was his own business." She shrugged. "For what it's worth, I liked him."

"You took him to your bed."

She laughed. "Is that a question? If so, it's indelicate."

"You told me you sold your maidenhead, how indelicate is that?"

"Fair comment, but for your information, no. We spent some time together. He was a guest in my house. I didn't take him to my bed, though it was not for lack of trying on his part. It's refreshing to find a man who understands a refusal is a refusal, though, and takes it in good part. Not all men do, you know."

His jaw may have dropped slightly. He shut his mouth quickly, feeling his teeth snap together.

"Ah, I see I may have hit a raw spot there, my friend. I'm sorry."

God's ballocks, had he been so transparent?

She shook her head. "I'm not asking questions of you, but I will say that casual liaisons are not my style." She gave him a level look and he wasn't quite sure whether she was warning him off or whether she was telling him he was safe. She smiled. "Let's just say Valdas was interesting on many levels. To learn later that he'd been in league with bandits—well—I thought my judgment might be slipping. I'd be relieved to know it was sound."

"Is that all?"

She set her mouth in a straight line. "Not exactly."

"Ah." Lind stiffened in his chair. "Go on."

"If Callender deliberately swindled me out of my goods on that journey—me and a number of other traders—I'd like to make sure that he doesn't do it again." She looked at Lind from beneath demure eyelashes. "Am I as good a judge of character as I think I am?"

She dropped a pouch of tolars onto the table.

Good, that changed their relationship. She was now his employer and her life was sacrosanct.

He half-bowed to her over his dinner plate. "You may well be, mistress." Ha! For an awful moment he'd thought she wanted his body. He was pleased to find she only wanted his professional skill. "But I work alone. You can't come with me."

What a remarkable woman this was. Jadzia was certainly not a victim. She was a woman who could look after herself. She could regain her virginity on her own terms and not come out of it damaged.

She'd gone through hell and come out of it whole.

Why hadn't he?

CHAPTER FORTY-EIGHT

Mirza

MIRZA INSISTED THAT she was fit to ride the following morning. Beneath her chemise, etched painfully into the skin above her heart, she had the raw salamander scar—a creature born of fire. She began to channel energy into the image to invest it with properties of protection, not for her, but from her.

An hour into the ride, she wished she'd decided to rest for a day. Every step her horse took jolted until her body felt as if it was on fire. She didn't know whether that was normal. Maybe it was real fire. Maybe she'd burn herself to ash.

Valdas stopped to rest and to let the horses graze by a trickle, barely big enough to call itself a stream. She didn't argue when he helped her down from her horse and sat her down against a scrubby sapling.

"I'm all right," she said.

But they didn't travel any further that day, and Mirza must have slept the afternoon away, for it was dusk when she woke, still sitting uncomfortably, propped up by the sapling, a blanket over her legs.

She slept through the night as well, but the following morning felt able to ride again. She saw Valdas glancing at her, assessing how much longer she could stay in the saddle, so she clenched her jaw, determined not to give in.

They still broke their journey early, but the following day she managed a full day, and each day after that became easier.

Once across the Tevecor Reaches, their first staging post was Sula, a city of four thousand people. Mirza wasn't sure which of them received the most stares as the road began to get busier, the imposing, outland warrior everyone took to be a man, or the woman with the terrible face. Valdas could have been the most sought-after criminal in the land and no one would have noticed him, which was a good job because they had to negotiate a guard post at the city boundary. Mirza nudged her horse close to Donkey.

"Routine," the officer said. "Checking where people are coming from and where they're going to. If you've nothing to hide, you've nothing to fear."

Mirza thought quickly and rode forward. In Igor Karel's cloak, if she spoke Zavonian with the right accent, the guard might not take her for a Landstrider. She tried to imagine how Valdas would say the words. It didn't come out quite as she'd hoped, but it wasn't obviously Bakaishan.

"I'm the reason we're traveling." She turned her ruined face toward him and leaned down from her horse to his eye level, ignoring the pricking of her half-healed scar and noting with satisfaction that the guard took a pace back. "Don't worry, it's not catching. I hear there's a doctor in Biela Miasto who cured a child of such a birth defect, and I hired these to see me there safely." She indicated Dahnay and Valdas. "Though they've already done a poor job. We were set upon in the Reaches, sergeant. Why aren't you out patrolling the roads there?"

"My apologies, mistress. That's what I've spent the last three years doing, and what I'd rather be doing now, but our troop was recalled to this duty a month ago."

"Your generals are insane."

"Mistress." He saluted politely and let them pass without commenting.

"What in the name of all the gods is King Gerhard up to?" Valdas said under his breath as they rode away. "Pulling troops out of the Reaches to stir up ordinary citizens on the internal roads is crazy. What's he looking for?"

"Maybe there's local trouble we're not privy to," Mirza said. "Or maybe he thinks Kristina is heading in this direction."

"All the more reason to have troops up in the hills where the roads funnel down to two or three likely passes. He's wasting his men as well as irritating the good citizens. You don't mobilize a whole army to look for one woman, even a queen. It makes no sense. We had troops in the Reaches for a reason."

They came level with a family in a farm cart, heading in the opposite direction. Dahnay did her usual you-don't-see-me freeze, but she didn't need it. A small child, maybe not more than four or five, of indeterminate gender, mouth and fingers sticky from some shapeless lump of foodstuff, took one look at Mirza's face and let out a wail. Its mother tried to hush it, but the woman's eyes kept straying toward her. The man nodded semi-apologetically and hurried his horse onward.

"We'll go round the city," Valdas said.

She'd have liked nothing better, but she needed to find a solution to her problem right now, even if that meant going against her principles. She gritted her teeth. "We will not! I'm going to find some Zavonian clothes and you two are going to come with me."

It took all of her courage to ride into the town, dismount from her horse, and walk down the street of merchants. Goodwives and servants alike all stepped aside for them. Mirza started to enjoy scowling at people and seeing their reaction.

Flanked by Valdas and Dahnay, she made her way to the nearest draper and used some of her diminishing coins to buy a Zavonian letnik and a soft linen rantuch, which she draped over her lower face like an Eastern-style veil. With her hair captured in combs, only her light brown skin gave away her Bakaishan origins, and there were plenty of women tanned to a similar hue by the outdoor life. True, they could arrest her for passing herself off as Zavonian, but if she did not say she was, it wasn't her fault if they made assumptions.

By the time they left Sula on the road to Koplarr, she was dressed as a respectable and modest veiled lady traveling with her husband and a trusted armsman in search of a mythical doctor.

It took another eleven days to reach Biela Miasto—eleven days during which they passed another two checkpoints and during which the pain of Mirza's scar faded to a smart and then to a raging itch and finally to a dull irritation.

It was a relief to see the walls of Biela Miasto in the distance. Mirza had heard Valdas talk about it—about the Basilica, the riverport, the immense curtain wall, and the Gura that reared three hundred feet above the Low City, topped by the Citadel—but in her wildest imagination she'd never seen a city that shone. It glowed not so much white as pale gold, in the low evening sun. The light reflected from the creamy sandstone of the bastions to the stucco walls of the grand houses clinging to the front of the silver-gray granite Gura.

They wouldn't make it before nightfall and hammering on closed city gates wasn't an option, so with two hours to go to the city and only an hour to the closing of the gates, they stopped at the Boundary Tavern and took a room for the night.

Mirza, face always veiled in public now, ate in her room, rejecting Valdas's offer to eat with her.

"No, go and eat in the tavern. You know you want to see if you can pick up gossip that might give us a head start when we arrive in the city. You, too, Dahnay. Don't feel the need to be polite. I shall be fine."

She wouldn't, she'd be lonely, but she'd manage. She veiled her face before the serving girl brought a tray with a bowl of indifferent soup garnished with dill, some watered wine, and a slab of dark rye bread. Ah, the joys of the road. Didn't anyone know how to souse a herring or roast a pig? Did the whole of Zavonia live on soup all the time? She supposed it was easy to make when you didn't know how many mouths you were going to have to feed, and yesterday's remains were always a good starter for today's pot. She eyed her bowl. On that principle, there could still be shreds in there that were weeks old. Months. Years. She put down the spoon and tore off a hunk of gritty bread.

She missed the swaying of her own wagon and the friendly chatter in her own tongue. Would she ever see her band again? Distance and experience had already begun to make their subtle insults fade. If only she could go home, she would calm her hasty tongue and cease to anger Stasha and belittle Boldo for his stupidity. Valdas and Dahnay were as good companions as anyone could wish to have in their family, but how she longed to be finished with all this and to go home to her wagon and her apprentice. How was Tsura getting on as shulam? Part of her hoped she was doing well, and part of her hoped she wasn't doing well enough. If Mirza managed to return to the band, she wanted her place back.

If only.

But the darkness hung over her head. She hadn't touched it directly for many days, but she still felt that it shadowed her. Every instinct told her that she was moving closer to it, yet she could find no argument that would turn Valdas from the Biela Miasto road. With Konstantyn's imperative lying on her, she wasn't sure she should.

A sense of doom still hung over her and the dread that there would be no return to her band.

Knocking softly on the door, Dahnay let herself into the room.

"Eat," Dahnay said, moving to warm herself by the fire they'd paid an extra two coppers for.

"Soup. I don't even know what kind, except there's cucumber in it."

Dahnay wrinkled her nose. "I've tasted better, but it won't kill you. Or shall I see if the kitchen has cold pork?"

"No, this is fine." She pushed the rapidly cooling mess around her bowl again and finally let go of the pretense. "Valdas?"

"Hoping for more city gossip. He's not happy with what he's hearing about people's reactions to this soon-to-be war. There's talk of conscription. Taxes are up, tempers are frayed. I can see he's worried, and he's set to drink three merchants under the table to get every last bit of information he can."

Dahnay eyed up the big bed and the narrow pallet on the floor. "Which do you want?"

"I . . . I'd rather sleep separate, if you don't mind. Valdas might turn in his sleep, might . . . I can't risk waking up to find I've . . . done something." She tried to read Dahnay's face. "I mean, it's not as if he'd do anything, at least not on purpose, but an arm flung in the wrong place while he slept and I might . . . But you'll be fine. I mean, he won't . . . try anything . . . try to force . . ."

"I know he's an honorable man. Besides, I do not lie with men."

"I never . . . Valdas was my first." She shrugged. "I hadn't intended him to be my only. He's a generous man in bed, you know, a healing spirit, once he stops talking and starts . . . working. I'm not . . . jealous, if you . . ."

"You misunderstand. It's not a choice. I cannot. I have sworn."

"Oh."

"It's no matter." Dahnay shrugged. "Do you want to see your salamander? The swelling will have gone down and the bruising faded, so it is time. I have borrowed a mirror from the landlord's wife."

"Yes, thank you."

Mirza unbuttoned her letnik and slipped off her loose blouse and shift. Dahnay handed her the small mirror and she held it at arm's length. In the soft lamplight, the head and front feet of a salamander crept out of her bosom. She held one breast aside and followed the body down to the curling tail across her ribs.

"Well?" Dahnay asked.

"It's beautiful. You're a real artist."

"I think I may have made a better job than Valdas could have done."

"Are you pleased with your handiwork?"

"Allah teaches us to take pride in our work, but modestly. I am even more pleased if it serves its purpose. Sleep next to Valdas tonight. You will not hurt him."

CHAPTER FORTY-NINE
Valdas

ON THE EDGE of the city, outside the walls of Biela Miasto, a shanty town had grown up. Overspill houses jostled for space with those industries that fed the city proper. A cattle yard nestled against a slaughterhouse on one side and on the other a stinking tannery that made Valdas's eyes water as they passed. Two flour mills sat almost side by side on the riverbank and a brewery, smelling strongly of fermenting hops and yeast, straddled a much smaller, swifter tributary stream between the bridge and the confluence where it poured into the Biela River.

Mirza wrinkled her nose. "It's as well these are outside the city or the air wouldn't be fit for your citizens to breathe."

Valdas grinned. "Oh, there's worse in the city, but you notice it less when it's masked by the stink of the people." He waved an arm to the brewery. "That one's illegal, run by botchers. Inside the city, only the guild is allowed to brew beer. Every so often there's a guild raid out here, but the City Watch mostly turns a blind eye, it being, officially, outside their jurisdiction. The legal breweries are well defended inside the walls, and woe betide any individual who sets up so much as a mash tub on his own premises."

Mirza stared at the city walls, the mile-wide silver river, the dome of the Basilica, countless church spires, the onion dome of a great mosque, tall tenements and townhouses, and behind it all the towering crag upon which was set a walled fortress. "I thought Norski was big."

Valdas shook his head. "Biela Miasto is five times the size of Norski, and it's older. The curtain wall was laid down before the Northern Crusades. The old keep was built up on the Gura at about the same time. No one is quite sure which came first. There are two stories, one that the Gura was raised by magic and the other that, before the keep, the defenders of this region lived in caves in the Gura itself. Wherever the slope isn't entirely vertical it's been covered with buildings, and many of them hide ancient tunnels. Even beneath the Citadel there are tunnels from the foundations of buildings long gone. They run right through the Gura itself. The New Palace, the king's residence, built by Konstantyn's father, King Aleksander, has cellars beneath it that are hundreds of years old."

"When you said how you didn't see that one man could avenge a king, I didn't actually believe you. I thought it couldn't be that difficult for an agile and careful man to slip inside the palace." She stared at the Gura and shook her head. "I see what you mean now. It looks impregnable."

"Yet an assassin did it. He got in and killed my king."

"Did he? Slip inside, I mean," Dahnay asked. "Might he not have been in there all along? Are you so sure that Konstantyn was killed by someone from the outside?"

"No, I'm not," Valdas said. "That's part of the problem."

"How are we ever going to find one woman among all these people?" Mirza asked. "Kristina may not even be in the city."

"We'll have a better idea when we've spoken to Trader Maksimilian," Valdas said. "But first we have to get through the gate."

"Remember to slouch. When you sit up straight you look like a soldier."

He'd thought that his hair flopping loose on his collar and a sevenday beard growth was a reasonable disguise, but she was right. He slouched.

Valdas saw Mirza press her fingertips to her forehead as if to ward off a headache.

"Are you all right?"

"It's the city. It presses down on me." She reached for her veil.

"You needn't do this. I know how much you hate—"

"It's the simplest way."

Mirza removed her veil for the city checkpoint. As usual, she drew all the attention, but they passed through without incident. As quickly as she could she pinned it back into place, stealing a sideways look at Valdas.

"Where now?" she asked when they were safely away from the gate. "I've never seen so many tall buildings in one place before. It gives me the ants."

"You'll get used to it," Valdas said. He glanced sideways at Dahnay, but she seemed perfectly comfortable with the surroundings.

The street was wide enough to ride three abreast, knee to knee. Valdas put Mirza between himself and Dahnay, in case she decided to turn her horse and bolt. He tried to imagine Biela Miasto from her perspective. The whole city smelled of unwashed humans, cabbage, and shit, not surprising when there was an open drain down the middle of the street.

"There's a tavern called the Winged Hussar . . ." Valdas said.

"Which sounds exactly the place we should avoid being seen in," she said.

"Agreed," Dahnay said. "We need lodgings where strangers with dark skin might pass unremarked."

"The landlord of the Hussar is Moorish himself, and there are plenty of dark-skinned people in the city," Valdas said. "Brown, black, and olive. There are even some of mixed blood, though the church frowns on that, of course. The most cosmopolitan area is the waterfront." Valdas pointed. "There are all kinds of people there from all across the world, including Africs and Hindians and people from places I've never even heard of. They all seem to rub along together well enough. Though there's little stabling, so we need to leave the horses at a livery in the Low Town. As for the Winged Hussar, I'll go on my own, later."

They settled their horses in a livery behind the Market Square and headed down a wide cobbled street toward the water, passing through another curtain wall, this one unguarded except for a Watch office next to the open gate. Valdas explained that this was not actually the city perimeter wall, but in the event of the city being attacked by water, it could be used as such, sacrificing the dock area to invaders if necessary. The river itself was the city boundary and every inch of river frontage was filled with cobbled wharves and wooden jetties. Warehouses, boat builders, chandlers, sailmakers, and even a fish smokery, clustered together. Noisome closes of rickety houses and tenements squeezed into the spaces between taverns and warehouses, with shanty shacks wherever there was the smallest gap.

After a few fruitless inquiries, during which Mirza stayed silent and let Valdas do the talking, they retired to a coffeehouse called the Dove. It was a cheap parody of the new ones in the fashionable part of town.

"So the part of town we came through is the Low City," Mirza said. "Yet it's above the docks."

"It's above the docks, but it's below the Gura," Valdas said.

"So shouldn't it be called the Middle City?"

"I can't fault your logic," Valdas said. "Biela Miasto is a city of contradictions. This, for example." He cast his gaze around the coffeehouse. "They don't mind women in here, though most of the coffeehouses in the Low City are for men."

Mirza glanced around the room. Every table was filled. Valdas was right. There were a few women, though the customers were mostly men. Some were obviously merchants, a couple of upper-class lords either slumming or conducting the kind of business best not seen in polite society. They'd been lucky enough to find a private booth, and the waiter had brought them a thick, bitter brew. Mirza lifted the edge of her veil to sip at her cup, shuddered, and placed it carefully back on the tray.

"We can cover more ground separately," Valdas said. "Mirza, you should wait here while Dahnay and I look for lodgings."

It said something for the way Mirza felt about the city that she didn't argue. "Don't be long. Too many cups of coffee and I'll be seeking a privy, and this place doesn't look as though it has one that's fit to use. Better a bush to crouch behind in the open air than the stinking sewers in this dirty place. You were right, Valdas, the tannery wasn't the worst stink we've encountered today."

CHAPTER FIFTY
Mirza

MIRZA HEARD THE bell of the Church of the Holy Martyrs ring twice before anyone returned. Valdas had explained that it rang every hour on the hour, day and night, with a little four-note peal, and the number of strikes for the hour. It was also the city's alarum, ringing in the case of fire or attack. The tower on the church was two hundred feet tall, with a lookout gallery perched on top. She supposed the lookout made sense. Fire could spread quickly in a city of this density, but the bell chiming every hour made no sense to her and was just one more example of how the Zavonians counted everything. What was wrong with watching the sun travel across the sky?

Valdas returned first with news of a tenement apartment for rent, but it was expensive. Dahnay returned soon after. She'd found them a cheap room above a stapler's warehouse down by the docks. They followed her down to the river frontage and along past the fish dock. The building occupied the block on the corner of Jadwiga Street and the Granary Wharf, with the entrance at the top of a dingy half-flight of steps, directly off Jadwiga Street. Their room was on a corner. The front window overlooked Granary Wharf and the river. From the landing outside their door, a small window on the side of the building overlooked the grain warehouse across the street.

Valdas sneezed. Mirza rubbed her own nose. The smell of raw wool for the weaving trade tickled her throat. Opening the window didn't help. Other pungent riverside aromas flooded in to mingle with it. She looked around, poking into corners. The room had been swept clean after its last occupant—well—swept, anyway. Clean was a matter of opinion.

The nearest water came from a communal well in the yard, and the nearest sewer was an open drain right outside the landing window and two floors down. A chamber pot stood in the corner, empty, thank goodness. The whole place was furnished, after a fashion, with two truckle beds, a table, and two mismatched stools. A large open fire-place served for warmth and cooking, though coals had to be bought from the dockside and carried up daily.

Dahnay disappeared and returned with an extra stool and an iron cook pot with a chain to hang it from the fire-crane.

"The pot I purchased. The stool is borrowed from the smith on Steep Street, an obliging fellow nearly as black as myself, but Moorish. He speaks Suomijian with a dense Ruthenian accent. I think he of-fered me the hand of his third daughter in marriage, but I'm not sure."

Valdas laughed, probably somewhat relieved that he wasn't the only one to mistake Dahnay's gender on first meeting.

Dahnay put the pot on the table and reached inside it. "Bread, onions, cabbage, and pork belly. You can be glad that I have some spices in my pack. I will start this pot simmering on the fire for to-night's meal, but don't expect me to cook every day."

Mirza inspected the beds and threw out both mattresses, having suppressed an urge to incinerate them on the spot the instant she saw something moving. That left two hard sleeping platforms and the floor for their bedrolls.

"How long do you think we'll be here?" she asked.

Valdas shrugged and settled the bucket of water he'd brought up the two flights of stairs. "I don't know."

Somehow, sleeping on flat wooden floorboards seemed different from sleeping outside on the hard ground, so the following morning Mirza sought out the stapler in his office downstairs. He didn't deal in sheepskins, only fleeces, but as she'd hoped, he did have some sam-ple skins in the warehouse. Her veil seemed to have an unsettling ef-fect. Berating him for the flea-ridden mattresses, she bullied half a dozen large skins out of him without even thinking about setting fire to anything. Ha! She touched her fingers to her breastbone and the salamander scar glowed warm. She was getting better!

Valdas excused himself on the grounds of going to see an old friend. Dahnay stood up to go with him, but he shook his head. "Not unless you want to be obliged to take a whore for an hour."

Dahnay shrugged. "You think I couldn't keep a whore amused for an hour without revealing my gender? What a straightforward world your mind inhabits."

Mirza was still laughing as Valdas mumbled something and left.

"Ah, Dahnay, you're getting the measure of that man at last. Keep him on the back foot."

Dahnay shrugged. "Does he always keep his brains in his trousers? It's as well to know."

Something in the tone of Dahnay's voice, wistful, maybe, alerted Mirza to her feelings.

"There's one way to find out his full measure, and I'll not stand in your way."

Dahnay shook her head. "I told you before, that's not possible."

"You've taken an oath?"

"I am a warrior and I am a virgin and I am still alive. My mother was one of our king's many concubines. She died when I was born. She was fourteen years old and had already borne my sister. Life is short for many women in my homeland. Short and brutal, and always ruled by men. The Cult of Kobiata takes young girls with promise and raises them in secret, trains them to fight, and then sends them to serve in foreign lands, often as personal guards to important ladies. We are whole women, we could not train and fight otherwise, but in return we take a vow of celibacy."

"Whole women?"

"Uncut. In my country it's common for girls to have their womanhood cut out and stitched over."

"Cut out their womanhood?" Mirza shuddered.

"Just as some men in high office are cut to remove . . . distraction."

"And your people think this is a good thing?"

"It is tradition." She shrugged. "But I have heard the screams of girl children, and I would rather be who I am than be like my sister. She was cut at the age of eight and died bearing a child at the age of thirteen. I am still alive at twice that age."

Mirza had so resented her own virginity that, with the zeal of the newly converted, she couldn't imagine anyone having that done to them. "You renounce your gender?"

"Not my gender, but I renounce all physical relationships."

⬦——⬦

Valdas returned before dark and slumped onto a stool at the table.

"Did you find anything?" Mirza asked.

"More than I expected, but not what I sought. The army is mobilizing. Talk has it that troops are massing in the southwest. There's much speculation, but no one knows for sure. If I had to guess, I'd say

Gerhard is planning to push through into Posenja, and since he's pulled troops out of the Tevecor Reaches I'd say he's already got an understanding with Ruthenia. Ruthenia wants its own port on the Narrow Sea. If Zavonia and Ruthenia combine forces to take Posenja, Ruthenia gets her port."

He frowned. "Though it's difficult to see the advantage to Zavonia apart from forcing out the influence of Karl Gustav of Sverija . . . which may in itself be enough, of course, because Gerhard's position with Sverija is uncertain whilst Kristina remains unaccounted for. Posenja offers wealthy coastal towns, and if Gerhard gives Ruthenia a toehold he must know that Tsar Ivan will have designs on the corridor of Zavonian land south of Jaunia and Viruter."

He thumped the table and made her jump. "Damnation! Zofia must have known when she sent us here." He turned to Dahnay. "What do you know of this?"

She shook her head. "Nothing. I'm not privy to war councils. All I've been told is that I must bring Queen Kristina and the royal heir to Tsarina Zofia in Bieloria, whether you wish it or not."

"With Gerhard's forces committed in Posenja, Ruthenia would be able to take the Tevecor Reaches with a troop of cadets, and I'll bet they have far more in reserve than that. Oh, yes, Zofia is Konstantyn's sister, all right. They both learned their strategy from the same teacher—King Aleksander! Having Kristina and the true heir under their control means they could annex all of Zavonia and have a whole coastline, not just a few Posenjan ports."

Dahnay nodded. "It's a logical plan."

"Does that affect us right now?" Mirza asked.

"Maybe. Maybe not." Valdas shrugged. "Troops are massing, but they aren't ready yet. The mood in the city isn't good. More taxes on top of taxes and a conscription for one in ten of the young men between the ages of eighteen and twenty-one. They're doing it by lottery, for God's sake!" He thumped the table with his fist again, making her jump and setting her heart racing.

"Sorry." He dipped his head. "All we can do is carry on. I set up a meeting with Trader Maksimilian first, and then I went to the Winged Hussar."

"Wasn't that a risk?"

"Not so much in an afternoon. I was looking for Aniela Kolano."

"I knew it, whoring!" Mirza said, rolling her eyes heavenward.

Valdas raised an eyebrow. He was beginning to get the hang of her humor, but didn't always know when she was teasing. There had been damn little to laugh about lately. He sat on a stool and rested both elbows on the table. "Whores have the best gossip. Besides, Aniela and I have known each other a long time."

"Ah, Aniela. I see. She's the one who helped you to escape; the one whose name was on your lips when you came round from near death."

"The one who stopped me from turning myself in like a sheep for the slaughter, yes."

"And?"

"She's disappeared."

"You're surprised? She's probably petrified someone will rat her out for helping you. She could end up being sawn down the middle."

"No, that's not it, she didn't disappear straightaway. She only left a few weeks ago, leaving everything behind." He pressed the palms of his hands to the rough wood of the tabletop. "She must have left in a hurry." Valdas looked worried.

"You like her, don't you?"

"Aniela? Well, yes, of course." He sat back. "She's Aniela."

She's Aniela. That seemed reason enough for Valdas. Mirza sighed. "You want me to scry?"

He looked hopeful. "Could you? I mean . . . does it work?"

"Of course it works, but . . ." Could she? She hadn't tried walking the spirit world since burning the bandit in the Tevecor Reaches. She wondered whether this *fire* inside her would make a difference. Would she be denied access now? Was she impure? There was still a dark cloud over the spirit world. It had tendrils that reached for her.

She nodded. "I'll try."

"What do you need?"

"A little water, my copper bowl. And some peace and quiet." She scowled at him. "You'll be worse than a basket of puppies, Valdas. Dahnay knows how to be still. She can stay with me and you . . ." She thrust his delja into his hands. "You can go and gather more gossip. I'm sure there are other whorehouses in the area."

She pushed him out of the door and turned.

"What do you want me to do?" Dahnay asked.

"Sit there and pour water if I start to burn."

"You're serious."

Mirza shrugged. "I don't know."

◦————◦

The flickering firelight poked holes in shadows gathering in the corners of the bare room as the afternoon light faded. Mirza hung a wool-sack over two nails above the window and lit a tallow lamp, which guttered and spat before settling down to a greasy burn. She set it on the table.

Dahnay filled two buckets with water from the well in the yard and stood them close to the table, then folded herself cross-legged on her sleeping skins. "May your gods walk with you," she said.

Mirza nodded and licked her lips. She dipped the shallow copper scrying bowl into the water of one of the buckets and took it to the table, where she placed it carefully and stood over it, looking directly down. It shouldn't have depths, but depths there were: the echo of a woodland stream and the muddy rush of a great river in spate; the pressure of being forced through underground rock, bubbling, at last into free air. The water touched everywhere.

Valdas had described the ruby ring, had even drawn it for her. He'd been less artistic about drawing Aniela Kolano. *Short,* he'd said, *about yea-high*—putting one hand to the top of his chest. *Round, not fat, but round. Soft and warm.* His eyes had gone dreamy when he'd said that. *With breasts a man could lose himself in.*

Conscious of Dahnay's expression, Mirza had asked about hair color. Trust a man to describe breasts before hair and eyes. *Blonde,* he'd said, *with a bit of a curl, and gray-blue eyes.* How old was she? He didn't know. *Not a girl, definitely a woman. Oh, yes, all woman.*

So that was the best description she was going to get, but she had the name and that counted for a lot.

"Aniela Kolano." She whispered the name. "Aniela Kolano."

"Aniela Kolano. Reveal."

She was walking through mists in a land that was one huge city. Streets radiated out from a dark hub, filaments, linked one to another by concentric rings—a spiderweb pattern. Gray shadowy buildings loomed up out of the mists and retreated as she passed. Dark alleys beckoned, but she didn't go down them.

"Aniela Kolano. Reveal."

Above her a darkness gathered. Glancing up, Mirza shivered. She'd seen it before. It gave her ants. The shadow hovering above the city. She tried to ignore it.

"Aniela Kolano. Reveal."

Something stirred. In a dark place a woman huddled, in pain, alone. She clutched her hand to her, a hand that wore a gold ring set with rubies, the rubies twisted inward and protected inside a clenched fist.

The shadow followed her. "Why do you seek this one?" The dark cloud had a voice. "And how do you seek her without blood?"

Mirza's head spun and the air left her lungs.

She had to reply. Hiding was not an option. "I seek through water and air."

The gray city swirled, and she was in a room high up looking down on the city. A man hunched over a table, standing, but with all the weight he could bear taken on hands splayed flat to the wood, hands incomplete—a little finger missing from the left. The scrying bowl directly beneath his eyes roiled with blood, his own. One sleeve was pushed up and red trickled against the pale skin of his arm where a vein had been opened.

"You seek through water and air, but your soul is bathed in fire," the shadow-man said. "You spirit-walk and do not bleed. And you have killed without sacrifice."

Oh, there had been a sacrifice. She raised one hand to her squashed blackberry face.

"That's no sacrifice. It's beautiful. A mark of power. The greater the mark, the greater the power. You are in my city. Come to me and I will show you."

Show her what? How to bleed herself in order to scry? How to cut off her fingers in order to kill?

No.

She felt heat building up in the pit of her belly.

No! No! I will NOT!

She gasped. Wet hair, wet arm, wet hand. Trickles of water dripping inside her chemise and down her breasts. Dahnay was standing over her, an empty bucket in her hand.

"What happened? What did I do?" She heard her own voice falter.

"Tried to set the place on fire by sticking your hand into the flame of the tallow lamp. Aren't you burned?"

"I . . ." She looked at her hands. "I don't seem to be. You were obviously very prompt with the bucket. Thanks."

"Did you find her?"

"Maybe. I think I saw her, but I don't know where she is. I found . . . someone else. I was right about the darkness over the land. It's up on the Gura. That's where he is. We have to get out of here. He's coming for me."

CHAPTER FIFTY-ONE
Valdas

"WE'VE GOT TO get out now!" Mirza said. "I don't know who he is, but he knows where I am and he . . . he wants me."

"What about Aniela? And wants you how?" Valdas, newly returned, was trying to take it all in. He could hardly deny it after the Tevecor Reaches, but most of the time he tried not to think about Mirza's magic, because admitting that something as primeval as magic existed had left his worldview shaken to its core. He believed in things he could see and feel, things he could smell and taste and hear. Magic was none of those things. Yes, he'd seen and heard and felt and smelled the result of Mirza's magic. A burning man assailed the senses in so many ways; none of them good, and all of them memorable.

"Wants me. For what I can do. Wants my power. Somehow. I don't know." Between staccato sentences, Mirza thrust possessions randomly into her pack.

"Aniela. Did you see Aniela?" he asked.

"Yes. No. I don't know. I think so, but I couldn't tell where before this shadow descended. I'm sorry, Valdas." She paused to put her hand on his arm and then tapped him lightly with it. "Hurry!"

He didn't argue and neither, he noticed, did Dahnay. She had packed her minimal possessions within minutes and had rolled up her sheepskins into a bundle, evidently unwilling to part with them. Valdas wasn't far behind.

"Listen!" Dahnay hissed.

She was right. Booted feet marched in step outside in the street.

"Does he know about us?" Valdas asked.

"Only about me." Mirza shook her head. "I know he's up on the Gura, which means he knows I'm here."

Whether Mirza's magician knew or not, some of the guards might recognize Valdas, with or without his mustache. Dahnay would be safe, though.

"Can you delay them on the front stair?" he asked Dahnay. "Give me time to get Mirza away."

Dahnay hesitated.

"Meet us at Trader Maksimilian's." He looked her in the eye. "Dahnay, I swear we'll be there."

She seemed to make up her mind and nodded, heading down to the front door. Valdas grabbed Mirza by one arm, shouldered her pack along with his own, and hustled her down one flight of stairs to the stapler's cavernous warehouse. Bales of fleece, stacked one on the other, made solid walls with alleys between. He was glad he'd stuck to his usual rule when entering any strange building—always know the alternative ways out of it. He steered Mirza to the right and they ran between tall stacks of bales, emerging at the head of a narrow stair that led straight into the yard with the pump and a close of small houses. The only entrance to the yard led out onto the main street where the guards now stood trying to gain entrance to the building. It was only a matter of time before they came sniffing around the yard.

Without knocking, Valdas shouldered a house door open and dragged Mirza inside. It stank of cabbage.

"Your pardon, ladies." He half saluted to three women frozen in various domestic poses. Grandmother stirring soup, mother spinning, and a child winding spun yarn. "We mean you no harm."

He pushed his way past them and out of a back door into an alley. Mirza ran alongside him, keeping pace without needing him to drag her along. What a blessing that she was so spry. Turning left down the alley then right at the end, followed by another two lefts and rights, through the unguarded inner wall, a couple of lefts and a right and . . .

He dodged into another alley, narrow and stinking of piss. "Rest here a second." He bent over, hands on knees, to get his wind back. The extra pack slipped sideways off his shoulder and Mirza grabbed it.

"I can carry that," she said.

"I won't argue." His chest smarted and all he could manage were deep gasps. "Need my sword arm free."

"Are we going to Trader Maksimilian's?"

"Yes. I don't know how far we can trust him, but at least, I'm sure he's no friend to anyone from the Gura."

"And Dahnay? I thought you said we had to get rid of her."

Dahnay intrigued him. Female, but unwomanly. He didn't want to get rid of her, but the time would come. "I'll take care of that when I have to."

Mirza put her hand on his arm. "Treat her gently."

"She's a warrior. Will she treat me gently? I can't make any concessions to her gender. She doesn't ask for that."

He lapsed into silence, which was probably a blessing.

"I think we're safe now." Mirza stuck her head out into the street and checked in both directions.

He did the same. The early evening revelers were beginning to gather in the taverns as dusk settled on the Low City, so a man and woman walking together would excite no comment. Valdas led the way to Trader Maksimilian's. The front doors were open for business and once inside they were accosted by a madame, easily forty, but still handsome beneath the excessively white makeup.

"Her kind aren't welcome here." She glared at Mirza.

"What's wrong with her being Landstrider?" Valdas asked, immediately rising to defend Mirza.

"Nothing. It's being female I have a problem with."

"It's all right, Martyna, these people are here to see me."

Maksimilian, tall and broad enough to block out the lantern light, appeared from a door further along the hall. "Come in, my friends. I was expecting you tomorrow."

"Trouble found us," Valdas said. "If you feel we're putting you in a difficult position, we can go again."

"Not at all. I have my eyes and ears on the street. Enough to know that you are one man short."

"One woman. Dahnay. She'll be joining us as soon as she can."

Maksimilian nodded to Martyna. "Tall, black. Very distinctive. Bring her in when she arrives." He turned to Valdas. "You'd better tell me everything."

Everything I can safely tell you, that is, Valdas thought.

⋄——⋄

Trader Maksimilian was a bear of a man, fully six and a half feet tall, though large around the girth as well as broad in the shoulder and thick in the neck. His black hair and beard were curled and oiled in eastern fashion and a spicy odor, not unpleasant, hung about him. Valdas sat across the table from him, trying to get the man's measure. Maksimilian was probably trained in intrigue, whereas he was only a soldier. God alone knew whether he was helping his country or knocking another nail in Zavonia's coffin. *Konstantyn, forgive me. I'm trying to do what's best. Your child's out there somewhere and this man knows where. What's most important: your heir's safety and happiness or the Amber Crown?* That one tiny baby should have to be both innocent child and monarch seemed cruel. *Help me to make the right decision.*

But he had no way of knowing if Konstantyn was watching this from the spirit world. Mirza had flatly refused to spirit-walk again. Konstantyn was out of his reach.

He blinked rapidly. *God's ballocks, I believe in that claptrap now.*

"A drink, my friend?" Maksimilian's Zavonian was barely accented, and if Valdas had had to guess, he would have said the man came from Suomija. A double-bluff, maybe?

"Coffee, if I may."

"Nothing stronger?"

"Just coffee." He needed all his wits.

"And for you, Mistress Mirza?" Maksimilian asked.

"Nothing, thank you."

"But I insist. My house is your house. We do not restrict our women to kvass here. May I offer you a local beer, guild-brewed, or spiced mead? Or I have imported Rhenish and Tokay."

"Thank you. I will have a spiced mead."

Valdas shot her a glance and she shrugged. "I'm still shaking. I don't feel entirely . . . safe. Something to dull the edge might help."

The drinks arrived and were served. Valdas sipped politely. Mirza downed hers in one gulp, sighed, and let Maksimilian pour her another. This time she nursed the cup.

"You said you wanted to discuss a very special lady called Kristina." Maksimilian opened negotiations. "I'm not sure I have a Kristina among my girls."

"A very special lady," Valdas said.

"It all depends on your tastes. We have whores specializing in all manner of . . ."

"Let's not beat around the bushes, Maksimilian. Christine Willenbach, Kristina of Zavonia, widow of Konstantyn is missing."

"The late king's queen? Missing? Is she?" Maksimilian's eyes opened wide. He was a good actor.

Valdas shook his head. "I'm Valdas Zalecki, lately Captain of Konstantyn's High Guard. I can't prove it to you, but if you go outside and cry my name you'll see me arrested for a sawing before the echoes have faded. I'd prefer that you not take that route, of course." He watched for Maksimilian's reaction, but the man was giving him the rope and waiting to see if he swung. Oh, well . . .

Mirza leaned forward. "Trader Maksimilian, the queen is in danger—and her baby."

That made Maksimilian sit up.

"How do you know about the baby?"

"Tsarina Zofia told me when she bade me find the queen," Valdas said.

"For Ruthenia?" Maksimilian scowled.

"It's a long story. Please trust me that the safety of the lady and her baby is my priority. Konstantyn was my king, my master, and my friend. Whatever you may have heard, I did not kill him or by willful neglect cause him to be killed. My loyalty is now to his heir and therefore to his wife. However, there's a complication."

"More than one, but we'll start with yours." Maksimilian kept his voice low.

"I came via Bieloria . . . that's a long story . . ." He looked at Mirza, but she didn't add anything to clarify. "Had it not been for Tsarina Zofia I wouldn't have known about the babe. That was a secret kept even from me. But the information came with a price. Zofia sent her own guard, Dahnay, to ensure that Kristina and the baby, if and when they are found, take refuge with her. As a loyal Zavonian I have no need to tell you that I don't think much to that idea."

"Indeed not, but you could have dealt with that problem anytime."

Mirza took a deep breath as if she was going to speak, but thought better of it and sipped her mead instead. Valdas continued, "It's not as simple as that. I bear Dahnay herself no ill will, and there may yet be an amicable solution. Besides, I prefer to have Zofia's agent—one I know—with me, rather than one I don't know watching me from the shadows."

"Agreed." Maksimilian nodded, and dropped all pretense. "But Queen Kristina is missing."

"I thought you'd have sent her to safety and know where she was."

"I thought so too. She came here for refuge, but the search through the city became too intense, so I had to send her away. I got her out of Biela Miasto with a man who stays here from time to time."

A mild disturbance in the hallway announced Dahnay's arrival. The door opened and the tall black woman entered and half-bowed to Maksimilian as he gestured her to a chair. In usual Dahnay style she sat, perfectly poised, refused a drink, politely but firmly, and took on a stillness so complete that it was easy not to notice her despite her stature. Valdas was aware that his every move was being scrutinized, as was Maksimilian's.

"Let me get this straight," Valdas said. "You had her here safely under your roof and you sent her off alone with someone you barely know?"

Maksimilian spread his arms wide. "What was I to do? Konstantyn knew who I was and tolerated me in the city as a courtesy to his wife. I wasn't sure whether Gerhard knew it as well. I daren't take her away myself, or send her off with any of my known agents. Balinski kept his own counsel, but he treated the girls politely, never bothered them, and always paid his bills on time. He did a little job for me once, quickly and efficiently. He's a man whose skills are for sale, but once bought he stays bought, or so I believed. The queen was anxious to leave. I advised against, but she decided to go with him after she'd met him. You know what she's like . . . headstrong . . . always has been."

"I'm sorry to say I didn't have the opportunity to know the new queen very well."

"Barely a slip of a thing, but very determined. She met Balinski and decided he was only interested in men, so she made up her mind to travel with him. Money changed hands. A bargain was made."

"Where did he take her?"

"A safe house. A place Konstantyn never knew about. It doesn't do to have all one's secrets in the open, and my master . . ."

"You work for Karl Gustav of Sverija."

"It's an honor to serve my king and his family."

"So you sent Kristina to a safe house."

"I thought so."

"What happened?"

Maksimilian spread his arms wide. "I wish I knew. The farmer and his wife simply disappeared. Their milk cattle were left unattended, the house unlocked." He raised both hands. "We didn't find out for some time, of course, because we couldn't make contact lest we drew attention. We'd hoped for a note, but when nothing arrived Martyna went and discovered all."

"And this Balinski?"

Maksimilian scowled. "A very good question. I have a lot of questions of my own to ask him when my agents catch up with him, but he seems to be more slippery than I suspected. Oh, there's a Ludwik Balinski, all right. Owns a small farm by Koplarr, just as he said, only the real one is sixty-seven years old and deaf as a post."

"God in Heaven!" Valdas shook his head.

"Indeed!"

"We have to find her," Valdas said.

"You're telling me old news. Tell me how."

Valdas looked at Mirza. She shook her head, her eyes wide with fear. How quickly he'd begun to take her magic for granted.

"If we protect you, you can scry from somewhere outside the city and we can have fast horses ready to move you out of harm's way."

Maksimilian looked at Mirza with new interest. "You can scry, Mistress Mirza?"

She shook her head. "Not with that dark-thing hovering over the Gura. He shadows the door to the spirit world, a beggar outside the feast, waiting—longing—to be let in. I can feel him. I don't want to be behind the door when he starts battering at the planks."

Maksimilian looked at Valdas, plainly puzzled.

"Mirza tried to scry earlier, but there's something—a user of magic arts maybe—she says he's haunting her on the spirit plane. Is that right, Mirza?"

"Near enough. I scry and he's watching me. He knows where I am. We barely escaped his guard today. Next time we may not be so lucky. Even now I'm not sure whether he can scry for me when I'm not even aware of him. Who uses magic in the palace?"

"Gerhard's chancellor, maybe?" Maksimilian asked. "I heard rumors."

"Zygmund Kazimir is no sorcerer," Valdas said. "He's all swagger, an opinionated leech, but that's all. Claimed to be a scholar when he first came to court."

"Well, someone up on the Gura has power," Mirza said. "And plenty of it."

Maksimilian nodded. "Kazimir is certainly not flaunting himself as a sorcerer."

Seeing Mirza's face, Valdas changed tack swiftly. She would either decide to scry or not in her own good time, but maybe he could put her mind at rest. "I know someone I can talk to, find out if there are rumors about him. Shall I do that? See if I can find out what we're dealing with?"

Mirza swallowed and nodded.

"This Balinski . . ." Dahnay's alto voice cut in. "How can we find him? Did he have any other contacts in Biela Miasto? Did he have a favorite out of your whores?"

"I never saw him talk to anyone, save maybe Klara, my cook. He was never more than polite to the girls. He doesn't seem to be interested in women. I assume he prefers men."

"You only have female whores here?" Mirza asked.

"The city ordinances forbid . . . and though the Justicia turns a blind eye when it suits them—which is most of the time for a consideration—any transgression would give them the opportunity to ask questions, and that's something I can't afford."

"There are many reasons why a man might not want a whore," Dahnay said. "Even though Valdas can't possibly think of one, as I noticed his pants twitching when I entered the room and I hardly think I am the cause."

Maksimilian laughed and clapped Valdas on the back. "I can see I'm going to make a good profit out of having you under my roof. Be good to my girls."

Valdas grinned. "Have no fear of that."

"Balinski used the room in the attic. If it pleases you, you may use the same one."

"Has it been touched since he left?" Dahnay asked.

"It's a room we don't use much."

"While Valdas questions your ladies, I'll try and get a feel for this man and see if I can do my own kind of scrying—the non-magical kind." She stood up.

"I'd like to start with your most buxom blonde?" Valdas glanced at Mirza and she shrugged almost imperceptibly—a tacit *go ahead, it's nothing to do with me*. He smiled ruefully, feeling his loins begin to heat up at just the thought. He took a deep, calming breath. "But I feel I should really discuss Balinski with your cook first."

"And I, my friend Maksimilian, would appreciate another spiced mead," Mirza said. "And can you tell me more about your Queen Kristina? What led her to conceal her pregnancy? Why did she believe she was in danger as soon as Konstantyn died? I want to know her likes and dislikes, her skills, how practical she is. I even want to know about her childhood ailments. The one possibility we all must admit is that she didn't survive the birth of her child. She may have had to give birth far away from the comforts she's used to."

CHAPTER FIFTY-TWO

Lind

LIND SAW THE white walls of Biela Miasto looming toward him. He was going to have to report Zalecki's death, but not by his hand. The Anglu Lord Callender had finally admitted to smashing the man's head open. It hadn't even been the honorable death that Zalecki deserved. Lind would have liked to give Callender the same kind of ignoble death, but clean kills were by far the safest. He'd retrieved Zalecki's sabre, though, and sent Callender to meet his maker with a stiletto to the heart. There hadn't even been much blood.

He'd collected a purse from Jadzia, which made her an accomplice and so ensured her silence, something which relieved him greatly. He really didn't want to have to kill her. She'd taken the confirmation of Zalecki's death with a pressing together of her lips and a frown, but she'd nodded approval at the report of Callender's end. Sensible woman.

Lind hadn't hung around after that, though staying would have been easy. Jadzia was a bright flame and he'd been out in the cold and the dark for a long time. He reminded himself that cold and dark was the way he liked it.

Returning to Biela Miasto, he noticed even more troop activity on the roads. The recruiters had been out and new conscripts were marching toward training camps, almost guarded by their sergeants in case they decided to make a run for it. It did, indeed, look as though King Gerhard was charting a course for war, though no one seemed to know why or think it a good idea.

He couldn't avoid the guards on the Biela Miasto gate, but as Lukasz Kowalik, he passed right through without hindrance.

Now he had to confront the thing that disturbed him. Having ascertained one of his targets was already dead, once he'd reported that fact to his employer, his next task should be to find the dowager queen and bring her back. He was still undecided about that task. Maybe he should quietly disappear. He had enough stashed away to set him up in any country he chose.

If he took Kristina's word that she wasn't behind her own husband's death, this order to find her meant that his anonymous employer must be either King Gerhard or possibly one of the ruling houses of Sverija, Kassubia, or Ruthenia. Any one of them could benefit from the destabilization of Zavonia, and from what he'd seen, the country was going to hell in a handbasket. He wasn't generally one for reviewing any of his actions with regret, but killing Konstantyn had begun a chain reaction that would make his own life more difficult. His only consolation was that if someone wanted Konstantyn dead they would have found another way if he'd refused the commission.

Why did they now want Kristina? Did they know she was pregnant? If it was Gerhard—and everything pointed in that direction—he would have tortured that information out of Kristina's women. That answered the why. Kristina wasn't the important one here, but Konstantyn's child was. If Kristina had been safely delivered, her child was potentially the fulcrum upon which anyone with a modicum of power could balance a lever to depose Gerhard. With the child safely dead, Gerhard would have no rival for the throne. So much resting on a head that must be barely a few weeks old.

Of course, the most sensible thing would be for Gerhard to marry Kristina and declare Konstantyn's son his heir. It would secure his throne from all comers in one easy move. Maybe that would be in Kristina's best interests, too—presuming the Father on Earth would give dispensation for her to marry her late husband's nephew.

If only he knew who he was working for.

He made his way through the city to the East Gate and found the North Star Coffeehouse on the corner of Podwale Street as he'd been told to do. It occupied the ground floor of a respectable, if faded townhouse in a row of eight such. Above the door was a plaque bearing the legend:

Let this nasty drink
Never sully a Christian mouth.

He smiled to himself. Long considered a pagan drink because of its Turkish and Arabic origins, coffee had now become respectable thanks to the patronage of the Father on Earth, but even the most respectable of establishments liked to play upon its reputation. It gave respectable citizens a thrill to drink a Satanic brew with no censure from their confessors, and it gave rakes an excuse to pamper their hangovers in the mornings instead of returning to the taverns early.

He was surprised to hear music as he opened the door. On the far side of the room a young man with a painted face played a clavichord passably well—not that he was any great judge of music. From the ripple of applause from a table of middle-aged gentlemen sitting close by, and the coins stacked on the edge of the instrument, he presumed they, at least, found it charming. Of course, it may have been the player who held the attraction, but Lind took one look at his pretty face and shuddered.

Sliding into an empty booth, as far away from the entertainment as he could, he ordered coffee and enquired casually for Chazon.

The young man waiting on tables acknowledged his request with a nod and pointed through a low doorway. "I think you may be more comfortable in our private room, sir."

"Of course." Lind crossed the busy shop, skirting past tables of respectable gents, professorial types, guild merchants, dubious-looking rakes, and even a party of individuals as dark as the coffee they drank, dressed in immaculate turbans and pale flowing robes. Everyone was seated in close proximity while managing to ignore each other completely. The coffeehouse was a good choice for a meeting. It brought all ages, all classes—above a certain level, of course—together in a melange that didn't exist anywhere else in the city.

The private room was small and plain, holding three square tables with chairs drawn up around each. He chose one away from the window and slightly in the lee of the open door and poured himself thick black coffee from a pot brought by a serving girl.

He wasn't kept waiting long. A middle-aged but wiry man, plainly dressed in a woolen zupan and matching sash, entered the room with both hands held empty before him. Lind wondered how many men his employer had trusted with his secret, or whether the last one was already dead. This man was younger than the last. His eyes were old, though.

"My master asks for news." He dropped a pouch onto the table that landed heavily with a metallic clink.

"Zalecki is dead." Lind didn't touch it. "Not by my hand. He was killed by a sly bastard of an Angluman on the road to Bieloria. I found the news in Dadziga."

"Zalecki didn't reach the border?"

"No."

"Did he meet with any agent of Ruthenia?"

"That I can't say. From what I know, I doubt it."

The man pushed the pouch toward him.

Lind pocketed it and sipped his coffee.

"What about the lady?" the man asked.

"My next job, but difficult without a starting point. If only I knew which city I should begin my search. She could be anywhere."

"That is why he's paying you."

And others, I'll bet.

They'd asked him to find her alive, not to kill her, so surely they didn't mean her harm. He suppressed a shudder. There were more ways to harm a woman than kill her, especially a vulnerable woman with a small child that held the balance of a kingdom in its tiny palm.

What would this man know? He was slightly built, a little smaller than Lind. The room was quiet. Lind could probably take him, but he couldn't extract information without making too much noise and once done he would have tipped his hand. He briefly considered trying to follow him, but he obviously wasn't dealing with a naive boy. He'd probably even got a guard waiting outside.

Lind nodded. The man got up and left.

Giving him time to get away from the building, Lind picked up his cooling coffee, bitter and black, but sweetened with honey. He sipped it again and grimaced. It really was an invention of Satan.

He didn't really care much one way or the other about the baby, except insofar as Kristina would care, but she had done nothing to bring trouble down on herself. Possibly the best thing he could do would be to run round in circles and fail spectacularly, but if there were others out hunting he ran the risk that someone else would find her first. If he wanted to see her safe, his only link to her was Trader Maksimilian.

CHAPTER FIFTY-THREE
Valdas

VALDAS NUZZLED THE breasts of a corpulent redhead. "Oh, my lovely girl!"

His sex life was on the up again. Literally. He never minded going without for a reason—at least his hand got plenty of exercise—as long as he knew the famine would end. He'd missed Mirza, as much for the warmth and companionship as for the actual fucking. Now he felt like a starveling who'd been given the keys to the pantry. Though it was a pity Aniela wasn't here.

"Valdas, you say 'lovely girl' to all the girls."

"No . . . don't." He stopped his tongue flicking across her nipple to answer. "Who says I do?"

"All the girls." She laughed and slapped his bare shoulder lightly. "Go on, Valdas, get out of here. Twice is enough for any man and I've got work to do. I should charge you double."

"Edyta . . ."

"Brygida . . . Edyta was last night. That settles it. Out. Go back to your own room, to your own women!"

"They're not mine." Valdas sat up on the edge of the bed and reached for his pants. He couldn't imagine either Dahnay or Mirza bowing their heads meekly to any man like a faithful hussif. "They belong to themselves."

"As do we all, sweet." She smacked his arm gently. "Beata says you can call on her tomorrow."

"Why do I get the feeling you girls are all comparing notes?"

"Because we are. I'll tell you what we like about you, my lovely boy? You haven't lost the joy of it. Every woman's as wonderful to you as your first."

"And here's me thinking I'm impressing you with my skill and all you want is my inept enthusiasm."

"Go get some sleep."

He finished dressing, saluted as he left, and boots in one hand, he tiptoed up to the attic. He didn't need a candle: the pale silver-blue light of the full moon shining through the rippled window glass showed Mirza asleep, snoring gently, empty mead cup by her bedside. He frowned. Four days of inactivity and she was dulling her senses against that magic other, wherever he was. It was obvious that she'd had a real scare. He believed in it now, but he didn't pretend to understand magic or what drove someone who used it. All he could do was to be guided by her. But, oh, that scrying thing would be useful right now if she could figure out where Kristina, if she still lived, had gone to ground, or where he might find the bastard Balinski. Whatever his name was.

Tomorrow he would go and see if he could find Tomas and glean some information about what was happening on the Gura.

A shadow unfolded itself and he gasped in surprise.

"Dahnay! You startled me. I didn't know you were still awake."

"You smell of sex." Dahnay crossed the room. "Come and look at this. I didn't spot it at first, but I've gone over every inch of this room and now I've started to look outside."

"Outside?" They were four floors up, what was she talking about?

She took his hand, hers warm, strong, and dry—*Oh, Dahnay, so reserved. What a waste of a woman!*—and led him to the dormer window.

"Look. Outside."

He looked out on planes and angles of roof and wall bathed in moonlight and shadow. Almost enough light to see the dull red of pantiles against the cream stucco or gray-brown stone of the walls, or was his mind telling him that because he knew the daylight colors? Across the way was a row of five-story tenements, similar but subtly different from each other. Their lower floors had been taken over by businesses, the upper ones rented out for accommodation. At least one was a whorehouse that Valdas knew by reputation only, none of it good. He'd never frequent a house where the girls worked under duress. Across and up the street a noisy tavern, the Rose, blazed lamplight out onto the cobbles through an open door despite the chill of autumn.

"What am I looking for, specifically?"

Dahnay pulled him into the small window opening, her body pushed up close. He could feel her against him, whipcord and ebony. No softness where a woman should be soft, but . . .

"Look!" She tapped him on the cheek to get his attention. "Or rather, feel."

He was feeling. Oh! She meant outside.

She guided his hand to just below the window frame. An iron hook, just big enough to hold a rope or act as a handhold, had been driven into the wood of the frame.

"And again down there. Look."

Where the roof tipped its rainwater runoff into a wooden gutter another spike similar to the first.

"And lean your head right out and look to the right to the next dormer."

She stepped away and the warmth of her was gone. Shaking his head to clear it, he looked. Another spike.

"Part of the roof construction?" he asked.

She shook her head. "Too new. Not rusted enough. Someone put those there in case they needed to make an exit across the rooftops. A quick exit, I imagine. I think our Balinski is a burglar and a thief, someone used to entering and exiting buildings four floors above the ground. I think we need to check with the Justicia to see if any notable thefts were recorded to coincide with his visit."

"Is this another hook?" He pushed his arm out of the window again, feeling downward.

"Where?"

She stepped in close and reached out, flattening her body against his. It was an easy thing, in the interests of allowing her to reach a little further, to casually rest the palm of his hand between her shoulder blades and draw her closer.

She stilled, as only Dahnay could.

Her face was inches away from his. He could blame the wine, except he'd had none. He breathed her in, intoxicating, spicy, dangerous, and . . . He couldn't help himself. He kissed her lips, gently, an inquiry at most.

She didn't respond.

But she didn't move away either. And she didn't try to kill him, which was a good sign. He bent toward her again and she gave a little shake of her head and stepped back.

"I'm sorry," he said.

She drew a deep breath. "I . . . don't . . ."

"Ah. This will never happen again, I promise."

He heard her breathing, felt her breath on his lips.

"You're a good man, Valdas Zalecki."

She stepped away and the emptiness rushed in again.

CHAPTER FIFTY-FOUR
Lind

LIND LEFT THE coffee cup half full, and thinking himself once more into the Ludwik Balinski identity he'd always used at Maksimilian's, he shouldered his pack and crossed the city to the slightly more respectable bad part of town.

He mounted the steps to the heavy front door, still closed at this time in a morning, and knocked loudly, the sound of his fist echoing throughout the building. He imagined sleepy whores mumbling and turning over in their beds. Heavy bolts slid back and the door cracked open on its hinges. He couldn't see who was on the other side in the gloom, but the door swung inward quickly. A large hairy hand grabbed him by the collar and dragged him inside. He was about to utter a greeting when Maksimilian's fist came hurtling toward the bridge of his nose.

Pain exploded his face open, and blackness sucked him through shattered shards of bone and down into a pit.

❦

Lind came to tied to a chair in a cellar.

God, no, not a cellar, for pity's sake!

He swallowed, but his tongue was parchment dry. The taste of blood lingered at the back of his throat. His nose was probably broken. He couldn't move. The chair back was wide enough to pull the inside of his arms and elbows painfully tight at full extension. His wrists felt raw where the rope dug into his flesh.

He allowed himself a moment of blind panic and then locked the feeling away.

"Where is she?" Maksimilian's face was in his, so close he could see the spittle on the man's beard, count the gray hairs in the ringlet at his temples, and smell the herring on his breath.

"What? Who?"

"You know damn well who. Where is she?"

"Roza? I don't know."

"Yes . . . Roza. You're going to tell me, you sniveling turd, or I will make you very, very sorry."

Pain followed, but it was only pain. He could cope with pain, divorce his mind from it as he'd learned to do when . . .

His mind slipped sideways to another place. A bad place.

He was drowning! No, it was only water, icy, painful, poured over his head in a steady stream from a height. He was on the floor now. The water woke him from the merciful blackness he'd sunk into, but it activated the bruises and cuts on his face afresh.

Push the edges of panic back. Roll them away.

Cold, he was so cold.

He had no clothes on!

No clothes!

A man stood over him. Maksimilian. Not Tourmine, he told himself. *Not Tourmine.* Maksimilian.

"What did you do with her?"

"Nothing." Lind managed to mumble the word through swollen lips.

Maksimilian left him alone. He heard movement, a door opening, several pairs of feet clattering down the steps. He tried to catch what they were saying but the words were low. He caught the tone, though. Surprise, a little anger, curiosity.

He understood that these new people might be deciding his fate, but one eye was crusted shut and they were out of his field of vision. He strained his ears. Were they arguing?

Heavy footsteps. Two pairs of hands under his upper arms lifted him bodily from the floor. Lifted him and carried him, his bare toes dragging across the icy cold of the flagstones. Then they dropped him onto . . .

No!

A barrel, his naked arse in the air . . .

Fifteen years crumbled to dust.

Oh, god, no! No! No! No!

Someone started screaming, a raw, primeval sound rasping from a desperate throat.

Oh, God! It was him.

Tourmine is dead. He held onto that thought. *Tourmine is dead!*

A hand touched his buttocks. He screamed again.

"I told you this was a bad idea. Get out, all of you. Leave him to me." A woman's voice cut through his screams.

He felt someone gather up his hands and hold them, cold and shaking, in her own warm ones.

Her face was on a level with his own as he raised his head uncomfortably, the barrel rough beneath his chest and belly. He could barely see her in the murk of the cellar and through swollen eyelids awash with tears, but he got the impression of dark eyes haloed with dark hair and a terrible wound on the side of her face.

"Tell me your name," she said.

"Ludwik Balinski," he managed through thickened lips.

"Tell me your real name."

"Konrad Nizin . . ."

"Your real name."

Breath escaped him. "Lind."

"That's better, Lind. My name's Mirza. Now, how old are you?"

That couldn't hurt, could it? "Twenty-eight, maybe . . . twenty-nine."

"Where were you born?"

Another answer that couldn't hurt. "Sverija."

"Where do you live now?"

He wasn't ever going back. He could tell her that. "Tepet."

"Where was the last place you were before you came here?"

God, she was asking him the answers to meaningless questions, getting him into the habit. The real ones would start any time now.

"Dadziga. I came from Dadziga."

"Was Roza Kushnir with you?"

That must be obvious. "No."

"When did you last see her?"

"Months ago."

He heard her draw breath. "Where did she go?"

"Who wants to know?"

"Was she alive when you last saw her?"

"Yes."

"Where did she go?"

He didn't answer.

"Did you sell her out?"

As if he'd answer yes to that. He shook his head.

"Then where did she go?"

He didn't answer.

Mirza touched his face, stood up, and let her hand trail down his neck. She felt along his back, making him wince at new welts. Then her hand came to rest on his buttocks. He clenched all his muscles, tightening himself as if that alone could protect him. She rubbed the cheeks of his arse impartially and then patted them as if he were a pet dog.

"Old scars, Lind, such a lot of old scars. And not all of them visible, I think. Did you kill Roza Kushnir?"

"What? No!"

"We're trying to help her. We need to find her."

"Yeah, right. Maksimilian . . ."

"You want me to get him?"

"Uh, na!" He shook his head. His words sounded garbled even to himself. "Bastard set me up. Nearly got caught. Could have done the job so much better if I'd known."

"Done what job, Lind?"

"Taken the little queen somewhere safe!"

He heard her suck in breath again.

He tried to get purchase to push himself off the barrel, but his limbs had no strength. He flopped forward again. "Bastard Maksimilian."

"Here."

She put her forearms under his and let him push himself backward until he was kneeling, then she rolled the barrel away from him and placed a blanket around his shoulders. The rough, scratchy wool smelled of lye soap and felt like heaven.

"Can you walk if I help you?"

"Think so."

She tucked her shoulder under his armpit, and with some maneuvering and some hands on his bare flesh, which he hadn't the liberty to object to, she helped him to his feet. One foot in front of the other, she guided him across the cellar and painfully, one at a time, up stone steps, then a wooden stair, and another and another.

"My room." He recognized the door she shouldered open, seeing it through one swollen eye.

"It was." Her breath came in gasps. "Lie down here."

A bed, more blankets, a wet cloth on his face.

"Tell me about Roza, about Kristina, Lind."

"She's pregnant, did you know?"

"Yes. Though by the one god's grace she may be a mother by now."

"Suppose so."

"But she was still pregnant the last time you saw her?"

"Dear God, I'd have run if I'd known what she was. She almost got us caught at the city gate. And that hair. Too recognizable. Wasn't hard to figure out, though, once the soldiers started looking for a flame-haired queen. Naive little thing. Such pretty hair, but so distinctive. Had to show her how to dye it. Hadn't a clue. Never had to look after herself a day in her life."

"You dyed her hair?"

"Brown. Much less distinctive."

"When did you see her last, and where?"

"Torek. We only stayed together for a few days. I checked it out— the farm she was going to had been taken over by the king's men. Only Maksimilian and her companion, Marilena, knew about it. One of them must have talked. Maksimilian?"

"Not Maksimilian. He's been going out of his mind with worry."

"Ahh, the companion, then. Kristina said she trusted her, but a good questioner can always find his victim's weak point . . . You found mine."

"We did. I'm sorry. I didn't know about the scars. How old were you?"

He squeezed his eyes shut and shook his head. It began to pound.

"That's all right," Mirza said. "It's none of my business. Tell me about Kristina. Where did you leave her?"

"She left me. I melted her plate into gold bars, sold one and gave her coin, told her to find a reputable Jew when she needed to sell another. I got her some henna for her hair, and clothes that were . . . more ordinary."

God's ballocks, his head was really pounding now. And his body was on fire, the weals on his chest and back burning. "I taught her all I could so she might disappear and make her own way to Sverija. I hope she was a fast learner. One afternoon I returned to the inn and she'd taken her things and gone. She'd left me two bars of gold." He shook his head. "I wasn't doing it for the money."

A pain stabbed through his right eye and he flopped back on the bed, able to see very little through his left. He could only see Mirza in outline until she turned to take something from a tall, black man and daylight fell on the most cruel birthmark he'd ever seen. He should have had such a mark. It would have been his protection and his salvation.

He reached up and touched her face as she bent over him with another wet cloth. "You're beautiful," he said.

All of a sudden holding on to reality was too much for him to bear. He let himself slide away into darkness.

CHAPTER FIFTY-FIVE
Valdas

"I THOUGHT YOU would have managed to get a posting away from Biela Miasto by now."

Valdas stood behind the young man at the busy bar of the Bell and crowded close as if by accident.

"For God's sake . . ." Tomas began to turn, but Valdas nudged him, trying not to grin. It was good to see an old friend.

"Outside. Five minutes."

Tomas nodded and turned to the bar.

The inn yard was pleasantly busy. A coach from Riyja had recently disgorged its passengers, and ostlers moved in patterns sensible only to themselves. Valdas found himself a corner by a pile of luggage and tried to look inconspicuous. It worked. Tomas walked past him twice until he whistled.

The young man's eyes widened. "I would hardly have recognized you." Tomas stroked his own mustache and grinned.

"Oh, the tash? Long gone. I'd almost forgotten it."

"Have you been in the city all along?"

"No, I've had a roundabout journey via Bieloria. Long story. I came looking for the queen, Kristina."

"You and the rest of the palace. She's not been seen since the king's funeral. The real king." He spat. "Chancellor Kazimir's new bully boys have been turning the place upside down. City searches and everything."

"Bully boys?"

"The Chancellor's Own Guard, recruited from . . . well, let's just say they'd make neither the High Guard, the Watch, nor the Hussars, but they think themselves above everyone and stick together all the time."

"How many of them?"

"Sixty. You'll recognize them if you see them in the street. Their mentes are dark red, wine colored, and they travel in packs. They are loyal to Kazimir, probably because he pays them well."

"Are you safe? No one has suddenly recalled you were High Guard?"

"I've not been drawing attention."

"They're still looking for me?"

"As far as I know, but it's a cold trail now, so we hear very little."

"Of course not. And what about the queen? Do they know they're looking for a pregnant woman?"

"What? No. At least, if they did, no one told us. Shit, no wonder she ran away." Tomas could weigh up the implications as well as the next man. "Is she safe?"

"I don't know. She might have had the baby by now. Hopefully she's found her own way to Sverija, but if not, it's my job to see Konstantyn's child safe."

"Of course. What can I do to help?"

"I need to know the inside gossip. Is there any mention of magic anywhere on the Gura? A mage or self-styled sorcerer maybe?" Valdas paused. "What? Don't stare. I know, I know. Magic doesn't exist, but I've seen things that—Oh, never mind, just take my word for it. I didn't used to believe, but now I do, all right?"

"If you say so, but—"

"What about Kazimir?"

"Would such a braggart be able to resist lauding his powers if he had them? Are you sure there's . . . I mean . . . magic?"

"Just take my word for it and hope you never see any proof. Any rumblings of discontent from the clerics? Cardinal Pieritz?"

"There's plenty of gossip, but not about magic. There are those who wonder just how close Kazimir is to King Gerhard."

"Close as in . . . ?"

"Lovers."

"What do you think?" If anyone would know the telltale behavior patterns it would be Tomas, whose close friendship with Henryk had been known, if not openly acknowledged.

"I don't see it, personally. That kind of relationship is played out subtly, but I can usually tell." He shook his head. "No, it's a rumor I'd discount."

"So what is going on?"

"Kazimir is the one issuing all the orders, on the king's behalf, of course. Gerhard spends a lot of time in his suite. There's no High

Guard anymore, just the Chancellor's Own. The generals run back and forth for their orders."

"So who's responsible for the ballocking mess in the Tevecor Reaches and this soon-to-be war in the south?"

"King Gerhard's name is on all the decrees, but . . ." He shrugged. "In the back corridors the servants are already talking about King Kazimir."

"Gods-poxed charlatan. Gerhard and his chancellor are well matched."

"Gerhard's no Konstantyn," Tomas said. "The Amber Crown weighs more than the head it sits on."

"Keep your eyes and ears open."

"You know where to find me. I come down here regularly—often with the Hecht brothers or Klavons and Kowalski. They're good men and still loyal to King Konstantyn's memory. This new king hasn't proved himself yet. In fact, he's gone a long way toward disproving himself."

"I'm not looking to start a revolution, Tomas."

"I'm not offering to join you in one."

Valdas felt the corners of his mouth twitch. *Of course not.*

They shook hands and parted.

CHAPTER FIFTY-SIX

Lind

THE FIRST TIME he surfaced, Lind was in a nightshirt, lying under warm blankets, and a gibbous moon shone in his eyes through the small dormer window. He knew the room, though the bed wasn't in the best position to be defensible. Not where he used to have it. He pushed the blankets away, swung his feet to the bare wooden floor, and sat upright. One wobbly step at a time, he tottered to the dormer, pushed it open, and reached out.

"Looking for your ironwork?"

He gasped and stepped back, smacking his head into the inside of the dormer. His knees buckled and the black man caught him awkwardly and half-carried him to the bed. He struggled to get away from those strong hands until Mirza came and took over. She rolled him into the bed and covered him, then brought a chair and sat beside him.

"Give her some rest, man, for God's sake." The black man bent over him, voice slightly effeminate.

Lind shuddered and rolled over, burying his face in his arms.

The next time he woke, Mirza was there alone.

"What are you going to do with me?" he asked.

"Do with you? That depends. Valdas is riding to Torek to see if he can pick up Kristina's trail. It's old, though." She sighed. "I might have to scry and I really don't want to do that."

"You're a witch. You bewitched the truth from me." Uncomfortable memories of magic surfaced.

"Alas, I didn't even need to. You talk in your sleep. Remarkably revealing. Tell me about Tourmine? Was he the one who gave you those scars?"

Lind clenched his jaw, but still he felt his eyes prickle. Tourmine was entirely his own business. "What's wrong with me?"

"Maksimilian was a bit too enthusiastic. The crack on the head gave you a brain fever for a couple of days. You're on the mend."

"I've spent two days spilling my guts to the world?"

"Only to me, and maybe to Dahnay when I had to get some sleep."

"The Ethiop?"

"She knows how to keep her own council."

"She?"

"Oh, heavens, you're as bad as Valdas. Though in all fairness he hadn't had his brains beaten in when he met her."

"Valdas?"

"You'll meet him later. I managed to convince him that you hadn't harmed the queen. He's very . . . protective."

"Valdas Zalecki?"

"Yes, do you know him?"

Lind began to laugh and laugh until the tears rolled down his face. It wasn't even funny.

◆ ── ◆

By the time Zalecki returned to Maksimilian's, Lind's face was as close to its normal shape as it was ever going to get, if not its normal color. His nose had been permanently resculpted by Maksimilian's fist. He supposed he was lucky. The man was as big as a bear. He could have smashed his nose right into his brain. The rest of his body had mended quickly, the hurts being surface only, and Mirza being an excellent healer.

He wondered whether Zalecki would recognize him from his days delivering fish up to the Gura, but if anything his new nose protected him. When he looked at his reflection in a glass, the pretty boy had been replaced with the face of a bare-knuckle pugilist.

"Good God, man, you look terrible!" Zalecki was obviously not a man to veil his words. "I'm sorry for what we did to you. We thought you had abducted the queen or worse still."

He'd been expecting . . . What had he been expecting? Abuse? Pain? He certainly hadn't expected Valdas Zalecki to apologize in such an open manner. How should he play this? What was going to let him get out of here whole?

"I know what you thought. I'd have thought the same, done the same." Lind took a deep breath and offered his hand. Zalecki took it without hesitation.

The Ethiop stood behind him. Lind bowed stiffly to her. "I thank you for your kindness, mistress, when I was not myself."

She inclined her head.

"Did you find anything?" Mirza asked the exact question he'd wanted to ask.

"A Jew in Torek bought two gold bars, one from a man—" He nodded toward Lind. "And another from a woman who, though she hid it beneath a full-cut szuba, was pregnant."

Trader Maksimilian lumbered up the stairs in time to hear the answer. "Did she say where she was going?"

"No."

That's my girl! Lind thought. He wondered briefly whether to come clean about his mission to find the queen and his suspicion that the person who wanted her had a sorcerer at his beck and call, but that would invite far too many questions and was hardly relevant to the finding of her right now.

"If she was trying to reach Sverija, she might have headed for Riyja. It's the most obvious port." Maksimilian offered a parchment map and they rolled it out on the small table, close to the window.

"She wasn't," Lind said. "At least not before the birth. She was worried about the sea-crossing and the difficulty of finding a reputable captain who would sail into what amounts to enemy waters with a pregnant woman on board. Sailor superstitions being what they are, she thought she stood a better chance after the birth. When we last spoke, her inclination was to find somewhere safe for her confinement and then travel with the baby." He leaned across the map and unrolled it to its fullest extent. "It's all guesswork. She could have gone to Ruthenia."

"No," Dahnay said. "Not as far as I know, anyway. Tsarina Zofia would have known."

Lind shrugged. "Ruthenia's a big place and I did warn her not to trust anyone. She could have gone via Dadziga and been in Ruthenia before the end of the summer. Once in Ruthenia she could cross into Sverijan-occupied Suomija and present herself to any garrison commander there. Or she could take passage for Sverija from Piotrsburg."

"If she headed the other way, for Posenja, she'd meet all the troops massing down there and find the border closed," Zalecki said.

"She might not have realized that until it was too late," Mirza said.

"What about the coast?" Dahnay trailed one finger across the map. "It's also possible to take a ship for Sverija from any one of a dozen ports."

"If Posenja is too dangerous, might she try crossing into Kassubia?" Mirza said.

"The border will also be heavily fortified and crawling with extra troops," Zalecki said. "Ah, it's all speculation. We don't know a thing. If she decided to have her baby first she might, even now, be heading for one of these ports—and we don't have a clue as to which one."

"If she headed for Ruthenia rather than Bieloria . . ." Lind stabbed his finger at the map. "She'd likely have still gone via Dadziga and taken a caravan. I have a contact there. There's not a caravan coming or going that she doesn't know."

Zalecki's eyes narrowed, brown yardsticks measuring him, and Lind realized why this man had risen so high in Konstantyn's service.

"Are you volunteering?" Zalecki asked.

Was he? He was certainly volunteering to find her; whether he came back and turned her over to them entirely depended on her. It also had the advantage of getting him out of Maksimilian's whorehouse with what remained of his skin in one piece. After that, he'd see.

"I'm volunteering."

"I don't trust him," Maksimilian growled and snatched his map back.

"Fine, wake me when you find her." Lind crossed to his bed, the bed he guessed must be Mirza's, and flopped onto it, closing his eyes and exaggeratedly sighing. Too much talk. If they'd let him go he could be in Dadziga in five days. He recognized with a small shock that the prospect of seeing Jadzia Lizovska again was not altogether displeasing. He found it difficult to hide a smirk. He could never tell Zalecki, of course, but he'd killed the Anglu merchant Callender for Jadzia, partly on the supposition that Callender had murdered Zalecki. Would Jadzia regret her commission if she knew Zalecki still lived? Possibly not. Callender had also transgressed the unwritten rule of business. *Don't cheat in the same place twice.*

"Of course, if Mistress Mirza would scry . . ." Maksimilian said.

"Mistress Mirza won't scry while the darkness haunts the Gura!"

Lind opened both eyes. This was something he'd not heard in Mirza's voice before, fear with an edge of panic. A witch afraid of magic? He could understand that.

"But if . . ."

Lind levered himself to his feet. "She said no!" He faced down Maksimilian.

CHAPTER FIFTY-SEVEN
Mirza

"SHE SAID NO!"

Mirza stepped back, surprised at Lind coming to her defense.

Dahnay put a restraining hand on Maksimilian's arm. "You didn't see what happened last time Mirza set out her scrying bowl, my friend, nor have you seen her power at full strength. I would hate to be close by if it came to a duel between shadow and fire. Let us find another way."

Mirza breathed again. It seemed that these people had become her friends—family—familia. Quite how and when it happened, she wasn't sure. Valdas's support was no surprise, but Lind stepping up to her defense had shocked her. Dahnay, too. The only other person she'd ever been able to rely on was Tsura. She missed Tsura, her common sense and undivided loyalty. She hoped Tsura was managing without her, but not so well that she couldn't regain her old place once this was done—if she survived what was surely coming.

Mirza looked from one to the other. Maksimilian implacable; Dahnay concerned; Lind fierce.

And she was just plain scared, because she knew that there might not be another way. She would have to scry if all else failed.

Valdas was watching Lind with some surprise on his face. He wasn't jealous, was he? No, Valdas was the last person to be jealous. He was open-hearted, but not possessive.

Maksimilian broke the silence. "We have to search, but the roads are thick with checkpoints and the ports are swarming with extra troops. I already have agents watching the shipping along the coast, so the smaller ports are covered. I also have . . . err . . . connections in Suomija. They've reported nothing so far." He stroked his heavy black beard. "Memel, maybe, though my money's on Riyja. It's the nearest and there are always mercanters who'll risk the crossing to Sverija for a price. My agent hasn't reported in, so I'll go there myself." He didn't elaborate.

Zalecki glared at Lind.

"I trust him, Valdas," Mirza said. She couldn't have explained why, she just did, and she always followed her feelings.

There was an uncomfortable pause and then Zalecki nodded. "All right, Maksimilian to Riyja; Lind to Dadziga; and I'll ride to Memel."

"Not without me," Dahnay said.

Valdas looked to Mirza. "What about you?"

"I'm going to stay here. I may not be able to scry or spirit-walk, but I can ask questions. I want to find out more about the magic up on the Gura. I may have to face it and I don't want to be ill prepared."

Valdas nodded. "Take care."

"Oh, I will."

◈———◈

Mirza dressed herself in her traveling clothes and pinned the rantuch to cover the worst of her squashed raspberry, then she went downstairs to ask where she might find an apothecary. Anyone performing magic might need supplies from an apothecary, so she simply had to keep asking and try to discover which ones might supply the Gura.

"An apothecary? Is he all right? Ludwik or whatever he's calling himself now?" Klara hefted an iron pan onto a hook and swung it over the fire in the iron range.

"His nose isn't pretty, but otherwise he's fine. He's riding out today, with Valdas."

"Valdas—didn't he used to be the king's bodyguard?"

"Yes, though are you supposed to know that?"

"There's not much I miss, but I tell nothing." She frowned. "So Valdas and Ludwi—Lind are riding together."

"Why not?"

"Oh, no reason. Did Maksimilian say anything?"

"Not to my knowledge."

"I'm sure it will be fine, then."

Mirza felt as though some subtext from the conversation had passed her by. "What about the apothecary?"

"Out of the kitchen door and through the side alley if you don't want to be seen leaving a whorehouse in daylight. Turn left down the street and go straight on until you come to the market square. There's an apothecary on the right-hand side, on the corner. Though you might want to talk to the dame in Rivergate Yard first. She makes magic potions, if you believe what she says."

"Thanks." Mirza crossed the kitchen but halted with her hand on the door. "Did you want to tell me something about Lind?"

"Nothing." Klara shook her head. "Nothing at all."

CHAPTER FIFTY-EIGHT
Lind

LIND RODE ALONG with Zalecki and Dahnay as far as Korek, where Lind planned to ride for Dadziga while the other two took the road south to Memel. Dahnay said little and seemed to have a knack of blending into her background, which was unusual for a six-foot-tall black woman with a scarred face like an ebony sculpture. With her along, killing Zalecki was not an option. In truth, Lind hadn't decided what to do about his commission. He'd already reported Zalecki's death, so presumably his employer had ceased to search. Lind would have the opportunity to kill Zalecki after they found Kristina if he needed to appease his employer by completing at least half his task, but until then the search needed all of them. He didn't dislike Zalecki, in fact he respected him, but that wasn't a consideration. It had never been a consideration. A job was a job.

In a way, the contract on Zalecki's head provided a bond between them that Lind found unique. Zalecki was an easy man to talk to, and the fact that whatever they discussed would likely end up in his grave made it even easier.

"Is that the best you can afford?" Lind asked Zalecki during one of their brief stops to rest the horses. Zalecki's ugly beast with the mule ears raised its head from tearing at a patch of grass and eyed him up in such a way he determined not to get too close to either its teeth or hooves.

"Donkey? He's as cussed as they come, but he saved my life. I fell foul of someone—I'm still not sure of the details, they say a knock on the head can do that to a man—but Donkey stood sentry for me while I was senseless. Mirza's people found me. She patched me up."

Lind could fill in the missing details, tell him he'd dispatched Callender on his behalf, but not without inviting way too many questions.

"Mirza seems good at patching people up."

"It's what she does. Her band calls her their shulam. To them she's a witch and a healer."

Zalecki sat on the sloping grass by the roadside and opened the satchel that contained their nooning. Dahnay headed across the road toward the nearest clump of bushes.

"And what is Mirza to you?" Lind flopped down beside him and took the cloth-wrapped pack that was being offered. He checked it: bread and cheese, an onion, and a generous handful of dried vinefruit.

"She's a friend. A good friend."

"You're not together?" He took a bite of his bread and another of cheese.

"We shared a bed for a short time. She won't have anybody right now, so don't think to try your luck." Zalecki started on the fruits. Typical of the man to gobble up the sweet first.

"I'm not . . . I wouldn't." Lind paused with the bread halfway to his mouth again.

"She's scared," Zalecki said.

Lind could understand that.

"Ah, my friend, I see from your face that you misinterpret. She's not scared *of* me. She's scared of what she might do *to* me." Zalecki put more vinefruits into his mouth and chewed. "We were set on in the Tevecor Reaches, a local band of thugs out for what they could get, and intending to share Mirza and Dahnay between them. Mirza burned their leader. I don't understand how she did it, but I know what I saw. She burned him with a fire made of magic."

Zalecki put out his hand palm first, and half closed his eyes as if touching the scene again in his mind. "He would have raped her, except . . . she screamed at him and . . . and his tackle started to smoke. And then flame. Then his body went up . . ." He flapped his hands upward. "Up in flames like oil-soaked kindling. He burned to ash in minutes—even his bones."

"Oh!" What would Lind have given for that ability and the opportunity to apply it retrospectively? His bread lay in his lap while he fed his imagination on the idea of Tourmine going up in flames, prick first.

"After that her face developed that mark," Zalecki said. "It was marked before, but only a red wine stain. She thought it bad, but it wasn't really."

Lind shrugged. "The mark doesn't matter. The person is worth more than the shell she's in."

"That's true; I've met some mighty ugly women in pretty shells." Zalecki grinned. "Anyway, since then Mirza's kept to her own bed. She says she's terrified of what she might do if someone else comes at her—even invited. I told her I'd risk it for one sweet night, but she thinks I'm joking." The grin left his face. "I'm not, you know. She needs to know someone trusts her. The men in her band already think that sleeping with her will shrivel their ballocks. If they'd seen what she did in the Tevecor Reaches they'd run screaming into the Northern Forest and not stop until they reached the great ice."

"And you'd risk bedding her?"

"She needs someone to hold her through whatever pain she has inside. Yes, I'd do it, even if I ended up a pile of ash. She's worth it."

The sincerity in Zalecki's voice cracked through to Lind's core. He had to turn away. Zalecki's hand on his shoulder brought him back to reality. He froze.

"Oh, sorry." Zalecki removed his hand and looked at it as if wondering how something so simple could cause offense. "I haven't worked you out yet, Lind. You don't seem to want women, but you sure as hell don't want men. Well, you've nothing to fear from me, I'm strictly a ladies' man. The more the better. I'd take on all of Maksimilian's whorehouse given half the chance—in fact, come to think of it, I might have done that already—one at a time, you understand. You've got to be honest with them, never let them come to rely on you for anything other than the moment, and never assume you have any rights over them. And always, always give them the respect they deserve."

"You make it sound simple."

Valdas shrugged. "I'm lucky. I had a good teacher, a handsome hunk of a woman almost twice my age. I was fifteen and that was a glorious summer. She broke my heart, of course. Turned her affections to the captain of a mercanter ship. But she couldn't wipe out what she'd given me. When it finished I joined the hussars, thinking the world was mine."

"Lucky." Lind felt his mouth twist. "I had a teacher too." He almost choked on his own words. "I was apprenticed to him."

"Him? Oh, I get it. So you do swing to the left, eh?"

Maybe silence gave Zalecki an answer he'd expected, but Lind felt as though he'd swallowed an egg whole and couldn't have responded to save his life. Zalecki's eyes narrowed and Lind tried to school his face so that it didn't give away all of his secrets, but he was afraid it was too late.

"God in Heaven! I have the right of it, don't I?" Zalecki cursed under his breath and for a few heartbeats said nothing. Then he seemed to gather himself together. "You know, a man—or a woman for that matter—should be the way they are born and not take any shame from it. The church is pissing in the wind. How can it be ungodly when God created man?"

Lind felt a fiery knot of rage tightening in his belly. How dare this vulgar fucker tell him . . .

Oblivious, Zalecki rambled on, trying to make it better. Making it unutterably worse. "You shouldn't worry about it."

Lind's mouth worked but no sound came out of it. Somehow Zalecki realized he'd said too much. And his voice died away. Lind took two deep breaths and eventually managed, "I don't . . . I'm not . . . I don't fuck boys. I don't bend over and take it from any man. Never again."

"Well, you certainly don't seem to fuck the ladies . . . Oh . . ." Zalecki shook his head. "You don't know, do you? You don't know whether you swing left or right, so you don't do either."

The look on Zalecki's face was a mixture of astonishment and pity. Lind wanted to shove his fist into it, but it wouldn't make the words go away. He shook his head, not wanting to hear it.

Zalecki started to reach out to touch his shoulder, remembered and thankfully stopped. "My guess is that whatever you might have done . . . whatever might have been done to you . . . if your cock doesn't know it swings left handed by now, if you don't rise at the sight of a good-looking man, then you're probably not. Whether you do anything with that knowledge is up to you."

Zalecki broke eye contact, stood, and busied himself packing leftovers into his saddle bag. Was he right? Did Lind rise at the thought of a good-looking man? He certainly didn't rise at the thought of Zalecki . . . or anyone else he could remember. Did he rise at the thought of a woman, though? He thought about the women he'd known. Once, only once. And that had been a disaster.

CHAPTER FIFTY-NINE
Valdas

LEAVING LIND AT Torek, Valdas and Dahnay turned their horses south on the road to Memel, a heavily garrisoned port some ten leagues north of the Posenja border, situated at the mouth of the Curian Lagoon where the Curian River flowed into the Narrow Sea. They skirted several checkpoints on the road and noted at least two training camps.

"Your king is definitely mobilizing for war," Dahnay said after the first one.

"Yes, but how many fronts is he going to have to fight it on?"

Zavonia had enjoyed prosperity under Konstantyn and a measure of safety thanks to the marriage treaty with Sverija. Since regaining the Tevecor Reaches, Konstantyn had made it plain to Ruthenia and to Kassubia that he was not interested in expanding his borders further, but that he would defend them with relentless force. Both Kassubia and Ruthenia had large standing armies, but it helped that they didn't trust each other enough to form an alliance, so Konstantyn had faced them both down individually.

Of course, if Dahnay found Kristina and the Zavonian heir, Ruthenia might take advantage. Valdas did not want to see Ivan Petrov of Ruthenia take the Amber Crown, even with Konstantyn's sister by his side. Under Konstantyn, Zavonia had become an enlightened nation reaching forward to embrace new arts, sciences, and liberal ideas. Under Ruthenia, they'd drop back a century. He could imagine it. All the Landstrider bands expelled; scientists burned for heresy. That was not a Zavonia Konstantyn had wanted to see and neither did Valdas. But if the alliance, through Kristina, was truly lost, Sverija might look toward Zavonia with hungry eyes. Then they would have enemies on three sides.

Valdas smacked the heel of his hand into his forehead. "What if Gerhard is smarter than he appears? What if he's already negotiating with Ruthenia? They could plan to carve Posenja between them. Ruthenia would get a port on the Narrow Sea, and an alliance between Ruthenia and Zavonia would put an end to the Sverijan threat altogether."

"That's a lot of speculation," Dahnay said.

"Count the troops massing on the Posenjan border."

Valdas slouched deeper into his saddle as they approached Memel. From the slight rise above the town he could see a forest of masts in the harbor and, squinting against the low evening sun, at least three more ships standing off the Curian Spit, the great bar of sand that enclosed the lagoon that Memel guarded. His heart beat faster and his palms began to sweat as they rode down into the town. The place crawled with soldiers, foot-sloggers, hussars, and marines too. He'd never had much to do with Konstantyn's sailing fleet, so at least they were not likely to recognize him, but his face was well known among the hussars and some of the infantry companies. Some troops were busy moving supplies to the ships, and plenty of officers with a few sergeants and corporals were going about official business. The rest of the rank and file were doubtless confined to their camps for fear of the unrest in the already overcrowded town. It was well known that marines and land-soldiers didn't mix well, or rather, mixed explosively, and since there were three ships of the line in port as well as some smaller frigates, the authorities feared drunken brawls at best.

Of course, hussars of officer status were not so easily kept confined, and daytime tensions easily turned to nighttime incidents.

Steering well clear of the massive Memelburg—the ancient castle with its slab-sided tower surrounded by ramparts and brick bastions—Valdas and Dahnay began to look for somewhere they could stay, but the inn rooms in the high town were all full. Down in the port, however, with most marines accommodated shipboard, they found a room in a tavern, the Lorelei, located down a side alley from the quay. Catering for the shipping trade, they had no stabling, but an obliging brewer nearby took three copper pennies a night for stabling their horses with his draft animals, demanding four nights in advance.

Valdas unsaddled Donkey and rubbed him down, leaving him with a full feed and hay in the rack. Dahnay was already waiting, her horse bedded down comfortably. Together they made their way on foot through crowded, noisy streets to the dockside.

A group of hussars, uniformed in red jackets, gold buttons glinting in the watery autumn sunlight, were supervising the unloading of their horses on the dockside. Poor sods, it was no fun shipping horses, especially when the seas got rough. A large carcass under a canvas sail testified to that. Some poor lad had lost his mount on the journey. Valdas felt slightly sick. A hussar was only as good as his mount. He thought of Donkey and smiled.

Valdas steered Dahnay away from the group, though he didn't recognize any of them. He had to raise his voice to make himself heard above the din even with her walking right alongside him. "If Kristina's here she must think she's stepped into hell. There's no way any mercanter vessels can even get near the quay with the navy in town. She'll be stuck."

Three ships of the line occupied deep-water moorings, the closest being a four-masted carrack, some two hundred and fifty feet in length and bristling with guns.

Dahnay eyed it up and shivered.

"There's a ship unloading on the fish quay, according to our landlord," she said. "He didn't know where it was from, though."

"We'll check."

The ship turned out to be unloading a cargo of wine from the Rhine, but when asked about where he was bound afterward, the ship's master spat over the side.

"I should have been bound for Kassubia with timber, but now I'm requisitioned to stand by for taking troops to Our Lord knows where. This isn't a passenger ship. I told 'em I could take a hundred maximum, and it would cost them. Do you know what they said?"

He was in full swing now and neither Valdas nor Dahnay even had to prompt him.

"Said I'd find room for three hundred even if it meant rigging a false deck in the hold—at my expense of course—and I'd be lucky to keep my ship let alone receive any kind of payment. I'd get a better deal from rutting pirates!"

Valdas made sympathetic noises.

"My friend, do you know where we might find any ship sailing for Sverija?" Dahnay asked.

"It's not a matter of where, it's a matter of when. Not until the king makes his move and the navy leaves us poor traders in peace. Two ships before mine were commandeered, and I've heard they're taking ships all along the coast as well. I wouldn't have pulled into port, but what's a poor sailor to do? My cargo was already spoken for here, else I'd have turned round and headed for Dantsig. I wish I had, now."

They left him still muttering to himself about the unfairness of it all.

"King Gerhard is making no friends." Dahnay stopped to read a paper nailed to a board at the entrance to the main dock. "It says here they're looking for volunteers to join the King's Fleet. Do they think the rabble they're likely to get can read?"

"Let me see that." Valdas scanned the paper quickly. "This is a license for the press gangs. They post these, nice and legal, and any poor bastards who get taken against their will are told that it's their fault for being on the dockside because the notices were posted."

"And we are . . ."

"On the dockside. Better make ourselves scarce."

They both pulled up their hoods to hide their age and began to shamble like grandfathers across the cobbles of the dock, skirting supply carts waiting to decant their loads onto naval vessels, trying not to catch anyone's attention. The Lorelei was across the far side of the quay, necessitating passing the largest of the carracks.

"Now's the time I'm beginning to wish I had a set of skirts with me," Dahnay muttered. "I really don't qualify as a sailor whichever way you look at it, but I don't want to have to prove a point."

"The only time I sailed with Konstantyn I heaved my guts over the side for the whole of the sea-crossing—and we only sailed from Riyja to Paviken—one of the shortest crossings to Sverija."

"That was to bring Kristina home?"

"To negotiate for her hand. She traveled in state a month later with her ladies and retinue."

"You don't really know her, do you?"

"Only by sight."

"Yet her fate means so much to you that you'd risk returning to a place where they'd saw you in half if they caught you?"

"It's not Kristina herself, but she's Konstantyn's Queen, and if by all the fates she has given Zavonia his heir, then I have a duty to him and to Zavonia to see that rightful heir on the throne."

"Why?"

"Isn't that obvious?"

Dahnay shook her head. "Not to me. Gerhard may not be a great king, but at least he's secure. You would remove a secure king and replace him with a baby who might or might not learn to rule well, and might or might not survive to reach his majority and beget heirs for himself?"

"What if Gerhard murdered his way to the throne?" There, it was out. He'd finally said it. There were other possible culprits, but Gerhard was by far the most obvious.

"Many kings have done that. It doesn't make them bad kings."

"He murdered Konstantyn!"

Would Valdas have been able to forgive him if he'd murdered a bad king? His thought had barely formed when . . .

"Well, you two lads look likely sailors."

A bo'sun dressed in the dark blue of His Majesty's Marines stepped out of a side street followed by half a dozen seamen obviously chosen for their stature.

"A sailor, sergeant?" Valdas said. Calling a bo'sun a sergeant was guaranteed to get him riled.

"Why, the only time I set foot on a ship I lost my breakfast over the side and that was before it left the dockside." Valdas nudged Dahnay and felt her adjust her stance slightly. "You'd get precious poor sailing out of me."

"What about your blackamoor?"

"Doesn't speak Zavonian or Ruthenian. Couldn't take orders."

"A lash would soon sort that out."

Valdas glanced around and spotted what he was looking for. "Besides, we're for the hussars."

"Wings! To me!" He roared out the rallying call he'd used at Tevshenna and smashed his right fist into the bo'sun's chin, bruising his knuckles, but hearing a satisfying crack as the man went down. Dahnay had already kicked another in the crotch and was bringing both fists down on his skull as he doubled over. The rest of the sailors rushed them, but perceiving fellow hussars in trouble, even one out of uniform, the officers who'd been unloading their horses on the dockside waded into the fray, followed by a group of sailors who'd been lounging outside a tavern, and a couple of civilians who'd been passing. Punch by punch the mayhem spread along the dock. Valdas saw Dahnay down on one knee prying a knife from the nerveless fingers of another of the sailors, and at her shout he turned in time to duck a belaying pin aimed at his head. He rammed his would-be attacker shoulder to chest and knocked the air out of him.

"Time to go." Dahnay swiped the man on the back of the knees with a stave she'd picked up and he collapsed in a heap.

"Right!" Valdas ducked into the side street the recruiting party had come out of and grabbed Dahnay's outstretched fingers, pulling her free of the melee. Hand in hand they charged down the alley, laughing, twisting and turning until they were all but lost in the backstreets of the city. At length he pulled her to him under an overhang protecting a loading door on the side of a disused warehouse. Laughing and gasping, he took her in his arms and hugged her to him. For a brief moment she let herself be hugged and then gave him a good-natured slap on the shoulder.

"Not a bad fight for an ex-hussar."

"Ex-hussar! I'll show you ex-hussar. Once a hussar, always—" He grabbed her in a headlock but she wrestled him out of it, and stumbling and laughing together they made their way through narrow streets to the inn.

"Hoy, you two. A big bo'sun with a bloody nose wanted to know if I had a Zavonian and an Afric staying here," the landlord accosted them on the way in.

"What did you tell him?" Valdas wiped the grin off his face.

"Told him I couldn't remember every face that came and went."

"Good man." Valdas flipped him a coin. "All the same, I think we'll be leaving. Keep the advance."

"And we haven't even slept in the beds, so you've no need to change them," Dahnay said, and under her breath muttered, "Not that they were clean to start with."

"One more thing, though," Valdas said. "I'm looking for a woman. A particular woman, I didn't suddenly get an urge. This one would have a very young baby, be traveling alone. About so tall, gray eyes, brown hair. Probably looking for passage to Sverija."

"Like I say, I can't remember every face that comes and goes." The man looked meaningfully at Valdas's purse.

Valdas kept his hand still. "You'd remember this one, my friend." He turned and walked out, knowing full well that the man would call out if he knew anything.

"Hey!"

"Yes?" Valdas turned back at the call.

"You need to talk to Erion."

"Erion?"

"The harbormaster."

"Where might I find him?"

The landlord half smiled until Valdas flipped him another coin, then he pulled open a curtain revealing a doorway. "In my back room, of course. Can't stand the navy."

"I'll get our things," Dahnay said as Valdas stepped forward.

"You trust me?"

"As much as you trust me," she said.

⎯⎯⎯⎯⎯⎯⎯⎯

The harbormaster proved unenlightening. Yes, he knew all the vessels that had sailed out of here for Sverija in the last three months and no, he didn't recall either a pregnant woman or a woman with a baby taking passage on any of them.

Valdas decided to try the whorehouses, about which the harbormaster was more enlightening. Apart from a flop-shop where streetwalkers and casual whores could rent rooms by the half hour, there were only three establishments in town run by the girls themselves.

They collected the horses and rode through the town, Dahnay holding Donkey in the street whilst Valdas checked each whorehouse.

Nothing.

"Can we do any more here?" Dahnay asked.

Valdas shook his head, his heart heavy. "We'll head back. I hate to say this, but I think we're going to have to persuade Mirza to scry. This is like hunting for a needle in two haystacks, and one alone would be impossible."

"This darkness of hers . . . she's not going to like it."

"I know. We must protect her."

"From what, men or magic?"

"Both—if we can."

The roads were quiet on the return journey to Biela Miasto, all the troop movements ceased, or completed. Valdas squashed down nausea. The whole country was going to shit and there was nothing he could do to stop it.

"Whatever he's going to do, Gerhard's going to do it soon," Valdas said as they successfully skirted a checkpoint on the Torek road. "He's either a brilliant tactician or he's going to lose half his army for nothing."

"What would you do?" Dahnay asked.

"Me?"

"You must have thought about it. You've been in enough battles in your day."

Valdas watched Donkey's rangy neck bobbing in front of him, ears flopping, as they trotted along at a pace he could keep up for miles.

"I'd be sending ambassadors to Sverija to assure them of my best intentions, reinforcing my borders, not planning any offensives. I'd be sending as many men as I could spare to the Tevecor Reaches. Their Majesties in Ruthenia may want a passage to the sea in the south, but they want the Tevecor Reaches as well. My guess is that while Gerhard is fighting in Posenja, they are planning an offensive into the Reaches. What does Gerhard hope to gain? Even if the Posenja campaign is successful, he's leaving his flank exposed."

Dahnay nodded.

"Do you know something, Dahnay?"

"I'm not privy to my tsarina's councils with the tsar."

Valdas scowled. "Of course, if you take home the Zavonian heir, they can simply take the whole of Zavonia instead."

She nodded. "It would save a lot of bloodshed, my friend, and whatever you think of Tsar Ivan and Tsarina Zofia, they are wise rulers, more than twice as wise together as they were before they married."

"Zofia is Konstantyn's sister. She learned her political strategy from the same teacher."

"I know you have no intention of returning Kristina to Tsarina Zofia. No, don't deny it. Why should you? But I urge you to consider that Konstantyn's sister on the throne of Zavonia might be better for the country than this crazy man Gerhard or a babe who may have the right, but not the might to hold the throne against all comers. Think about it."

"I am thinking about it. That's the trouble."

CHAPTER SIXTY
Mirza

THE DAME IN Rivergate Yard was distinctly unhelpful, but Mirza could tell in an instant that there was nothing magic about either her or her potions. It was all strictly herbal, though there was nothing wrong with that. There was a kind of magic in the way people believed in cures.

She trudged around every apothecary's shop in Biela Miasto asking for orris root and mandragora. Some of the apothecaries had no knowledge of what she was asking for. Others gave her a strange look but said no, they'd no call for that. One kindly gentleman invited her into his consulting room and then gave her a lecture on how experimenting with "deep" magic would damage her soul, but when she showed him her face and said she was trying to undamage her body, he sadly told her she was walking a dark path and that the only apothecary he knew who might be able to help her had recently met with an untimely end.

Without actually scrying for the shadow-thing, she could do no more, so she decided to search for Valdas's friend Aniela instead. She'd thought it likely that the whore had sold the ring and run off to start a new, well-funded life, but when she'd looked into her scrying bowl, an instant before the shadow had found her, she'd seen Aniela in a cellar, not the sort of surroundings that someone in possession of a small fortune would willingly seek out.

She thought about the cellar. What could she see or sense?

Fear was the first thing. Aniela was scared and hiding out from something or somebody. She wasn't in the cellar out of choice. Second—ah, right—Aniela's hands were bandaged, or at least the third and fourth fingers on each hand. It was common enough to strap up a broken finger to its good neighbor. How did someone manage to break both pinkie fingers? The answer: they didn't, not without damaging a lot more. Two pinkie fingers broken likely meant they'd been broken on purpose.

Ah, and there was a gold band on her middle finger.

So someone had damaged Aniela's fingers deliberately, but hadn't robbed her of the ring.

Now all Mirza had to do was to narrow it down to the right cellar.

CHAPTER SIXTY-ONE

Valdas

VALDAS AND DAHNAY arrived in Biela Miasto before Lind, which, considering his journey was shorter, was worrying.

"You don't think he's run out on us?" Valdas asked Mirza when she met him at Trader Maksimilian's door with a smile on her face.

"I don't think so," she said. "In many ways he seems to have no connection to the world, no ties of loyalty or friendship, but Kristina somehow got through to him. She may be the first person to do that for a long time and I think he's fastened on to the idea of her in the same way that a duckling will cleave to the first thing it sees upon coming out of its shell."

"And that makes you smile?"

"No, something different. Come in and warm yourself by Maksimilian's excellent fire. I have a present for you."

"You found Kristina."

"No, sorry, but perhaps the next best thing, at least as far as you're concerned." She almost dragged his cloak from his shoulders and bundled him down the hallway to Maksimilian's sitting room. There, in a chair by the fire, looking much the same as he remembered her, was . . .

"Aniela!"

She leaped out of her chair so fast it slid backward across the wooden floor.

"Oh, Valdas!" She threw herself into his arms.

"Aniela!" He hugged her to him, his face buried in her blond curls, breathing her in, a mixture of carbolic and cheap perfume. *Aniela! His Aniela.*

It must have been a good ten minutes before he realized that Mirza and Dahnay had left them alone.

"Come, lover, sit and tell me what you've been doing." She drew him to the fire and he sank into the chair across from hers.

"This and that. What about you? I went to the Hussar and you'd gone. No one knew where you were."

"I was hiding. A man. Came looking for you. I . . . I tried not to tell him but . . ."

She held out both hands, and the little fingers on both were crooked.

"He broke your fingers? God in heaven, let me find him. I'll kill him for you myself."

"They're healing."

"Not well. Have you let Mirza look at them?" Valdas looked around, but Mirza had withdrawn and left them alone.

"She . . ." Aniela swallowed. "She says she can make 'em straight, but she'll have to break 'em again and I don't think I can stand that."

"Oh, Aniela." Valdas knelt at her feet and took her hands, kissing each in turn.

"He . . . the man who did this. I thought he was one of the chancellor's men—they've got a bad reputation—but I don't think he was. He asked if you knew who'd killed the king."

"He did?"

"If he'd been one of the chancellor's men he'd have been convinced you'd done it, stands to reason. I . . . I think he did it, Valdas. He asked if you knew who'd poisoned the fish. How could he have known it was fish that was poisoned? I didn't know. Did you?"

"No. I didn't." Valdas sat back on his heels, the heat from the fire scorching his face. "And when was this, Aniela?"

"A month ago, maybe a bit more."

"And you've been hiding since then?"

"I daren't go to the Hussar. I found a cellar room, down by the docks, used the last of my money on food and a few coals. I daren't even go on the streets."

"Thank Heaven you didn't, sweet. You know how street-whores get cheated, and misused."

"I can look after myself."

Valdas took both her hands in his and ran his thumbs along both pinkies.

"You won't have to in the future. I'll look after you."

"Don't make promises you can't keep. You've all on to keep your own head on your shoulders. And the queen's more important than I am. Yes, Mirza told me what you were about. I've asked Maksimilian to take me in. It's not as good as working at the Hussar, where I was my own boss, but he's a fair man in his own way and he keeps his house in good order and his girls clean."

Valdas squeezed her hands gently, avoiding pressure on the damaged fingers, and stood up. "I owe you, Aniela. I won't forget it."

"I know you won't."

"So how did you find me?"

"I didn't. Mirza found me. Said she'd seen me in a scrying. Knew I was in a cellar somewhere, thought about it a lot and recognized sounds from the harbor. She must have checked every cellar close to the quay before she found me. I didn't believe you'd sent her at first until I asked her some more personal questions. Stands to reason you wouldn't have traveled alone with a young woman and not have fucked her, given half a smile's worth of encouragement." She touched his cheek. "A lot of men wouldn't have gone near a woman with a face like that, but I knew you'd have been looking at the woman underneath and not what was on the outside. When she said you took her cherry and called her your lovely girl as if you really meant it, I knew it was you. I told you before, you're a generous soul in bed, lover."

"Aniela . . ."

She stood and dropped a kiss on his hair. "Come and see me tonight. I'll be working 'til midnight, but see me after. I'll save you a squeeze, and you know how I can squeeze. Second floor, back room."

They heard a sharp rap on the front door. One of the girls, Edyta, opened it cautiously. As Valdas reached the door into the hallway, Lind came through carrying a bag and stomping the dust from his boots.

He cast his usual cautious glance around and nodded a greeting. "Valdas! God's ballocks, man, I'm glad to be back. Dadziga is full of God-damned hussars. There are no caravans moving through the Eris Gate in either direction and nobody I talked to had seen Kristina with or without a baby . . . Oh!" His eyes focused on Aniela, who had followed Valdas out of Trader Maksimilian's parlor.

"That's him!" Aniela tugged on Valdas's arm, her voice rising to a wail. "That's the bastard who killed the king!"

The man who killed his king! The man who tortured Aniela for information about him. Why? The man who said he wanted to find the queen safe. Fury boiled in Valdas's gut.

"Lying bastard."

Valdas pushed Aniela safely away, heard her stumble up the stairs, and drew his sword.

"I never lied!" Lind threw his bag at Valdas and backed away, reaching for his own sword.

The bag thwacked into Valdas's thighs and he shoved it with his left hand, failed to push it clear of his feet, and leaped over it. He raised his blade, but the hallway was too narrow, and he snicked the tip against the newel post as he sliced toward Lind's head. It slowed down the momentum and gave Lind time to draw his own side-sword to parry, otherwise it would have been over before it had begun.

He leaped sideways as Lind thrust a stiletto at him with the other hand. Where had that come from? His heel hit the bag. "Damn!" He stumbled and caught himself. He snatched a cloak from a peg and flipped it around his forearm to block the deadly little blade, but he had to pull his arm back in order to launch another attack at Lind, otherwise he'd have lopped his own hand off. *Christ on a pig, the man's good.*

Lind parried, twisting his hand so that the guard of his sword prevented Valdas from lopping off a few fingers. He lunged back. Valdas barely blocked in time. He was panting, not with exertion but with shock. He'd started to like Lind. How could he have been so wrong?

They separated, both coming to en-garde positions, Valdas high and Lind low. Valdas's heart pounded and blood throbbed in his temples. "You killed my king." Valdas's breath already rasped in his throat.

This wasn't going to be easy. The man was a swordsman, a duelist maybe, assassin certainly, classically trained. Well, he'd find that Valdas had learned a few dirty tricks in the field.

"No!" Lind took two paces back and then thrust forward. "Well, yes."

"Bastard!"

"It was just a job."

Valdas heard footsteps on the stair and Mirza's voice screaming for them to hold. He shoved her out of his mind. Concentrate on the damned blades.

"I'll give you just-a-job. He was my king." Slash. "My friend." Clash!

Behind him the door into the yard burst open. Maksimilian's voice added to the confusion, but the words didn't register.

Lind pressed forward, Mirza screamed again, and Valdas gave way, feeling the shocks of blade hitting blade, the clang of steel on steel almost deafening. He let Lind drive him back and back, parrying, ducking, barely glancing behind him until he passed the door frame and spun and leaped into the yard, where he could swing his blade much more effectively. Lind pressed home the attack, but now Valdas had the room to give as good as he got, parry, thrust, block, slash, thrust, trying any way to get his blade into flesh. Valdas went for a breast cut from below and felt the feather bite. A diagonal line of red seeped onto the front of Lind's slashed zupan, but Valdas knew it was neither deep nor disabling. It would have been an end to a first-blood contest.

This was not a first-blood contest.

They engaged again. Valdas pressed home his advantage with a low thrust to the belly. Lind parried then feinted then lunged again. The tip of his blade glanced off Valdas's sword and sliced Valdas's upper arm. It wasn't a deep cut, but Valdas felt his arm going numb with reaction. He pushed through the sensation, forced his grip to tighten.

With the dagger in his left hand, Lind was better able to thrust than slash. Valdas swept Lind's dagger aside and the two of them locked swords for vital moments and then whirled apart again, both breathing heavily.

Lind stabbed obliquely. Valdas parried, saw the deadly dagger too late. He took the point on the bundled cloak as it was on its way toward his ballocks. Cold steel bit the back of his wrist through the bundled cloak. He twisted and wrenched the knife out of Lind's hand and hurled knife and cloak away. He launched a series of major cuts, pressing Lind back.

"Stop!" Mirza's voice cut through the anger still roaring in his ears. "For God's sake . . ."

Valdas's sword grew hot in his hand. Hot, hotter, burning. The quillions almost glowed. He flung it away. It flashed into bright white light, flamed and was gone.

Shit!

He turned to find Lind also disarmed, rubbing his right hand with his left.

Mirza screamed again. "If you're going to kill each other at least make it personal!"

Kill. That was it entirely.

Valdas's vision clouded with red. Rage chased away the last remnants of strategy. He heard a roar, realized it was his, and ran at Lind. They crashed together and the frenzy took over.

CHAPTER SIXTY-TWO
Mirza

MIRZA HADN'T KNOWN she could fly until she heard the commotion down in the hallway and heard Aniela's desperate cry. She hurtled out of their little top-floor room and took the stairs three if not four at a time, grabbing up her skirts and barely touching foot to stair tread. Dahnay pounded close on her heels.

Valdas and Lind were going at it with blades and looked likely to kill each other. She hadn't seen either of them fight—seriously fight—before, and it was now that she realized the difference between civilized sparring and the real thing. Someone would end up dead on the floor.

Aniela grabbed her arm. "He's the one. The one that killed the king. Oh, Sweet Jesu and Mary the Mother! Valdas!"

Mirza grabbed Aniela in time to stop her from throwing herself between the two of them. She screamed for them to stop, but it was like spitting into a storm. Behind Valdas the door crashed open and Maksimilian appeared in the doorway, blocking the light and yelling for them to put up their weapons. Fat chance.

She waved him back. "Give them some room!"

Whether he heard her or not above the clash of steel, he stepped back and left the way clear into the yard, an enclosed space with a stable, outhouses, and a gated archway into the alley.

Valdas backed out, giving ground cautiously. Lind followed, sword moving faster than Mirza could follow. She rushed to the door. Dahnay started to draw steel, but Mirza held out a hand to stop her.

Without even considering the dangers, she drew on her newfound power and poured fire into both swords equally, seeing each man fling them high, seeing them flame to nothing.

That should slow them down.

"If you're going to kill each other at least make it personal!" she yelled, and was immediately horrified by how personal it got. The two of them crashed together like stags in rut, punching, kicking, gouging, biting, each trying to get a throttle-hold on the other. She couldn't see where one man started and the other stopped. At this rate they'd both end up dead.

When they could no longer stand, they fought each other on their knees.

Only when both fell face down in the dirt and neither could get up again did the gut-punching stop.

Maksimilian turned Lind face up. "Still breathing," he said.

Dahnay knelt by Valdas, who rolled over and groaned. Blood trickled from his mouth.

Please, the one god, not his ribs again. Mirza started forward, but Valdas sat up and wiped his mouth on the back of his hand. A cut lip. She breathed.

He made as if to reach for Lind, but she stomped between them.

"Enough!"

"He . . . killed my king." Valdas's voice cracked.

"But he saved your queen!" Maksimilian said.

"You . . . knew!" Valdas's left eye was closing fast.

"I suspected. I didn't know for sure."

"And you let her go with him?"

"We were desperate." Maksimilian shrugged. "It wasn't an easy decision. They'd started a house-to-house search. He didn't want to be caught up in it either. I figured they could get each other to safety. Kristina agreed."

"She knew?"

"Like I say, we suspected."

"How could you trust him?"

"He's a professional assassin. I knew that from the very first time he came here. I have my contacts in Tepet."

"Ludmila Korolenko, Madame Lucille." Lind spat a clot of blood and ran his tongue along his teeth as if checking they were all still there. "Is nothing sacred between a whore and her customer?" He sounded tired, defeated.

"You never had more than a room from the madame."

"He doesn't do sex." Valdas turned and glared at Lind. "Got sodomized as a boy. Doesn't know whether he wants to do women or men so he doesn't do either."

There it was! Lind's deepest secret spilled for anyone to hear.

Mirza had known—she'd heard Lind's nightmares while he'd been recovering from the brain-fever, but she hadn't realized Valdas knew. Judging by Lind's face, it was the deepest cut of all. Lind's eyes half-closed and any fight that was still in him evaporated. He was a pretty boy again at the mercy of powerful men.

Mirza wanted to scream and beat her fists at Valdas's chest. *You might have let him have some dignity. In all his life it's all he's ever craved.*

But Valdas hadn't finished. "Give me your blade, Dahnay, and I'll do him with three feet of steel."

"Here." Lind fumbled with the drawstring of his trousers. Still unable to stand, he rolled over onto his knees, flipped the skirt of his zupan up, and let his trousers fall. Bending over, face in the dirt and naked arse upward, a lattice of old white scars crisscrossing flesh, he said, "Go on. If it will make you feel any better. Do it. Finish it now! If it means anything, I'm sorry I took the gods-poxed commission in the first place, sorry it was me that killed your king. It was nothing personal. A job. Country's going to hell without him. That wasn't my idea. I can't even tell you who hired me. I'm a useless bastard. Put me out of my gods-poxed misery."

Valdas looked at Lind, and looked at Mirza. Back and forth from one to the other. She could usually read the man, but not this time.

"Valdas, think about it," Mirza said. "He's a hired assassin. Yes, he killed Konstantyn, but if I shot you with a pistol, is the pistol to blame or am I? He was just the weapon. If it hadn't been him it would have been someone else. Who hired him? Ask yourself that. You need him alive."

Time passed.

Valdas looked as though he wanted to bellow. Everyone else was frozen into position. In the end, Lind cleared his throat.

"Are you going to kill me or shall I just stay like this until I freeze to death?"

Valdas drew a deep breath. "Cover your arse. You look ridiculous."

A round of applause drifted down into the yard from above. Mirza raised her head. Fifteen girls at least were hanging out of every available window.

"Valdas, if you're not going to kill him we'll take care of him," one of them shouted down.

"Cute little arse."

"Soon find out which way he swings."

Valdas nodded.

"No!" Mirza shook her head. Lind was already shredded and this would surely finish him.

Lind looked across at her. He seemed calm. Calm, not rigid. He shrugged. "There's nothing they can do that's worse than what's happened in the past."

Half a dozen girls in various states of dress and undress came down to the yard and bore Lind away.

Mirza offered her hand to pull Valdas to his feet, but Maksimilian cleared his throat and stood a few feet away. Surely he wasn't going to get all nervous of her now?

"What is it?" She sounded a little short tempered even to her own ears. She forced a smile to her face.

"Mistress Mirza," Maksimilian said. "What you did . . ."

"I won't do it again. I promise. Your house is safe from me."

"It was magnificent. Truly magnificent. I don't suppose you would consider—"

"I don't suppose I would. Please excuse me."

She hauled Valdas up to the attic, one step at a time. As they passed the room where the whores had taken Lind, she paused outside to listen. There were no screams of pain or terror so she decided to let it be.

CHAPTER SIXTY-THREE
Mirza

"HE KILLED THE king," Valdas said for the fifteenth time as she bathed his face.

"Not his king." Mirza wondered whether the cut above Valdas's eye needed a stitch, but decided it didn't. "How are your ribs? Take off your shirt." She ran her fingers down his side, pressing each individual bone.

"Ow!"

"That wasn't a loud enough ow. Nothing broken. Thanks." This to Aniela as she brought another bowl of boiled water and some fresh towels up from the kitchen.

"He's an assassin! He kills for money."

"And what do you do, Valdas? Eighteen years a soldier, first man across the line at Tevshenna. Is it any different? Didn't you kill for money?"

He didn't answer.

"I don't know why," Mirza said, "but I feel he's important to this venture, just like Dahnay is. Keep them both close."

"Keep your friends close and your enemies closer still."

"Huh?"

"It's from an ancient text," Valdas said. "Konstantyn used to quote it. Unfortunately he kept at least one enemy too close."

"Lind might help us to unravel that. He really does have Kristina's best interests at heart, you know. You can trust him on that. He needn't have come back."

"Like I can trust a viper."

"I'm done." She considered her handiwork. "You'll live. Aniela, take him away and bang some sense into him, will you? That's if he can still get it up."

"Please." Valdas managed to look offended. "Has there ever been a time when Valdas Zalecki hasn't risen to the occasion?"

"There's a little herb . . . I'm sometimes tempted to slip it into your food just to take down your ego, and your kok. Go on, get out." She threw the bloodied towel at him.

Aniela took Valdas's hand and led him away. Mirza watched him move. He'd be massively sore tomorrow, but she doubted any lasting damage. What about Lind? She was tempted to go and kick the door down and demand the girls give him up to her care, but when she listened through the door she couldn't even hear whimpers. Maybe she'd see what sort of man greeted her in the morning.

Dahnay peered round the edge of the door.

"It's all right. They've all gone," Mirza said.

"I kept out of the way. I didn't know what to do."

"Nothing much you can do in a situation like that. Hope that they work it out between them."

"You like Lind, don't you?"

Mirza sighed. "Like? I don't know if there's anything in there to like. I feel sorry for him. Does that sound stupid? I feel sorry for a man who could kill me in an eyeblink and probably would if someone gave him a tolar."

"I could kill you in an eyeblink!"

"Yes, I feel sorry for you, too."

Dahnay laughed softly. "Actually I could kill you providing you didn't turn me to a cinder first. Nice job on the swords. I thought you were scared of using that power."

"I was. I am. I just didn't think. I can still feel it buzzing inside me." She put her hand up to her face.

"Don't fret. The mark's no worse." Dahnay sat down on her own bed and pulled off her boots. "You're not upset . . . about Aniela and Valdas?"

Mirza started to clear the debris from ministering to Valdas. "Upset, no. Should I be?"

"I thought you were taken with him."

"He's a good man, but I never saw myself as being with him permanently. It just ended sooner than I expected. I can't ask him to cleave to me when my cleaving days are over." She sighed. "Truth to tell, Dahnay, I've had this feeling right from the beginning that this was a one-way journey. There are bad things happening, a darkness gathering, and . . ."

"You're afraid."

"Yes. Horribly afraid all of the time. I just don't let myself think about it, otherwise I wouldn't be able to function." Her voice sounded small, even to herself. She sat down next to Dahnay. "I don't think I'm meant to survive this, somehow. The dead don't care about the living. We're a means to an end. I'm carrying out the wishes of a dead king. It's a king's job to spend the lives of his soldiers and that's all I am to Konstantyn."

"Nothing is predetermined. Don't think yourself into an early grave."

"How do you manage? To be so brave all of the time, I mean?"

"Brave? Me?" Dahnay shuddered. "In the Tevecor Reaches I was pissing myself with fear. I couldn't move to save myself, I was so frightened. You were the one who saved us all."

"I've seen you wield your sword."

"I'm strong. I've trained for years so that my reactions are automatic, but I'm not infallible, and I'm not free of fear. I just know how to hide it away. Like you say you are doing."

Mirza began to shake. "I was so frightened tonight. I thought Valdas and Lind would kill each other. Why should I care about two pig-headed men?"

"Because we have formed a band of our own, a kinship, bound by a common purpose." Dahnay put one arm around Mirza's shaking shoulders. "You're frozen. Here."

She lay down and pulled Mirza down onto the bed, Mirza's back to her belly, covering them both with a blanket. Mirza felt the warmth and solid companionship gradually begin to warm her bones.

"Do you like what you do, Dahnay—what you are?" Mirza asked.

"I don't know. I've never known anything else. I'm loyal to my tsarina because she is my tsarina and I have sworn on my honor to do my duty, but . . ."

"You have doubts?"

"Yesterday I walked down the Street of Artisans by the Littlemarket and I met a potter and his wife. She was tall and black, like me, and carried herself well. I saw the pots she had decorated, each one well-nigh perfect. She took such pride in her work, and for a moment I wondered what it might be like to be a maker, not a destroyer."

"You could change your life, walk out of here tomorrow," Mirza said.

"I could, but I have sworn an oath, and on my honor I will keep it. You could change *your* life."

"Not without denying the dying wish of a king."

"It seems we must both follow our present path for a while."

"Are you so very lonely, Dahnay?"

"Sometimes. I'm used to being alone, though."

"I'm not," Mirza said. "I've always been part of the band, even though I didn't always like them much and they didn't always like me. I find I miss them, Boldo and Stasha, Himali and Rafal. The only one who likes me is Tsura, my apprentice. I miss her most of all."

"You'll see them again." Dahnay patted Mirza's arm and Mirza felt her breath warm on the back of her neck as the tall black woman drifted into sleep.

Mirza knew she wasn't going to be able to sleep. As the sounds in Trader Maksimilian's faded out one by one she lay awake, warm in Dahnay's sisterly embrace. The whole day was still spinning around in her head. What had happened to Lind in the past, and his fear of sex, had been no surprise to her, of course. She'd nursed him when he'd been having fever dreams and she'd lived through the worst of his nightmares with him. There might be hope for him, yet . . . and if Valdas hadn't killed him today it was likely he wasn't going to.

She wondered who Ewa was. A lover maybe. He'd screamed for her in his sleep, seen her dying over and over again. She'd been tempted to spirit-walk into his dreams, but spying on him would have been too much of an intrusion, even if she did it with the best of intentions.

Part of her wished that it was her with him tonight.

She closed her eyes and let her mind wander off on a fantasy where she was entirely normal and Lind was a carefree young Bakaishan with a wagon of his own and a glint in his eye. She sighed. That took all of ten minutes and the night stretched out ahead of her. She turned her mind to the memory of those few days with Valdas when nothing existed except the road during the day and Valdas's kok at night. Ten more minutes.

It was no good, she was going to have to face it. No one had found any sign of Kristina. Darkness or not, she was going to have to scry.

She sat up and swung her legs over the edge of the bed.

She thought Dahnay asleep, but as soon as she moved, the black woman unfolded like a shadow beside her.

"I'm coming with you," she said.

"How do you know where I'm going?"

"You've decided to scry for Kristina. It's the only option left. And you can't scry from here in case you endanger Maksimilian's house, so you need to be somewhere safe, somewhere you can get away from in a hurry, and somewhere where you won't risk exposing any of us."

"Am I that obvious?"

"I told you, it's the only option left."

Mirza nodded. "What do you think? Inside the city or out of it?"

"Inside gives you more cover, more places to hide. Outside means you can have a horse standing by and get away at full gallop, but there are fewer places to run to."

"Inside the city means I can do it tonight. Outside means I have to wait for the city gates to open in the morning."

Dahnay nodded. "Inside, then. How about Soldiers' Fields?"

"The memorial? Not afraid of ghosts?"

"No. That's your province. I don't have experience of scrying, but I'm told it's like traveling in the place above, where you see spirits."

"It can be. It can also just be like looking through a mirror at a world in miniature. You never know until you open yourself up to it."

"You'll need someone with you."

"I would be very grateful."

CHAPTER SIXTY-FOUR

Lind

UTTERLY SPENT, LIND allowed himself to be carried up two flights of stairs into a room with a large bed. His mind was mush. Surely he hadn't flung away his own sword? How had that happened? One minute he'd been confident of filleting Zalecki, the next he'd been gut-punched into the middle of next week. He must get his sword back. Not right to leave it in the yard.

He was only dimly aware of hands touching him in all manner of places. They dropped him on the bed where he flopped, boneless, completely drained, curled on his side. He'd never been more comfortable in his life. That part of him which was shrieking to run away was locked inside a tiny box in his head where it couldn't do any damage.

Running away was not an option, and if this was his punishment he'd suffer it.

"Come on, sunshine."

He didn't know the girls individually. He'd always managed to keep them at a polite distance, and except for Ruta, who often helped out in the kitchen, he'd never bothered to learn their names, so with his eyes swollen shut, he didn't know who was speaking or whose hands were doing what. Better keep it that way.

They had him stripped in next to no time, turning him this way and that. One of them ran her hands over his body impartially, even grasping his balls and his prick, not teasing, more like a physician checking for damage. They turned him over. Rubbed his arse as if cataloging scars, and turned him onto his back again, running their hands down his flanks and across his belly, stirring rivers of pain across fresh bruises, probing as if he was a prize horse they were planning to buy. He groaned involuntarily.

Would they like to see if he had all his teeth?

Apparently they would.

He felt a light sheet drop onto his body and fingers began to poke his face. God's ballocks, that hurt!

"All right, sweetheart. We've got you now."

That's what he was afraid of.

"Come on, sit up."

Arms behind his back levered him into a sitting position and soft pillows held him in place. He felt a cool cloth on his right eye, dabbing, wiping, soothing. And the left. Then his nose, his poor battered nose, and his jaw and mouth. He ran his tongue around. Yes, he did still have all his teeth, though one of them felt a little loose.

"Here, this will help."

A bone medicine spoon touched his bottom lip and he opened his mouth as he had not done since he was a child. Bitter sticky liquid oozed onto his tongue. It almost needed chewing before he swallowed. Christ, it stuck to his teeth and gums like tar.

"It's vile, but it will ease the hurts. Here. Water. Wash it down."

A cup touched his lip and he managed to raise both hands, still violently shaking, to grasp it, swallowing gratefully, but regretting it as cold water followed the medicine into his churning stomach. He began to retch, but someone put a hand on his shoulder.

"Breathe. Keep it down, you need it."

The cup magically disappeared and someone took his right hand.

"You'll be lucky if you haven't broken something. What a mess."

Each hand in turn was tweaked and turned, fingers bent and straightened, joints squeezed.

At one point he bit back a scream, but it was soon over. Then each was soaked in soothing balm and bound lightly around the knuckles.

"You're lucky. Nothing broken."

Finally he lay in the soft feather bed and no one was touching him at all.

If he didn't move, nothing hurt, and he felt as though he was floating on a cloud, soothed and safe. What was in that vile stuff they'd given him?

His whole world marked time.

He listened, suspecting someone else was in the room with him. Finally he heard a soft sigh. Slowly, painfully, he opened his right eye and then the left. At the bottom of the bed, sitting with hands clasped around knees drawn up to her chin, was a young brunette, dressed in only a thin muslin shift, which was more clothing than he'd feared.

"He's awake," she called softly.

"Good, get this tisane down him before he drifts off again." An older blonde, sitting by a fireplace in which a fire burned red and cheerful, took a cloth, grasped an iron pot, and poured something into a cup. She handed it to the younger girl, who had scrambled across the covers to Lind's side.

"Shout if you need anything." The older woman left.

"I will." The brunette didn't take her eyes off Lind's face as she held the cup to his mouth.

"I can manage." His voice sounded wobbly even to his own ears. He cleared his throat and then said, "Thanks."

"You're welcome. Name's Cecylia. Like the old queen what died. Cylia for short."

Whatever was in the cup was warm and sweet. It trickled down his gullet and into his belly without making him gag. Cylia took the cup from him, reached over and put it on a small table by the head of the bed.

"Thanks."

"It's Maksimilian's recipe for what ails you. One way and another we get to do a fair amount of doctoring here."

"I'll bet you do."

"That's how I came here. Got knocked about, knocked up too as it turns out. My family threw me out. Wouldn't believe it was my uncle. Said I was a slut. Came begging to the kitchen door and Klara brought me in. Fixed me up. Sorted out my little problem. She's nice."

"And now you're a whore, taking it every night."

"Maksimilian made me work in the kitchen 'til I was fifteen. Then he said it was up to me. Now I have a choice. Figured if I was going to be called a slut I could earn my living from it. It's not so bad when it's your choice. The men who come here, they ain't got power over me. It's when they got power over you that it makes you feel so helpless you wonder if you'll ever be able to be you again. Sex for money, it's not real . . . It doesn't touch you here and here if you don't let it." She touched her forehead and closed both hands over her heart.

Someone else had said that to him . . . Jadzia.

"I dunno what love is. One day I might find out, but until then it's a job, and I'm good at it. But I couldn't do it if I 'adn't left that sleazy uncle behind me. It's like it happened to someone else."

She pushed her hair off her face. "You was raped," she said.

He nodded.

"Up the arse?"

He nodded.

"How old was you?"

"Eleven the first time. It hurt so much I thought I was going to die. And then I wished I had."

"I was twelve." She thought for a while. "I ent never taken it up the arse, though. My choice."

"Good choice, Cylia."

She swiveled round and slid off the bed. With one quick movement she pulled her muslin shift over her head. She was short and dainty, beautifully proportioned with breasts heavier than he'd have guessed, a little round belly and a thick dark bush.

"What are you doing?" He heard his own voice rise in panic.

"Nothing you don't want me to." She lifted the cover and slipped into the bed beside him.

It said a lot about his physical state that he didn't immediately leap out of the other side.

"No need to flinch." She stretched down beside him. "Turn over."

"What?"

"Turn sideways, with your back to me. We'll sleep chairs."

He started to shake.

"Trust me. I ent got no power over ya. I ent gonna touch ya like that. Just like this." He turned to face the fire, its warmth on his face. Cylia fitted herself like a second skin at his back, her knees drawn up around his arse. She draped her arm across his waist, her hand cool against his chest next to the scabbed-over cut.

"Did I tell you I was going to charge you for this?"

"No."

"Well, I am."

"Should be half price. 's money for nothing."

"Yeah?"

"No fucking."

"You want to fuck me an' get your money's worth?"

"No."

"Good." She snuggled up closer. "All right?"

"Yes."

And it was, for now.

When he awoke in the morning, the fire was out and cool autumn sunlight streamed in through the window. Somehow they'd both turned together in the night and now his knees were drawn up behind hers, his hand rested lightly across her, cupping one generous breast, and his prick was pressed up against the cheek of her arse, flaccid as usual, except . . . No, he just needed the outhouse. He rolled off the bed in one movement and looked around for his clothes. There they were, on a chair.

As he finished dressing she yawned and stretched.

"There you are," she said. "What time is it?"

"Early. I heard the matins bell a short while ago. Go to sleep. Thank you, Cylia."

"Tonight? Just the same. No expectations nor nothing."

He nodded and stepped out.

CHAPTER SIXTY-FIVE
Mirza

EVEN IN THE dead of night there was an energy about Soldiers' Fields. The land had been a cemetery when the city had been more scarcely populated. Now the buildings had encroached on all sides and it had become a small park, planted with trees and surrounded by a wall. Mirza and Dahnay walked on memories, the pathways being paved with old headstones bearing foot-worn inscriptions from two or even three hundred years ago. Set upright or laid flat on the ground beneath the trees were more recent carved stones and engraved brass plaques, most darkened with age, bearing the name and date of death of Zavonia's battle-fallen; not all, of course, only those who had family or friends to pay. For those who didn't, a statue, or rather statue-group, towered on a plinth in the center: a hussar, an archer, a marine, and a humble pike-man to represent all of Zavonia's spilled blood.

"So many . . ." Mirza said as the clouds split and a half moon lent its pale light.

"Spilling the blood of his armies is a king's job." Dahnay bowed her head to the statue as they came to the middle. "I know Valdas believes that the babe is the rightful king, but when you find the queen . . ."

"If we find her."

"When! When you find her, consider that the protection of Konstantyn's sister may be the best thing for her and the babe, and that even if it leads to Ruthenia annexing Zavonia . . . No need to look at me like that. I know what Valdas fears. Think on this, Mirza. Even if Ruthenia takes Zavonia, Kristina and Konstantyn's son will be safe, and it is more likely to be a bloodless coup, or at least, less bloody than a war on two fronts. You can see that, can't you?"

Mirza nodded. "I can see. It's one way, and not a bad way, but . . . I'm not Zavonian."

"And Valdas is."

"Break his bones; you'll find Zavonia written in the marrow."

Dahnay sighed audibly. "I was afraid of that."

Mirza licked her lips. "You won't . . . try anything tonight, will you? I need to know you're at my back before I can scry."

"What can I do? I'm at your disposal. You know I'm a foreign agent. That's never been a secret between us. Until the queen and the heir are found safe we have entirely the same objective. Afterward, well, I have my job to do and Valdas has his duty."

"That day will be . . . interesting."

"Yes." Dahnay gave her attention to helping Mirza set up the copper scrying bowl, tipping a little water in from one of the two skin bottles they had brought. The remainder of the water and the second bottle were set ready in case Dahnay needed them to douse Mirza. Mirza fervently hoped she didn't.

"Do you need me to do anything else?" Dahnay asked.

"Stay close and stay watchful. This time you'll be watching for interruptions from the outside as well as watching out for me."

They'd taken a turn around the area, disturbing a few vagrants, before entering Soldiers' Fields, and Mirza had a fair idea of the latticework of streets and where they might dart for shelter. The early-morning workers would be abroad within the hour, confusing any search. Luckily, vagrants believed this place too haunted to use it for a sleeping place.

Mirza lit a stub of candle and placed it on the statue plinth and placed her bowl on the ground below so that the flame reflected in the water when she knelt over it. She cleared her mind of all distractions, or tried to. She prayed to the one god. *Please let Lind and Valdas be all right.*

No. Don't think about your friends.

Focus on Kristina.

I can't do this. Yes, you can.

What if the Darkness comes back?

Dodge. Run. Don't let his shadow touch yours.

Just do it!

Think about Kristina.

She concentrated on finding a lone woman and a baby. She'd never seen the queen, but Valdas had described her and Lind had given away more in his ramblings. Finding someone on the spirit plane or in the scrying bowl was about more than appearance. And at least she had a name to fasten onto, two names, in fact, since the queen had changed her name to the Zavonian form when she'd come from Sverija. Christine of House Willenbach had become Kristina of House Zamoy. Mirza decided to use both.

"Christine Willenbach, Kristina Zamoy, reveal!"

The water didn't even stir.

"Christine Willenbach, Kristina Zamoy, reveal!"

She took ten breaths and tried again.

"Christine Willenbach, Kristina Zamoy, reveal!"

A faint ripple disturbed the water. She knelt a little straighter. Felt her breath puff out in a little "Ha!" of satisfaction. The bottom of the bowl had vanished. She saw below the surface. Deep, deep, deeper and deep.

And no Shadow!

Her relief at that was palpable.

"Kristina!"

A woman looked up from where she huddled over a wrapped bundle.

"Who wants me?" she mouthed.

In the candle light Mirza saw the face staring up. Below it a pale breast, and fastened determinedly on the nipple an unmistakably healthy baby.

"Oh! Beautiful baby!" Mirza breathed the words. She needed to find out where mother and child were. Not far away, she thought. "Dahnay, they're in the city."

The water stirred again as if some celestial artist swirled a carmine brush in its depths. Trails of red dissolved as she watched, bright drops of ruby blood.

"No!"

But it was too late. Gray-silver spider-silk spanned the bowl, anchored at compass points round the rim, crossing and crisscrossing to support the weight of an enormous shadow, spidery with limpid human eyes. Instead of being outside looking in, Mirza was now inside looking out. Looking up at the surface of the water and the swirls of blood, dark shadows in the half-moonlight, wrapped about her, roiling with intent.

Fear such as she had never known took her breath and chilled her blood all in an instant. She didn't even have time to call out to Dahnay. She felt herself collapsing forward.

Dahnay's hands were on her shoulders, hauling her up, dragging her along the ground so her boot heels scraped in the grass and bounced over the surface roots of the memorial trees. She tried to move her feet, to help Dahnay along, but it was as if the spider-silk had caught her fast like some fat bluebottle.

"Leave me."

"I will not."

"Tell Valdas she's in the city."

"Tell him yourself."

Another tug and a jolt. Dahnay was strong. Mirza heard the snick of steel as Dahnay drew her blade. She felt herself swung bodily across the Ethiop woman's shoulder and bounced along at a stumbling run, held with one strong arm round her thighs.

Yes, they were going to make it!

But the shadow tightened around her and Dahnay slowed as if mired. The world spun and Mirza was pitched onto the cold ground, a frosted tree root beneath her cheek.

"Dahnay!"

She heard blades clash together, though she couldn't see any opponent because her vision clouded in on itself. The shadow squeezed tighter. She fought for air. With each wriggle her bonds tightened. Above her the entity turned his hungry eyes in her direction. She screamed out her remaining breath and her chest locked tight. Her muscles sucked against unyielding iron.

Air! She must have air!

Her body panicked and kicked, using up all the goodness in her last breath, yet her mind set itself aside in a tiny still room. *This is it. I'm going to die. I knew it was coming.* The dark night grew darker still, and the dizzying swirls of black blood enclosed her face completely, filling nose, eyes, mouth, ears, flooding inward, filling her with poison.

I'm dead already.

At least I hope so.

CHAPTER SIXTY-SIX

Valdas

VALDAS SLOWLY OPENED his eyes, or tried to. Only one opened and the low, morning sun blazed into it through the east-facing window. He blinked it shut again. Screwing his face up told him exactly why the other eye would not open.

"Ow!"

A warm body next to his rubbed against him.

"Good morning, lover."

"Aniela."

She leaned over him, her nipples against his chest, and kissed the tip of his nose. "It's the only place that doesn't look as though someone's set about it with a club."

"Uh-huh." That was the extent of the conversation he could manage this morning.

"Want to go again, lover?"

Her hand rested low on his belly with the promise of working its way down. He felt a tightness that was nothing to do with sex.

"Need a piss." He flung the covers off the bed and she made a grab for them, snuggling down, her naked shoulders tantalizingly over the top.

"Romantic as ever. There's a pot under the bed."

"Nah, I'll go down to the outhouse." He dragged on his pants and undershirt, splashed water from her washbowl onto his sticky eye, and experimentally prized it open. God, it hurt. So did his whole body. He felt as if he'd been pounded to within an inch of his life.

He had.

But he'd given a good pounding back. "Does that make us even?"

"What?" Aniela said from the depths of the bed.

"Oh, nothing. Just thinking out loud."

"Are you coming back up, lover? Shall I wait here?" She stuck one delicately shaped leg out of the covers and it was obvious that she'd got her legs open and her hand . . .

"Uhhh!"

He sat down on the edge of the bed, took her by the shoulders, and kissed her forehead. "Of course I'm coming back, lovely girl. Try to stop me. Just . . . not this morning. Get some sleep, or some breakfast, whichever you fancy."

"Aww." She flounced out of bed without a stitch on and his resolve very nearly broke, but he really did need that piss. He fled the bedroom to the sound of her sticking her tongue out and blowing a mouthfart at him. He could hear her laughter as he took the steps cautiously, one at a time.

Outhouse visited, he headed for the kitchen, where Klara was stirring kasza in a pot.

"Good morning, lovely lady."

"Valdas! Oh, my! I didn't hear you creeping up on me. Don't give a poor old lady the vapors, boy."

"Boy!" He laughed. "Thanks, Klara, but no need to play the matron with me. I know you pretend to be older than you are so no one will invite you to try the front parlor job."

"And what would my husband and sons say to that if I did?"

"They'd say you're a fine figure of a woman."

"Get on with you, flatterer. Take a bowl of kasza and eat it through there." She nodded to the front of the house.

At this time in the morning the front parlor, where the girls sat and waited or paraded their wares before potential customers at night, was turned into a breakfast room. Three gate-leg tables stood end to end in the middle of the room to make a board for all comers, but few of the girls roused for breakfast this early.

One figure hunched over a bowl of kasza.

"Lind!"

Lind looked up warily and nodded. His face was a mess.

Valdas waited for the fury to rise in him.

It didn't.

Curiosity overcame him. What had happened to Lind last night? The asexual Lind and fifteen whores, now that would have been something worth paying to see. Lind wasn't even twitching. He seemed well enough in control for someone who'd faced a nightmare—maybe not his worst, but a nightmare all the same—and yet lived.

"I've seen you look prettier," Valdas said, and sat opposite, the muscles in his chest feeling as though each one was pinging against his ribs as he came to rest.

"I could say the same about you," Lind said.

"You pack a decent punch."

"When I'm desperate. Fist fighting's not my style."

"No, I'm sure."

"Have . . . Have we got a truce?" Lind asked.

"For now," Valdas said.

"Good. After we've found Kristina, kill me then."

Valdas nodded. "Thanks. I probably will." He cleared his throat. "Can you pass me the honey, please?"

Lind pushed the jar across.

⊸————⊸

It wasn't until after breakfast and ten minutes of sluicing himself off under the pump head in the yard that Valdas finally climbed the steps up to the attic room, expecting to find Dahnay and Mirza still fast asleep. Both beds were empty and cold. He checked the pegs. Their cloaks were both missing.

With a sickening feeling in his gut, he checked beneath the bed. Mirza's saddlebag was unbuckled, the scrying bowl gone.

Oh shit!

"Maksimilian! Aniela! Lind!"

He bolted down the three flights of stairs, yelling as he went. Aniela ran onto the second-floor landing dressed only in a thin chemise and, pulling a shawl around her shoulders, leaned over the rail; Lind appeared from the breakfast room where he'd lingered over coffee, and Maksimilian came from his parlor, already fully dressed.

"Mirza's gone out to scry. Dahnay's with her, I think, or else she's gone after her. Their beds are cold."

"Their beds would be cold inside half an hour. There's no telling how long they've been gone, lover." Aniela padded down after him, barefoot.

"She's right." Maksimilian shrugged. "Maybe they left at dawn."

"I've been in that kitchen for four hours already." Klara came up the hallway dusting flour from her hands. "It's the only way I can get the bread made before all you lazy-arses are up for breakfast. No one's come in or out this morning, not since I lit my first candle."

"I got up in the middle of the night for a piss," Ruta called down. By now they were all awake and coming out of their rooms in various states of undress. "Thought I heard something, so I looked out of the window. Saw a couple of people in the street, but . . . well . . . Trader don't like us to see things, so I figured I didn't see nothing."

"How long ago?"

"I dunno. After the midnight bell, maybe six hours gone."

"Six hours! Good God! While we were sleeping, those two were out there. Why didn't they wake us?"

"You know that, lover." Aniela touched his shoulder and looked across at Lind. "You survived the night, I see."

"Yes, mistress."

"You both look as though you're trying to outshine each other's beauty. Go out like that and dogs'll bark and children burst into tears at the sight of you. Let's have both of you in the front parlor dressed and ready by the time I count to a hundred."

Valdas turned and looked at her. "What are you babbling about?"

Aniela gently cuffed him on the shoulder. "You're going to want to set off to look for Mirza and Dahnay and you've both got faces like leavings in a butcher's yard. Get dressed and I'll cover the worst of the bruises up for you before you go. Go on, get on with it!"

Valdas didn't argue. When had Aniela got so bossy? Uh, all right. She'd always been bossy—or at least a woman who knew her own mind. He liked that in her, and though he hadn't looked in a glass this morning he must look awful. Lind certainly did.

It was more than the count of a hundred, but he finished dressing quickly, pulling on his zupan and buttoning it as he walked into the front parlor. The breakfast things had been shoved to one side and two chairs had been set up facing the window. Aniela had a pot of cream and some brushes. Ruta hovered, trying to be useful.

"Sit you both down, this won't take long."

Aniela started to mix cream and pigment in two little flat dishes, matching it against each man's skin color. She gave a dish to Ruta and pointed to Lind. The women began to smooth the pigment over bruises.

"Don't get it in any open cuts and don't, for God's sake, rub it into your eyes. This stuff is for emergencies only," Aniela said.

"What is it?" Valdas's nose wrinkled at the smell.

"A secret recipe, passed from one whore to another for I don't know how many generations," Aniela said. "There are times when we need to cover up bruises or we lose custom. We always want to look like the pick of the crop, not windfalls."

"Oh." Valdas's voice was small. "I'm sorry. I didn't think." He felt stupid.

"That's 'cos you'd never beat on a woman, lover, but there's plenty that do. This place is better than most; Trader Maksimilian won't have it, or at least he stops it whenever he can."

She smacked his hand away as he tried to touch the cool cream that she was smearing into the tender swelling on his cheekbone. "Don't touch, I said."

He returned his hand to his knee.

"Where to?" Lind asked. "Where would be the likely place?"

Maksimilian came to the doorway to watch the progress of the cover-up job. "I've sent out runners to the people who usually know what's going on. Give them a few more minutes. Let's see if there have been any disturbances in the city overnight."

Impatient as he was to be outside and looking, Valdas recognized the sense in Maksimilian's words.

"There." Aniela stepped away to examine her handiwork and held a glass up for him to see. "It hardly looks like you, Valdas. Your nose is thick and your cheeks are so puffy it's changed the shape of your face. With all the bruising covered and that cut twitching your eyebrow out of shape, you're a new man."

"Let me have the glass." Valdas took it from her and grunted at the stranger who looked back at him. "Good disguise. Even if it's a painful one." He turned to look at Lind. "You, too, I guess."

"I could have done with the secret of this a time or two, myself, mistress." Lind stood and inclined his head.

The sound of a runner, one of Maksimilian's trusted message boys, hurtling in through the kitchen door caught all their attention. The child bent over to get his breath.

"Gabrjel says . . ." He took three more rasping gasps. "That troops from the Gura—the Chancellor's Own—were swarming over Soldiers' Fields just before dawn."

"What else?" Maksimilian heaved the boy upright.

"Nothing. That was it. Body pulled out of the river late last night, but it was only one of the vagrants and it was too early to be who you're looking for."

Maksimilian flipped him a coin. "Go to Klara and get some breakfast. You did well."

"Soldiers' Fields." Valdas stood.

Lind stood as well and stretched carefully with his hand on his chest where Valdas had cut him.

Serve him right. Valdas allowed himself a moment of smug satisfaction before his own breath caused a shooting pain through his ribcage. Damn! He hurt all over, too.

"Well, at least no one will recognize either of us," Lind said.

CHAPTER SIXTY-SEVEN

Mirza

SHE WASN'T DEAD.
Being dead should hurt less.

Mirza breathed in. Every rib bone creaked and popped. She didn't get beyond half-filling her lungs before her chest stabbed as if a knife was buried to the hilt in it. She moved her hands to feel, ran them from belly to breast. No knife hilt, no puddled blood.

She wanted to laugh with delight, but the first "Ha!" shot her through with agony. She wouldn't try that again in a hurry. Where was she? Not Soldiers' Fields. She was definitely not lying on the frosted ground, but she was lying on something cold and equally unyielding. She felt with one hand. Stone, smooth and flat, slightly slimy with moisture. Not a breath of breeze on the dank air. *Inside.*

"Dahnay?" Her voice wobbled. She tried to steady it, and said again, "Dahnay?"

Better.

But still no response.

Could she open her eyes? The question occupied her for an unknown length of time and eventually she answered it herself. *If I don't try, I'll never know.* One by one she opened them, at least she thought she opened them, but her world remained steadfastly black.

Blind!

Her moment of panic was overtaken by rational thought. *Or I'm in a place that's very, very dark.*

Wait until she knew which before starting to panic. She could put up a witchlight, of course, but she didn't want to use magic here until she knew where she was and what was happening.

She gathered her thoughts. What was the last thing she remembered? *Falling to the floor from Dahnay's shoulder and lying face down across a tree root with the air being squeezed from her lungs.*

"Hello?"

No answer, but her ears told her part of what she needed to know. From the echo she was in a fairly large room with hard surfaces to bounce the sound back at her. She thought it had a tallish ceiling, too. Nothing disturbed the air, so either a room with all doors and windows sealed tight, or a room far from the penetrating breezes of outside. A cellar, maybe, which would certainly be consistent with the stone beneath her back.

She'd lost her cloak and she was cold, maybe close to dangerously cold. She rolled sideways, intending to try to haul herself to her knees and then her feet, but she clanged into something . . . bars . . . Magic fizzed painfully through her, as if she had bubbles in her blood.

She cautiously reached out and touched the metal, but quickly jerked her fingers away as it stung. Wriggling across the damp floor, she quickly came up against a rough stone wall. Stone on one side and spell-strengthened iron bars on the other. A cell of some kind.

Somewhere a long way off, muffled footsteps sounded. She thought she could hear voices, but they quieted again. Then a key in a heavy door, somewhere up and to her left. Another scrape and . . .

She wasn't blind!

Torchlight flickered from a door some twenty feet up. She blinked. It seemed bright, but it barely made a dent in the darkness. It revealed a high, vaulted, windowless room, and a long flight of descending stone steps hugging the end wall.

There were muttering voices outside the room. A man entered and the door closed behind him, shutting off the torchlight. The only illumination now came from his lantern. Mirza could just about make out the man's upper half. He held a large canvas bag in one hand and the lantern in the other. It cast lurching shadows as it swung with the rhythm of his descent.

Step by step, the lantern revealed a dungeon. King Gerhard's dungeon, no doubt. Barbaric instruments of torture lined the walls, some pushed together higgledy-piggledy as if no longer used. *Please let that be the case.* The man reached the bottom of the steps and raised his lantern high.

She wasn't the only prisoner.

CHAPTER SIXTY-EIGHT
Valdas

SOLDIERS' FIELDS WAS deserted now except for its ghosts. Valdas didn't believe in ghosts the last time he'd come here. Now, he wasn't so sure. He remembered Mirza's answer to his question about whether she saw ghosts all the time. *Only when I look.*

Gods, he hoped she was all right.

The sun had risen to half-mast, pale and watery as clouds drifted in front of it. The grass crunched underfoot with the remains of an early autumn frost.

"I'd hoped to have a respectable plaque here one day." Valdas shivered as they walked on the gravestone pathways past the neat memorials.

"When I go, I don't even want to leave marks where I've been," Lind said.

Valdas grunted and bent over to examine one plaque.

"Found someone you know?" Lind asked.

"In a manner of speaking. These threads could be from Mirza's cloak."

They looked around, examining the ground, both paths and grass. Eventually they worked their way to the memorial, walking all the way around the four marble figures on their plinth.

Lind sat down on the edge and rested his elbows on his knees, bending his head forward to pinch the bridge of his nose between thumb and forefinger. "You think they were here?"

"Possibly." Valdas sat next to him and held up the thread of cloth.

"Plenty of people have cloaks."

"True." Valdas leaned forward to where paving gave way to grass.

"But how many people leave the stub of a good beeswax candle behind them?"

"You don't know how long that's been there."

"I do." Valdas rolled the burned end of the wick in his fingers and they came away sooty. "It rained yesterday afternoon. Wouldn't have been any dry soot on this wick if it was here then."

Lind sprang to his feet and reeled slightly. Shrugging, he said, "You look as bad as I feel." He held out his hand.

Valdas glared at him. *Whose fault was that?*

The hand didn't waver.

It was as if Valdas looked at Lind through his left eye and saw a comrade in arms. Look through his right eye and he saw an enemy, the man who started this whole sorry mess and plunged Zavonia into chaos. Open both eyes and he didn't know what he saw. Just a man, maybe. One who'd been offered limited choices and had made the wrong ones.

He took the hand and let Lind haul him to his feet.

"What now?" Lind asked.

"We scour the streets. See if we can find anyone who saw anything. There are plenty of vagabonds who sleep in corners and alleyways. Perhaps one of them had his dreams disturbed."

"Split up?"

"Split up," Valdas said. "Meet here just after every toll of the hour. If one of us isn't here, take it as a sign that something's been found and head straight for Maksimilian's."

"Right."

While Lind headed for the west side of Soldiers' Fields, Valdas walked purposefully, but not too fast, to the east side. Starting on the Shambles, he checked every doorway and alley. It wasn't so late that all the vagrants would have departed their nighttime quarters. The butchers were all setting up their shops, but it seemed unlikely that any had been here during the small hours. He narrowly missed a dousing in bloodied water from a scrubbing bucket as some careless apprentice sloshed it out into the noxious drain that ran down the center of the street.

The hour bell rang and Valdas headed to Soldiers' Fields. He saw Lind from a distance; they waved an acknowledgment, *Nothing yet*, and each turned back to their own search.

Valdas was halfway down Milliner's Row before he found the alley. Tucked behind a water butt, close up to the side of a building that had once been much more genteel than it now was, he saw a still figure bundled in a good cloak. So still, and the angle was all wrong. He bent to roll the body over, breath held, terrified that he might see blind eyes staring up at the sky out of a black, scarred face.

He almost laughed when the face was the pale putty-gray of death visited upon a fair-skinned man by a cudgel to the temple. With the efficiency of a battlefield corpse stripper, he checked the pockets.

He found nothing, but what did that prove except that the man was poor?

A scrape behind him made him turn. Seeing nothing but empty alley, he drew the loaded flintlock pistol in his belt, pulled the dog-head back, and took three cautious steps forward.

Silently a ragged figure staggered out of the shadows, took a pace toward him, and collapsed.

He jerked his finger from the pistol's trigger as he recognized the black face. "Dahnay?" But she was past responding, unconscious.

Heart pounding, he stripped the filthy rag cloak from around her shoulders, saw the drying blood on the front of her zupan, wadded up his kerchief and pressed it over the oozing wound. Squashing down a knot of fear, he scooped her up into his arms, not caring what sort of glances he drew as he made his way to Maksimilian's, kicking the front door open with a bang and delivering the too-still figure to Maksimilian's waiting arms. Then he sank to his knees, exhausted and trembling.

"Dahnay." Getting his breath, he half ran, half crawled up the stairs behind Maksimilian, four flights, seeming like a mountain until he reached the top gasping for breath. Maksimilian had laid Dahnay on Mirza's bed and was undoing the button at her throat.

Valdas lurched into the room.

"I'll do it." He elbowed Maksimilian out of the way. "Tell Lind I found her in an alley in the Street of Milliners. That's where he's to start searching for Mirza."

"M'za . . ." Dahnay's eyes flicked open briefly but then rolled back in her head and she passed out again.

Valdas had had enough experience of battlefield injuries to make a passable job of stopgap treatments. The chest wound, just below her left breast, was small but deep, and by the blood on her lips, serious.

He stripped off her zupan and undershirt, cut the binding round her small breasts without even thinking about her gender, then cleaned the wound with water and cloths Klara had brought and applied gentle pressure. It was still oozing but not bleeding freely. That didn't mean that she hadn't lost a lot of blood before he found her. Keeping up the pressure, he applied a clean pad and wrapped a bandage around her torso as gently as possible. Ignoring old scars, he checked neck, ribs, spine. There were bruises, though they didn't show up so obviously on her dark skin.

He pulled the drawstring and removed her boots and pants without looking too closely at her mound. He was relieved to find no more fresh injuries. He covered her with a light sheet and a warm wool blanket, chafed feet and hands to restore some circulation. He tried to drip some water between her lips, but she was too far gone to swallow and he feared to choke her. Not knowing what else to do, he pulled up a chair by her bedside. This needed Mirza's expertise.

Light footsteps on the stair and a scratching on the door announced Aniela's arrival.

"What do you need, lover?" She rested her hand lightly on his shoulder.

He covered it with his own callused one. "A miracle, I think." He leaned forward and wiped spittle from Dahnay's lip. It was flecked with pink.

"Shall I send for a surgeon?"

"It's a stab wound. It's gone into her lung. A surgeon will do nothing except shake his head and offer condolences."

"Shall I sit with her awhile?"

He shook his head. "No, I will, but thanks."

Twice during the morning Dahnay stirred, but lapsed into unconsciousness again. Valdas wiped her face and hands with a damp cloth, dribbled a little water between her lips, gave her a second blanket when she appeared too cold, removed it when she appeared too hot.

Aniela delivered soup at the nooning and left again. The whole house seemed to have gone quiet. His only notion of time passing was by the steady tolling of the hour bell. By five the light was already fading and the street outside beginning to wake. He could hear preparations for the night's activities. On the floor below one of the girls giggled and was shushed by a comrade.

Laugh as much as you like, I don't think she can hear you.

Dahnay's breathing was ragged. Valdas heard her lungs rattling. He wiped her mouth again.

Aniela brought a thick slice of roasted pork on a trencher of bread and a wedge of cheese big enough to feed a family. With it was a pot of weak beer.

"Got to keep your strength up, lover."

He pulled a corner of the pork off in his fingers and chewed it to oblige her. It might have been ashes. "Any news from Lind?"

"No, nor from any of Maksimilian's men neither." Aniela took a candle from the box by the fireplace, lit it from the fire, and placed it in a holder, topped by a glass chimney. "If Mirza's on the streets no one has seen her, and if she's anywhere up on the Gura no one saw her being taken, save maybe for the Chancellor's Own."

"Gods!" Valdas let his head fall forward and rubbed his eyes. They began to sting from the remains of Aniela's camouflage cream.

His cheeks were wet.

"Why didn't they wake us?" he asked. "Mirza said scrying was dangerous. And I was going to ask her to do it despite that! Now look. Instead of finding Kristina we've lost Mirza and . . ." His voice caught in his throat so the last word came out in a whisper. "Dahnay."

"Well, you didn't ask. This wasn't your fault." Aniela pulled a cleanish rag from her pocket, spit on it, and wiped his eyes.

"Neither was Konstantyn's death, but if I'd been a little more watchful I might have prevented this whole gods-poxed mess."

"Not so!" Her voice took on a sharp tone. "Whoever hired Lind would have hired someone else and someone else until the job was done."

He sighed. "You're right."

"Course I'm right. If there's one fault with you, Valdas Zalecki, it's an overabundance of melancholy. You can't take on the responsibility for the turning of the world, nor the guilt should it cease to turn."

He sighed. "I know."

"Aye, you might know, but you don't really *know*—not here in your heart." She leaned over his shoulder and placed her hand on his chest. "You've done so much already. Don't lose your focus now."

Dahnay muttered and Valdas leaned forward and took her hand, but she stilled again. "Damned if she hasn't got the knack for being the stillest, quietest woman I know," he said under his breath.

Aniela rubbed his shoulders, offering what solace she could. "The front doors will be opening soon, lover. I'm required downstairs. I could tell Maksimilian not tonight."

"No, it's all right. Go ahead."

"I'll come by after I've finished with the customers."

He nodded.

"She means a lot to you, doesn't she?"

"She's Dahnay."

"Of course she is."

Aniela dropped a kiss on his head. "I'll see you later."

He heard her footsteps receding.

"Oh, Dahnay. Don't die. Don't die."

"Not dead yet." Her voice was so weak he could barely catch the words.

He was on his knees by her side in a second. "Dahnay." He took hold of her hand. "What happened? How do you feel? Does it hurt?"

He was asking too many questions. Start again. "You're safe." He squeezed her hand, pleased to feel her fingers twitch to squeeze his in response.

"Safe. Not. No one safe."

"You're safe. I promise."

She twisted her head sideways.

"What can I get you? Water?"

She made an incoherent but positive sound and he eased her into a sitting position, cradling her head so she could drink. Three sips was all she managed before she gave up trying and her breath bubbled in her throat. She couldn't even support the weight of her own head. He laid her down gently, cold with fear. God, he needed Mirza's good sense and healing skills right now.

"Mirza," Dahnay said.

Valdas crouched down beside her, his face close to hers. "Mirza, yes. What about Mirza?"

"Taken. Chancellor's Own."

"Where?" Stupid question. She wouldn't know.

"Gura. Heard them. Played dead."

"Was Mirza injured?"

"Scrying. Carried her, but . . ." Her fingers twitched in his again. "I'm broken."

"You only need to rest."

"No. Broken. Inside." She twitched his hand toward her bandaged chest.

"Dahnay . . ."

"Find Mirza."

"I will."

CHAPTER SIXTY-NINE
Lind

"**S**HE'S MADE IT through the night."

The news misted through the whorehouse like a sigh. Girls appeared at their doors and on landings to ask if it was true. Someone, Klara, Lind thought, came down into the parlor, still redolent with the fumes from drink and cheap perfume, and lit a single candle. Maksimilian and four of the girls joined her to pray.

How did he feel about it? Lind wasn't sure. Dahnay had never been anything but fair toward him. He began to climb the steps, his feet leading him to the top of the house, though he barely knew why.

Aniela sat halfway up the stair to the top floor, a small and lonely gatekeeper. She'd avoided him, of course, since giving his identity away to Valdas. Well, he could hardly blame her for that. They'd moved in and out of Trader Maksimilian's as if they were existing in different places. He'd caught the occasional glance, wariness tinged with fear, but mostly she didn't look at him.

"Aniela." He stood at the bottom of the stair and looked up to her, not quite tall enough to meet her eyes on the level.

She looked at him, looked through him, really. Hardly seeing.

"Has she said anything about Mirza?"

He thought at first that Aniela wasn't going to reply, then at length she focused on his face, swallowed, and shook her head.

"Will she be all right?"

"I don't know."

Get it over with, man, now or never. "I'm sorry."

She nodded distractedly.

"Not about Dahnay . . . I mean I'm sorry about her too, but I mean I'm sorry about your fingers."

"Sorry's an easy word to say." She held her hands out in front of her, casting long shadows up the wall from the lamp on the landing below. Her little fingers were both crooked, the left slightly more than the right.

"Not for me."

"You don't scare me anymore, Lind."

"Sometimes I scare myself."

"With all the thing about killing the king . . . I never thought . . . Why did you want to find Valdas?"

"A commission. Someone wanted him dead."

She started to rise, but he waved her down. "I could have done it anytime we were on the road together if I was going to. He's safe, at least from me."

"Why?"

"Why what?"

"Why kill Valdas?"

"Does an archer tell the arrow why? I'm given a purse and a name."

"Does he know?"

He shook his head. "I'll tell him. No more secrets."

"I know I'm only a woman, but . . ." She leaned forward so her eyes were on a level with his. "If you hurt Valdas, or knowingly let him be hurt, you'd better do more than break my fingers, because this world will be too small a place for you to hide."

He put his right hand, palm flat, over his heart. "I swear to you, Mistress Aniela, that no action or inaction of mine will harm him."

"And I should believe that because?"

"You don't have to believe it. I believe it."

"Are you willing to swear it on the blood of Our Lord?"

"I am."

She sucked the tip of her right thumb, reached forward and drew a cross on his forehead. "I baptize thee anew into our company, Lind, but don't expect me to be your best friend."

He half-bowed in acknowledgment. New christened in the spit of a whore. Didn't that beat all?

CHAPTER SEVENTY
Mirza

IN THE OPPOSITE diagonal corner of the room, a cage matched Mirza's, and in it was a young woman with a baby. Lantern light glinted off copper hair! Kristina! Hell's teeth, how long had they been looking for her while she was here? When the woman didn't even look up, Mirza's anger turned to concern.

She concentrated on the man. He didn't look dangerous. His hair was already turning to silver and he wore the livery of a palace servant with the only sharp steel about him his own table knife.

He had a peculiar look in his eyes, as if he wasn't really seeing what was in front of him. He walked carefully, mechanically, negotiating the steps almost as if they weren't there. He stopped in front of Queen Kristina's cell and delved into his bag, bringing out a water skin, which he pushed through the bars and set on the ground, retrieving what must be an empty one.

"Hey!" Mirza called to attract his attention.

He might not have heard her for all the good it did. He never faltered in his precise movements, pulling out a linen bag and pushing it through the bars to rest next to the water.

"Hey! Water Man!"

At that Kristina looked up and stared with pupils too big and dark to be natural. Drugged in some way, Mirza guessed. Maybe the water. The man passed a third bundle through the bars. Fresh linen napkins for the baby by the looks of it.

"You! Water Man! Hey!"

Still nothing to indicate that he'd heard. Was he deaf? A deaf jailer might make sense, but . . . if she could only get a look at his face again. She had nothing to throw to attract his attention.

"Kristina, lady, make him look at me. Turn him around."

Kristina looked in her direction at last, eyes dull, but at least it was some kind of response.

"Turn him around."

Mirza put the full force of her will behind that quiet command.

Kristina cradled the baby in her right arm, but with her left she reached through the bars and tugged on the man's sleeve, breaking his steady concentration for the first time. Without saying anything, she pushed against his arm so that he turned and at last Mirza was able to catch his gaze.

It was like looking into a bottomless pool with no perspective, no spark of humanity.

A creeping dread assaulted Mirza's spine. Bespelled, she thought, as surely as the iron bars of her cage were. She took a steadying breath.

"Here. Look at me. Yes, you, look at me. Come here."

He took a faltering step toward her as if not quite sure she existed.

"Yes, that's it. Here."

First she persuaded and then she coaxed. When coaxing failed she snapped out an order. It took minutes instead of seconds, but gradually she brought him across the floor, closer to her bars.

Close enough for her to reach out between the bars, being careful not to touch the metal, and touch his clammy fingers, feeling the wrongness. She almost recoiled but forced her fingers to curl around his. A spell, but one not set there naturally with gentle persuasion. This was a harsh twisting of the man's self-will. It was a sickness invading his body. Mirza flushed with sudden confidence for the first time since waking here. She knew how to deal with sickness. It was what she did.

Concentrating hard, she winkled the wrongness to the surface, drawing it toward the fingers that she held. Down, down and . . . out. She pulled the spellworking out of him and shook her hands to let it dissipate.

She felt a surge of triumph. Yes! She'd done it!

He blinked.

"Do you know where you are?"

"Yes, I'm . . ." He looked round. "No. Yes." He shook his head as if trying to piece things together. "This must be the dungeons under the old keep. Tunnels go on for miles, they say. It's a labyrinth. How did I . . . ?"

"What's your name?"

"Piotr. Piotr Aniekin."

"See that lady in the cell behind you, Piotr?"

He turned, looked, and shook his head dumbly.

"She's your queen . . . Kristina . . . and that's King Konstantyn's child, the rightful heir to the Amber Crown."

He stared at her, eyebrows drawn close together in a frown. "I saw her once at her wedding. Bright red-gold hair and so dainty."

"Yes, that's right. Take a look at her. It's the same woman. Are you a loyal subject of the crown?"

He straightened up. "Of course."

"Good. That little babe is your king. You must take mother and child to safety. Quickly, man!" She put all her will behind the firm instruction.

"Kristina. You must go to the same place you ran to before. Do you understand? To the man in your brother's employ."

The queen's drug-glazed eyes barely flickered in her direction.

"Piotr, when she comes round, tell her to go to the same place as before."

"Same as before." He nodded, crossed quickly to the queen's cell, and began to check the door, a center panel of bars. He couldn't see an obvious lock, but he spotted a winch handle on the side wall, pulled out a locking peg, and began to crank it. The bars groaned and shuddered. He put more muscle into it and they lifted off the ground by an inch or two.

"Well done, Piotr. Keep going," Mirza said.

"Yes, Piotr, keep going. I'd be interested to see if it's possible for one skinny old man to raise that on his own."

The bars crashed to the floor. Piotr jumped back and stood like a child caught with his hand in the honey jar. He wouldn't meet the eyes of the man at the top of the stairs. Mirza had no such inhibition. She felt queasy as soon as she looked at the newcomer. A palpable aura of menace clung around him, dark with tendrils of power reaching deep into the stones of floor and walls as if drawing energy from the building's dark places.

Oh, kak! Kak! Kak!

Hardly able to take her eyes off him, Mirza watched the man descend. Just looking at him felt like a violation. She wanted to flee, but she was trapped. Suffocating.

Breathe.

She sucked air into her lungs and tried to think rationally.

Was he dangerous? He wasn't even armed unless he was carrying hidden weapons beneath the long, fur-lined delja. A fringe of dark hair escaped the velvet kolpek on his head. They were court clothes, fine and yet warm against the dank chill. His regular features, not handsome, but distinctive, were not unlike the statue of the old king, Aleksander, Konstantyn's father, that she'd seen in the Market Square. King Gerhard was the son of Aleksander's sister, so with such a strong family look this must be him. Was King Gerhard himself the powerful mage?

Whoever he was, and whatever he was wearing, she instantly recognized this man as a predator. *Never run from a predator, he'll only chase you for the sport of it and then tear out your throat for fun.*

With barely a quick glance at Kristina and the baby, the man snapped his fingers. Piotr stood as if turned to stone. Then the man-who-might-be-Gerhard turned his attention in her direction as he descended the stairs.

"Awake, I see, and getting into mischief already."

When she didn't answer, he shrugged and continued down the steps and into the room. He lit lamps around the wall using a taper set alight from Piotr's lantern, then touched the taper to sticks and coals already laid in the hearth.

Would a king light his own fire? Probably not.

"Of course, we could light this quicker with your power; then we'd both be warmer," he said quietly, as if to himself.

She stiffened. Exactly how much did he know about her power?

"Now, what are we to do with you, and more importantly what are we to do with poor Piotr? Poor deluded Piotr."

It wasn't a question she felt a need to answer. Anything she might say would only hurt Piotr more. Never ask for mercy from a predator.

He sighed. With barely a wave of his fingers, Piotr jerked upright as if someone grasped him by the upper arms. Two someones maybe. His invisible captors dragged his arms behind his back and almost carried him to the stone wall opposite. She saw a length of chain and shackles move and apparently lock around Piotr's wrists. A crank above his head began to wind the chain shorter . . . and shorter. His arms were pulled up and up behind his back until he leaned forward against the chain to try and ease the pain. The screaming started before the sickening crunch as first one shoulder and then the other dislocated and Piotr's useless arms were pulled out of their sockets until he was hanging by them.

"My boys are quite creative, don't you think? Highly trained soldiers . . . Well, they were while they still lived. I'm surprised you can't see them with your talents."

Mirza looked. Really looked. Beyond the world of living flesh she could see a shadow of a red *mente*, the uniform of the High Guard. She'd seen them before, but not in the world of the living. Were these Valdas's men bound beyond death to this man's service? She knew him for a powerful wizard. Was he also a necromancer?

She struggled to swallow, mouth dry. Piotr had passed out and his screams had subsided, but she guessed the man-who-might-be-Gerhard wasn't finished with him yet. Those arms. If Piotr lived he'd likely be crippled. And if Gerhard freed him, would the memory of the queen stay hidden?

Piotr was a dead man.

She'd killed him. Sorry didn't begin to cover it.

"Kazimir, let the old fool go, please. It was not his fault." Kristina spoke from the shadows of her cage with a wavery voice. Her pupils had contracted. Maybe the drug was wearing off a little.

She'd called him Kazimir. Not Gerhard, then. King Gerhard's chancellor.

"Drink, my sweet. You must be thirsty." Kazimir turned to Kristina. At his suggestion she bent to retrieve the water bottle, almost draining it in her eagerness to gulp down the contents.

He nodded. "You're tired now. Sleep."

Carefully she cradled the too-quiet child and sank to the floor of her cell.

Kazimir nodded in satisfaction.

"Let him down." The instruction was to the empty air, but two red-uniformed spirits, still barely shades, winched Piotr down until he was lying on the ground, groaning.

"Watch and learn," Kazimir said. "By the feet, boys. Strip him first."

Ghostly hands worked on Piotr's body, dragging off clothes and attaching fetters to his ankles. He groaned pitifully when they pulled off his shirt, and when they hoisted him aloft, his arms hung down like broken wings, the line of his shoulders all wrong. His eyes opened, beyond desperation, beyond pleading.

Kazimir took a small copper bowl from a shelf, about twice the size of Mirza's scrying bowl. He placed it carefully on the floor beneath Piotr's head. He took a slim-bladed knife and began to draw the point of it over Piotr's skin. First a slice to the crown, then the forehead. The blood began to drip into the bowl. Next the throat, not a deep and fatal wound, but another slice across the skin. Above the heart next and then stomach, belly, and finally genitals. With each cut Piotr whimpered. With the final one he howled as the knife jabbed into his stones and the blood trickled sluggishly down over his belly to join the steady stream drip-drip-dripping into the bowl.

Kazimir was following the body's own centers of power as set out by eastern medicine, draining life-energy.

"Piotr Aniekin, I bind you to my service, in life and in death."

Piotr's whimpering ceased instantly, but his eyes opened wide, and his mouth opened as if he were screaming a silent scream.

"Piotr Aniekin, I bind you to my service, in life and in death."

Mirza opened her other sight to the spiritual maelstrom around Piotr's body. His life-energy swirled and his ethereal body bucked and writhed. The third call would be the charm. It would draw Piotr's spirit from his body to do Kazimir's bidding, leaving his body as carrion. It was her fault. She'd cost the poor man his life. She mustn't cost him his death, too.

The spirit of Konstantyn hovered close by. He stretched out his hand and nodded.

"Piotr Aniekin, I bind you to . . ."

Mirza reached out on the upper plane, took Piotr's hand, and drew his spirit from his body, putting his cool fingers into Konstantyn's safe grip. Both spirits vanished with a suddenness that left her weak as she dropped back into her own body. Kazimir finished his sentence, but Piotr's corpse hung lifeless. His eyes stared at nothing.

CHAPTER SEVENTY-ONE
Valdas

VALDAS SAT WITH Dahnay all night, dozing lightly in a chair and coming instantly awake every time she groaned or moved. With first light he rose and called Aniela.

"She's a strong woman—still hanging on. Can you sit with . . ."

"Of course." Aniela squeezed his arm. "You go and get the bastards who did this."

"Whoever . . . from the Gura. Must be working for the king. Chancellor's Own took Mirza. You stay with Dahnay."

"Don't worry. I'll keep her safe and private."

He nodded, knowing he could trust her. "Lind?"

"Waiting downstairs. I told him . . . Oh, it doesn't matter. He knows and that's what counts."

Valdas nodded.

"So there's just me and Lind."

"Good job you didn't kill him after all."

"Looks like it."

"Are you going to?"

"Not yet."

CHAPTER SEVENTY-TWO

Lind

BY THE TIME Valdas came downstairs, Lind was ready for him. He ushered him into Maksimilian's parlor, away from the vigil in the breakfast room.

"Sit."

Lind pushed him into a wooden chair at Maksimilian's table, then went foraging in the kitchen. Klara wasn't there, but the porridge pot was bubbling over the fire. Lind took the ladle and slopped a generous dollop into a bowl.

Klara came into the kitchen as he straightened up and made to leave. She waved the honey at him. He held out the bowl. She plopped a large spoonful into the kasza, stirred it round, and nodded, jerking her head toward the door. Lind didn't need telling twice.

"Eat, man." He pushed the bowl toward Valdas. "You need your strength and Klara has robbed a beehive for all the honey in this kasza."

Valdas picked up the bowl and spoon like a man in a dream, or a nightmare. His eyes looked haunted, hollow. Well, it was going to get worse yet by the time Lind had finished.

"What did Dahnay say?" Lind asked.

"The Chancellor's Own took Mirza. She's up on the Gura somewhere."

"God's ballocks!" Lind pinched the bridge of his nose. "I guess that confirms what we suspected."

"Yes." Valdas took another spoon of kasza, then pushed the bowl away.

Lind pushed it back. "Do you want to have to explain that full bowl to Klara? She pounded the millet herself."

Valdas took the spoon up again.

"Ideas?" Lind asked.

"I can talk to Tomas again."

"Surly fellow. I met him once when I was looking for you."

"Huh?"

"You think it was coincidence that I was here in Biela Miasto? That I'm looking for the queen? Come on, Valdas, you're smarter than that."

Quickly he told Valdas the whole story, from the time when he'd lately kept a room in the Old Town of Tepet and done business on a bridge above a waterfall.

"I . . . greatly fear that my paymaster had a sorcerer working for him," Lind said. "Maybe it was the same as Mirza's shadow. I don't know. I wish to all the gods I'd never taken his purse, but what did your king mean to me, then?"

"How . . . did you?"

"You walked past me nearly every day for six weeks," Lind said. "Delivering fish to the kitchen."

Valdas studied his face, obviously searching for a pattern to recognize.

"Even without the broken nose and the bruises I doubt you'd know me. I told you, I'm good at my job. My hair was longer; I had a beard, brown with gray streaks. Plumpers padded out my cheeks. I even walked with a bit of a drag on one leg."

"God's ballocks! I deserve sawing in half."

"If it's any consolation, it took me so long because you were never off duty. You were always sniffing around. Anyhow, you know about me using this place as a bolt hole and Trader Maksimilian seizing the opportunity to send Kristina out of the city with me. I didn't know who she was at first. Then when I realized, she scared the shit out of me."

"You could have killed her."

"Strange as it may seem to you, I'm not a murderer, unless someone is a direct threat to me. Besides, she was pregnant."

"And you wouldn't kill a pregnant woman for money?"

He shook his head. "Got to draw the line somewhere."

"An assassin with a conscience."

Lind shrugged. "After Kristina left me I kept my head low and eventually returned to Tepet where, to my surprise, the same employer, via another servant, offered me two purses. One to kill you . . ." He heard the indrawn breath, but plowed on regardless. "And one to find Kristina, alive, and deliver her to him."

"You know where he is?" Valdas was half on his feet.

Lind shook his head. "Nothing so simple. I'm to leave a message at a certain coffeehouse. I'm sure that's not where we'll find anyone of any importance. It's only one end of a messenger chain."

"Why does he want to kill me? Surely I'm old news by now."

Lind shrugged. "I don't know."

"How did you know where I was?"

"I didn't."

"Huh?"

"By the time I came here I'd convinced myself that you were dead. I followed your trail to Dadziga, to a shining star of a woman called Jadzia Lizovska."

"You didn't . . ."

Lind held up one hand, palm outward. "Relax, she's all right. Or she was a few days ago. I saw her again when I went to Dadziga."

"She was your contact?"

He nodded. "She's branching out. She made a good profit on re-mounts for the hussars who are gathering to push through Eris Gate."

"They're going to try and take the pass with winter coming on? Gerhard's a bigger fool than I thought. I wish Jadzia's profit wasn't at the expense of all the lives they'll lose."

"She was pleased to hear you still lived. You made quite an impression. Did you do it without fucking her?"

"A gentleman never tells."

Lind pushed a long bundle toward him over the tabletop.

"What's this?" Valdas unwrapped it. "My sabre? My sabre. It is! Where?"

"Jadzia said you'd signed on with an Anglu merchant called Callender, but the pack-train was attacked and you were slandered for being the bandits' inside man."

"I never . . ."

"Jadzia didn't think you did, though she was glad to have proof. She was also aggrieved, mortally aggrieved, that Callender had cheated her and, she believed, was planning to do so again." Lind sat back and smiled. "You should never cross that young woman. She paid me to put Callender out of action—permanently—and since I had my own business with him I was pleased to serve her wishes, but only after my own. Under some duress, Callender finally admitted to having one of his thugs smash in your head from behind during the attack. The only reason that they didn't cut your throat as well was because of your damned horse."

"Callender. Oh, gods. Last thing I remember was an attack, and my horse, the good one, taking three arrows . . . Nothing after that."

"I'd say your good horse is the one that saved you. I believed you were dead, so I reported that in all good faith to my contact at the coffeehouse. That meant my next job was to find Kristina and deliver her to them."

Lind waited for Valdas to react to the *deliver* part of what he'd said, but when no outburst arrived he continued, "I hoped that as long as they thought that I was still looking, they wouldn't send anybody else."

Valdas nodded. "So they think I'm dead."

"That's what I told them."

"Do you think they might have anyone else looking, either for me or the queen?"

"I don't know. For the queen, possibly. I'm thinking a trip to the coffeehouse might flush out someone."

Valdas sat back. "Let's be very clear. Does anything you've seen or heard lead you to believe that your orders to kill Konstantyn came from the Gura? Is there a connection between the king's death and Mirza's capture?"

Lind shook his head. "It's a leap of logic. My orders definitely came from the same source both times even if they were delivered by different men. Who else but Gerhard would want his nephew out of the way, the heir under his control, and you and all the High Guard dead so no one could contest it all? If he were to get papal dispensation and wed Konstantyn's widow, he could adopt the child as his heir and it would eliminate any last doubts about his claim to the throne."

Valdas frowned. "Well, first off, he didn't know about me. As far as he knew, I'd run off."

"Valdas, he's got a magician working for him. There's someone on the Gura with power. Power and politics. Not a good mix."

"I'll make contact with Tomas, see what he knows. He's a sharp lad."

"And I'll away to the coffeehouse."

"What if you told them you had a lead on the queen's whereabouts? What if you could finesse someone out into the open—someone who might lead us up that message chain?"

"My thought exactly."

Lind stood and then paused. "You haven't seen my sword, have you?"

"Which sword?"

"The one I was trying to gut you with."

"Mirza flamed it along with mine. Glad you hadn't given me this fellow back." Valdas patted his old cavalry sabre.

"Flamed it? I thought my brain was playing tricks. How did she—?"

"Magic." Valdas shook his head. "I didn't believe either, not at first, but it's hard not to when you've seen it for yourself."

"Do you know how hot steel has to be before it melts?"

"Hot, I guess."

"And to burn it . . . I've never seen steel burn. And Mirza—"

"Yes, she did, and when we get her back you won't treat her any different. She's still Mirza. She might be a witch, but she's our witch."

"I'd guess she's her own witch."

"You might have a point there," Valdas said. "You realize she saved our lives? One of us, anyway. Not sure which one, and I'm not going to take a guess."

"We probably wouldn't have stopped until one of us was dead on the floor."

"Don't suppose we would," Valdas said. "There's one on the hall table."

"What?"

"A sword. Maksimilian left it for you. He says not to get it melted."

CHAPTER SEVENTY-THREE
Mirza

KAZIMIR STEPPED OVER Piotr's corpse and turned on Mirza, but her body let her down. She started to throw up the contents of her stomach—precious little—and barely made it to the open grate in the floor.

"You did that!" he accused.

Bluff it out, girl. She wiped her mouth. "Did what? You killed the poor man."

"Did I? I think I need to use something extra to contain you."

He took the bowl of Piotr's blood and trickled a thin line on the floor around the outside of her cage, then he muttered something under his breath and the blood burned blue and disappeared into the stone. She pushed against the magic with her mind and found it an effective barrier between her and the rest of the cellar.

She'd known instinctively that Kazimir couldn't do the things he did without blood magic, but to see him bleed Piotr and then use his blood so set up a cold itch between her shoulder blades.

Kazimir had his invisible servants take down Piotr's body.

How did you do that—bind the ghosts of the High Guard?

He actually chuckled as if it were a fine joke. "I claimed them as mine before I had them hanged. A spell written on paper and placed in their mouths, tied closed with a kerchief, before the rope was placed around their necks. They were thrown from the curtain wall of the Citadel on a long rope. A mercy, really. No slow choking death, just one quick snap and they were mine."

"But I saw them on the other side."

"They come when I need them. I have only to call."

"You planned that in advance?" Mirza felt anger well up. How would Valdas feel if he knew the souls of his men, his brothers-in-arms, had been perverted?

"Clever, aren't I?"

She didn't answer him. Clever was not a word she would have used.

"If I had your talent for fire, disposing of poor Piotr would be a simple matter," he said. "I don't suppose you'd care to cremate him for me?"

She shuddered.

"No? I didn't think so."

The body was carried out, seeming to float on its own up the steps with a red shadow at head and feet.

Kazimir dragged a chair in front of her cage, a pace behind his new barrier, and sat. She expected reprisals for the death of his potential spirit servant, but got none. It didn't stop her shaking.

"What do you need for scrying?" he asked.

"What do you mean?"

"To scry. What do you need? Bowl? Knife? Herbs? Flame? Blood? Salt?"

"You bring me here, put me in a cage, kill a man in front of me, and then ask me about scrying? What is this? What am I accused of?"

"I'm sorry, haven't we been properly introduced?" He rubbed the point of his chin. "Ah, well, never mind. You're in my territory. Using powers. I want to see them working. I want to understand them."

She wrapped her fingers around the bars of her cage, felt the sting and jumped back. "Let me out and I'll show you."

"I think not. And before you try any of them on me, you've obviously noticed that cage is spelled. The wall between us is impervious to your magic. Not to mine, of course. Your powers can't penetrate it. Do you want to try, or will you take my word for it?"

She said nothing.

"I know you scry. I've seen you on the plane above, and I know you killed a man with fire. I felt it."

"Do you know why?" she asked.

"Tell me."

"Maybe it was for locking me in a cage."

The wary look in his eyes, quickly suppressed, told her that for an instant he had considered that possibility. That meant he genuinely didn't know why she'd burned the bandit. Keep it that way. And he didn't know the extent of her powers. That made two of them.

"I will also point out that, should the barrier prove less effective against your magic than I believe it to be, that you will never be able to open your cage from the inside. This room . . ." He waved one hand. "You can probably tell what it is—or was; the torture chamber buried deep so that the screams of the dying didn't disturb the living. It hasn't been used in anger in half a century at least, not since King Konstantyn's grandfather tore out the . . . but you don't want to know about that. I'm told it was a family matter.

"No one comes here willingly anymore except those who serve me, and even they forget as soon as they leave. Gossips say it's haunted, and with good reason." He glanced at the rack and the iron maiden and a chair with horrific iron spikes, now rusted to the color of dried blood. "If by any chance I don't return from here, I left instructions that the door be sealed. If I die, it will condemn you to a slow death from starvation, trapped in that cage."

"Maybe taking you with me will be worth my life."

"But will it be worth theirs?" He nodded to the queen and her baby, still both frighteningly silent. "Besides, I think if you could burn a man to death without ritual sacrifice of some poor creature, or a body part of your own, then you would have done it when my guards came for you. So which is it? Your own blood or some other creature's?"

"I don't know what you're talking about."

He blinked twice as if, wrapped in his own thoughts, he hadn't heard her denial. "Hold out your hands. Come on, I only want to look."

She backed into the corner of her space, pressed up against the stone.

"Don't do this the hard way."

He stood and gestured. The invisible hands of his spirit guards picked her up and propelled her forward, pushing her up against the bars that fizzed and stung her thighs, belly, and breasts. An invisible hand pressed against the back of her head and shoved her face, the good side, up hard against the cold iron, firing up her skin with the sensation of a thousand red-hot needles where it touched her cheekbone and brow.

She screamed. And the invisible hand pressed harder so that her eyelid touched the metal and she screwed up her face to keep the bar from her eyeball.

Kazimir reached through the cage and took her hands one at a time in his. The pressure eased. She drew away from the bars, shaking, but his spirit servants held her firm. He was missing a little finger on his left hand. He turned her hands over and back again, running his thumbs over her finger joints as if to ensure he wasn't looking at an illusion.

"Your feet. Quick, remove your boots and stockings." His voice raised a notch with excitement or anticipation, she couldn't tell which. He dropped her hands and motioned impatiently.

She didn't move.

"You're in no position to refuse me, you know."

He was right, of course. She half turned away while she raised her skirt and removed her boots and her stockings, one at a time. The stone floor felt like a sheet of ice under her toes.

"Put your feet through the bars. Do it!" He didn't even give her time to hesitate.

One by one she put her feet through for examination, taking care not to touch the metal.

He held each one in turn, twisting it so he saw every angle. If nothing else, she was grateful for the warmth of his hands, and relieved he took care not to brush her skin against the bars again.

He stared at her and chewed his lip. "Take off all your clothes."

"What?"

"I want to see any damage to your body: marks of the scourge, strips of flesh cut away, perhaps."

"I don't have any marks."

"There's only one way I'll believe that."

"I will not . . ."

Invisible hands grasped her arms. One began to paw at the drawstring of her blouse.

"Stop it!"

"Undress or my boys will do the job for you. Or maybe I'll have them hold you still while I do it."

She was about to tell him he wouldn't dare, but she knew that he would.

"A trade," she said. "I'm so cold I can't think. Your fur-lined delja as recompense for my embarrassment."

"Done! A fair trade. You'll see I'm not a cruel man."

She rubbed her face, which still tingled from contact with the iron.

"So why am I in a cage?"

"I'm careful . . . and you, mistress, are a powerful witch. Fear not. This is scientific inquiry."

"Your delja first." She reached through the bars.

He shrugged it off and pushed it through. She had to tug the bulk of it between the bars, but finally it came and she dropped it to the floor and stood on it, feeling the residual warmth soaking into her bare feet.

"I'm waiting."

She pulled the drawstring on her blouse and let her mind reside elsewhere as garment by garment she stripped herself of clothing while trying to retain dignity.

"Turn, please. Hold your hands away from your body. Quickly; this is investigation, not titillation."

She began to shiver. "Of course it is."

Had her voice betrayed sarcasm? She bit her lip.

Without warning the invisible hands shoved her forward against the bars, bare thighs, belly, ribs, and breasts burning with spell-shock.

"What's this?" He reached through the bars and traced his fingers across the salamander scar, then laughed. "Salamander. The symbol of fire. Is this how you got your talent? Did you carve it into yourself, or did some master imbue you with the power?"

If that's what he wanted to think, let him.

"And what is there on your back? Come, I am not a patient man," he said. "Turn."

Without giving her the opportunity to move, he stepped up to the bars and gut-punched her away from them so that she folded up over her belly, retching. The invisible hands pulled her to her feet.

She turned, unsteady on her legs.

"Face me. Arms above your head."

She saw the look on his face and wanted to crawl away. He could say this was a scientific inquiry, but he wasn't immune to a naked woman—especially one in his power so completely.

"All right, turn again, face the wall, feet apart, bend over."

She hesitated and an invisible hand pushed her head down toward her knees. She wanted to die, but embarrassment was rarely fatal, and as soon as the pressure released her, she stood up, grabbed her chemise, and dragged it on over her head.

"Ha!" He stared at her as if she was a puzzle to be solved. He paced the floor, then turned.

"No other scars," he said. "Only the salamander and that thing on your face, and that's not self-inflicted."

"I told you."

"Now, let's discuss the nature of magic and sacrifice."

She wanted to fling herself as far away from him as possible and cover her head with her arms, but he was a predator. She mustn't show fear. "How about we discuss the nature of food and getting out of this cage?" she asked. "If you don't have the authority, take me to King Gerhard."

She ignored his smirk and wriggled into her stockings and boots again, then pulled the heavenly delja up around her shoulders, where it enveloped her right down to her ankles. With warmth came a little courage. She silently thanked the god of all small creatures for the souls of the foxes who had given up their lives for her warmth.

"Tell me what you do to balance the blood debt," Kazimir asked. "Is it linked to your monthly flow? Is it something to do with the mark on your face?"

"I don't know what you're talking about."

"Come. Two practitioners of a dying art, comparing notes. What could be more natural?"

"Why should I talk? You can walk out of here at any time and leave me to starve to death."

"Oh, you are far too fascinating to kill. I have too much to learn and perhaps something to teach, if you could see the value of an alliance."

Was that fanaticism on his face? She contemplated the fire inside her. She'd done so much to still it and now . . . Could she burn him through his spell-strengthened barrier?

She didn't know. She'd fought so hard to prevent her fire from burning anyone. It wasn't her way. *It wasn't her way.*

But oh how she wanted to.

"You are Kazimir." The warmth from the delja gave her more courage.

"It's not my true name, of course."

Oh, he was one of those who believed that you could get power over someone if you knew their true name. Well, she had news for him. A name you used all the time was stronger than one kept hidden.

"King Gerhard Zamoy is your master."

He snickered, not quite a laugh, not quite a sneer. "Enough questions."

He pulled his chair a little closer and sat again. "Who trained you?"

She didn't answer.

"Where's your spell book?"

Now it was her turn to snicker.

"You think I can't scry for it?"

"What do I need a book for when I don't have the reading or writing? All I have is in my head."

She saw surprise on his face. He hadn't even considered that. Had he thought that he could find her secrets by reading them?

He stood quickly. "I have an appointment with my king. You have until tomorrow morning to contemplate the advantages of cooperation."

And the disadvantages of non-cooperation, no doubt.

Mirza waited until the door was firmly closed behind him and she'd heard the key turn in the lock and footsteps retreat along a stone-flagged corridor, then she put up a witchlight, a soft, gently glowing ball of light no bigger than her fist. It didn't take much energy; she could keep it there for hours if she needed to. She wanted to establish a rapport with the queen. How long would it take for the drug to release her?

At length she whispered, "Are you well, Majesty?"

The figure in the other cage didn't move, but by a slight stiffening of her shoulders Mirza thought she'd got the young woman's attention.

"Kristina?"

The queen raised her head a little and looked out from under a heavy curtain of unkempt hair, bright copper-gold again despite Lind's henna, an easy trick for a sorcerer. She glanced at the door and back to Mirza.

"Who are you?"

"My name's Mirza. We came to find you. You've got friends."

"I hope they are better positioned than you are."

So did Mirza.

"Does the babe thrive?"

The queen shook her head. "I don't know. Kazimir spelled him to silence because of his crying . . . How do I know when he's hungry or in pain if he can't tell me?"

"Does he feed?"

"Sometimes. Enough, I think. It's difficult to tell how time passes in this place."

"How long have you been here?"

"A week, maybe two. I should have listened to Balinski and gone to a whorehouse. The Holy Mother of the Abbey at Metzer took me in and sent word to the chancellor while I lay in my child-bed."

A scrape outside the door silenced them both. Kazimir? A guard.

The queen lowered her head again and Mirza understood she'd get no more from her tonight, so she snuffed the witchlight and curled up on the stone floor of her cell, wrapped in her fur-lined delja, with her knees pulled up to her belly to preserve warmth and ease the ache from Kazimir's fist. She doubted she'd be able to sleep, but she dozed for a while until she judged it to be late.

CHAPTER SEVENTY-FOUR

Lind

LIND MADE HIS way to the East Gate, where he watched the North Star Coffeehouse and the surrounding buildings for a full hour before entering. There were no empty booths, so he caught the eye of the young man waiting on tables and mouthed, "Chazon."

With an almost imperceptible nod of the head, the young man directed him through the busy tables to the private room as before.

"Beg pardon, sir." The young man came through after him. "Chazon is not here. May I offer you coffee while you wait?"

"How long?"

"Within the hour, sir."

Lind tapped the table. "I'll take coffee, thank you."

While the boy was out he moved a table and chair so he could sit in the corner of the room where he could see both the door and the window that looked out over a small enclosed yard. The door opened into the room, masking whoever entered until they stepped beyond it, and the boy had left it open. Bad design. He would have changed the hinge so that the door opened against the far wall.

The boy brought him coffee, a small cup of oily black stuff and a pot of honey to sweeten it. Lind spooned the honey into the cup and stirred it round, then paused. Someone was listening outside the door. Listening for what? He stirred the coffee round again. Yes, he was sure they were still there.

He looked at the coffee, picked up the cup, and sniffed. It smelled only of coffee with a faint honey overtone. That was no guarantee. There were any number of poisons that had no scent.

He picked up the cup as if drinking, clanked it down on the table, waited a few seconds, and made a choking noise. Then he stood and pushed over his chair, thumped the table with his fist as if a body was falling on it, and took two light paces to stand behind the door. Someone moved on the other side. He took the door handle and smashed the door sharply into whoever was coming through, then wrenched it open again, drawing his knife at the same time.

The coffee-boy doubled up, clutching his nose, a kitchen knife in his other hand.

Lind grabbed him by the shirt and dragged him into the room, downing him and punching the knife up under his ribs, into his heart, in less time than it took to breathe. The boy died silently, blood puddling slowly around the wound. There would be someone close behind him, someone with more experience. Lind didn't waste time wiping his knife, but quickly checked the tiny corridor outside. He could see the coffee-room along the passageway, still full of guests, many of them wealthy merchants or minor officials as befitted the type of house. At the other end was a stair and beyond that a door into an enclosed yard.

He debated whether to risk the yard, or stroll through the full coffee room, bold as anything, and rely on the fact that they would not risk starting a melee with so many customers. His third choice was the stair and making an exit through the roof. He'd checked from the outside. If he could get up to the attic, that way was clear.

He dashed for the stair, yanking open the outside door as he passed. They'd look outside first. Light on his feet, he kept his weight to the outside of the treads so as not to make them creak. This building was tall but narrow and had an attic with dormers, much like the dormers at Trader Maksimilian's. On the first landing he stopped. One door was wide open, showing a front room furnished as a sitting room, but empty. He ignored the next floor, stopping on the one below the attic. The door to the back room was closed. He tapped on it, ready to burst in should anyone answer, but it was quiet. Good.

At the top of the building the stair opened directly into a single attic room, the stairwell protected by a rail. He crept up and popped his head above floor level. There were three beds, a table, a chair, and two stools, basic enough to be servants' quarters. A middle-aged woman turned and saw him. As she opened her mouth to yell, he jumped up three steps and threw the dagger. She looked surprised as a red flower blossomed across the front of her apron. Lind caught her before she hit the floor and lowered her soundlessly.

He wiped his knife on her skirt and sheathed it, heart hammering in his chest.

There were dormers at the front and back. Both windows opened easily, and though he'd only surveyed the front, he exited at the back, pushing the window open and pulling himself up and through with his hands. His damned sword caught on the window architrave, but he pulled it free and with a twist was out on the rooftop, face down on the pantiles. *Up, go up.* His body ached all over. New bruises pressing on old ones. He tasted blood from yesterday's cut lip—now reopened and bleeding. He sucked at it so the blood didn't drip onto the roof. He inched up the tiles by the side of the dormer, having nothing to keep him in place on the steep slope except friction and his own weight. Wriggle, inch. Wriggle, inch. He passed the dormer, then had the angled top of that to support his weight as he gained the ridge with his hands. Pulling himself up, he heard horses in the street and peeped over. Half a dozen of the Chancellor's Own at least. That answered his question and probably answered Valdas's question about his employer: either the chancellor or the king, or maybe both together.

With his elbows firmly over the ridge, he started to work his way sideways across the roof of the coffeehouse, on to the building next door and then the one next to that. Three doors down was a private house. He'd checked it at the same time as he'd watched the coffeehouse. No one had come in or out in that time and he trusted it was empty—if only temporarily. It was four stories, but thankfully because of the pitch of the roof only about six feet lower than the roof he was presently on. He glanced sideways, rewarded by the sight of a jutting window. Thank God! A dormer on the back matched the one on the front.

Getting down to the lower roof proved to be more difficult than he thought. With nothing to anchor himself to, he ended up slithering precariously on the slope, praying that his feet didn't find a mossy patch or a loose tile. Thatch. Why the hell didn't they use thatch? He could have anchored his knife into thatch and made a decent handhold.

He lay on the pantiles for some time, hearing a commotion down below. Hopefully they were wasting time casting about in the yard, trying to work out which of the sheer walls he'd scaled. They'd know which way he'd gone when they found the body in the attic.

He reached the dormer, finding it wouldn't yield at first, but the wooden frame of the window was so rotten that the catch gave with minimal force on his part. In a rush to get out of sight, he wriggled through head first, got his bastard sword caught again, and ended up sliding ungracefully down onto something soft below.

"God's ballocks!"

A dreadful stench, uniquely repulsive, assailed his nostrils, and he almost screamed as his face landed on a straw mattress right next to something grotesque that might once have been human. He leaped sideways, coming to rest against the side wall of the attic room in which someone's life could be read like a book, a very sad book. One chair, one table, one cookpot, one pisspot—crusted over and stinking—one empty coal bucket beside the ashes of a fire long since burned out. Hanging on a hook behind the door was one rag that might have been a decent delja once. A chest maybe contained what personal possessions the now dead resident of this room had owned.

The bed that he'd landed on contained the corpse of an elderly woman, at least five days dead, sunken eyes, still open wide in surprise, but almost buried beneath swollen eyelids, her skin darkened around the lips and blotchy and already seeming to slip like an ill-fitting glove. He saw no sign of foul play, though truly it was foul to both his eyes and nose. She'd died here, unloved and undiscovered, another one of the city's lonely people.

He started for the door, but heard horses outside and the echo of footsteps three floors down. A loud hammering on the door and, "Open up in the name of the Amber Crown!" Either the Chancellor's Own or the City Watch, no doubt.

A commotion began downstairs, an angry woman's voice and an insistent man's. Lind jumped up and looked to the dormer, wondering whether to exit onto the roof, but this was the last house in the row. He'd run out of options.

He hadn't bet on such a swift house-to-house search, but if they'd found the woman in the attic, they'd know he was on the rooftops.

He pushed the broken window closed, and trying not to breathe in the stench, he brushed the flakes of rotten wood off the bed.

Screaming inside, he slid under the bed, hoping that nothing was dripping through the mattress. Heavy footsteps clattered up the stairs, halting on the floor below. More voices, irate, angry.

Footsteps coming up to the attic level.

"Beg pardon, mistress," a deep man's voice called from outside the door. "We're looking for a man."

He thought about answering and telling them that he was a sick old woman and not to disturb him, but that would likely not send them away. He heard a woman's voice calling up after them, "She's an old besom, don't mind her scolding tongue."

The old besom wouldn't be causing any more problems for her neighbor unless she was going to haunt the place.

"Mistress, in the name of the Amber Crown, open this door."

With no answer forthcoming, the sharp sound of boot against door frame heralded a splintering crash as the old wood gave easily. The door slammed open, all the way against the door frame, sundering the hinges as well as the lock.

"Holy Mother of God!" Lind heard the deep male voice rise to almost a shriek.

"Jesus!" another voice said. Someone retched.

By the voices, there were at least four of them. Deep Voice was obviously in charge. He heard feet enter the room, but they showed a reluctance to come too far in. He didn't blame them. If they came any closer, surely they'd hear his heart trying to hammer its way out of his chest.

"Been dead for a few days at least," Deep Voice said.

"Best send for the Watch, Cap. This is what they're paid for."

"Ain't no one paid enough for this," a third voice joined in.

"Janek, search the room."

"What?"

"You heard me. Litorski, finish searching on the floor below. Lech take the ground floor. I'll go and make arrangements with the Watch."

One pair of heavy boots almost ran down the stairs. When he'd gone, the one he'd called Janek said, "Tell me I don't have to stay in here with that, Sarge?"

"Our good captain said search and so you search, but make it quick."

"I reckon he's puking in the street by now."

"Maybe, but that's none o' your business. Get on with it. Come on, Litorski."

Two more sets of footsteps retreated. The unhappy Janek was obviously still in the room.

Lind fingered the slim-bladed dagger at his side, wondering if he could unsheath it silently, but deciding not to try. He drew in his breath, hoping he wouldn't sneeze. He heard footsteps cross the room and fancied Janek was looking through the front dormer. The footsteps crossed to the back dormer. God, he was standing directly above. If he bent and looked under the bed now all was lost.

The door closed and footsteps retreated down the stairs. Lind didn't move, and neither did his savior in the bed above him. He wondered how long he had until the Watch arrived. They wouldn't rush. It took them long enough to answer an urgent call.

He was beginning to think the corpse smelled of roses. He stifled a sneeze, but didn't emerge from under the bed until he'd heard all the Chancellor's Own leave the building.

"Thank you, old mother," he said to her tufts of gray hair.

Her eyes appeared to stare at him despite being filmy.

"What? You want to know what I'm doing in your boudoir? If I told you, I would have to kill you." He cut off a laugh that sounded hysterical even to his own ears.

"It's like this, old mother," he said in a low whisper.

He told her. Everything. From his mother dying to his stepfather, the man she'd entrusted him to, selling him to Tourmine, probably knowing what apprenticeship to the blacksmith, and sometime assassin, meant for a pretty boy, yet not caring. He stumbled over the bit about Ewa. The old woman said nothing, but still she stared, rapt. He began to find it oddly comforting.

"After I killed Tourmine, I went looking for my stepfather, but the plague had robbed me of the pleasure of buggering him before I killed him. I'd have liked him to know what it felt like. That . . . intrusion. That . . ."

He lost his words. "I think you know."

He thrust his hand through his hair, already starting to curl as it grew.

"Once I was free I ran for the nearest port. I'd learned enough, between the buggerings and the beatings, to know how to forge a blade, and how to handle one. I found good trade for an assassin in Zavonia. And I am good. Better than Tourmine ever was. I'm the best. I killed the king. Oh, it wasn't my idea. I was paid."

Did the corpse forgive him? Had she grieved for the loss of her king? Had she died because she couldn't afford a cabbage at the new prices?

"Old mother, if I hadn't done the job, some other assassin would have. Though . . . maybe no one else is as good as me."

Don't flatter yourself, boy, there's always someone better. It was as if she spoke in his head.

"Yes." He shrugged. He finished his story, leaving nothing out, including the breaking of Aniela's fingers and Dahnay's life hanging in the balance.

She listened quietly, and when he'd finished, her eyes asked, *And what do you feel about that?*

"I don't know. Numb. Empty. Hollow. Dahnay didn't deserve to be hurt."

Are you perhaps a little bit angry?

His vision clouded and two wet tracks rolled down his cheeks. "I'm gods-poxed furious."

He sank to the floor and leaned against the wall, weeping silently but inconsolably.

"I'm sorry to intrude on your grief, sir."

Lind jumped up, his hand already reaching for his dagger, but the young watchman didn't even have a weapon drawn.

"Sorry. I didn't mean to startle you. A relative, was she?" He nodded to the mound on the bed covered by a thin gray blanket.

"My old mother, sergeant." The youngster certainly wasn't a sergeant, but he puffed up a little at the implied compliment. "I just heard the news. I've been out of town. No need to worry the Watch. I'll make arrangements myself."

"Best you do it soon, sir. She's not getting any sweeter. No offense."

"None taken." Lind climbed to his feet. "Perhaps you could show me where I can find a reliable undertaker?"

"There's one on Kirchma Street. It's not far. I'm walking that way. I'll walk with you."

"Much appreciated."

Lind left the house, strolling apparently unconcerned, side by side with the young watchman. They turned away from the coffeehouse, where half a dozen military horses were still tethered outside. Lind didn't push his luck by asking what was going on there.

At Kirchma Street he parted from his unknowing guardian, and feeling so grateful to the dead woman, he went into the undertaker's shop and paid a silver tolar to have prayers said, and to have her buried with all possible haste.

CHAPTER SEVENTY-FIVE
Valdas

VALDAS SOUGHT OUT Tomas, waiting on the busy street corner outside the Bell under the pretext of buying roasted chestnuts, and chatting with a couple of early-evening whores, a boy and a girl barely halfway through their teens and both made up with heavy dark smudges around their eyes, too-pale lips and too-pink cheeks. They were for sale individually or together, but it was too early for real trade and they were pleased to pass the time, especially on Valdas's purse.

They perked up when Tomas approached, but quickly retreated when Valdas gave them the rest of the chestnuts and shooed them away gently.

"They get younger," Tomas said, watching them drift through the crowd hand in hand. "That boy's already getting himself a reputation for innovation. Don't look at me like that, he's too young for my taste."

"Did you find anything interesting?" Valdas asked.

"Not about magic. Are you sure that's a thing?"

"I am now."

Tomas gave a noncommittal grunt.

"It took me a while to admit to believing it, too," Valdas said. "What have you discovered?"

"There's something going on in the tunnels under the old keep. The Chancellor's Own wouldn't be guarding the doors so heavily otherwise."

"The labyrinth?" Valdas had once mapped out the tunnel system for Konstantyn. He'd suspected it linked the old keep, the heart of the original fortress built on top of the easily defensible Gura, with the new palace, begun by Konstantyn's grandfather and finished the year after the old man's death. Valdas had found the route through, but he'd thought no one knew about the palace access except Konstantyn and himself. The labyrinth, however, could be entered from the dungeons under the old keep, though that end had been closed off when last he'd been down there. In the bad old days of the wars with Kassubia, the labyrinth had been used as a prison and had a reputation unsavory at best. Supposedly haunted, no one was entirely comfortable in the dark atmosphere, and eventually a new cell block had been built close to the curtain wall.

"You may already have answered my second question. I've lost a witch and I think King Gerhard may be holding her somewhere on the Gura. In the cells, I hope, not the old dungeons."

"A witch?"

"A Bakaishan shulam by the name of Mirza. Anyhow, shulam or not, Bakaishan or not, she's with me and she's been taken to the Gura. I need to get in."

"You'll be recognized."

"Are you sure?" He tilted his chin up for closer examination.

"Hmm, maybe not. But security is tighter than a duck's arse."

"Can you check the cells for me, see where she is and get me in there?"

"Meet me here tomorrow at noon."

"Not here. Come to Trader Maksimilian's."

"Maksimilian's. Right."

"So, I never got my answer. Why didn't you get yourself posted to the Tevecor Reaches?"

"I tried, but they've withdrawn all but a few border patrols."

"Stupid bastards. Does Gerhard want to see it in the hands of Ruthenia?"

"It's hard to know what Gerhard wants. I've never seen a more ineffective monarch. Kazimir could do better without him. And I'm not the only one who's saying that. Better to have a strong, wrong king than a weak, right king."

Later that night, lying in his lonely bed, the words echoed through Valdas's mind.

Kazimir could do better without him. And I'm not the only one who's saying that. Better to have a strong, wrong king than a weak, right king.

It was no good, something didn't fit, but he didn't know whether his nerves, and maybe his confidence, were shot to hell by Dahnay's condition and Mirza's imprisonment.

It had been a day of frustrations and revelations, the former out-weighing the latter. He'd kept himself busy, not letting himself think about Dahnay, because the more he did the more angry he felt and that anger was all mixed up. She was still hanging on by a thread and hadn't regained consciousness.

Mirza's empty bed accused him of negligence, too.

He closed his eyes. It wouldn't do any good, he'd never sleep.

CHAPTER SEVENTY-SIX
Mirza

NIGHT. THIS MIGHT be the opportunity Mirza needed. If she could spirit-walk her way into Valdas's mind, she might let him know where she was, and that the queen was here, too. She could see soft flickering shadows on the room's stone walls from the fire's glow. With that and the fur-lined delja she was almost warm again; hungry, though, and thirsty, and scared half to death. In this state she was hardly fit for spirit-walking.

She took a deep breath and cleared her mind. Pity she had no salt, but all she really needed to walk the spirit realm was the confidence to go there and trust that she could return again. She had to do this. Her friends needed her.

Valdas, desperate to do the right thing and redeem himself.

Aniela, stronger than she believed. Steady as a rock.

Lind, a deep well from which she may yet draw pure water—if he hadn't been driven completely over the edge in the arms of fifteen whores.

Maksimilian, a strong link in the chain.

Dahnay . . . What had happened to Dahnay? Had she run? Was she imprisoned elsewhere? Was she injured? Was she dead?

By all the gods, she hadn't wanted Dahnay with them on this journey, but the woman warrior had quickly become . . . friend was too small a word to use. Familia. Band. Sister. If she was hurt it was Mirza's fault.

She pushed all that out of her mind. If Valdas was asleep she might be able to walk straight into his head. She had to try, anyway.

The spirit world was different each time she entered it. This time it was a maze of bare stone corridors, lit at intervals with guttering torches set in sconces that were at the same time at head height and so far above her that she couldn't reach them. She walked along, hoping for a door or an opening into a room, but all she found were turns and junctions, none of them making any sense.

She had no inkling of where she might find Valdas's living mind. This seemed to be a world of shades, not of dreams. She went where her feet led. After the seventh turn she found a door. It was locked, but if she stood on tiptoe she could peer through a tiny window to a barracks room, now empty.

Seven more turns and the door this time led into a king's chamber. A figure bent over a writing desk.

"Konstantyn? Your Majesty?"

The shade looked up at the sound. "You are close, Mirza of the Bakaishans, but it may already be too late. Zavonia faces war on two fronts, and all for some madman's idea to win popular support."

"I know where your son is," she said.

"Unless you can save Zavonia from this lunatic, there will be nothing left for him to inherit. You can't take a country so close to the brink and prevent it from falling. He doesn't understand."

"Who doesn't? Gerhard?"

"He thinks to be hailed as a war-leader and a savior. He's wrong. Soon, there will be nothing left to save."

"I'm looking for Valdas's dreams. I need to tell him . . ."

"You'll not find Valdas here, not again, not until it's his time. Take seven more turns, Lady Mirza. You will find *someone*." King Konstantyn bent over his paper again, pale and ghostly.

She took seven more turns. The next door looked out onto a vast landscape of low-lying land. She could taste the dry heat. The sunlight was so bright that it hurt her eyes. There were groves of trees she could not identify close to a green oasis. A tall black woman, far in the distance, was walking toward her. Time slipped sideways and now the woman was much closer. Dahnay. Another slippage and she was barely ten paces away. This was a less solid shade than Konstantyn. She wasn't dead yet. "Dahnay?"

The woman's smile lit her scarred face, now augmented with painted patterns. "Mirza?"

"Dahnay, I . . ."

"Tell my tsarina I died in her service."

"You're not dead yet. And you weren't serving your blasted tsarina, you were helping me. Don't go noble on me now. Stay focused."

"It's not your fault."

"It will be if I leave you here. I have to lead you back to your own body."

"Go back? But it hurts."

"I know. I'm sorry. Tell Valdas."

"He knows you were taken to the Gura."

"Tell him I'm in the dungeon below the old keep. Kristina is here too, and the baby. I don't know if he can get to us. He'll have to find a way. Tell him he'll have to be a hero again."

"I'll carry your message."

"And Dahnay . . . I'm sorry."

"It's not your fault . . ."

"But it is. Here, take my hands. Take my strength. You must fight Lord Death, Dahnay. Live, for all our sakes. Live."

Mirza felt Dahnay's ghostly hands taking the heat from her own. First her fingers turned chill, then her palms and her wrists. The icy cold crept up her forearms toward her elbows. When she looked, she could see through her skin to the bones below, and even they were becoming insubstantial.

I'm turning into a ghost.

But she couldn't stop before she'd infused strength into Dahnay. "Live, Dahnay, live!"

"Enough." Dahnay dragged her hands out of Mirza's frozen ones. "You must live, too."

Suddenly Mirza was back in her own body, the echo of Dahnay's voice in her head. Her hands were freezing. She hardly dared look at them in case they were ghostly, but they looked solid enough, though so pale as to be tinged with blue. She pulled the delja tight and clamped her frozen hands under her armpits. She shivered. Her fingers began to tingle and ache as blood returned.

Dahnay was right. It wasn't her fault, it was the fault of the ones who struck the blow.

King Gerhard and Kazimir.

CHAPTER SEVENTY-SEVEN
Lind

LIND LAY IN Cylia's arms, her breasts to his back and her hand pressed against his chest. The fire in the hearth burned patterns through his closed eyelids as he concentrated on the rise and fall of her breathing and the rise and fall of his own.

"You were dreaming. You cried out."

Was there ever a night when he hadn't had the dream? He doubted it. Would there ever be? Cylia was warm against him. For the first time he allowed for the possibility that there might—if he lived long enough; if he ever found the right woman to sleep at his back. Cylia wasn't the right woman, neither of them pretended that she was, but he found her undemanding presence comforting. Expensive, but comforting.

"You're not coming back again, are you?" she asked.

He thought for a moment. "One way or another, I doubt it."

Valdas had made it sound so easy. Lind knew it wouldn't be. Mirza was scared of the magician on the Gura for a reason. It wouldn't be all head-cracking and blade-work. They were going into something totally outside of their experience.

"I know you'll not tell me what you're doing, but is it dangerous?" Cylia asked.

He nodded. "Probably."

"You and me, we could slip out tonight. Be out of the city by morning. Never come near again."

"Thank you."

"For what?"

"For the offer, but you know I can't."

He felt her hair brush his neck as she nodded.

"Let's do it," she said. "You're not scared of me no more and I got to earn my keep."

She started to move her hand down his chest. He grabbed it, momentarily panicked.

I could walk out of here now and never see her again. No one would know, she wouldn't tell.

But I would know. I have to do this. Prove something . . . to myself. Prove Tourmine isn't in charge anymore.

He let her hand go, feeling it travel down his belly and down. Small fingers, but confident, warm, determined.

"Come on, my lad, get up for Cylia. That's it."

He'd been so afraid for so long.

"You've got to let it go or it'll kill you," she said.

What the hell. He was going to die tomorrow anyway. He felt heat in his groin and a sudden infusion of dizziness. He turned to face her.

"Here, like this."

She placed his fingers in her wetness, arching against his hand when he found her spot.

"Come on in from the cold, lover. You can't stay out there for the rest of your life." She pulled him between her legs and cradled him between bent knees. With one hand she guided him deftly, then, transferring both hands to his scarred buttocks, pulled him all the way inside.

Sensations overwhelmed him. He was fourteen again, in the hayloft with Ewa. Loved.

"That's the way," she whispered. "Ah, yes . . ."

Instinct took over. He groaned and began to thrust.

CHAPTER SEVENTY-EIGHT

Valdas

SOMETIME BEFORE DAWN, Valdas sat bolt upright in his empty bed as someone knocked on his door. It was Ruta.

"Aniela says Dahnay's awake. You'd better come."

He dragged on his trousers and boots and, still fastening the neck of his shirt, slipped quietly into the room where they'd taken Dahnay.

"Valdas." Aniela held out her left hand to draw him closer, but held on to Dahnay's fingers with her right. "She's very weak. She asked for you."

He stepped close and saw the fine sheen of sweat on Dahnay's forehead. Her color had an underlying grayness beneath the dark brown-black, and as her eyelids flickered open, her eyes seemed glazed and distant.

"Dahnay?"

Aniela relinquished her place to him and placed Dahnay's hand in his. He leaned in to her, bending close as she began to speak.

"Mirza . . ." Dahnay's voice was so low it was barely there.

"On the Gura. You said."

"Dungeons . . . below the old keep. Mirza says . . ."

He knew the place. Konstantyn had locked the heavy door and thrown away the key, sealing in ancient instruments of torture and hundreds of years of pain.

"Kris . . ."

Kris?

"Tina. Baby . . . a boy."

The queen was there as well! No wonder they hadn't been able to find her! Christ on a pig!

Tears prickled his eyes. "Thank you, Dahnay." He stood up to re-linquish Dahnay's care to Aniela but she clutched his hand. He sat down again. "You go get some rest, Aniela. I'll stay with her."

"Do you think it's right, what she says? What if she's only dreaming?"

"Mirza's spirit-walking into her dreams. She's already halfway to the next world. Maybe if Mirza were here Dahnay could be saved, but . . ."

"We've done all we can. I think she was right when she said something was wrong inside. Her heart's fluttering like a little bird."

He felt Dahnay's grip tighten. "I'm here." He leaned across her. "What do you want? What can I do for you?"

"Call me if you need me," Aniela said as she slipped quietly out of the room.

"Find Mirza," Dahnay whispered. "Be a hero."

"I will. Of course I will." Valdas squeezed her hand.

"Cold."

"I'll get you a blanket."

"No. Just stay with me awhile longer. It will soon be over."

He kissed her forehead, very lightly, very gently, then, trying not to jostle her, he lay down on top of the covers, stretching next to her, sharing warmth. He slid his left arm under her head and cradled it.

"This all right?"

"Hmmm."

"Not hurting?"

"No."

"Oh, my lovely girl." He kissed her forehead again and let his large blunt hand rest lightly on her flat belly.

She sighed and was still again.

Sometime in the middle of the night he realized that she'd slipped into her very last stillness.

He lay unmoving, not wanting to disturb her.

With first light he rose, used the water Aniela had brought to wash her body, laid her out in her best trousers and tunic, and placed her sword on her chest with her hands closed over the hilt. With her face in repose she looked merely asleep.

The door opened and Aniela tiptoed in.

"She's dead, Aniela."

"I know, lover. I came in hours ago. You never even noticed."

She held her hand out and he took it, crumpling over to cry silent tears on her shoulder.

"Sorry. Not very manly."

"That's all right, lover, you wash it out of your system, then get the bastards who did this."

"Stay with Dahnay, please. She's to have a warrior's funeral . . . and a plaque on Soldiers' Fields."

"I'll tell Maksimilian."

He nodded, knowing he could trust her.

"Lind?"

"He knows. They all know."

Valdas nodded, strapped on his sabre and settled it comfortably.

"I still don't trust the bastard."

He ran down the steps.

"Lind!" His roar echoed through the whorehouse.

"Shut your racket, Valdas, you'll disturb the all-night customers." Ruta hovered by the stairs on the second floor.

"Where's Lind?"

"I don't know. I thought he was in the attic."

A door opened on the third floor landing. "I'm here, what's the matter!?"

"Huh?" Valdas caught a glimpse of a bare body in the shadows behind him, but he couldn't make out which of the girls it was. Oh well, he didn't have time to wonder now.

"I know where Mirza is, and the queen. This changes everything."

CHAPTER SEVENTY-NINE
Mirza

KAZIMIR RETURNED THE following morning. At least, Mirza thought it must be morning. She'd slept long enough to need to relieve herself over the hole in the floor. As he descended the stone steps, she could almost see the darkness writhing about his head. It was so wrong that it made her want to run, but she had nowhere to run to.

Queen Kristina seemed resigned. She didn't even look at him as he pushed a cloth bag and a water skin through the bars of her cell. Mirza had tried to get her to talk, but she wouldn't. All she would do was look at the door as if she expected someone to be there. Maybe she suspected someone was listening. Since the queen had been here longer than she had, Mirza gave her credit for knowing how things were. Perhaps silence was the best for both of them.

Kazimir pushed a small canvas bag through the bars to Mirza and followed it with a small water skin. She took care not to scrape her knuckles on the spelled iron, and trying not to tremble, she thanked him politely as she opened the bag, finding two apples, some shelled nuts, hard cheese and salt pork, plus a half loaf of bread. She chewed on a strip of pork, toying with the urge to call on fire. She'd take the punishment of slow starvation if she succeeded, but she couldn't condemn the queen and the little king. Valdas might never find them.

Kazimir ignored both his prisoners while he lit a new fire in the ashes of the old. Mirza watched him. *Bide your time, girl, see where all this is leading. Hope that Dahnay can get a message into Valdas's thick skull.*

Kazimir tipped a few more coals on the fire and dropped a gnarled log into the grate from a stack by the hearth. He was wearing another delja.

Good, he won't be wanting this one back.

He pulled up the wooden chair from where it still stood in front of Mirza's cage and drew it a little closer to the hearth, sitting close enough to the fire for the flames to illuminate the left side of his face. It was the kind of face you might easily trust, but her belly still hurt from yesterday.

"Tell me," he said. "About the carving of the salamander. Tell me about blood."

Blood. Did it all come down to blood in the end? Is that all his magic relied on, blood and sacrifice?

"What about it?" Her voice shook.

There followed a long question-and-answer session—far more questions than answers—about the nature of her magic, how she trained and how she came into her powers. And though the questions were all his and the answers all hers, she learned a lot about his use of magic from the presumptions he made about hers. The more she learned the colder she got. Inside.

She answered what she could answer truthfully, because she had a growing conviction that whatever she told him wouldn't make any difference. It was obvious as he spoke that his magic source was so far away from hers that he'd never be able to draw on natural magic any more than she could draw on the power of blood.

Her skin crawled beneath the fur-lined delja and the salamander scar began to itch fiercely. Kazimir thought she had something he could learn, something he could take for himself and use. What would he do when he found out he couldn't? She had to keep him guessing, play for time.

She tried to consider every answer carefully, drawing it out, but his questions were coming faster. Her answers excited him and his speech grew rapid, sometimes too fast for clarity, and then she'd slow him down by asking him to repeat something.

"Enough, please, you're making my head spin." She rubbed her eyes. It didn't take much play-acting to look washed-out and exhausted.

He nodded sharply. "Tomorrow we begin again."

He turned and left her.

He was a conundrum. His personal power depended upon blood magic. It was something that could be learned. Spells, lore, sacrifice. Give enough of yourself and you could get a return for your pain and suffering. Mirza's flesh turned icy. She wondered who had died when he'd cut off his finger. She wondered how many scars there were on his body, and each one a death or disaster for someone. Had he cleared a path to the throne for Gerhard with a trail of bodies? She thought of Queen Cecylia's four stillbirths and shuddered.

Natural magic, her magic, was an innate talent, not taught so much as nurtured in those who showed potential. It was a magic that leaned toward healing and light . . . or at least it had until that moment in the Tevecor Reaches. She'd shied away from thinking about the nature of that too closely, but now she'd have to sort it out in her own mind.

Ultimately it would be her fire magic that Kazimir wanted, but she didn't see how he could possibly take it for himself, and nothing he could do would persuade her to use it on his behalf—even if she could.

After all the sounds in the corridor had died away, Mirza put up a witchlight. It hovered in the vaulting, casting a gentle glow over the cold stones. She tried not to let her eyes dwell on the instruments of torture, draped about as they were with sad old ghosts, all but faded now, and quite benign.

Highness? Majesty? What was the correct form of address for a queen who was no longer a queen? She knew nothing of Zavonian nobles and how to address them. She opted for not being polite. "Kristina! Can you hear me? Are you awake?"

The queen was so still, especially when Kazimir was in the room, that sometimes Mirza thought she was suffering bouts of catalepsy, but in the dark she would hear sounds of the baby feeding and soft little murmurs from mother to child.

"Kristina, Ludwik Balinski is coming for you."

"What?" The young woman sat upright and at attention, cradling the baby in her arms.

Mirza spoke quickly and urgently. "Balinski, and . . . friends." Better not give real names in case anyone was listening. "Have courage. Stay whole and healthy."

"I'll kill myself rather than be whole and healthy to be Kazimir's bride."

"Kazimir?" She must be scared out of her wits. Marrying the old king's widow to the new king and making the baby the new heir would make much more sense. Secure the throne.

"Surely King Gerhard plans to wed you himself?"

If Gerhard didn't marry her and claim the baby as his own, then the child was far too dangerous to the throne to leave alive, and so was his mother.

"Haven't you worked it out yet?" Kristina asked. "Gerhard's a puppet. Kazimir's making him dance."

"To what benefit? He's already chancellor. What more can he want? It's not as if Kazimir can take the throne."

"Can't he?"

She moved the baby to her shoulder, held him with one hand, and pulled herself upright on the bars. Hers were obviously not bespelled.

"Kazimir is the old king's bastard, never acknowledged because his mother was a high-ranking lady who had him in secret and wanted nothing more to do with him. He has old King Aleksander's blood in his veins. Had he been legitimate, the throne would have been his, not Konstantyn's. And he means to make it his now. Has always meant to do so. He's played a long game and now it's almost done. He plans . . ."

The door flew open and Kazimir entered at the head of a small procession: a bewildered but determined-looking servant woman, plainly dressed, followed by four guards, their faces as incurious as the man Kazimir had killed . . . was it only yesterday or the day before?

Kazimir took in the witchlight, glanced quickly at Mirza, and then turned his attention to the queen.

Mirza's breath caught in her throat.

"I see I should have bespelled *your* mouth closed as well, my dear." He nodded. Two of the men worked the winch and raised the door.

"Take the child!"

The other two men stepped forward, and for the first time Mirza saw that the little queen's spirit was not broken. Cradling the child to her, she spat defiance at the hapless guards and shrieked abuse at Kazimir that would have done a fishwife proud, but it was all to no avail. Taking an elbow each and a firm grasp of her shoulder, the guards quickly had her pinned, and the servant woman stepped forward and took the child easily. Mirza felt for Kristina. What could a mother do? To grab hold of her child and use him as the rope in a tug-of-war contest would only hurt him, but to let him go must feel like the worst betrayal. Kristina's knees gave way as the baby left her arms. Only the guards kept her upright.

The woman hurried out, one guard leaving with her. Mirza saw their faces as they turned to the steps. Their eyes were spellbound, the pupils large, even for this level of illumination.

The queen crossed her arms over her breasts and began to weep silently.

"You'll see him again after our wedding," Kazimir said. "Shall we make it soon?"

Kristina raised her head and stared at him through a veil of tears.

Mirza could only see the back of his head, the determined set of his shoulders, but the look in Kristina's eyes was enough.

Kazimir nodded once. "Good. I see you've reached a sensible decision. We'll solemnize our vows on Sunday morning. Cardinal Pieritz will officiate. A nice public wedding, I think—in the Basilica—and the king will recognize me as his uncle and his heir. A nice touch, don't you think? The throne will go from nephew to uncle."

"And how long then before you inherit at Gerhard's expense?"

"Kristina, my dear, that's in God's hands."

"Like Konstantyn's death?"

"God moves in mysterious ways . . ." He stepped back. "Take her to the East Chamber. No one is to pass, either in or out, except me. Understand?"

They saluted, fists hitting mailed chests simultaneously. The two flanking Kristina tried to lead her forward, but she wouldn't walk.

"Carry her." Kazimir turned to the third guard, a bear of a man.

"My lord." He inclined his head, picked up the queen, and threw her over his shoulder as if she were a rag doll.

"Until Sunday, Your Majesty."

Kazimir followed the little procession up the stair, taking the light with him as the heavy door swung closed. Mirza heard the key turn in the lock and bolts slide across on the outside.

⊰———⊱

Though the queen had hardly been company, the high-vaulted room felt achingly lonely. Eventually, Mirza heard the lock again and Kazimir returned.

She didn't give him time to talk. "Where have you taken Kristina? What have you done with the baby?"

He didn't answer, just paced the length of the room.

"She's a new mother," Mirza said. "Inexperienced. She'll need someone to show her how to deal with breasts too full of milk and no baby to feed. Right about now she'll be in agony. You don't want her leaking milk through the front of her wedding dress, do you? Take the babe to her for feeding."

He reached the far end of the room, turned, and waved one hand dismissively. "So passionate. Tell me how you killed that man in the Tevecor Reaches."

Self-defense, she wanted to scream at him. *And defense of others*. Oh.

Something clicked into place. She hadn't killed in anger or in vengeance. She'd killed protecting herself and Dahnay, and probably Valdas as well.

Oh, oh, oh . . . and the second time she'd used her fire magic had been to disarm Valdas and Lind, to prevent them from killing each other.

Maybe this power wasn't uncontrollable. Maybe it was part of her healing magic. Healing. Protection. Maybe it had always been there, but she'd never needed it before. Oh, how she wished she knew more.

One thing she knew for certain, hers was natural magic. So Kazimir could never use it, because he didn't have the talent. His magic was powerful—and dangerous—but its source was so very different. Magic of the head, not magic of the heart. But telling him that gave him no reason to keep her alive.

Kazimir started to smile. "I think it's about meshing the physical and the spiritual." His face held open desire, but also calculation. "The magic of passion. The release of energies. Oh, yes."

A cold clamminess that had nothing to do with the temperature in the room settled on her skin.

He turned on his heel and left, plunging the room into darkness as the door slammed and locked behind him and his lantern.

She closed her eyes, feeling sick. He was talking about torture or sex. Or both. She'd heard that blood-mages used either pain or passion or a confluence of the two. If he tried to rape her, would the fire come to her call whether she willed it or not? She thought about the bandit in the Tevecor Reaches.

Once Valdas knew where she was, he would come for her, and if he met Kazimir's magic and the shades of his own High Guard, he would die. Maybe there was a way she could prevent that. Though it wasn't going to be easy or safe. And it certainly wasn't going to be pleasant.

CHAPTER EIGHTY
Valdas

"TOMAS IS COMING here?" Lind's voice was incredulous; he didn't need to add the rest of the words that were in his thoughts.

He turned and leaned his forehead against the thick, rippled window glass of the attic's dormer and stared down at the street as if expecting to see a troop of guardsmen hurtling toward them.

Valdas nodded. "I trust him."

"With our lives as well as yours? You might have consulted first." Lind turned.

"I wasn't aware this was a committee. He's a good man. High Guard." He wondered whether Lind would be nervous—no, nervous probably didn't cover it—about Tomas being left-handed when it came to partners. Best not to mention it.

"We'll meet in Maksimilian's parlor. He should be here any minute now. I'm going down. Don't come if you don't want to."

He heard Lind on the steps behind him.

Valdas waited by the front door at noon.

Tomas grinned as he handed over a package wrapped in oiled cloth. "I thought you could use this."

Valdas opened a corner. It was an old friend. "My flintlock."

"It was still in the armory. There's powder and balls, too."

"Thank you." He led Tomas straight into the parlor where Aniela, Lind, and Maksimilian waited.

Tomas nodded politely to Aniela, shook Maksimilian's offered hand, and eyed Lind with a certain amount of suspicion until Valdas introduced him as *working for the queen*. He saw Lind's eyes flash a question at him, but it was the closest he could come to an explanation that Tomas would accept. He noticed that although Tomas offered his hand, Lind didn't take it. Lind was nervous; Valdas could tell by looking at him.

"What have you found?" Valdas asked.

"Nothing," Tomas said. "Your Mirza isn't in the cells. There's no record of her having been taken by the Watch, but if it was the Chancellor's Own, well, they seem to make up their own rules. Sometimes squads get sent out, nothing is written in the log, and memories slip if anyone asks."

"She's in the dungeon under the old keep," Valdas said. "I had . . . new intelligence . . . last night."

Tomas frowned. "The Chancellor's Own guard is stationed there. We've all had orders to stay away unless we're called on, and there's nothing we'd rather do. That old place is cursed. There's a guard on the outer door, four men; two static on the door and two patrolling."

"We can deal with four," Lind said.

"We're not going to the keep," Valdas said.

"What?" Everybody seemed to say that at once.

"Mirza's in the keep, and the queen," Lind said.

He nodded and let the atmosphere settle so they were listening to him properly. "And Gerhard's in his suite—without the protection of a High Guard. We'll never have a better chance to put the rightful king on the throne." *And I'll never have a better chance to keep my promise and avenge Konstantyn.*

"The rightful king is a baby. What chance has he got of holding the Amber Crown?" Lind asked.

"We'll bring Chancellor Skorny out of retirement. He's no more sick than I am. He's just keeping out of sight while it's politically expedient."

"Don't discount the queen." Maksimilian spoke up for the first time. "She may be young, but her mother and brother trained her well."

Tomas took a deep breath and said, "Getting you in to rescue your friend is one thing, but this is high treason. I'm sworn to the Amber Crown."

"To the rightful crown, man," Valdas said. "Not to some power-hungry idiot who would lose half the kingdom—or worse—to a war on two fronts within a year. Only yesterday you said yourself that King Kazimir would do a better job than Gerhard. You were seriously thinking that you'd let him if he stepped in. What's that if not treason?"

Tomas's eyes looked glazed. Things were moving too fast for him.

"I don't know what's right and what's wrong anymore. I trusted Henryk. Henryk trusted you."

"I let him down," Valdas said.

"No! King Gerhard let him down."

Valdas nodded. "We sneak into the grounds, find the king in his apartments, and secure him against all comers. We'll need to draw Kazimir there as well and get them both under our control. Then Tomas, with orders signed and sealed by the king, can go to the palace guard. Not the Chancellor's Own. They will have access to the keep and can bring Mirza, the queen, and the baby to us. Lind will have to go too. Both the queen and Mirza will trust him. It's vital the rest of the palace doesn't realize what's happening until it's too late.

"Once we've got the queen and the baby safe, we declare the baby to be the rightful king. Neither Gerhard nor Kazimir have got popular support. We can swing this if enough of the hussars will declare for Kristina and the baby."

"And Gerhard?" Tomas asked.

"What do you think? He's too dangerous to leave alive."

Tomas shook his head, not so much a *no* as an *I don't know*.

"We'll keep bloodshed to a minimum," Valdas said. "I'll not kill honest guardsmen unless I have to. It's not their fault they're caught up in this. Though from what you say, the Chancellor's Own may be more difficult to convince."

"God's ballocks, man, that'll hamstring us, leaving squealers behind," Lind said.

"Just a few months ago they were my men, and I was trying to stop people getting into the palace and killing the king. It's important we don't tip the balance and bring them out against us."

"I can help with that," Maksimilian said. "There's a potion—we call it *Goodnight*. A couple of drops will knock a man out for an hour when inhaled from a kerchief. We use it occasionally when customers get out of hand."

"Guaranteed?" Lind asked.

"Guaranteed. So don't breathe it in yourself."

"Tomas, are you with us?" Valdas asked.

The young man took a deep breath and nodded. "I am."

"Good man! Do you have people you can trust?"

He nodded again. "A few. Enough."

"You're forgetting something," Aniela said. "If the king has a magician, maybe guards are the least of your worries." When Lind and

Valdas both turned to glare at her, she shrugged. "Just thought I'd mention it. Someone at the palace is causing Mirza's darkness, and she was plenty frightened."

Valdas nodded. "We shouldn't discount it. Any more rumors, Tomas? Who is it?"

Tomas shrugged. "Maybe someone imprisoned in the dungeons too. Kazimir goes there regularly. His servants are notoriously close-mouthed. You know me. I'll believe in magic when I see it, and I've seen nothing yet, but . . ."

"But what?"

Tomas shrugged.

"Well, we'll find out soon enough," Valdas said.

"But first we have to get up to the Gura and inside the palace," Lind said.

"Saturday night," Tomas said.

"Saturday?" Valdas tilted his head slightly to one side.

"Saturday!" Aniela jumped up. "Oh, yes. I am going to have my work cut out for me between now and then."

"What?" Lind said.

Valdas realized what Tomas meant by how Aniela was starting to laugh. "No, you can't be serious. That's . . . wrong . . ."

"What?" Lind said again.

"Saturday night is the night we conspire to let in some gentle companionship," Tomas said. "Brother officers turn a blind eye for each other while the whores come through the postern gate."

"No one's going to believe that great tree of a man is a female whore." Lind eyed up Valdas.

Valdas felt himself bridle. He softened his voice, raised it several tones, and lowered his gaze demurely. "You mean I'm not pretty enough for you?"

Aniela choked back her laughter. "Ladies, leave it up to me and my paintbrush." She frowned. "And of course, I'll have to come with you."

"No!" Valdas and Lind both answered at once.

Valdas's head buzzed. There was no way he was going to let Aniela put herself in danger.

"Yes," Aniela said. "I might be able to make you look like great strapping farm-girls from cabbage country, but you'll never get the voices right, Valdas just proved it. I'll get you past the gate. I'm sure Tomas can find me a real customer after that to keep me out of harm's way. I'm not mad. I know I wouldn't be much use against the Chancellor's Own."

It made sense, but he didn't have to like it. Valdas nodded agreement while thinking of all the ways it could go horribly wrong for her.

"One more thing," Lind said. "There's a woman called Marilena. She's Queen Kristina's chief lady-in-waiting. She came with her from Sverija. They've been together for years. She was the one walking veiled in the queen's place in the funeral cortege while the queen escaped. She's probably the one who told Kazimir about the queen's safe house. We need to protect her, too."

"There's a limit." Valdas raised both hands. "We'll have enough to think about with Mirza, the queen, and the baby, and if this woman betrayed the queen . . ."

"I don't believe she did it on purpose." Lind glanced sidelong at Aniela's crooked fingers. "Gerhard's questioners would have had the truth from her. You know it happens." He looked at Aniela again, but she shook her head minutely. "If Marilena still lives, Kristina will want us, command us, to free her. She . . . they . . . were lovers."

"Oh," was all Valdas could manage.

"You mean she was sold to Konstantyn as a political bride, a brood mare, and she doesn't even like men!" Aniela said. "Did Konstantyn know?"

"I think he did." Valdas had a sudden insight into the reason Kristina had spent so much time in the Queen's Court with her ladies. "He was a wise man who asked her to do her duty in getting an heir, but no more. There was a certain accord between them. I think they were friends."

"So we rescue Marilena as well?" Lind asked.

"If we can. If she still lives."

CHAPTER EIGHTY-ONE
Mirza

MIRZA SANK TO the floor of her cell. She examined the fresh information from all angles. Kazimir wasn't working for Gerhard, he was manipulating him. Valdas and Lind had the wrong man in their sights. If they somehow managed to get inside the castle, they'd go searching for King Gerhard, who, by the sound of it, was almost as much a victim as Konstantyn had been. If Valdas and Lind went after the wrong man, that gave the right man, the dangerous one, time to . . . what? Kill them? Have them imprisoned—which meant they were as good as dead, but probably would die more painfully, or more publicly.

Could she spirit-walk into Valdas's dreams? She doubted it, from what Konstantyn's shade had told her. There had never been a bone-head like Valdas.

She tried once more to access Dahnay in the spirit world. As before, she moved along gray corridors, and turned a corner into a hot land lit by a yellow sun. Dahnay stood as before, but this time much more ghostly. She smiled at Mirza and whispered words that Mirza heard inside her head. *Now I am ended. Tell my tsarina.* She turned and walked away, fading into nothing as she did so.

Dahnay was dead. Mirza felt a sob rising inside her and pushed it down. She mustn't get distracted now. She took several deep breaths to calm herself, trying not to think about the woman she had come to regard as a *sister*.

How about Lind? Could she reach him?

She closed her eyes and sought him out. This time she thought she had some success. Lind's sleeping mind tickled the edge of her consciousness. She opened herself to him to reach into his dreams, but found herself yanked cruelly into a cellar beneath a forge, not this high-vaulted dungeon, but a low-ceilinged place with walls that had once been lime-washed, but were now darkened with splatters of . . . blood. She recognized the charnel house reek beneath the smell of charcoal, soot, and cinders.

She's not herself anymore, she's a boy—she's Lind . . . Lind's done something terrible. It was only for comfort. How was he to know . . .

Thwack! A cane across his back. Thwack across buttocks. Thwack. Thwack. Thwack. A kick to the ribs. He gasps for air. He's flung over onto his back, knees drawn up, hands between his legs to protect himself. The monster grabs both ankles in one massive hand and drags him over the stone slabs of the floor, straightening his legs, leaving his genitals exposed and . . . Thwack! He can't breathe for the blazing agony. Thwack! He might never breathe again. In the dim light of the single oil lamp the blackness threatens to overwhelm him. This is it. Tourmine is going to kill him this time, and he's not sure he cares . . . not for himself . . . but Ewa. He should protect Ewa . . . and their baby.

Tourmine looms over him with—oh gods, no—a knife. "I should chop 'em off, boy, and slice your prick in twain from stem to stern." He nearly shits himself. Tourmine jabs the point of the knife low down into his bruised belly and slices a shallow cut downward until the blood flows. He knows what's coming next. Ewa screams. Tourmine's attention wavers. Lind is crying, snot and tears smeared over his face. His skinny legs are jelly. He's paralyzed, unable to even crawl away. Convulsions course up his body in waves from toe to scalp.

Ewa screams again.

Tourmine likes screams.

The monster kicks him into the space between the wall and the keeping slab.

That slab.

He starts to retch, spasms wracking his body.

There's a timeslip.

Tourmine grasps Ewa by a thick handful of hair. Thwack. The cane across her swelling belly, the only part of her that's not scarecrow skinny. Thwack. Thwack. Thwack. He tries to beat the babe out of her. Thwack across the belly and breasts with his stick until bruising skin splits. She doubles over, pukes, whimpers. Begs him to stop.

It can't get any worse, but it does. Tourmine pushes her forward across the stone slab. Lind can see her face from this angle. He's shivering in a heap, curled around his own throbbing balls, arms and legs not answering his attempts to move. He tries to crawl, but what can he do?

The monster pulls on the draw-cord and drops his trousers. Pain thrills him. He's a big man, built like a bull, strong from the forge and athletic from the swordplay. She's so tiny. Tiny and pregnant and . . . breakable. As Tourmine slams into her from behind and starts to rock and moan in pleasure, her face contorts and her breathing is all gasps through clenched teeth as she tries to hold back screams.

"Ewa!" Lind draws her attention. Their gazes lock. Tourmine never lasts long when he's in a lather. It'll be Lind's turn next, then they can both crawl away to heal, but never together. Not again. He'll not make that mistake twice.

Tourmine grunts louder, hips thrusting faster now. His eyes glaze over. He's nearly there. He drags Ewa's head back. With one sweep of his right hand and a flash of steel he slices open her throat. He laughs— an inhuman sound of giddy joy. "Two deaths for one cut. A bonus!" Blood arcs across the gap. It spatters over the limewash of the cellar wall. It's in Lind's eyes, in his mouth. Metallic on his tongue.

Tourmine climaxes inside her while her life's blood pumps out.

Ewa!

Tourmine rolls her body off the slab and she crumples to the floor, ungraceful in death, like a child's doll discarded.

"Fuck your dead meat now, boy. See how you like her. You're mine. You'll always be mine. Don't forget it again."

The cellar door slams and all is quiet save for Lind's own whimpers.

In the low gleam from the grating set high in the wall, he crawls to Ewa inch by painful inch. He tries to straighten out her twisted limbs. She's grinning at him, a hideous gaping smile across her throat. Her skin is still warm. He kneels by her side, weeps into her breasts and pillows his head on her flaccid belly. Then he feels it. The final flutter of butterfly-wing beneath his cheek. His child is dying unborn.

Mirza came back to herself dry-heaving. She couldn't get into Lind's mind through that turmoil. Was this what he dreamed of every night? With her head spinning, she curled up with her knees pulled tight against her belly and folded the fur-lined delja around her feet for warmth, wondering if she'd ever be able to sleep. When sleep came it was more like unconsciousness.

And that was the last thing she remembered.

The night passed too quickly. She awoke feeling violated and nauseous—the aftereffects of walking Lind's dream-world. She sat with her back against the stone wall, feet drawn in close, knees hugged to her chest and her cheeks wet with tears. She'd known in her head, but never really understood in her heart, what a terrible furnace had been used in the forging of Lind's soul. How could anyone suffer that and still be sane? Perhaps he wasn't.

Maybe she wasn't either, not now.

CHAPTER EIGHTY-TWO

Lind

THEY SPENT THE day in preparation, cobbling together outfits from clothing lent by the more generously proportioned girls, and thanking their luck for drawstrings. Lind patted down the skirts on top of his trousers. His sword hung beneath them, wrapped to muffle any telltale click or rattle of sheath against boot. A flintlock pistol was tucked in the back of his sash, ready primed. He hoped he didn't look as ridiculous as Valdas, but Valdas was taller and broader.

"Gah! I'll never make a believable woman," Valdas said, priming his own pistol.

"I used to be such a pretty boy, you know," Lind said. "It got me into all sorts of trouble."

Listen, I'm making jokes about it, now.

"Well, you're not so pretty now. That nose is set wrong."

"No matter."

Aniela acquired two wigs. Lind avoided the fair one. The curls were too reminiscent of his own hair. *Maybe I'm not quite cured yet. Maybe I never will be, but I'm getting better. I'm leaving it behind. I win, Tourmine. In the end I win, even if I die tonight.* In the brunette wig, curls pulled down to hide some of the bruising on his cheekbone, he looked in the mirror and began to think that, in the dark, they might just get away with it.

Valdas looked stupid in the yellow wig with the dress barely laced across his broad chest. He scowled at his reflection, but sat while Aniela applied cosmetics. When their disguises were finished, Klara was called in to inspect them.

"Pretty." She pursed her lips and blew them a kiss. "Don't stay out too late, girls."

Lind managed a passable curtsy but Valdas nearly tripped over his own skirt. Klara began to laugh.

Aniela pursed her lips. "You're not a good advert for Trader Maksimilian's establishment. Say you work at the Rose Tavern if the guard asks," she said. "No, on second thought, don't say anything at all. Let me do all the talking."

"I'm still not sure about you coming in with us," Valdas said.

"There's not much choice, lover. Someone's got to get you in there."

But when it was time to leave, there were four girls besides Aniela. "We thought we'd take a bit of hussar action if it was on offer," Ruta said.

"Is Maksimilian making you do this?" Lind asked.

Ruta shook her head. "It's the thought of all those lovely boys in uniforms with money in their pockets."

So it was a party of seven that climbed the Gura's narrow crookways on the Serpentinas and approached the postern gate after dark, Lind and Valdas in the middle of them, trying to minimize their height. Aniela gave her Rose Tavern story and said she'd been told to ask for Tomas. True to his word, Tomas had arranged for his brother officer to ignore the party, but all the same it raised a question from one of the guards when Tomas arrived.

"Ladies, Tomas? Not changing your mind about the fair sex, are you?"

"I owe Radofski. Lost a bet. They're not for me."

The guard scowled. "One of 'em might be. You needn't disguise your boys quite so elaborately."

Tomas shrugged and reached for Valdas's arm. "If it's that obvious, I'll take this one now."

The guard muttered something under his breath, but Tomas turned away.

Once through the gate, Tomas pointed the whores to the barracks while Valdas and Lind dodged straight into a store room he'd unlocked for them. They stripped off their dresses. Valdas was quick to wipe his face clean of rouge.

The door creaked.

Lind's hand flew to his knife.

"Tomas?" Valdas stepped behind the door and called softly.

"No. It's me."

"Aniela? You're supposed to be going about your business," Valdas hissed at her as she stepped inside.

Lind breathed out and eased his knife back into its sheath.

"Someone's got to find Marilena," Aniela said. "I'm going to the Queen's Court."

"That wasn't part of the deal."

"Let her do it," Lind said. "Aniela, here, have this." He took a slim-bladed knife, one of two strapped to his chest beneath his shirt. "I've got plenty more. Don't get into any fights with it, because you'll lose, but in an emergency—between the ribs and angle it up. Don't stab downward. If you miss or it glances off a bone, you'll gut yourself."

"And if I miss this way I'll stick it in my eye. Well, I suppose it's a quicker way to go." She took it and slipped it into her sash.

Valdas took her face in his hands and kissed her quickly. "Find Linnea Petrana. She's one of the old queen's chief ladies who still has residence there. She's got no love of Gerhard, I'm sure. Tell her we think Gerhard murdered her mistress. After that you're on your own."

"Linnea Petrana, right."

"Take care."

"Let's go," Lind said. "We're wasting time here."

"Lind." Aniela gave him a level look.

"I remember, mistress. Don't worry."

Quietly they slipped out of the store room and across the inner courtyard and to the door in a long low wall that led into the private gardens. Their best entrance into the palace opened from the garden into one of the public reception rooms, now in darkness. It would be locked, of course, and guarded. Valdas and Lind inserted themselves into the dense shrubbery and watched. A guard patrolled the strip of garden in front of their door. Lind fingered his belt knife, but Valdas took out Maksimilian's little bottle of Goodnight, sprinkled some onto a kerchief, handed it to Lind, and slipped into the shadows.

"Who goes?" The guard was sharp.

"A ghost from your past, Fryderyk."

Valdas's familiar voice was enough to confuse the guard into sufficient hesitation. Lind got behind him with the kerchief, and held it over his mouth and nose until he dropped unconscious.

They dragged him under a rosebush together, and in silence Lind applied his skills and his skeleton key to the door. It swung open and they slipped into the building.

So far, so good.

CHAPTER EIGHTY-THREE
Mirza

KAZIMIR WOKE MIRZA in what she thought might still be the middle of the night. His ghostly minions dragged her to the bars and thrust her against the bespelled iron.

"You still resist me."

Her body spasmed involuntarily while Kazimir pulled several hairs from her head and sliced a sharp knife lightly lengthways along her left wrist, not a deep cut and not into tendons or artery, but enough to bleed her into a bowl. Maybe as much as a cup of blood before the vein became sluggish and Kazimir let her arm go. Mirza sank away in relief when he left her. She gripped her wound tightly to close it, but hours went by, and then more hours, and she had nothing to distract her from the angry smart.

The wound began to scab over. Unbound and without clean bindings, it was better left alone. She got up, paced her cage, sat down, tried to sleep, failed, got up and paced her cage again. She knew Kazimir was spellworking, she could feel it. He wasn't far away. Somewhere in the old keep's labyrinthine dungeons he was spinning his tangled web of deceit, murder, politics, and raw ambition.

She should have run far away from Zavonia the first time she felt his dark presence; but instead, she'd played right into his hands. She'd outdone herself in stupidity and it was likely to prove fatal. Yet if she couldn't stop Kazimir, no one could.

She considered her options, heartened by the thought that she still had options. None of them was good, but if she was going to die she could at least take Kazimir with her.

She could flame him and by doing so leave herself, dying by degrees, walled up in this place. At least the queen wasn't here now, so she would only be condemning herself to a lingering death. Wasn't that better than letting him work his dirty magic on her? He wanted her fire magic and she wouldn't let him hurt her friends.

Or was it better to capitulate? Should she pretend to give in and become his acolyte? Would he even believe such a sudden about-turn? Would she have the opportunity to kill him? How long had it taken Lind to turn on the master who used him so badly? Four years.

If Kazimir intended to marry Kristina on Sunday, then—if she'd calculated correctly—today was Saturday and she had a few hours at best.

She needed to know whether she could push her fire magic beyond the bespelled bars and whatever barrier Kazimir had set up. She concentrated on the cinders in the small fireplace. Could she ignite what was left of them?

She called on fire, drawing her magic into the very center of her being, and held it while it grew and surged in the pit of her belly. The fireplace. Flames. Concentrate.

Bring. Forth. Fire!

She felt the barrier that Kazimir had set to protect himself, but pushed, and pushed, and pushed at it until it gave. With an audible pop, flames blossomed in the fireplace.

She grinned and let them die back, breathing heavily as if she'd run a race. She could do it.

And knowing that she could do it, she practiced again and again. Each time, passing Kazimir's barrier became easier and easier. She was weakening it.

With luck he might not even notice until it was too late.

If only she knew why he had taken her blood and hair.

He'd talked about passion. She shuddered. There were superstitions . . . Take the witch's maidenhead, take her powers. It was an old tale and patently false, since Valdas had taken nothing from her that morning in the tumbledown barn except her ignorance. But Kazimir's knowledge of magic was twisted. If that was what he believed, then that would guide his actions.

Sexual energy was almost as powerful as death in anguish. He might be planning to harness both. Use her and kill her painfully. She wasn't going to let that happen.

She would not be a victim!

She trembled inside, and pushed down her fears. Concentrate on the options. For every plan of Kazimir's she needed a counter plan.

Think.

His knowledge of natural magic was limited. If he was constructing a ritual, using blood and dark magic to take her fire, he was courting danger.

Oil and water. They didn't mix, but add fire and that changed the game. Pour water on an oil fire and you got an explosive backlash . . . It was unpredictable and dangerous. If Kazimir tried to absorb her natural magic and couldn't hold it, it might kill him.

Of course, it might kill her, too.

Of all the ways she might die, she feared fire the most. Besides, she wanted to live. She wanted to go back to Tsura, to Stasha and Boldo and the rest of the Bakaishans; leave her sharp tongue behind when they went to the next moot and bargain hard for a husband, even an old one or a maimed one—she couldn't be picky with her face—but oh how she wanted a child, a family of her own. Maybe in time she could have a whole family consisting of relatives by marriage and her children's children.

Or maybe not.

She'd long had a suspicion that this task Konstantyn had settled on her would be her death, and now it looked as though she'd been correct. Her chances of surviving were small. All she could hope to do was to sell her life dearly before Valdas and Lind blundered in and got themselves killed.

She sat in her cell and let the whole sorry business unravel in her mind. How had Kazimir planned all this? He'd played the game so patiently, inserting himself years ago into Gerhard's household while Gerhard was still so far from the throne that his retainers were no one's business but his own.

Mirza shuddered. All those murders—the king's younger brother, Queen Cecylia's unborn babies. She wondered why Kazimir had chosen to have Konstantyn assassinated, but it didn't take her long to come up with an answer, or two answers. Firstly, the toll on Kazimir's body would already have been heavy. She'd seen the missing finger and noticed his slightly uneven gait, which probably meant he was missing toes as well. He'd examined her hands and feet, checking for missing parts, and then her whole body, even her private parts. That alone was a sign that he carried more scars himself. How many body parts could one man shed? The death of a king would demand more than a toe or a finger. Maybe to kill Konstantyn he'd have had to sacrifice a much more significant organ, maybe an eye or a hand or a more tender part.

In addition, the actual crime of hiring an assassin would be easy for him to pin on Gerhard whenever he needed to, which would show Gerhard to be corrupt as well as incompetent, and strengthen Kazimir's reason for stepping in—as Konstantyn's bastard half brother—to right Gerhard's wrongs and rule in Konstantyn's name.

Queen Cecylia's suicide must have seriously upset his plans. When Konstantyn took a young wife who might prove fertile, he'd had to act quickly before she conceived. He'd already been too late, but he hadn't known it. Still, it wasn't too late to turn the unexpected appearance of Kristina's child to his advantage. Marry her, kill Gerhard or discredit him, set the heir on the throne with himself as regent and, two or three years down the line when the child died, who would question his right to rule?

Oh, he was clever, she'd grant him that. As soon as he gathered the reins of power he was ready to send the country to war—and there was nothing like a war to cement a strong leader firmly on the throne.

But he was only one man. One man and the Chancellor's Own guard. She doubted that he had a strong political power base yet. Kill him now and it was done. She hugged the delja closer to her body. That chill had nothing to do with the temperature in the room and everything to do with mounting dread.

Who would do the deed if she didn't?

The next time a key turned in the lock, Mirza was ready. She stood to face him as he reached the bottom of the steps and crossed the floor.

He opened his mouth to speak, but Mirza didn't give him a chance. She gathered her fire, feeling the heat rising and rising inside her. Then she pushed the flames at him.

Smoke began to rise from the hem of Kazimir's delja. A tiny flame ran up the cloth. More flames began at the sleeves and neck.

Yes! She'd done it!

But Kazimir laughed and cast off the delja to burn in a heap on the stone floor. The rest of him was untouched.

"I am protected," he said, opening the front of his zupan and undershirt.

On his chest, crudely cut, but recognizable, was a mirror image of her salamander, its back daubed in blood. It called to her. Her own blood.

"Your fire can't hurt me, but it will come to me so very soon now." He looked up to the top of the steps. "Come!"

The woman who had taken Kristina's baby came down the steps.

"Step away from the bars."

Kazimir's invisible guards grabbed Mirza by the arms and slammed her against the wall so hard that she heard the dull thud as her head hit the stone and felt her brain rattle inside her skull. She saw a shower of sparks painted across the inside of her eyelids. Thank goodness for thick hair.

Kazimir unlocked her door and stepped through. Flame him, now!

Again she tried to use the murderous fire, found it simmering like a kettle on the embers. The salamander scar itched. She gathered herself and pushed the flames at Kazimir.

Nothing happened.

Kazimir had the grace not to laugh in her face, but she could tell that he was amused. He held up a thin silver band, shot through with streaks of blood-red—her blood—and covered in marks that might be written words or indecipherable ancient runes. She had no talent for reading.

"I told you," he said and turned to the woman. "Take her hair."

The woman stepped forward with a pair of iron shears. The invisible guards obligingly moved her far enough away from the wall to let the woman get behind her. Mirza felt her long curls gathered up and pulled tight behind her. Three quick snicks with the blades and what was left on her head fell short around her ears and flopped over her forehead.

Kazimir stepped forward and snapped the silver band around Mirza's neck. She felt it taste her skin and fuse itself to her with a fizz.

Damn!

He held out his hand and the woman handed him the thick skein of Mirza's dark curls, which he wrapped in a silken scarf and placed inside a pouch secured at his waist.

Was he planning more spellworking?

Options. What were her options?

Mirza's chest tightened as if a giant hand squeezed her heart. The salamander scar throbbed. She took a deep breath. If she wasn't careful, her own fear would do her more harm than Kazimir could.

"You will go with Radmila. A bath awaits. Don't make this harder on yourself than it needs to be. Do I have to tell you that the collar holds your powers in thrall, and that my boys will not be letting you out of their sight? Be nice to Radmila. She won't remember any of this when she goes back to her husband and child. If you break the spell I've set on her, I'll have to kill her. Understand?"

She didn't reply.

"Understand?"

"Yes." Her voice cracked on the single word.

She followed Radmila out of the room, invisible hands still at her elbows.

"Where are we going?"

Radmila didn't answer, but she led Mirza along stone corridors very similar to those in her spirit-walk. They walked too far for this to be the vaults beneath the old keep. These tunnels were hollowed in solid rock, deep in the Gura itself. They might be under any of the buildings inside the curtain wall of the Citadel.

Radmila reached a door and opened it, then stepped aside to allow Mirza through. The room was warm and lit with at least a hundred candles burning in nooks and on shelves all around the walls. In the center of the floor stood a large wooden tub, big enough to lie down in, steaming with its burden of scented hot water.

Why a bath?

Oh, right. That's what he was planning. He wanted her clean for their coupling. Blood magic and sex magic, just his style.

Not her style.

Radmila stood expectantly. When Mirza didn't move, she reached for the clasp at the neck of Mirza's delja. Mirza brushed her hand away.

"I can do it."

The woman stepped back.

"You too." She addressed the spirits. "Let go, boys. No touching. Turn your backs."

If she imagined they had turned their backs, she was able to quickly strip off her delja, skirts, and chemise. How long had she been wearing them? Three days? Four? Quickly she stepped naked into the tub. She didn't want to sit in the water. The thought of sitting in her own filth was repugnant to her, but she liked the idea of standing naked in front of Kazimir's ghostly guards even less, so she sat down, grateful for the warmth and the fact that the sides of the tub hid her from view. If she stayed in the water until her skin wrinkled, would Kazimir come and fetch her himself? Better not risk it.

Using the bar of scented soap and washcloth that Radmila held out, she scoured her body. The salamander scar glowed blood red, heated by the water. She soaped, rinsed and soaped her hair again, then spluttered as Radmila poured clean warm water over her head to wash away the last of the soap scum, but it floated on the surface of the water. Hurriedly she climbed out and stepped into the large white drying sheet that Radmila held. The woman helped to dry her off and gave her a comb for her shorn locks. With no mirror, all she could do was tease the short tousled curls into place with her fingers. "I've seen a better job on a sheep, Radmila."

But she'd probably be dead before the night was out. What was the sense in worrying about her hair?

"I don't suppose you can tell me where Kazimir took the baby?"

Radmila might not have heard. She handed Mirza a voluminous, ermine-lined, white over-robe with long bell sleeves. It draped around her body and clasped at the neck, but had no other fastenings.

She pulled the edges so that they overlapped and held the robe closed over her nakedness.

"Right, boys, you can turn round now, I'm decent." There wasn't a whisper in the steamy atmosphere of the room. She didn't let herself think of the two shades—if there were only two—watching her. Some things felt plain wrong.

She followed Radmila out into the corridor, and as they passed a branching passageway she caught the faint cry of a hungry baby and hesitated, but an invisible hand propelled her forward from behind. Barely a hundred paces further on, they stopped in front of an oak door that was a little more elegant than the other functional ones. Mirza wondered whether the choice of oak was coincidental. Its physical properties were strong, but its magical properties provided a balanced energy, neither light nor dark. The door swung inward at Radmila's knock. Radmila halted, but the two guards, still at Mirza's elbows, herded her through.

The room inside, though windowless, was furnished as sumptuously as any rich man's house: an upholstered couch with carved arms and feet, a polished side table, some wooden chairs, dark with age, carved with initials with an obvious crown above them. Too old to be carved for Konstantyn; maybe they'd been his father's or his grandfather's. Kazimir's father and grandfather, too.

A small accident of birth seemed to count for so much among the Zavonians. Kazimir was so near yet so far from the highest power in the land. She could almost have sympathy for his position, but she couldn't countenance his willingness not only to murder his way to the throne, but to put his land and people in danger in order to establish himself. A king should look after the little people all of the time, not only when it suited him.

An inner door swung open. "Bring her in."

CHAPTER EIGHTY-FOUR
Valdas

VALDAS KNEW THE palace better than anyone. Just the smell of it overwhelmed his senses. Familiar, yet alien at the same time. He knew these rooms, these corridors, every twist and turn, every servant's stair and curtained arras. It had been his job to find every possible source of danger and set a guard in it. His successor hadn't done his research properly. Valdas led Lind through the garden room, around containers of exotic plants, to the inner door, pausing briefly to check the corridor, which was empty. A narrow servants' stair gave them access to the floor above and Valdas mentally gave the officer in charge of the Chancellor's Own a firm dressing down for his mistakes. They could cost the king his life. In fact—tonight—they *would* cost the king his life.

His lips drew back from his teeth in either a grin or a grimace. He thought it might have been a mixture of both. He was no assassin, to dispatch a man and think nothing more of it than a pleasant fullness in his purse. Gerhard already weighed on his conscience and the deed was not even done yet.

Keep your mind on the goal. Rescue Mirza, rescue Kristina, restore the rightful king.

Close to the top of the steps, Valdas motioned for Lind to pause. From here any guard would be able to see the main stair in its entirety and also guard the servants' stair. He could hear footsteps, regulation boots on the tile of the corridor.

Lind had a stiletto in his hand.

Valdas frowned, made eye contact, and shook his head slightly.

Lind shrugged and mouthed something that might have been, *Insurance.*

Valdas pointedly tipped a few more drops of Goodnight onto the kerchief. Whether this guard was one of the unpopular Chancellor's Own or not was something they'd have to ascertain later. Kill indiscriminately, and Tomas's promised support would dissolve quickly enough. Without it they were lost. They might kill Gerhard, but they'd be dead before they could set Konstantyn's son on the throne.

Lind jerked his head in the direction of the corridor and calmly scraped his boot heel on the top step. As the guard came round the corner to check the noise, he stepped in front of him with the stiletto, drawing the man's eyes away from where Valdas waited with the sleeping drops. It was an easy matter for Valdas to close in behind him, and in two breaths they were lowering him onto the steps.

Lind stripped off the man's red uniform mente and dragged it on over his own tunic. With a quick glance he stepped into the corridor and began to make realistic choking sounds, dropping to his knees and bending his head forward in such a way that the guard at the other end of the corridor could only see his boot soles and his back.

"Droski? What's wrong?" The other guard came at a run and Valdas mentally cursed his stupidity. He should have been shouting for help in case his partner was choking over a knife in his throat or a topical poison. But the stupidity worked in their favor. Once more, Valdas stepped in with the Goodnight drops, and the second guard joined the first.

According to Tomas, inside the king's suite there would be at least four of the Chancellor's Own and Gerhard himself, of course. Even soft Gerhard should be counted as a threat if his life was in danger. Valdas slipped the Goodnight into the pouch at his waist and loosened his sword. He raised an eyebrow to Lind, who licked his lips and nodded once.

On Valdas's sharp nod they each kicked in one of the grand double doors, catching two guards completely off balance. Valdas saw Lind in action at his side, but blocked his progress from his consciousness. Lind would either deal with his two guards or he wouldn't, and if he didn't, Valdas would know soon enough. All things considered there weren't many men he'd rather have with him right now. That thought flashed through his brain, barely acknowledged, as he came nose to nose with his first guard. He was almost quick enough to gut the man before the dreaded pike turned his blade. It was all or nothing. His primed pistol was good for one shot. As his blade bit into the shaft of the pike, he swapped the hilt to his left hand, pulled the flintlock from his sash, and discharged it into the guard's face, fighting the kick of the recoil. Tossing it aside, he grabbed the sabre with his right hand again and leaped over the fallen man's ruined head, ducking to one side as the second guard raised his own weapon and fired.

His head rang with the noise and his eyes stung from the black powder smoke. He felt the ball snatch fabric from a fold of his right sleeve, but it passed him by. Pray the guard only had one pistol.

He lunged with his sabre, feeling the jar all the way up to his shoulder as the guard blocked his blow. Finesse gave way to murderous hacking and thrusting, searching for an opening, never letting up. The guard was a swordsman, a duelist by the feel of his bladework, but the High Guard would have made a much better showing. This man probably hadn't been in many real fights where his life was on the line if he lost.

He lost.

Valdas pressed him back and back until his heel caught against a side table. The momentary hesitation killed him as surely as Valdas's blade into his chest. Valdas pulled the blade free, feeling flesh suck at steel, and he turned for the next target to see Lind dealing with the last guard standing. The guard had been good enough to get at least one cut in. Lind had blood dripping down his forehead into one eye. Before Valdas could decide which was the best way to intervene, Lind parried steel to steel, stepped inside the arc of the man's blade, turning, and sliced across the man's unprotected throat with his knife.

"I thought you said we do this quietly," Lind said. His own pistol was still in his belt.

Valdas shrugged. "Hurt?"

Lind wiped blood from his eye with his sleeve. "Scalp wound. Bleeding like a pig. Not serious. King Gerhard?"

Valdas nodded at the door opposite the one they'd entered by. It was wide enough for one person, and if Gerhard had a pistol, likely the first one through would know about it.

In the distance Valdas could hear running feet. They had seconds. He kicked open the door, crouched and rolled through it, waiting for the flintlock blast that never came. Straightening up, he grinned sheepishly as Lind strolled in.

"That your villainous king?" Lind asked.

On the high bed a pale figure in stained linens and nothing else tried to raise himself from the pillows and flopped down again, rattling his short chain as he did so. A sour smell filled the room: sickness and neglect.

"God in Heaven!" Valdas stuck his sabre, point down, in the floorboards by the foot of the bed and leaned over the usurping, bastard king that he'd been dreaming of filleting for months.

"Lord Gerhard! Are you all right?"

Gerhard's eyes were half-closed, but what Valdas could see of the pupils were dilated, a sure sign he'd been drugged, or worse, bespelled. On his chest, lying in a pentagram scorched into his flesh, was a stick doll, arms and legs lashed to his torso with twine, and the whole thing, except for a crown made of gold wire, stained dark rust-brown, the color of dried blood. The king's wrists had dirty bandages around them stained the same color. Valdas felt sick. Magic! Here on the Gura. Mirza had been right all along. He cut the twine and tried to move the doll, but it was firmly fixed, though he couldn't tell how.

"Hurry up, we've got company." Lind drew his flintlock and turned to the door.

Valdas didn't know what to do with the stick figure. Would trying to move it or destroy it break the spell or damage Gerhard further? Did he care?

"That's far enough!" Lind bellowed toward the outer room. "We have the king. Stand down!"

If it wasn't Tomas, as planned, they were dead.

For a heart-stopping moment Valdas waited for the sound of pistol fire, but none came.

"Tomas?" he yelled.

"Yes!" The younger man answered him from the outer room.

"Can you trust your men?"

"I can."

"Get in here fast."

Lind let Tomas past with a nod.

"How long since you've seen your king?" Valdas asked.

"I don't know. A week? Two maybe." Tomas stepped up to the bed.

"Did he look like this?"

"Mother of God! Is he sick?" Tomas reached out to touch the stick figure on the king's chest, but stopped halfway.

"Spellbound, I think, but he's been chained here for long enough in a puddle of piss to get bedsores."

"Chancellor Kazimir?"

"Who else?"

Tomas's stream of invective would have done the High Guard proud.

Another man hovered in the doorway, jaw open. Valdas looked up.

"Piotr Hecht, I might have guessed. That means your brother Pawel isn't far behind."

"Gone to the chancellor's suite with ten men, Captain Zalecki."

"I've got twenty more men, hand-picked," Tomas said. "Longin Klavons and Serafin Lukov are here as well and . . ." He reeled off a list of names. "None of them volunteered for the Chancellor's Own, even though the wages are half as much again. They were all loyal to King Konstantyn and . . . to you."

Valdas cursed under his breath. "I told you I'm not here to start a personal revolution, I'm here to get justice."

Lind tsked and shook his head. "I think I'd rather have a self-serving revolutionary than an idealist."

"Look, we haven't got time for this. Where's Kazimir?"

Pawel Hecht entered the outer room at the head of his men. "The chancellor's suite was empty, sir. Only two guards and we dealt with them."

Valdas cursed. Having Kazimir loose was the last thing they needed, especially if he had access to magic, his own or anyone else's. "We need to find Mirza and the queen before Kazimir—" Before Kazimir did what? What was he planning? What did he hope to achieve? Did he honestly think he could make himself king without any claim of blood? Surely he'd already risen as high as any commoner could hope to.

They're already calling him King Kazimir.

"Christ on a pig!" Valdas shook his head to clear it. Taking charge as if they had already won the day might carry the rest of the troops in the Gura with them.

"Get someone to search the bodies out there and see if any one of them has a key for this shackle," he said. "Make this poor bastard comfortable, but don't move the spellstuff, it might hurt him. Though you might send for a surgeon and maybe Cardinal Pieritz. Tell him to bring his best exorcist. Don't let anyone else in here, especially any of the Chancellor's Own or—it goes without saying—the chancellor himself. If anyone sees Kazimir, don't get too close. Don't let him open his mouth. Shoot the bastard."

Valdas ran over possibilities in his mind. It was now or never. "Use the king's seal. Send Klavons and Lukov to the duty officer and the captain of the City Watch. Tell them there's been an attempt on the king's life and the king orders that all the Chancellor's Own are to be apprehended and held until further notice. Tell the duty officer, very specifically, to replace the guards on the old keep with men he trusts."

"And the chancellor?" Tomas asked.

Valdas drew a deep breath and looked at Gerhard on the bed. "On the king's order, kill him if they can, but tell them to be careful. He's got resources . . ." Any lingering doubts about Mirza's claim that there was a magical power on the Gura dissolved in an instant. "I don't know whether telling them he's a sorcerer will help. Most of them won't believe it. I didn't."

"You're still going after Mirza and the queen?" Tomas asked.

"This changes nothing except that the real enemy is not who we thought."

"I can spare six men. We can hold the king safe here with the rest. Pawel, Piotr, pick four more and go with Captain Zalecki."

"Do we know where we're going?" Lind wiped the blood from his sword and dagger with remarkable disregard for the expensive comforter that had fallen to the floor.

"I'm afraid we do." Valdas crossed to the fireplace and put both hands on the panel beside it. "And unless we're very lucky I expect the chancellor will be waiting for us." The panel clicked and slid backward and to the side. "There's a passageway from here all the way through to the old keep. It's a bit of a maze, but I mapped it years ago for King Konstantyn. Only he and I knew about it. I doubt Gerhard did, or Kazimir. Bring oil lamps."

CHAPTER EIGHTY-FIVE
Mirza

MIRZA FALTERED IN the doorway but received an inelegant shove from behind. Kazimir was waiting. He wore a blood-red robe similar in style to her own, but belted, presumably for modesty, as she could see bare feet and ankles. The room was draped with rich tapestries, but the floor was tiled with stone slabs, carefully jointed and polished to a smooth surface. On them, in something dried and suspiciously dark, was a large circle and a five-pointed star inscribed with symbols she neither knew nor understood. They gave her ants.

There was the sickly sweet scent of incense and beneath it something more earthy, hops and barley and the salt-iron tang of . . . blood. Her own blood called out to her.

In the center of the markings stood a bed with head and foot board of plain hazel wood. Hazel, the bringer of change. On a table by its head were two turned wooden goblets and a slim-bladed knife.

If only she could reach the knife, she might avoid what was to come.

She lunged forward, but it was as if the air around the table turned solid. Kazimir watched with amusement.

"I told you I am protected. Come, don't make this difficult. Think of it as your wedding night. I have no wish to take your maidenhead unwilling, but I will if I have to. Am I so repulsive?"

"Your looks have nothing to do with it, but as for taking my maidenhead, you're too late."

"You lie."

"No, but I have lain." She allowed herself a smirk to irritate him. "He had a kok bigger than yours and knew how to please a woman."

"My kok is big enough, and I have no need to please you."

Good, she was getting to him. She didn't know what good it might do, but if she could only keep him off balance he might make a mistake.

Kazimir took one goblet, full to the brim with a rich dark beer, and held it out. The cup was birchwood—for wealth, and the achieving of goals, for exerting willpower and with an affinity for fire, but it was a wood that could quickly lead to rash impulse. It lacked the steady balance of oak. She didn't think he'd chosen well.

He reached across and checked the silver collar tight about her throat, then let his fingers brush over the hideous squashed-raspberry mark on her face.

"Drink," he said.

She ignored the goblet. "Aren't you afraid that if you take my power, you'll also take my mark? It wasn't always like this, you know. It grew when I used my fire to kill a man. You asked me why I killed him. He came at me with his kok, ready to pierce me through with it. My fire answered the call. He burned. Oh, it wasn't a clean burning. His screams . . . Terrible. Do you know which part of him burned first?"

Kazimir didn't answer.

"Guess."

She thought she might be winning the war of words.

"Since then I have not lain with a man, for fear that in my passion I might burn him from the inside out. Do you think you have the skill to ignite my passion, Kazimir? Do you think you are protected enough to try?"

"Drink!" He pushed the goblet against her lips, maybe to shut her up. She thought that her words had started him thinking.

The beer smelled heavy and heady with the sweet perfume of malt and an underlying burned caramel, while the hops added a spicy, lemony note. Her stomach, empty since yesterday, growled. Even if it had been straightforward beer, she would have refused it, but that cup contained more.

She shook her head, lips tight.

"But I insist."

At his nod, her invisible guards twisted her arms behind her back, pulled back her head, forced open her jaw, and poured beer into her mouth until it was swallow or choke. She managed to spill a lot of it over the expensive white robe, but enough went down her throat. Almost immediately her head began to spin. She realized that the position she was in had allowed her robe to fall open.

Kazimir stepped toward her and slid his right hand, the one with the regular number of fingers, beneath the fur and traced the salamander scar. This close he smelled of sandalwood and musk. Fire flooded her belly, but it was neither passion nor *her* fire coming to call, it was whatever had been in that wretched brew.

She staggered. The invisible guards held her upright. It was the work of a moment for Kazimir to unclasp her robe and let it fall open. He threw off his own and kicked it to the side. His pale skin carried old white scars of scourging and newer livid lines, too, barely healed weals and cuts. Mirza concentrated on his proud kok, and drew on her memory of the bandit in the Tevecor Reaches. She needed to flame Kazimir now.

Kazimir drew his fingers over her salamander scar time and time again, as if by memorizing it he could learn its magic.

He held out his right hand. A slim-bladed knife flew from the table and landed handle first in his palm. Mirza saw a shimmer of red. One of his corrupted High Guards, no doubt.

"Hold her steady, boys," he said. "I thought we could do this with sex, but maybe not. It will have to be blood, then."

He jabbed the point of his knife into the hollow at the base of her throat, just far enough to let the blood flow. Far enough to hurt, but apart from a gasp of surprise, she didn't cry out.

He reached out with his left hand and one of his invisible guards held a goblet. He dipped the first two fingers of his left hand into it. Blood. Her blood?

"My blood to your blood," he said and daubed a line down her body from her chin to her mound, and then another down his own from throat to kok, and for good measure slathered the remainder over his genitals.

Options. She must have options.

This was it. Let him come at her with his proud kok, and she would burn him. That's what her magic did.

Please let that happen.

Now.

Please . . .

Nothing.

Was it the drugged beer or the band around her neck? Why didn't the fire protect her now?

Sick and dizzy, she flopped against her two invisible guards. It was as if the glow in her belly sucked heat from her scar. A deadly stillness wrapped her, body and mind.

Think!

She recalled the fire.

She drew on the nature of steel, the heat of the forge, hot as the sun in the sky, until she could smell the sulfur of burning coals.

The silver band around her throat squeezed. Gasping, she let the flames die back. She wanted to retch.

"Not yet. Not yet," Kazimir murmured. "I will have your fire, but only when it's time."

He began to chant.

"*Per permixtionem sanguinum nostrorum.* By the mingling of our bloods." The collar held her in thrall and she stared in horrified fascination. The knife dipped quickly and he sliced a shallow cut down the middle of her salamander scar. She winced as the blade bit, but she couldn't move. Then he made a shallow cut above his own recent salamander, tossed aside the knife, and bent to her body, touching wound to wound.

"*Sanguis meum ad sanguinem tuum.* My blood to your blood."

"*Sanguis tuum ad sanguinem meum.* Your blood to my blood."

His words became more impassioned.

At the back of her mind something beat at the bars of her cage with bleeding fists. That was it. She needed to let that panic sweep through her, otherwise she'd never be able to draw on fire. She tried to use the memory of the bandit in the Tevecor Reaches.

Let the fire come . . . Now.

Now!

But it didn't answer her call.

She sucked in a breath and waited . . .

And waited . . .

Nothing.

She was out of options.

If she'd thought she was beyond struggling and fighting back, she suddenly found that she wasn't. She twisted and turned, trying to get her knee close enough to that ghastly bloody kok to do some damage. Her heart pounded and her breath came in shallow frightened gasps. She forced him back, caused him to twist away from her jabbing knee and to break the rhythm of his chanting, but he whispered a word and her collar tightened again.

Kazimir pushed his body up against hers and he grasped her in a fierce hug. She stamped on his feet. He swore and squeezed her tighter. She could feel the stiffness of his kok jumping against her belly.

"*Per contactum corporum nostrorum omnia tua ligo.*" His voice was a throaty whisper. "By the contact of our bodies I bind all that which is yours."

She felt every fiber of her body buzz, as if a layer of her soul was being peeled away with a knife.

He was stealing her soul, her power.

She had only one chance left. One option.

Take what's happening and use it.

His own magic was so different from hers. Mixing the two magics in one body should not be possible.

Let him have it, but on her terms, not his.

She was dead either way, but at least she might save Valdas, Lind, the queen, her baby, and Zavonia. It was a small price to pay.

With his lips close to her ear Kazimir continued the unholy chant. *"Per contactum corporum nostrorum omnia tua ligo."*

She wanted to retch, to struggle, to hit out, scratch, bite, anything, but she let her body go limp and concentrated on keeping her soul together, using the patterns of her life to hold on to that which was hers. Think of Boldo, of her wagon, the Bakaishans, the endless plains of grass, her pony. Think of Tsura and Stasha Hetman. Think of her apprenticeship with Luludja, her duel with Esmaralda. She was not powerless. She knew what to do.

She must hold her power back. Hold back and build a dam, so that he couldn't draw the magic out of her slowly. It had to be a surge.

Everything at once.

Overwhelm him.

He continued chanting, his words coming out in gasps. Words in a language she didn't recognize.

And then she felt it.

On top of a welter of physical sensations the salamander scar flared white hot. The fire that had been hers was ready to leave her.

A shriek rent the air—hers.

Now!

"Per contactum corporum nostrorum omnia tua ligo."

The third time was the charm. She fell into that quiet place inside herself that could still reason. Instead of holding back her magic, she gathered it together, hot and strong. Gathered it. Held it. Held it. Held it . . . and . . .

Released.

The dam broke.

She channeled everything she had into the salamander and thrust with all the power she had.

Her throat ached with unvoiced screams.

Kazimir gasped and she felt him shudder as he grasped her power and sucked it into himself through his own salamander.

This was it.

If he couldn't hold it she'd be in the middle of a conflagration within seconds. She screwed up her eyes and turned her face away.

"Don't turn away, woman. Look at me. Am I not the most powerful wizard in the land? What a marriage of powers this is! I can feel it! I can feel it!"

He stepped back and spread his arms wide. Naked and bloody he glowed with power, every inch of him the scion of a king. But the weakness that shook Mirza's limbs told her exactly who this man was. He was a thief twice over, a murderer and a usurper.

The power should kill him.

Why wasn't he dead?

Why wasn't he burning?

She'd failed. How could he hold both magics in one body and live? A bitter bile rose in her throat. It had been her last chance and she'd failed. She'd unleashed her magic into him, exactly as he wanted. Her last mistake.

His eyes shone with fire.

She didn't think he was entirely human anymore.

"I thank you for your gift. Now it's time to test it." He raised both hands above his head as if gathering flames between them. This was it. She waited for the fire to envelop her, desperately wishing she hadn't let her friends down.

CHAPTER EIGHTY-SIX

Lind

LIND FOLLOWED VALDAS down narrow stone spiral steps
built into the thickness of the palace walls until he guessed they
were well below ground level. Piotr and Pawel Hecht were close behind, followed by more nameless hussars, two of them carrying lamps
from the king's suite. Valdas ignored several branching corridors at
the foot of the steps and led them to one blocked by a heavy oak door.

"Can you open this?" Valdas asked.

"Probably. Move over. Give me room to work. Bring a light up close."
Lind bent to the lock and inserted a probe, then a second one, feeling
for the mechanism. It yielded more to force than finesse, and soon they
were all through, and running along a tunnel carved through solid rock
and floored with level sand. At the other end was another door. He
knelt and reached once more for his lockpicks.

"Good man. I'd have had to chop through it with an ax." Valdas
stood close behind, almost jittering from one foot to the other.

The lock yielded as before and they rushed through, straight into
four of the Chancellor's Own. Still putting his lockpick in his belt
pouch, Lind would have taken the first blade had it not been for Piotr,
who blocked it.

"Thanks. I owe you."

"You owe me twice." Piotr parried high, opening up the guard's
middle for Lind's deadly knife. "I remember your face from the Bell,
a marathon drinking session maybe a month ago. You listened when
we talked about Captain Zalecki and never turned up at the barracks
to enlist as a hussar."

The guard fell to the floor and they stepped over him.

"It's a long story."

"I order you to live to tell the tale." Piotr grinned.

A shout ahead announced more of the Chancellor's Own, but the eight of them had made short work of the first four, and with Valdas in the lead—exactly where he liked to be—they all ran forward.

Six guards were almost as easily dealt with, except they lost one of their own men to a blade across the throat. Piotr's brother Pawel hesitated over the downed man, but Piotr grabbed his elbow and pulled him away.

Ahead was a door, but shining a lantern through it showed nothing but an empty cell. They passed three more before the corridor branched.

"Kristina, it's Li . . . Ludwik Balinski. Where are you?"

They listened intently but heard no reply.

"So much for the element of surprise, then," Pawel growled.

"A bit late for that, I think," Valdas said. "Besides, how many guards does Kazimir have down here? How many in the Chancellor's Own?"

"Um . . . sixty," Piotr said.

"Shit, way more than the High Guard, then."

"Way more—though not as good." Piotr grinned.

"Four in the king's chambers, ten here, so far. Even with half of them on duty at any given time we've dealt with fourteen. There should be at least another four up on ground level at the doors of the old keep." Valdas counted them off. "No more than another twelve down here and seven of us. Not bad odds."

"And Kazimir himself," Lind said.

"I was trying not to think about him or what he might be able to do."

"We need to split up. Search for both women at once," Lind said.

"Splitting up is about the most stupid thing we could do," Valdas said.

"Second stupidest." Lind scowled. "Being here is the most stupid."

"Fair point. Split up. Still got your flintlock?"

Lind touched the pistol at his belt.

"Fire it if you get into trouble or if you find them both, of course."

"What about you?"

"Such touching concern."

"My pistol's primed," Pawel said. "We can do the same."

They split into two groups. Lind, Piotr, and a heavyset young man, introduced hurriedly as Cyril, watched the other four continue straight along the corridor before picking one of the side corridors to start the search.

Three side corridors later, Lind shouted again and this time was rewarded by a faint cry and a man's voice cursing. They came round a corner to find themselves face-to-face with two guards.

"Molnek." Piotr obviously knew one of them. "Save your own life. The chancellor's discredited. The Chancellor's Own disbanded. Put up your blades and we'll not harm you."

Molnek didn't reply. He drew steel and stood ready to defend the door. Three against two.

The odds were not in favor of the guards, but they launched themselves at the intruders with wild abandon, not hesitating when they took small injuries. Piotr took down the nameless guard while Lind and Cyril got in each other's way in the narrow corridor, facing Molnek. In the light of the corridor sconce Lind could see the man's eyes, pupils dilated with magic or drugs. He stepped to one side and let Cyril take him with efficient economy.

He ran to the door. "Kristina. Kristina."

"Here. I'm in here!"

"Are you hurt?"

"Hurting, but not hurt. They've taken my child."

Lind dropped to his knees by the door lock and set about picking the mechanism.

"Here, look."

Lind turned to see Cyril standing over Molnek's body, and where his sword had sliced through Molnek's uniform mente, a stick doll, like the one on the King's chest, poked through.

"Poxed Devil spells!" Cyril brought his sword down on the stick figure, cleaving it in two and hacking into the dying man beneath it. As the stick man sundered, a rotting flesh stench hit the back of Lind's throat and a small coil of greasy black smoke twined up from the blood of the now dead man.

Cyril went rigid for a second, and when he raised his head, his pupils were dilated. It was the only warning they had as he lunged forward, sweeping his blade sideways and catching the back of Piotr's shoulder, slicing it to the bone.

As Piotr fell, Lind dropped his lockpick and pulled out his sabre, stepping between Piotr and Cyril.

"Cyril. Stand down!"

Piotr was rolling on the floor, cursing, while a series of ever more frantic questions came from the grill of Kristina's door, all basically asking the same thing. "What's happening?"

"Cyril!" Lind tried the command-voice that Valdas used as soon as he wanted to be taken notice of, but either his version of command-voice didn't work, or Cyril was past commands from anyone but the person who set that spell. His eyes were dead. The Cyril who had run and fought solidly by with them wasn't there anymore.

Lind found that while he'd killed many men and a few women anonymously and for money, killing Cyril was far different. The man had been—however briefly—a comrade in arms, and this bastard spell thing wasn't his fault. Cyril was a good swordsman, maybe not great, but competent and strong. Could he injure him and leave him alive or would that be asking for trouble?

As yet the man hadn't remembered that he still held an undischarged flintlock, as did Lind, but he wouldn't use it if doing so called Valdas from his quest to find Mirza. He could deal with this, but he doubted it would be to Cyril's advantage.

Cyril's eyes narrowed and his hand went to the pistol in his belt. In an instant all choices were stripped away. Lind's hand went to his knife and using an underhand throw he hurled it at Cyril. It embedded itself in his throat as the man was still thumbing the doghead back. He fell choking. Lind scrambled forward, thinking to slice across Cyril's throat and end him as mercifully as he could, but he thought about the black smoke and the split doll and decided not to touch the dying man, even to retrieve his own knife, in case the spell was infinitely transferable. It would be over soon enough. It was all he could do.

He turned to find Piotr, his own pistol held in a shaking hand, propped against the corridor wall.

"I hope that's not for me."

Piotr let the pistol drop. "He cut me."

"Yes. Let me see. One moment, mistress, please," he shouted as Kristina's yells increased. "There's a man bleeding here."

He quickly took off his own over-tunic, sliced a sleeve out of it, and wadded it up over the deep gash over Piotr's shoulder blade. "You need to keep pressure on this."

"Right, I'll hold it, shall I?"

"Good to see you've not lost your sense of humor. Lean on the wall. Trap the pad behind you. Don't move."

Piotr didn't answer. He closed his eyes, his face as white as his shirt. Lind cast around on the floor, looking for the lockpick he'd dropped. Finding it kicked partway down the corridor, he went back to Kristina's door.

The queen almost fell into his arms, her eyes wild. "Kazimir has taken my baby boy."

"We'll get him back."

She nodded. "I heard him crying. I'm sure he's close by." Her hands went to her breasts, laced tight beneath her simple *letnik*. There were damp patches where milk was leaking. She was probably not exaggerating about hurting.

"Piotr?" Lind turned to the injured soldier.

"Go, just don't forget to come back for me."

Lind nodded and grabbed Kristina's wrist as she rushed past him. "There are things . . . people . . . here, mistress, who are not right, not rational in the head. Don't trust anyone."

"Not even you, my loyal assassin?"

He shook his head and pulled out his flintlock. "You know how to use this?"

She nodded.

"It's primed. If I . . . change . . . if you believe me to be a threat . . . don't hesitate. That dead man back there was one of us until some foul magic of Kazimir's touched him."

She looked at him steadily.

"I mean it," he said. "One shot will bring help. You know Captain Zalecki?"

"I thought him dead with the rest of the High Guard."

"He's here and he's loyal to you and your child. I doubt even Kazimir's magic will turn Valdas Zalecki, he's got a heart as big as a bucket. He's gone to look for Mirza."

"The witch with the . . ." She gestured to her own face.

"You saw her?"

"She told me you'd come. I thought she was mad, yet who else but you could have told her that we spent those few days together?"

Lind led the way down the corridor. "Maksimilian is standing by at the Wharf Tavern with a river raft and horses in case we need to get out fast. Hush."

He made Kristina hold back until he checked each turn and junction for safety. She pointed to a corridor in the direction he'd come from, but he shook his head. He'd already checked that when he was looking for her. He pointed ahead instead.

He put out his hand and eased himself toward a junction in the stone-walled corridor, peeking round quickly and snapping back out of sight. He put up two fingers and mouthed, "Two guards."

She nodded and half raised her pistol. He shook his head and put out a hand to stop her.

She tapped his elbow and put her lips close to his ear. "Get ready."

He frowned briefly, but she stepped from the corridor's opening and began to sing a simple lullaby, her voice sweet and clear.

He pulled another knife from his boot, tucked in behind the corner of the wall, and waited. Sure enough, the sound of footsteps came toward him, only one set. Good. That meant they were curious, but not alarmed. As the guard stepped past his position, Lind reached forward, grabbed him from behind, and drove his knife between his ribs and into his heart. He eased the body down quietly and stepped right away from it.

Kristina's song faltered. He heard her gag, but she recovered herself, wiped her eyes and her mouth with the back of her hand, and began to sing again, her voice trembling now.

"Hey?" The remaining guard called for his partner, but he made no attempt to leave his post. "What's happening?"

Somewhere close by, probably in the room behind the last guard, a baby began to wail. Holding her pistol behind her skirts, Kristina stepped out into the corridor. Lind tried to grab her, but she was too quick for him.

"Your friend's been called away by Chancellor Kazimir, my betrothed. Did you know it's the wedding tomorrow? I'm allowed to have my baby back tonight."

"I've had no orders concerning that."

Nice try, Kristina, but it wasn't going to work. Lind heard the dog-head of a flintlock pistol being pulled back. God's ballocks! He stepped out into the corridor, his own pistol held away from him as if he were surrendering.

"No need for rash actions, my friend. The king sent us. Chancellor Kazimir is discredited, the Chancellor's Own disbanded." He kept talking, low and even, while he walked steadily forward to catch up with Kristina, all the time seeing the telltale darkness in the guard's eyes. "If you wish to save yourself, put down your pistol now. We mean you no harm. This lady is your rightful queen and the babe your rightful king."

A brief look of confusion crossed the guard's face, but he started to sight down the barrel of the pistol. Three quick steps and Lind stepped in front of Kristina and put his arm out so she couldn't run past him. The guard's finger tightened on the trigger.

CHAPTER EIGHTY-SEVEN
Valdas

VALDAS JOGGED ALONG the dank stone corridor. Pawel Hecht and the two hussars, Iwo and Michal, ran behind him, sabres at the ready. It was good to be doing what he was good at for a change. He wasn't good at waiting; he despised politics, but give him three feet of sharpened steel, hussars at his back, and he was the man for the job.

"Steady." Valdas held up his left hand and slowed them all down. The maze of corridors began to twist more from here on, and he didn't want to run full tilt into trouble. He swept his arm across. "Fan out, stay ready."

The rattle of metal ahead and the definite snick of a sword being drawn told them that they were about to have company. In case the guards ahead hadn't heard them yet, Valdas motioned the others to be still and silent and crept to the corner of the corridor, kneeling and risking a quick glance with his head low to the floor.

Nothing.

He stood up. "I could have sworn I heard . . ."

Iwo screamed as something slashed his sabre arm from his torso. For a moment he stood frozen into position, then he juddered as if he'd been run through. For a split second, the hilt of a sabre projected from the front of his mente, then vanished. Bright blood blossomed on his chest. He choked and blood trickled from his mouth. Like a puppet whose strings have been cut, he folded to the floor.

His attacker, whoever it was, whatever it was, was nowhere to be seen.

Vanished, said Valdas's rational mind.

Invisible, said his imagination.

Ghost, said his guts.

Michal took one step toward Iwo, but Pawel yanked him back. "It's a haunt!" His voice came out squeaky.

"Back to back," Valdas snapped, and they formed up, sabres at the ready, facing outward.

"Did you see it?" Pawel asked.

"S-see what?" Michal could barely keep his voice steady. They revolved steadily, moving round sideways, one step at a time, gradually wheeling clockwise.

"I saw a sabre," Valdas said. "Only for a second."

"I saw nothing," Michal said. "Mother of God, these dungeons are supposed to be haunted by the ghosts from before the first Konstantyn's time. Do you think—"

"It was a much more recent haunt," Pawel said. "I recognized it. It was Eberhard Brunner. The High Guard has come back to haunt us."

"But why would the High Guard want to kill hussars?" Michal asked.

"Brunner. Are you sure?" Valdas's guts felt frozen. He took another sideways step, gradually wheeling them away from the remains of the unfortunate Iwo, progressing down the corridor, slowly but surely. He didn't believe in ghosts, but a man's blood was soaking between the flagstones and *something* had killed him. "Brunner was one of my boys, a good swordsman and honorable. Tell me why he would wish to return from the grave and harm old comrades? It makes no sense."

"My grandmother saw ghosts and it seems I have her gift," Pawel said. "I don't know why the dead wish to harm the living. Maybe because we are still living."

"Th-they are not in their graves," Michal said. "The High Guard, I mean. They were never buried. Their bodies were burned and their heads were . . ."

"On pikes, I know. Mine should have been with them. Maybe it's me he's after."

The sound of steel being drawn was the only warning they had. Valdas felt the swish of air that precedes a sabre cut and parried high without thinking. The clash of steel on steel jarred his arm all the way to his elbow. He swept his blade low and diverted a cut on the return. Michal yelped and grabbed his thigh with one hand while randomly swiping his blade in front of him with the other. Blood oozed between his fingers.

"I see him," Pawel yelled. "Get behind me. I can see to fight him." He broke formation and stepped forward, sabre held en garde.

"Don't be stupid, Pawel. You might be able to see him, but you can't kill a dead man. Get back here."

But Pawel was fighting for his life. Valdas thought he could see the occasional flash of metal as the ghost sabre struck sparks off Pawel's blade.

"Aieee!"

Beside him Michal dropped to the ground, his other leg spurting blood from the knee. Valdas whirled to face another of the damn things. Were they really his boys, returned to claim their revenge on their commander who'd let them die alone?

"Pawel! Who?"

Pawel whirled away from his ghostly opponent and glanced up quickly. "You're fighting Brunner. I've got Smetona." He turned to the ghost and stabbed forward with his sabre. "I've killed him twice. It doesn't stick."

Brunner. Valdas parried again, guessing where the sabre would swing next and luckily guessing right. He had fought Eberhard Brunner many times in training sessions. He was a good man, handy with a sabre or a knife. He'd married a girl from the palace kitchens last Christmastide. They'd got a baby girl. Yes, he could understand why Brunner was jealous of the living, but the Brunner he knew would not have taken revenge in such a way.

"Brunner! Ten-SHUN!" Valdas tried his parade ground voice, but Brunner didn't seem to hear.

Valdas stopped trying to see what was happening and let his hearing and his senses work for him. Fighting blind wasn't an exercise he'd ever enjoyed, but the armsmaster had insisted on it, though with wooden sticks, not with blades. He sensed the next blow and parried it, and the next, fighting defensively. There didn't seem to be much sense in offense since their revenant spirits couldn't be killed again.

His next parry was clumsy and the feather of the ghost blade ripped his sleeve and sliced a long shallow cut into the muscle of his left forearm. He cursed. "What do you want, Brunner? Show yourself. This isn't an honorable way to fight. Where are your manners, man?" He kept his voice light, wondering what, if anything, might make a difference. "You were never a coward in life!"

That seemed to do the trick. All of a sudden he could see the red haze of a uniform mente and the flash of ghostly steel. Now he knew what he was fighting.

Blood soaked into his sleeve and he felt that curious numbness that radiates from the shock of a battle wound. Fighting it down, he whirled under a ghostly thrust and slashed his own sabre across Brunner's belly. The blade bit deep, but without any of the resistance of a blade cleaving through meat, and no let-up in Brunner's attack.

With a sickening feeling, Valdas knew that it could only end one way. It wouldn't end yet, but eventually he would tire and Brunner would lay him open to the bone.

CHAPTER EIGHTY-EIGHT
Mirza

KAZIMIR'S HANDS WERE poised, fire at the ready. This was it. Mirza saw the power coursing through his body and knew the flames would envelop her within seconds. She wanted to beg, to weep, to plead, but it wouldn't do any good. He'd won. She should welcome the long dark.

She'd walked the spirit world before, but always in the knowledge that she could return. This time there would be no coming back.

She'd led people over, but now that it was her turn, something inside her said nothing was worse than death. While she had breath in her body, she needed to keep fighting, because Kazimir must not be allowed to keep what he'd stolen.

The invisible guards who had pinned her were still holding on. Mirza leaned into them, brought both feet up and kicked out. She caught Kazimir in the gut and hurled him backward onto the markings on the floor.

She shook off the guards at last and pulled the white robe around herself to cover the blood smeared down her body. She reached deep into her soul, searching for any remnants of power that he'd left her.

Nothing. She was drained dry.

Kazimir leaped to his feet, gathering fire into his hands.

She felt the heat in her body rising. Sweat ran down her naked skin. The sliced skin above her scar flared unbearably hot beneath the clotting blood, hers and Kazimir's. She clenched her teeth, determined not to give him the satisfaction of dying screaming.

The salamander scar sprang from her skin, whole, and hovered before her, etched blood-red in the air.

Kazimir's hands faltered and shook. He flung them in front of his face as if to ward off a threat. His hair began to singe.

With a whoosh and a whump of acrid air as solid as a wall, his whole body burst into flames. His unholy screech battered her ears. She wanted to fall to her knees, but she couldn't take her eyes off him as his flesh blistered, his lips charred back against long, uneven teeth, and his eyeballs burst. She didn't know what kept him standing, but it was an age before his body collapsed in on itself and he shriveled down to the stone-flagged floor. Only then did she fall backward against the bed, and retch up the foul drugged beer until she had no more retching in her.

CHAPTER EIGHTY-NINE

Lind

LIND SAW THE guard's finger tighten on the trigger. Behind him
he heard Kristina whimper and behind the door a baby wailed.

This was it. The end. It hadn't been much of a life, had it?

An inhuman shriek echoed down the corridor, ricocheting off the
walls and freezing the tableau. Lind's spine felt as if someone had
rubbed ice down it. In this place it was almost impossible to tell where
it had come from.

The guard's eyes rolled up in his head and he dropped boneless to
the floor. The pistol discharged the ball into the ceiling with a crack
that made both Lind and Kristina cringe. Inside the room baby wails
turned to howls.

Kristina ran past him and pushed open the door. By the time Lind
got to the threshold, she was reaching into a wooden cradle for a noisy
bundle, alternately laughing and crying to herself. A woman lay unconscious on the floor, fainted away, her blouse open low and the top
of a stick figure showing between ample breasts, rising and falling
with each breath. Lind bent over to look. This little doll was different.
Whereas the last one he saw had seemed ringed around with power,
this one was nothing but a bundle of dirty sticks and twine.

Had Valdas succeeded? Was the sorcerer defeated? Dead?

"Don't stand there, help me!" Kristina dragged his attention away
from the woman. One-handed, she was trying to undo the lace on her
tight corset.

"Here." He was too wise to offer to hold the squalling baby. Kristina would never let him go. Instead he sliced through the lace that
had become knotted, and loosed the corset at the top. He guided her
to the stool and eased her down. As she pulled one ripe breast from

the top of the loose neck of the letnik, milk was already beading on the rosy nipple. The baby latched on and began to suck, then let go, letting fine jets of milk squirt in three different directions. Kristina laughed, held the baby close, and pushed the nipple back into his mouth, whereupon his cries ceased as he fastened on. Kristina rocked, her face blissful, but she was dangerously near to collapse. Lind moved to stand behind her, supporting her against his belly and pulling her loose hair away from her face.

After a few minutes she swapped the baby to the other tortured breast, gasping as his gums clamped on and he began to suck.

"Thank you, Ludwik." She patted the hand, which he'd not moved from her shoulder.

In that moment he fell in love, not with the queen, but with motherhood. This was how a parent should feel for a child, and nothing on God's good earth should ever threaten that circle of protection. Life was hard, parents died, but always there should be someone to take on that mantle of trust, to protect the little being until it could protect itself.

His own mother had trusted Lorcan and he'd let her down. Tourmine should have protected his apprentices; instead he preyed upon them and corrupted them. Well, here was one of Tourmine's apprentices who would stand and say, *no more.*

He almost felt giddy with relief. He'd found the man inside. Tourmine was his past. The little king was his future, if the queen would allow it.

He squeezed her shoulder in reassurance. "There is nothing to thank me for, Majesty. I think it might be what any decent man would have done."

"Are you a decent man, Ludwik?"

Was he? He could try to be.

"I wasn't, Majesty, but I am now. I'll serve you and the little king faithfully, if you'll have me."

"Ludwik Balinski, kneel and pledge yourself to my service and let all your previous crimes be expunged."

Heart light, he knelt.

CHAPTER NINETY

Valdas

VALDAS TWISTED AWAY from Brunner's blade. He almost fell over Michal, who was stretched out on the flagstones. He lost his balance and staggered into Pawel. Only the ghostly Brunner was visible to him, and then only as a haze. Brunner came in for a high attack, Valdas's sabre was low. This was it.

As the blade swished toward his shoulder he heard a mortal scream. The blow never landed. Brunner faded to nothing. By his side, Pawel leaned on his sword as if it were a walking cane, panting heavily. Michal groaned and rolled over, trying to get up. Pawel offered his arm and pulled him to his feet.

Valdas smelled smoke on the air and heard another scream.

"No. No. No! Mirza!" He began to run toward the sound, Pawel close behind. He almost tripped over four unconscious guardsmen as they rounded a corner.

"Michal, take their weapons and secure them. Stay here and try not to bleed to death." Valdas barely broke his stride.

A pall of smoke hung in the air outside a heavy oak door. Two more guardsmen lay unconscious.

"Careful." He held up a hand to slow down Pawel and pushed the door open cautiously. Beyond the first room, flames filled the whole suite with the stench of burning hair and . . . skin and meat. He choked down his gorge. Huddled on the stone floor in the second room was a blackened, twisted corpse.

"Pawel!" Coughing and spluttering on the smoke, his eyes stinging, he grabbed a small rug and began to beat out the flames. Pawel joined him, and when the grisly thing was nothing but a smoldering mass, he went to fetch water to damp it down.

"Tell him he'll find a bathhouse down the corridor."

Blinking through smoke-gritted eyelashes and wiping tears and snot from his face with the back of his hand, Valdas looked across to where the voice had come from. The bed was miraculously untouched by the fire, and sitting against it, white robe clutched around her, covered in blood, was Mirza.

"Mirza!" He started toward her to scoop her up and hug her tight, but she scrambled to her feet. As she turned toward him, Valdas could see that her face, for so long marred by the squashed-fruit birthmark, was now completely clear. Left and right sides matching, skin smooth and golden. Even through the tear streaks her beauty was breathtaking, but her body shook all over.

He didn't want to look into her eyes, but he forced himself anyway, only to find she was staring at a fixed point somewhere beyond the wall behind him. Whatever she was seeing had nothing to do with the sudden arrival of help.

"Mirza." He stepped forward, arms outstretched.

Her right hand shot out toward him, palm out, fingers splayed, not only a stop gesture but a *take that, you bastard!* Her robe fell to the floor. She stood naked and defiant, the salamander scar glowing red, poised to flame any man who came too close. Any man.

"Kazimir is dead!" Mirza said.

Valdas faltered and stopped, resisting an urge to clutch his crotch in self-defense. It hadn't done Kazimir any good. His naked body was now just so much burned meat.

"Mirza, it's me, Valdas. You're safe now. It's over."

"Valdas? Oh . . ."

Recognition dawned in her eyes. She slipped to the floor, almost gracefully, and passed out.

He checked her heart was beating steadily, turned her sideways to ease her breathing, and covered her over with the bloodied robe. He let his fingers brush the side of her face that had been so strangely marked and now was not. What had happened here?

"I found the bath house." Pawel came in with two buckets and they damped down Kazimir's body so that it wouldn't smolder dangerously. Kazimir was dead; no need to continue to cook him.

Between them they laid the contorted body straight before the rigors of death set him in such an ugly position. Valdas wondered what had happened, but said nothing. The bandit Mirza had burned in the Tevecor Reaches had burned away to ash. This was a much dirtier immolation. Still, he couldn't fault her for it.

"What's that stench? Oh! Is he dead?" Queen Kristina, carrying a bundle carefully in the crook of her arm, entered closely, followed by Lind, covered in blood that was probably not his own.

"Very." Valdas pulled a blanket from the bed and dropped it over the ex-sorcerer.

"Good."

"Is that . . . ?" Valdas leaned toward the bundle.

The queen turned slightly so that he could see the child, not sleeping peacefully, but wide awake and staring round him.

"Konstantyn's son," she said. "Bazyli."

It meant king.

"Your Majesty." Valdas dropped to one knee before his liege and bowed his head.

"Where's Piotr . . . and Cyril?" Pawel asked, a tinge of alarm creeping into his voice.

"Piotr's injured," Lind said. "Not badly, don't worry—at least not fatally, though he's lost blood and needs a surgeon. Cyril's dead. I'm sorry. You seem to be short a few men, yourselves."

"Iwo's dead, Michal injured." Valdas still barely knew how to describe what they'd had to fight. "Majesty, with your permission, we should go to the king's chambers while we can. The Guard will be down soon and there's nothing more we can do here. We'll collect Piotr and Michal on the way."

While she was still unconscious, Valdas scooped up Mirza in his arms.

It was a tired but triumphant little procession that made its way up to the king's chamber via the spiral stair. Valdas carried Mirza every step of the way, though Lind offered to share the duty. Pawel supported Piotr, and Lind ended up half-carrying Michal up the last few steps.

They emerged into the king's chamber to find Tomas's hussars holding off an assortment of courtiers in the hallway while Tomas and Sulislaw, the grizzled duty officer, watched the king's physician bending over the still form of Gerhard.

Tomas stepped forward to take Mirza, but when Valdas shook his head, he moved cushions on the king's daybed and stood aside while Valdas set her down.

Sulislaw kept his face impassive. It had only been minutes since he'd been admitted, and he didn't yet know what to make of it all, so he nodded cautiously at the man on the top of his most-wanted criminals list.

"How is Lord Gerhard?" Valdas didn't refer to him as the king.

"He'll survive, I think," Tomas answered. "He went from that awful spellshocked state to plain unconsciousness and then woke a few minutes ago. He says Kazimir is the old king's bastard, Konstantyn's older half brother. Now he's drifted off again. The physician's pretending he knows what he's doing, but he hasn't a clue."

"I heard that, young man." The physician looked up. "It's his heart, it's not regular. He needs rest."

"Will that cure him?"

"Sadly, no, though it might prolong his life for a year or two."

"We need help here," Pawel said as Piotr collapsed onto the floor.

"See to the wounded, doctor. I'm not dead yet." Gerhard's voice, weak but clear, came from the bed.

"But, sire . . ."

Gerhard waved him off and sat up against his pillows, face gray, but eyes clear. "M'lady." He gave Kristina as much of a bow as he could in a clean nightshirt and from behind a fresh down-filled comforter. His eyes strayed to the bundle in her arms. "It's true, is it?"

"Konstantyn's son. The rightful heir," she said.

"Oh, thank God and all His angels for that." The relief on his face was palpable.

On the daybed Mirza began to stir. Valdas sank down onto the floor so his face was on a level with hers.

"Valdas." She began to cry. "I didn't know . . . He was so strong. He took it all. Took it right out of me."

"Hush, love, time to talk about it later. No need now. You're safe."

"You don't underst . . ."

A scuffle behind him and Aniela, five foot two of blond curls, breasts almost popping out above her working clothes, shouldered her way into the room through Tomas's men, dragging an elegant lady by the wrist. As soon as the woman saw the queen, her eyes lit up with a look that Valdas hoped one day to see in the eyes of a woman looking at him.

"Mari!" Kristina rushed into the woman's arms with much weeping and laughing and kissing of cheeks and gabbling. The two of them whirled each other into the corner by the door, eyes for no one else except each other and the baby.

Mirza tried to sit up. Her robe fell away, and Valdas tried to cover her again but stopped when she flinched away. "You don't understand, Valdas. It was my decision. I let him take it all. It was the only way."

Valdas wasn't sure what to say to that. She must feel as though some part of this was her fault, when she was probably the most blameless.

Aniela dropped to her knees and pushed him roughly away. "Later, lover. Much later. Right now it's time for girl-talk." She rearranged Mirza's robe.

"Come with me, sweetheart." She sidestepped Valdas and looked around. "Is that the door to the king's fancy bathhouse?" she asked Tomas.

When he nodded, she glanced at the king in his bed. "Begging Your Honor's pardon, but please order your bathtub filled and buckets of clean water on hand for rinsing—women servants, mind—and keep everyone else out until I say so. Understand?" She glared at him.

"Yes, mistress . . . er . . ."

"Introductions later. Do it quickly. And fresh linen would be good, and a complete outfit . . . skirts and a decent szuba . . . something nice . . . something . . . modest." The last phrase she called over her shoulder as she drew Mirza to the door, clearing their path with a look.

Valdas let them go.

CHAPTER NINETY-ONE

Lind

LIND WALKED SILENTLY along the tiled floor of the upper colonnade and stopped in the middle, the most exposed point. He leaned on the balcony rail, taking in the manicured garden below, the central fountain, the clipped bushes and the bright spots of late-blooming flowers.

This was a part of the palace he'd never seen when delivering fish for the king's supper. How different from the plain stone corridors in the kitchen and store rooms, half hidden below ground. This garden was designed to catch the sun and funnel it for the appreciation of kings and queens, not for the likes of him.

He resisted the temptation to look over his shoulder. He wouldn't normally present his back to all the approaches, but today was different.

It was time.

He heard heavy footsteps approaching.

Valdas. The man didn't know how to walk silently. Lind supposed he'd never had to sneak around a day in his life. Soldiering was such a noisy occupation. Unsubtle.

He didn't look around as Valdas approached and leaned on the rail by his side, elbows almost, but not quite, touching.

"Are you waiting for me?" Valdas asked.

They'd seen each other every day since Saturday, but always at meetings to discuss, and inform, and consider aspects of all that had happened since the whole sorry tale had begun, not on the day Konstantyn was assassinated, but on the day Kazimir, Konstantyn's bastard half brother, had inserted himself into Lord Gerhard Zamoy's household nine years earlier. The story had unfolded slowly and the convolutions of that twisted mind had turned Lind's stomach more than once.

All the time he'd been in and out of the palace, setting up the kill, his employer had been walking these hallowed halls, closer to his victim than Lind had needed to be. Kazimir could have done the job himself, but that wasn't his way. Oh, he'd killed with magic, but always at a distance and always at a cost.

But he'd paid for it.

And Lind had not.

Yet.

"Waiting . . . Yes." Lind drew a deep breath but didn't turn to look at Valdas. "You said after this was all over that you were going to kill me."

"I did, didn't I?"

"I wanted to say that if you still want to go through with that . . . I won't stop you. I've made my peace with the man I used to be."

There was a long pause.

Very long.

Lind could almost hear Valdas thinking.

He kept his eyes on the beauty of the garden. If he had to die here and now, he'd like it to be the last thing he saw. He listened for a snick of a dagger being drawn, or the swoosh as Valdas's sabre left its sheath. He flexed his fingers on the rail, willing his hands to be still. Whatever happened, he would not defend himself.

Death might have come for him anytime during the last fifteen years, and though he never sought it out, he might not have minded. He reflected on recent events. He didn't want to die, not now he had a purpose.

Valdas drew a shuddering breath. "The queen might have something to say about it."

"She'll get over it. She's safe now."

"Do you want to die?"

"No, I don't. Not at all."

A servant approached. "Ludwik Balinski, the queen will see you now in her suite."

Lind nodded.

"Balinski?" Valdas raised one eyebrow.

"It was the name I gave her when we met, and I never told her otherwise."

"I see. This Ludwik Balinski, is he an assassin or an honorable man?"

"Can't a man be both?"

"I don't think he can."

Lind knew what he wanted to be. "He's honorable. He'll never go back on his word."

"Ah," Valdas huffed out a breath. "There's your answer. I wanted to kill Lind, the man who assassinated my king. If I ever meet up with him again, I'll run him through in an eyeblink. But I have no quarrel with Ludwik Balinski, the man who saved my queen."

Lind nodded.

"Don't ever give me reason to change my mind."

"You know I won't."

"I know."

CHAPTER NINETY-TWO
Valdas

A LOT HAD happened in the last three days. The Amber Crown might still sit on Gerhard's head, but he held it for little Bazyli, the Amber Prince—at least for as long as Gerhard lived, which might not be long, according to the physicians who'd attended him since the rescue. His heart had lost its rhythm. It was failing. It might be months or a few years, but Gerhard was dying.

Konstantyn's son would be a child king. His mother would be regent, a good regent, too. Chancellor Skorny had been recalled to court, his illness suddenly cured. The wise old man and the young queen would not only rule well, but they'd raise Bazyli to be the king Konstantyn would have wanted him to be, wise and just, but also clever, and the guardian of his people. God willing, when the child came of age, he would inherit a settled kingdom.

Valdas smoothed his uniform mente and checked his reflection in the glass. This wasn't his room. It wasn't even his uniform, but it would do for now. He ran his fingers over his top lip, wondering whether to grow the mustache again. He quite liked the clean-shaven look.

"Do you have to go, lover?" A sleepy voice from the bed told him Aniela was awake.

"Yes. It's time."

She sat up, blond curls falling chaotically onto ivory breasts. "You know what I think about it all."

Valdas leaned over the bed, pulled down the sheet exposing her rosy nipples, and kissed them one at a time. "I do, and I'll bear it in mind."

"You're sure you won't stay in the palace, take back your old job?"

He shook his head. "Lind will do that better than I ever could.

There isn't anything an assassin could try that he hasn't tried himself. All the time I was guarding the king, the assassin moved freely in and out of the palace, and Konstantyn's worst enemy walked around these halls, facial features half-hidden beneath a beard."

"You couldn't have known."

"I failed. I failed in the worst possible way. I failed my men and I failed my king."

"You rescued the queen and Bazyli. You stayed faithful to Konstantyn."

"Not alone. I was only part of it. Mirza, Dahnay, Lind, Maksimilian, you."

"You held us all together, Valdas. Your strength of purpose never wavered."

He shrugged. "I've been told to be available to see their majesties at noon. I'll find out then what the rest of my life is going to be. I will accept Queen Kristina's judgment, whatever it is. If I go now, I have time to bring Mirza to the palace for that meeting."

"Do you want me to come with you?" Aniela threw off the sheet.

By Perkunas, she was lovely from the top of her head to her delicate toes.

"No, sweet, I'll do this on my own. Cover up or I might change my mind and stay here instead."

She giggled and drew the sheet up to cover her nakedness.

Valdas stalked up the corridor toward the colonnade where he'd met Lind yesterday. *Ludwik Balinski,* he readjusted his thoughts.

He paused and stared out over Konstantyn's gardens, the fountain and six young pear trees Konstantyn had planted himself the year before last. There was the bench where he'd loved to sit with a book in the few quiet moments his life gave him. Would he approve of what they'd done?

Of course he would. He was a practical man and he loved Zavonia. Even he knew that a baby couldn't hold a throne.

There had been a wedding after all. Queen Kristina had married King Gerhard without waiting for the papal dispensation, but with the cardinal's blessing and reassurance that His Holiness would grant one retrospectively. The papacy was more obliging to its remaining loyal monarchs as the danger from Christian reformers was felt ever more strongly.

Gerhard had declared before Cardinal Pieritz and the Lord God Almighty that Bazyli, posthumous son of Konstantyn, second of his name, was his adopted son and legitimate heir to the Amber Crown. That was important. Bazyli's succession was assured.

The queen had made it quite clear that, though she would be queen in public, in private, her affections and her bed would only be shared with Marilena, a discreet arrangement, a secret that her ladies in waiting would guard with their lives, as they had been doing since her marriage to Konstantyn.

Gerhard knew his time was short. He'd pledged to rule with Kristina by his side, equal in all things, though from what Valdas had seen of the little queen, she'd more likely be one pace in front. She'd been trained by Karl Gustav. Sverija was one of the richest trading nations on the Narrow Sea, and the Willenbach political and business acumen was legendary.

He smiled. Her first act as co-ruler had been to remove all taxation on cabbages.

Envoys had already been sent to Ruthenia, Bieloria, and Kassubia, suing for peace. Though it would take more than one envoy to pull Zavonia back from the brink of the war that Kazimir had mistakenly believed would cement his position on the throne, it was not yet too late for talk and trade, and a few concessions to save face.

That wasn't Valdas's job. He was a soldier, not a politician or a courtier. Whatever happened next, his time in the palace was over.

Thankfully, Chancellor Skorny had been ordered to the capital. The grand old man had a good ten or more years of politicking in him yet, God willing.

The country was in safe hands.

Valdas had an hour before the audience with his monarchs; time to go and see Mirza if he was quick.

Stablemaster Vronski smiled. "Good to see you back, Captain Zalecki."

Was he back? Maybe. He'd know after this morning's audience. Until then he was a visitor. Captain Sulislaw didn't know whether to congratulate him or hang him in irons. Vronski, however, was not so reticent. Instead of Donkey, he led out Zuma, Valdas's expensive gray war-horse that he'd thought lost forever.

"Hey, boy, pleased to see me again?" he asked the gray, but Zuma remained remotely polite, while a couple of stalls down, a big soup-plate-sized hoof connected with a wooden door and a ridiculous braying whinny announced that someone didn't want to be ignored.

He left Zuma with Vronski for a moment while he went and fed

Donkey an apple he'd picked out of the feed bin. "Don't worry. The pretty one's only for show. You're my best boy."

Donkey's evil yellow teeth snapped together a whisker away from Valdas's face, and his ears flattened to his coffin-shaped skull.

"I love you too." Valdas pulled Donkey's head down with the headcollar, rubbing his neck until the horse's ears relaxed and lolled sideways again. When he scratched behind them, he almost thought Donkey whickered with pleasure, but it must have been his imagination.

"Make sure you give this old fraud the best of everything, Vronski. He deserves it."

"He's nothing to look at. You don't want me to put him in the pool of available mounts?"

"Never. Ask me when I have more time and I'll tell you how he saved my life."

He mounted Zuma and left the stable yard to Donkey's braying protest.

It only took ten minutes to ride down the steep cobbled slope of the Serpentinas to the Low City, past the Basilica, where Konstantyn lay in peace, and along by the Market Square to Maksimilian's.

Even this early in the morning, the breakfast room was busy as yesterday's all-nighters ate up, paid up, and left, one by one. Mirza wasn't in sight, but Ruta jerked her head toward the stairs.

"How is she?" Valdas asked.

Ruta shrugged. "She'll be better for seeing you, but treat her gently."

"Of course." He'd never do anything else.

CHAPTER NINETY-THREE

Mirza

MIRZA HEARD FOOTSTEPS on the stair and knew it was Valdas, come to see how she was. She'd refused accommodation at the palace, saying that staying anywhere near the Gura made her nervous. She'd kept to the little attic room, resisting all Maksimilian's attempts to persuade her downstairs to eat breakfast and lunch. The girls had been taking it in turns to sit with her, which was kind of them, but she didn't really need their company.

She heard Maksimilian ask, "How's everything up on the Gura?"

"As well as it could be." Valdas's heavy footsteps paused briefly. "Better, in fact. Good. Yes, good."

"Should we be hunkering down ready for a war?"

"Not if Queen Kristina has anything to do with it."

"Don't ever underestimate her." Mirza heard the pride in Maksimilian's voice.

Valdas's footsteps began again.

She sat up in bed as Valdas knocked and opened the door.

"It's only me. I came to see if you were ready to talk yet. I have an audience with Queen Kristina and King Gerhard this morning. You should come with me."

She shook her head. "I'm finished with palaces and kings and queens. I'm going home. Back to the Bakaishans."

"The king and queen want to reward you. They owe you so much."

"They owe me nothing." She swung her legs out of bed and stood up, smoothing her shift. "Look, Valdas, if I tell you everything, you can pass on whatever you see fit. I . . . I don't want to have to explain myself. I feel . . . dirty."

"You can't help what he did to you."

"Men! You think it's all about sex, but it isn't. It's about power. Aniela told me some things, and I figured out the rest for myself. It wasn't about Kazimir's kok. He didn't put anything inside me except drugged beer. In the end, the only power I had was to give him what he wanted in the hope that he wouldn't be able to hold it."

"And in doing so you saved us all."

"Yes, but . . . It's gone, Valdas." She rubbed her face. "I used to hate that old mark. It made me different. It meant I couldn't have some of the things I wanted. It meant I had to do things that I didn't want to do. I could see things I didn't want to see. But it's all gone now, the power, the sight, everything."

"But you're a healer."

"Oh, yes, I know remedies and plants, and I can deliver a baby and bind a broken bone, but I'm no longer a shulam. I've lost my connection to the spirit world. I came to Biela Miasto with you because of Konstantyn's ghost. He called in a debt and told me to come. Well, I did as he asked. His son is set to inherit the Amber Crown when Gerhard dies. The country is safe in Kristina's hands until the boy comes of age. I think all Konstantyn wanted me to do has been done—by others if not by me—but I'll never know because I can't spirit-walk anymore."

She scrubbed her eyes with the heels of both hands. "Konstantyn is lost to me. The souls of your High Guard are lost to me as well. Though I think the ones Kazimir enslaved are free now. Blood magic spells don't survive the death of their maker."

"They were enslaved?"

"Yes."

"I thought . . . I thought they'd come for me because I hadn't died with them."

She sighed. "No, I can tell you that in the spirit world they wished you well. The revenants only did what Kazimir told them to do because he bound them."

She drifted to the window, looking out of the narrow dormer across the city's rooftops. "It's my fault Dahnay died. If I hadn't gone out to scry at a stupid time in a stupid place . . ."

"Hush, don't say that. You knew we would have to ask you to scry. Don't judge yourself harshly with hindsight. None of us knew about Kazimir then."

"I did. I sensed someone dangerous on the Gura. Oh, I didn't know who, and I didn't know why, but it stank of danger. When I found out what he wanted and why he wanted it, I was so scared."

Valdas nodded. "Kazimir was a true viper in the cradle. Old King Aleksander was apparently quite a man for the ladies, though he always acknowledged his bastards—or so everyone thought. The king couldn't acknowledge this one, though, not without angering a very ancient and very rich family of Zavonian Jews. Kazimir's mother is still alive, I believe. Kazimir—named for our most noble first king—was brought up as a good Catholic by a couple who were paid to take him into their family, but he was persistent enough to find out about his real parents, and determined to get his due. He's been working his way ever nearer the throne since the day he first entered Gerhard's household nine years ago. All Queen Cecylia's stillbirths, the death of Konstantyn's younger brother—I don't know how he did it, but it wasn't just luck. Gerhard was supposed to acknowledge Kazimir as King Aleksander's bastard son, and name him heir. Marrying Queen Kristina was the final part of his plan to establish a legitimate claim."

"But why kill Queen Cecylia?" Mirza asked.

"He didn't—at least not directly, though he caused her death right enough. She killed herself. I found the note, but Konstantyn ordered me to keep the knowledge quiet so that she could have a Christian burial. She asked him to find a new queen who could give him sons. Four dead babies and so much resting on the birth of a live heir. When Konstantyn married Kristina, Kazimir had to move quickly before she became pregnant, but he made a mistake when he commissioned Lind to do the killing. Lind's reputation—among those who knew such things—was that he was the best, but not the fastest, because he always set everything up meticulously so he could get in and out again without anyone suspecting him."

Mirza shook her head. "So without ever intending to, Lind saved the situation by taking his time."

Valdas grunted. "I'm still confused in my own mind about how much I owe that crazy assassin. Ex-assassin." He corrected himself. "The only thing that still puzzles me," Valdas said, "is why Kazimir hired an assassin in the first place. His magic had already killed the king's brother and the queen's babies. Why didn't he kill Konstantyn himself?"

"Blood magic is expensive," Mirza said. "Not in money terms, but in pain. It requires sacrifice. Often the sorcerer's own. Blood for small things, a toe or a finger for something larger. The sacrifice for killing a king would have been more than he wanted to bear, a more important body part, a hand, an eye, a foot, or maybe his kok and stones."

Valdas shuddered. "I still don't really understand magic. I hope I never need to again."

"Blood magic is thirsty and it makes its users greedy. They always want more power. That's why Kazimir wanted my fire."

Valdas reached out and gripped her work-hardened hand in his own blunt-fingered one. "You're not still blaming yourself for anything, are you?"

"If I hadn't been here . . ."

"We would have failed. No question. You were the one who defeated him in the end."

"He wanted what he could never have. Blood magic and natural magic don't mix, can't mix."

"And that's why you killed him?"

She shook her head. "I told you before. I didn't kill him; the magic did. He absorbed my power. At that moment I thought I'd misjudged it and created a god. Then he tried to use the power on me and . . ." She put her hand to her breast. "The salamander that was supposed to stop me from hurting others protected me. The fire rebounded on him. I had nothing to do with it."

"You had everything to do with it. The queen is in your debt. Mirza, you saved Zavonia, single-handed. Kristina isn't going to forget that."

She shrugged. "I'm still going home."

"You shouldn't travel alone. I'll come with you."

He would, too, if she'd let him. If she took him home with her it would be hard to let him go, but the world, or rather the queen, must have other plans for Valdas Zalecki.

The Basilica bell tolled and he looked up in alarm. "Time to go if I'm not going to keep their majesties waiting."

He dropped a kiss on Mirza's head. She tried not to flinch away, but she wasn't the same woman who'd seduced him in that faraway barn. Or had he seduced her? It had been mutual, she thought. The best kind of seduction.

"Go to your meeting, Valdas. You don't need to prove anything to me. Aniela, me, Dahnay. We've been the three most important women in your life for the last few months. You love us all, Dahnay none the less for her being dead. I know you care, and I love you for it, but it's time to part."

CHAPTER NINETY-FOUR
Valdas

"CAPTAIN ZALECKI, THEIR majesties will see you now." Valdas's foot had hardly hit the top step of the stair to the colonnade when Arofski, the same quiet servant who'd spirited Lind away yesterday, appeared at his elbow. He followed the man to the small state room where Queen Kristina and King Gerhard waited among the trappings of their office.

Chancellor Skorny, attended by his daughter, Danute, sat to one side below the dais.

Valdas bowed low, going down onto one knee and smiling to himself to see that matching thrones, equal in every way, had replaced Konstantyn's lonely seat.

"Rise, Captain Zalecki." It was Kristina who spoke.

As he rose he managed to lock a fleeting glance with Chancellor Skorny. The old man winked. It was good to see him back. The queen would need his solid political acumen, though from what Valdas had already seen, she had a significant ability in that direction already. It seemed likely that she'd be as enlightened and forward thinking as Konstantyn had been.

Gerhard dismissed Arofski and the bevy of servants and minor officials with a wave of one hand, all except for Skorny, his daughter Danute, and Lind, who stood behind the queen's throne.

"We have now pieced together the whys and wherefores of this whole sorry incident," Queen Kristina said. "I'm pleased to say we have decided to put it behind us and move forward with our lives for the good of all Zavonia, but we wish to reward those who have served us."

Valdas hadn't been seeking a reward. He felt that he'd barely redeemed himself. He certainly didn't want his old job back.

The queen smiled as though she knew what he was thinking. She indicated Lind. "Ludwik Balinski is my new protector. Responsible for my person and that of Bazyli, and King Gerhard, of course." She added Gerhard almost as an afterthought. "There will be no more High Guard, but there will be the Queen's Own—persons we trust."

Lind half-bowed in acknowledgment and raised an eyebrow as if to say, *I didn't expect this.*

Valdas inclined his head. *Good thinking. Set an assassin to ward off other assassins.*

"And you, Valdas Zalecki. What would you ask for yourself as a reward?"

Yes, what? His freedom from responsibility? Wealth? Retirement while he was still young enough to enjoy it? He cleared his throat. "Majesty, I ask only to serve."

"I hoped that might be your answer. I . . . we . . ." She glanced sideways at Gerhard, who waved his hand to signify that anything she decided was fine with him. "We are worried about the Tevecor Reaches. Our late husband's sister in Bieloria was most gracious in offering her hospitality during our recent troubles. However, we felt the need to decline. It has come to our notice that our forces were rashly withdrawn from the Reaches. Nature abhors a vacuum, and ambitious neighbors could easily take advantage. I want you to take three companies of hussars and five companies of infantry, General Zalecki, and establish a military presence that will be a deterrent to our good sister, but not onerous on the people there. You will be our military governor."

General Zalecki! Military governor! Valdas's brain slipped several cogs before he felt it mesh. "Majesty, as you wish." He bowed, thinking furiously. "May I request . . ."

"You may."

"King Konstantyn enriched the province with roads, hospitals, and even schools. Is this to continue?"

"Would it be advantageous to us?"

"I truly believe it would."

She nodded. "Put your proposals together, General. And might I suggest that when selecting staff you look favorably on Lieutenant Tomas Gaida, and the brothers Hecht. I believe we have it in our purse to raise them all to captains at your discretion."

He bowed in acquiescence.

The queen's face clouded over. "The foreign spy, Dahnay."

"Hardly a spy, Majesty. It's not as if she ever pretended to be anything other than what she was."

The queen acknowledged this with a nod of her head. "We will write to our sister queen in Bieloria to commend Dahnay's actions on her last mission, and she shall have a plaque on Soldiers' Fields."

"Thank you, Majesty. My men . . . the High Guard, executed by Kazimir . . ."

"I can't bring them back, but that is a barbaric tradition that ends here," she said. "Their remains, such as they are, will be given Christian burial, and they'll have a single plaque on Soldiers' Fields with all their names. And may their souls rest in peace at last."

"Thank you." He hoped their souls would indeed rest in peace.

"And what of Mirza?" Queen Kristina asked. "I had hoped she would be well enough to accompany you today."

"She's asked that she be allowed to return to the Bakaishans."

"I know little of them."

"The ones I saw were good people. I truly believe that the superstition regarding them is mostly misplaced. They certainly steal to live on occasions, but it's largely forced on them because in some regions the locals will not trade. And they are stolen from as often as they steal."

"We shall continue to grant them passage through Zavonia. They shall have grazing rights and campgrounds upon common land."

"If I may be so bold, Majesty, they need more than that. They need a place where they can settle. Somewhere to call home. There is space in the Tevecor Reaches, vast tracts of land uninhabited. They have no love for the Tsar of Ruthenia, and would owe their loyalty to the Amber Crown. If I am to be governor there . . ."

"A persuasive argument. I leave that up to your discretion. But for Mirza herself?"

"She's lost her connection to the spirit world, and possibly her status as shulam, but she still wants to return to her band, to her apprentice. She won't ask, but if I might suggest, you send her back with a fine living wagon and horses so that she won't be dependent upon the charity of the band. And there is a debt, a purse of twenty tolars for Stasha, the band's hetman."

"She shall have a hundred and twenty silver tolars. And horses are as good as coin, yes?"

"Among the Bakaishans, certainly."

"She is to have a living-wagon and pair, plus six mares from the royal stud, each of them in foal to a good stallion. Make sure she picks suitable animals."

"I will, Majesty."

"There is one more debt—the lady Aniela."

Aniela would laugh to hear herself called a lady.

"She's a woman who is not shy about taking coin." Valdas grinned. "Though I suspect your coin will finance the best—" He'd been going to say whorehouse, but that would be more than indelicate. "The best business in Zavonia."

The queen's face flickered with barely suppressed amusement. She was ahead of him.

"What of Trader Maksimilian, Majesty?" Valdas asked.

"Who?" One elegant royal eyebrow arched, and Trader Maksimilian's interest in the whole affair was erased from the record books—which was exactly what he would have wanted.

"I think we have said all we need to say on this matter. We leave the details in your capable hands. We are going to be busy negotiating with Kassubia and Posenja over the matter of large numbers of our troops massed close to their borders. Removing some of them to the Tevecor Reaches will be an excellent first step. Thank you, General Zalecki, you may go."

And that was it. The interview finished, Valdas bowed low, nodded to Skorny and his daughter, and left the royal presence. His next few years were going to be interesting. He set off with a light step to find Aniela. He hoped that she'd see it as he did. The Tevecor Reaches was an area sorely in need of a good whorehouse. Along with new roads, schools, and hospitals, it would be another social amenity.

CHAPTER NINETY-FIVE
Mirza

VALDAS HAD VOWED to accompany Mirza to the Bakaishans. Since this was the time of year the band passed close to the Tevecor Reaches on their way back from Djanganai, she couldn't prevent him from making good on that promise, but he didn't need to. She chose to drive her new wagon at the rear of the army train, separated from Valdas by three companies of hussars, five companies of infantry, their baggage, the holy brothers and holy sisters from teaching and healing orders, and a small administrative staff. Immediately ahead of her were Aniela's three wagons of pretty whores, and immediately behind her, the horsemasters with the remounts and her own mares. She would arrive home with much wealth.

She'd said her goodbyes to Lind before they'd left Biela Miasto. He seemed more relaxed now. She'd never told him about her spirit-walk into his nightmare. There were some things a man didn't need to know, especially one who seemed to have, at last, turned a corner in his life.

In a way she wished she could have said a clean farewell to Valdas too, but he found time to visit her on a daily basis while they traveled, and made sure she had a pair of courteous and attentive ensigns to help with the horses or to drive if she wanted to ride or visit Aniela while they rolled along.

Valdas wasn't responsible for her losing her powers, no matter how guilty he felt. He wanted to make it up to her, and was unnecessarily attentive. With Aniela along on the trip, Valdas was hardly going to lack for companionship. She'd noticed that since Aniela had come back into his life, he'd stopped seeking other women.

That could only be good.

And what about her? Did she want to make love to him? He was a big handsome man, and if she was going to test herself to make sure she had not one scrap of fire magic left, then Valdas was certainly a good choice.

Five nights into their trek, she invited Valdas to her wagon for one last night together, making a nest big enough for both of them and turning the oil lamp down low.

The band would never know whether she'd given her virginity to him or not. They'd take her in. She was, after all, Bakaishan. They'd gossip and speculate for a while until they got used to the idea, but she could cope. She'd have her wagon, her horses, and maybe, one day, she'd find a man who cared for her.

A man, a family, an unmarked face, it was all she'd ever wanted, yet now she wasn't sure she still wanted it. She had her healing knowledge, but her connection to the spirit world was dead, and that would take some getting used to. It was as powerful as a bereavement. She might never truly get over it, but she would learn to live with it.

"Have a care what you wish for. It might come true."

"What?" Valdas raised himself up on one elbow beside her.

"Nothing. Just thinking out loud."

He ran a gentle fingertip over the salamander scar, now a quiet pale pink. "You're sure you're ready for this."

"I'm sure."

"You're not going to flame me to ash?"

"Not if you do your job properly."

He tried to look offended and she laughed softly. "I know," she said. "When did Valdas Zalecki not rise to the occasion?"

As if to prove a point, he slid his hand beneath the blanket.

"Oh, my lovely girl!"

She let him kiss her, and responded, but it never exceeded friendship or entered the realm of passion.

"Why do I get the feeling that this is a farewell?" Valdas asked.

"Because it is. We have separate lives to lead, you and I."

"Stay with me, Mirza."

"The Landstrider and the general? No. Besides, you have Aniela."

His eyes clouded. "Aniela's going into business. It's what she does."

"Have you talked to her about it?"

"It's her life. Her decision."

"She loves you, Valdas."

He was silent and then said, "I think we're friends."

"Of course you are, but you're also more than friends. Why do you think her new business venture is in the Tevecor Reaches?"

He shrugged. "It's a good business opportunity—all the military, plus the locals."

"And do you think she'd be on this trip if you weren't here?"

"I . . ."

"She loves you. Talk to her. You might find she's ready to let her girls run the business without participating."

"You think?"

"I know. I've seen the way she looks at you when you're not watching."

He nodded.

"You love her."

He nodded. "I always have. That's not to say that I don't love you as well."

"Oh, Valdas, you love us all. You'd love every woman in the world if you could, but there's only one that you keep going back to. Don't fight it. Marry her while you have the chance."

"I've often thought . . ." He sighed and sank back on the pillow. "Do you think she'll have me?"

"Oh, Valdas, for an intelligent man you can be unbelievably dim." She leaned over his chest and gave him a peck on the cheek. "Can we stop pretending now? We don't have to do this. I don't need it, and your head is full of Aniela. Hold me until morning and we'll call all debts paid."

He pulled her into his arms and tugged the blanket round them both.

"Sorry. First time Valdas Zalecki hasn't risen to the occasion."

"Oh, I don't know about that."

His body relaxed as she curled against him, and soon he began to snore softly. She turned half toward him and kissed his cheek. "Have a happy life, Valdas."

He mumbled in his sleep and his hand drifted to her breast, warm and comforting.

ACKNOWLEDGMENTS

This book has been a long time in the making. Though an author's name goes on the front cover, behind the scenes many people work to bring the book into the world. I owe a huge debt to my editor Sheila Gilbert, managing editor Joshua Starr, and all at DAW, as well as copyeditor Shoshana Seid-Green, proofreaders, and publicists. They are simply the nicest people to work with.

Also thanks to Donald Maass, my agent, whose writing advice is always excellent, and always valued.

Thank you to my beta readers and people who have addressed specific research questions, including Carl Allery, Mihaela Marija Perkovic, Sue Thomason, Martha Hubbard, and Scarlett de Courcier. Some of those research questions ended up with me taking things out of the book rather than adding them in, but that's okay. Also to my longtime friend and bandmate, Hilary Spencer, who takes it as a personal challenge to find as many typos in my manuscript as she possibly can!

(Band? What band? See artisan-harmony.com if you're curious.)

Thank you to the members of Northwrite SF who suffered through many versions of this: Gus Smith, Terry Jackman, John Moran, David Lascelles, Tina Anghelatos, Shellie Horst, Liz Sourbutt, Sue Oke, Tony Ballantyne, and Cheryl Sonnier. Special thanks to Kari Sperring for helping me to find the right title.

Also thanks to attendees of Milford SF Writers' Conference (MilfordSF.co.uk) who critiqued chunks of this at different stages of its development, from the first twinkling of an idea in 2006 to the final revisions.

More than thanks are due to my family, who put up with a lot when I'm obsessively up to my ears in a manuscript. Love you.

A huge thank-you to you for reading. If you haven't already, I encourage you to read my other novels, the Psi-Tech trilogy and the Rowankind trilogy. Details of my books and short stories are on my website, jaceybedford.co.uk, where you'll also find my contact info. I'm always happy to hear from readers, writers, and reviewers. I do answer all emails personally, though not always immediately. You can also follow my writing blog at jaceybedford.wordpress.com, my Twitter feed at @jaceybedford, or my Facebook page at facebook.com/jacey.bedford.writer.

But mainly . . .

I would really love for you to sign up to my mailing list: jaceybedford.co.uk/contact.htm. I promise I'll not flood your inbox with emails, but I will send news of new short stories and books.